Heading

Home

Heading

Home

Clayton Carlson

Published by First Page Solutions
Kelowna BC, Canada

Cover Photographer: Lawrence Kessler

The future is surrounded by a riddle, wrapped in an enigma.

Contents

Introduction

It had been over ten months since Isaac left the Bible College to help his parents run their small family company. His father had a serious industrial accident leaving him debilitated. Not wanting to diminish the student numbers, the college dean counseled Isaac not to return home until the semester was over. He confirmed to Isaac there would be no rebates on money received for tuition or living expenses and that all his school records would be graded as 'incomplete'. The Dean reassured him that his parents would get along fine on their own. Unsettled in his heart, Isaac felt compelled to reject the Dean's advice and returned home as soon as he could, despite his lack of money or lost school course credits.

Full of youthful certainty he started to hitchhike home. Catching a ride with an apparent sinful trucker heading his way, Isaac was not shy about informing the old trucker about his sins and where they would lead him. Unoffended by Isaac's remarks, the trucker turned out to know more about biblical topics than Isaac had given him credit for. Needing to stay awake on the day long trip, the old trucker kept Isaac engaged in heated discussion over church doctrines Isaac had believed all his life. Realizing his beliefs were not as biblically supported as he had thought they were, Isaac vowed to himself to only follow beliefs with unwavering biblical support. The sting of seeing his cherished religious beliefs disproved through

Bible scripture by a grubby old trucker left his faith in those doctrines shattered.

Believing the Bible to be the sole source for Godly understanding, Isaac was obsessed with conforming his beliefs to match what he found the Bible to be declaring, rather than follow Christian tradition. Spending all his spare time in this sole endeavor once he returned home, alienated his old friends and family who did not understand his need to biblically prove their time-honored traditions. Dissatisfied with his status quo, Isaac was fully committed to following his savior in love and truth. We pick up his story after another long night of scriptural analysis.

Note: The full story of Isaac's ride home with the sinful trucker is found in 'The Eden Conspiracy'.

Chapter 1

"Isaac! Isaac it's time to get up now." Mum sang up the staircase. "You don't want to be late for class."

Isaac had always been self-motivated and conscientious, she never had to prod him to get going in the mornings when he was younger. It had been eight months since Pa's funeral and Isaac still hadn't gotten back to his normal self.

"If I don't hear you moving around soon, I'll have to send Rosy up there to get you and you know what that'll be like."

Several minutes go by before the kettle slowly starts its faint whistle. Mum opens the kitchen door, standing to one side she snaps her fingers, then points up the stairs. The cues aren't missed, as a large Irish setter bounds in through the open door. Paws flailing on the linoleum at twice the speed of its body, finding traction the big red dog gallops up the stairs bursting through a partially closed bedroom door. Jumping onto the bed, Rosy frantically digs at the covers, trying to reveal her beloved master.

"Ugh, yes rosy I love you too." Isaac groggily responds. Sticking an arm out from under the quilt, he finds a floppy ear and scratches it until Rosy settles down beside him on the bed.

"Now that's better." Isaac says, sensing he will be safe from Rosie's exuberance if he gets out of bed.

Flipping the blankets back he sits up on the edge of the bed with his feet snugly planted in the deep pile of his bedside mat. Reaching for his clothes on the chair where he had left them, he dresses quickly while being sure to give sufficient attention to keep Rosy pacified.

Standing to pull up his pants and tighten his belt, Isaac quickly finishes dressing. Looking at his faithful friend he says with excitement, "Okay, lets go get something to eat."

Rosy leaps off the bed and spins a few tight circles then follows closely behind Isaac as he vaults himself past his bedroom door and down the flight of stairs three steps at a time. They both spill into the kitchen in a whirlwind of energy.

"Well that didn't take long." Mum said with a grin in her sing song morning voice. "I knew you couldn't stay asleep with Rosy up there. I've made some porridge."

"Thanks." Isaac heads into the bathroom closing the door behind him leaving big sad eyes on the waiting redhead. Drying his face with a towel Isaac soon emerges. Giving Rosy a pat on the head, he tosses the towel back onto the bathroom counter.

"That's better." He says. "Did you sleep well last night Mum?"

"Oh, not really." Came the weary reply. "I've not had a good rest since Pa...," Mum paused, unable or unwilling to talk about her husband's death. "Sleeping alone again takes some getting used to, but I'll get there."

Isaac gives her a hug. For the first time she seemed vulnerable to him. Snuggled in his arms he's struck by their reversal of roles, remembering the times she had comforted him as a child. Now it was his turn to do the comforting.

"I know it's not the same, but Rosy could at least keep you warm." Isaac says with a smile.

"Thanks, but I can do without all the long red hair in my bed. Besides that, there's no telling what she'll get herself into during the day and bring back into my bed at night. You know how she loves to run wild in the fields. I'll be fine alone."

Moving over to the stove Isaac dishes himself a bowl of porridge. Mum tops it off with crushed walnuts, raisins and brown sugar. They sit at the table quietly, Isaac eating, Mum drinking her morning coffee.

"That was good. Thanks Mum." Isaac says wiping off his mouth with a napkin. "I better get going, I need to find out about my new classes today. I took an English course and some easy class to top up my credits."

"I'd hate to see you waste your time on some impractical subject. You've always liked rocks. Wasn't there an earth science class you could take? You never know, you might go prospecting someday." Mum says thoughtfully.

"Ya, I found something like that. I hope it's an easy credit, one I can breeze through, but it all depends on the teacher."

"Well I suppose easy is ok, but if it's something you're interested in, it won't seem like work, you'll enjoy it and probably get a good grade anyway."

Isaac frowns. "You're probably right as usual Mum, we'll see how things turn out."

Toot, toot. The sound of a car horn drifts through the window into the kitchen. Isaac looks past the kitchen curtains to see a familiar faded blue Corolla parked in the driveway. The driver coiffing her long blonde hair in the rearview mirror with a brush.

"Hey, Becky's here. She must be here to give me a ride. That's great! I gotta run Mum. Thanks for breakfast."

After picking a binder up off the table Isaac gives his mom a kiss. Pausing at the door he slips into his shoes and coat, then rushes out into the brisk morning air. Slowing to a walk Isaac gives Becky a cheerful wave and smile. Opening the car door, he beams a toothy grin.

"Glad to see you Beck. I didn't really want to walk. I need to find out which courses I got for this second semester, I hope I get the profs that I wanted, some have pretty bad reputations and I was hoping for a few easy credits."

"Well if you had signed up earlier like I did, you would have been assured of the prof."

"I was waiting for my transcripts to see which courses I needed to complete my degree. Dealing with that Bible school was like pulling teeth, I think the dean's been out to get me ever since I left there."

"Dad's good friends with the dean. Dad says the dean went out of his way and did all he could for you when you decided to come home and help your mom and dad. The way I hear it, you blew off every offer of help he gave you."

"Oh, he went out of his way all right, but it wasn't to help." The tone in Isaac's voice was heavy with sarcasm as he did up his seatbelt.

"He wanted me to finish the school year. If I hadn't come back home when I did, I wouldn't have gotten to see Pa before he died. As it was, I wasn't here helping him with the business very long at all before..." Isaac's voice trails off. "I Just had time to finish off the jobs that were on the go and had to be finished. Then out of the blue, Pa had complications from his fall and dies." Isaac was upset with having to explain himself to Becky. He had confided his personal struggles with the dean to her when he got home from Bible school. He felt close to her, like she really understood him and what he was going through. Now he found himself beginning to question that assessment.

Isaac and Becky had always been good friends growing up in their small local church, where her dad was a respected leader and deacon. Their parents had always been friends and shared common interests that brought both families together on many occasions. Pa had a modest painting business that kept him busy and supplied the family's needs. When he got behind, Mum and Isaac would pitch in to help get the jobs done, it was after all, a family business. Isaac and Becky had dated seriously in high school. When he left for college their parents talked them into parting as friends until Isaac's schooling was over. Now that he was back, he was hoping they might get back together.

"You've changed, sometimes it's like I don't understand you at all." Becky said harshly. "You seem to question and mistrust everything and everyone. Like on Friday night at young people's group, grilling my Dad for Bible scripture to support long established beliefs. Doctrine that you used to be a fan of. I just don't get you sometimes."

Isaac sits thoughtfully for a couple of minutes as Becky makes her way onto the road heading towards the college.

"I wasn't trying to be rude to your dad. He was leading the Bible study! If I can't ask for a Bible reference during a Bible study, when can I?"

"Well he gave you a reference. One that everyone knows. One that you've used before and supported. But no" Becky says mockingly, "that's not good enough for you anymore, now you need better proof!"

"You know I've been studying our traditions and beliefs a lot lately. They aren't as Bible based as I had once thought, they seem to be based on misunderstanding a very basic Bible truth. I think the belief that people have an immortal, or possess an eternal soul, is wrong and not Bible based. I believe this doctrine has led us down the wrong path. Knowing our true nature is as fundamental to Bible study as knowing two plus two equals four is fundamental to doing math."

Not heeding his inner voice of caution, Isaac continues. "After looking into Genesis 2:7, I believe God created us mortal, just like the other animals. If we were created with an immortal soul, then banishing Adam from the garden, keeping him from the tree of life, would have been useless as Adam would already have been in possession of eternal life. He wouldn't have needed to eat from the tree of life to have immortality. The belief your dad was teaching only works if we have an immortal soul."

"Do you hear yourself?" Becky asked with alarm. "Your study, your understanding, your belief! It all revolves around you. Have you sought out advice from others with different insights?"

Isaac sits up straighter in the passenger seat looking intently at Becky. "I have been trying to. No one seems interested in discussing the topic with me. So, I ask questions when the subject comes up, I try to be appropriate. Isn't a Bible study a good place to ask questions and discuss Bible topics?

"You seem to have all the answers, don't you?" Becky's voice is cold.

"Would you rather I have none of the answers? I don't have to be right; I just can't be indifferent!" Pausing, Isaac turns and watches the dirty snow-covered fields go by. looking back at Becky he softly continues.

"Your right, I have changed. I think I have changed for the better. I will no longer believe things just because I'm told them by those in authority. I want to see the proof for Christian beliefs for myself, from the Bible." Isaac looks at Becky with determination as she drives. "I told you about my ride home from Bible school. It really made me think."

"Ya, I remember. Is this about that crazy old conspiracy man again, the one with all the wacky ideas about everything?" Becky is still on a slow boil. "I talked to Dad about him and he thinks you should put his ideas out of your head. They'll only get you in trouble. Dad said that even your mom is worried about you."

"Mum always taught me to base my beliefs on sure Bible footings. That's all I'm doing. I'm only asking for the Bible proof for our beliefs. No matter how established those beliefs are, I want to be sure." Isaac's response was soft, trying to deflect some of Becky's bitterness.

Becky wasn't responding as he had hoped. "I thought we would get back together like we had planned before you left for school. Dad had some jobs lined up for you to build our future on and he thought that before long you could really be someone of importance at church. Maybe get on the board with your Bible school training and all. But now, with quitting Bible school and coming back home with a head full of nonsense, I'm afraid that he won't let me see you anymore." Tears start to well up in Becky's eyes as her heart aches for the relationship that seemed to be slipping away.

Recognizing the true source of Becky's anxiety and worry, Isaac does his best to reassure her of his intentions.

"Becky, I want our relationship to grow too. But I can't, no, I won't compromise my belief that the Bible is the inspired word of God and it will not contradict itself. If the scriptures conflict, then we aren't understanding them properly. Doctrine that isn't supported by the Bible, is a doctrine of man and should be taught as such. Look, let me talk to your dad. He has always been keen on scripture as the basis for faith. It will all work out. I'm not as crazy as everyone seems to think I am. I've been doing a lot of Bible study over the last eight months and I feel like I'm being led by the Spirit. Trust me."

He reaches over and gives her hand a squeeze. Smiling weakly, she pulls her hand away as she steers the car into the college driveway around a slow bend to the parking lot and into an empty stall.

"Ya, but what Spirit?" Becky says with a teasing tone and a wink. Then her voice turns serious again. "Ok, I'll trust you. Dad should be home tonight after supper, come by and see him. I hope you're right."

Isaac softly wipes an errant tear away from Becky's cheek. "I'll be over tonight. Come on, let's find our classes."

A small group of students are milling around a bulletin board in the college front foyer. A tall lanky boy with an acne pot marked face turns to Isaac as he and Becky approach.

"Hey Bible boy, you're in Speckle's geography class with me. This should be fun as he's an ardent evolutionist and you're, well, you've always been Bible boy. I can't wait for the fireworks, it should be an interesting semester." After having a good chuckle at Isaac, the lanky boy makes his way down the hall towards the cafeteria.

"Ugh." Isaac groans to Becky. "Speckle! So much for an easy credit. Maybe I'll get lucky with English."

"I'm sure God will give you what you need." She whispers with a smile.

"I can't find my name on any of the English classes." Isaac says with concern.

"Oh, here you are." Becky pipes in, pointing to a list at the edge of the bulletin board. "Looks like you'll be doing some creative writing. They must have been filled up and gave you an alternate course. You'll still get your English credits though. It wouldn't have happened if you had registered when I did. I got all the classes I wanted, with all my preferred professors." Becky is smiling teasingly now, her voice light, as she pokes fun at Isaac's presumed misfortune. "I have to get going to meet Sherry. You better go face the music."

"Ya, I suppose you're right. I'll catch you later and tell you about it."

"Ok, but I don't want any crying. You know it's your own fault."

Becky walks away, breezing down the hall, her tight jeans swaying with her hips. Isaac turns the other way, optimistically heading towards his first class of creative writing. Arriving to a partially filled classroom, Isaac picks a desk near the back and slides into it. Valencia Molindes is boldly printed on the black board at the front of the class. In front of it, a woman with short, spiky, orange and blue hair, sits behind the teacher's desk. Several facial and ear piercings are adorned with bits of twisted metal contrasting her bohemian midcentury party dress, giving her a punk-art, avant-garde look. She checks her phone for the time, then stands to address the scantily filled classroom.

"Good morning!" Her voice is firm and confident. "This may be my first semester as an instructor, but I want to make it your best." Her voice may have been confident, but it was high pitched and squeaky, making it hard to listen to for very long. "There's not many of you here yet, I am expecting more, they may come a bit later. Let me introduce myself and give you an overview of this class. As some of you may know, I am an active playwright, having multiple shows open in New York and London. I currently have one being produced on Broadway, which I go help direct from time to time. This semester you will be primarily concentrating on writing a play of your own. It doesn't matter what your play is about, but I encourage you all to heed the adage to write about what you know. Make it something you're passionate about and your ideas will come easy and flow effortlessly.

I like to describe my teaching method as freestyle, so I won't be micromanaging you, rather, I'll be giving you the freedom to explore your individual artistic style on your own. In our more formal lessons, we will be studying works from renowned authors, unveiling their techniques so you can utilize them in your own work. Your play will count for ninety percent of your final grade, the other ten percent will come from periodic test results, based on author studies. This class is to help you all become proficient authors by practicing the craft. So, you will be writing."

After fielding a series of questions from the class, Val supplies a book list of required reading, then sends the students off with encouraging words about finding spiritual liberation through creative writing. Isaac wonders what he's gotten himself into. It wasn't the English class he had been hoping for. Collecting his binder, he heads for his geography class with trepidation, praying as he goes.

"Oh father, I know you are in control of this world's events and my life, guide my paths at school this semester, let it all be for your glory." Isaac prays silently as he walked down the hall. "You have always been faithful to me, help me to always be faithful to you in all I do and say. I desire to proclaim you to those I interact with. Please help me to demonstrate your love to others more by what I do than what I say. Whether they agree with me or not, help me be faithful to you and your word in everything I say and do. Thank you for the insights you have already given me, and please continue to open my eyes to your wisdom. Please work things out for Becky and I."

Speckle's class was almost full when Isaac walked through the open door, the only empty seats left to choose from were in the front two rows. Isaac sits in one close to the door. Classroom chatter comes to a hush when Mr.

Speckle strides through the door and up to the large oak desk from where he ruled his kingdom. Surveying the crop of fresh minds waiting to be shaped, his bright blue eyes sparkle with delight. Dedicated to the scientific method for understanding the world's mysteries, he relished his job of guiding his charges into intellectual enlightenment through scientific discovery.

"Good day everyone, I am Mr. Speckle. You may address me as Mr. Speckle." Standing behind his desk, Mr. Speckle's domineering personality looms larger than his physical presence. Standing five feet five and weighing a slight hundred and twenty-three pounds, Mr. Speckle had spent years honing his skills as a dictatorial leader, proving to those around him that, intellectually speaking, size doesn't matter.

"This semester we will be covering the processes that built our world and how those processes are still actively shaping it today. Knowing how the world started will help shape our understanding of how it works now and how it will likely react in the future. Most of the curriculum's modules will be investigated and studied in small groups of four or five. Your theories will be individually marked and you each will have to supply supporting evidence for those theories. Your mark will reflect how well you support your theories using the proven scientific method of research."

"The scientific method! Hey, how are you going to like that Bible boy? I hope I'm not in a small group with you! Bill Nye step aside, Isaac is the science guy!" came a loud sarcastic commentary from the back of the class. Stifled laughter was interspersed with, 'ya, I don't want to be in his group either'. It appeared Isaac had past encounters with several students in the class, where he publicly took a vocal stand on the Bible being the best source for truth and knowledge.

"That will be enough of that!" Mr. Speckle said, forcefully gripping his pointer. "I don't care how you may behave in your other classes, but that kind of outburst will not be tolerated in mine. Are there any questions, or do I make myself perfectly clear?" The room was quiet in response to Mr. Speckle's question.

"As I was saying, this semester will require group effort. As a senior member of the faculty, I am, however, sympathetic to my students' worries and concerns. Something tells me that not all of you have the same degree of belief in the scientific method of study. In response to my sympathy for those concerns, I think it best we hold a debate of sorts. For our next class, we will devote the time to discuss the merits of the scientific method along with other ways humans have used to discover how our world works. Knowing the beliefs and prejudices of the others in your small groups may prove helpful when interpreting their research and points of view." Mr. Speckle looks intently at Isaac. "That will be all for today. You can pick up your required book list and assignment schedule at the door as you leave. Next class come prepared to defend your convictions." he tells the class. Then, again looking at Isaac, he adds, "If you have any that are worth defending?"

As the students disperse helter skelter into the hall, Isaac is jostled by a few of them as they rush past on their way to somewhere important.

"Way to go, Bible boy. Your reputation seems to have preceded you. You sure got Speckle worked up. I hope he doesn't take it out on the rest of us just because of your archaic beliefs." The lanky, pot marked faced boy, gives Isaac a hard push on the shoulder, almost knocking him over.

"What do you mean me, Bob? If it wasn't for your comments Speckle wouldn't have even noticed me, or my convictions. I could have attended this class without any conflict."

"Oh, boo-hoo, blah, blah, blah!" Bob mockingly cries. "What did you expect? I've been your nemesis since kindergarten. You should've let me go down the slide first, not punch me in the nose."

"You butted in! We were supposed to wait properly in line. You pushed in where you shouldn't have. I was only five and you were being a bully. You always do things out of turn. You always go out of your way to make things hard for me."

"Well then, you should be used to it by now, Bible boy. See you in class. I can't wait to hear you defend your convictions, if you have any worth defending." With that parting comment, Bob is lost in the crowd.

Having only the two classes to attend, and needing time to think about his day and clear his head, Isaac takes the wooded path and walks home rather than waiting for Becky to give him a ride. She has a full course load and would be busy until the end of the day. He had much to consider, from figuring out what play he should write, to how he would scientifically defend his belief in the Bible as the source of wisdom. He pondered these questions as he slowly walked down the well-worn snowy trail towards home.

It was late afternoon as he lay on his bed stoking Rosie. Staring up at the ceiling, lost in thought, he remembered he was supposed to meet with Becky's dad after supper.

"Oh, thank you." He said out loud to God "I had forgotten, please give me the right things to say." With that he got up and started getting ready to go. Rosie yawns and puts her head back down on the bed knowing she will probably be left behind.

Chapter 2

After straightening his hair Isaac reaches out and knocks on Beckie's front door. Opening the door a moment later, Becky greets Isaac with a smile.

"I missed you after classes, but I figured you would have been done early. You really need to get a cell phone. Then we could text and keep in touch easier."

"Ya sorry, I had a lot to think about. It doesn't seem like I'll be getting any easy credits this semester. I'll get a phone soon. I just made the last payment on my Bible School student loan so now I have more financial flexibility. I promised Mum I would be debt free before I took on any frills."

"I suppose it's what you value. My phone is a necessity." Becky said firmly. "You live so frugally, like you were impoverished or something. You have to learn how to spend your money and live a bit like everyone else. Don't worry, I'll help you with that." She says twisting her curls in her fingers. "No one else worries about being in debt, get with the program."

"Ya maybe, but that's just not me. I enjoy the freedom being debt-free brings." Changing the subject away from another contention he had with Becky, Isaac asked. "Is your dad home? You said this morning that he would be home after supper. I wanted to talk to him about my Bible questions, like you suggested."

"Oh, I had forgotten about that. I thought you were here to see me." Becky looked surprised. "Ya, I think he's free, come in and I'll check." Becky turns and shouts down the hall. "Dad Isaac is here to see you, are you free right now?"

"Ya! That would be ok, send him in." Came a response from deep within the house.

Isaac leaves his coat and boots by the door and makes his way down the hall and into Matt's office. Becky follows him to the door, then leaves Isaac with her dad and heads off to the living room to watch Wheel of Fortune with her mom.

"Come in and sit-down Isaac, what can I help you with? Matt was smiling friendly. Matt had always liked Isaac and thought Isaac would be a good future husband for Becky. Providing, he had the opportunity to mold Isaac into the proper man for his Becky.

Isaac sits in the chair across the desk from Matt. "I would like to bounce some thoughts off you, get your ideas on them."

"Sure, the more I can pass my wisdom onto future generations the better. What are you thinking about?"

"Well I have been doing a lot of Bible study on the doctrine of Man's immortal soul. I haven't been able to find support for it in the Bible, which leads me to believe it's not true. I'm afraid that believing it takes us away from the truths of God, leading us into false doctrine in a wide range of topics. Having this one wrong belief, distorts our concept of what God is planning to achieve through mankind."

"Whoa, that's a mouthful." Matt leans back in his chair, crossing his arms. "I'm glad you came over; your mom is worried about you and your ideas. She asked If I could talk to you about them and help you get back on the right spiritual track. She told me your new ideas have led you to believe our church beliefs are part of some giant evil conspiracy. You know our church denomination was founded on the authority of the Holy Bible. We acknowledge the supremacy of the Bible over man's laws, that's written right into our church constitution. Why would we teach anything unbiblical?"

"That's why I find it so hard to understand. I can't find any biblical support for our denomination's doctrine of the immortal soul. I think it is a Satanic conspiracy. I believe it all started with him." Isaac was unaware of his mum's concerns; he was annoyed she hadn't talked to him about them. "Our doctrine of when man received an immortal soul, as I have been taught, comes from Genesis 2:7 in the Garden of Eden."

"Ya, I think that's the right verse. I'd have to get out my Bible to be sure though."

"That's what I thought. But we're wrong. That's not what the Bible tells us, if we seriously investigate the verse. Many Bible translations don't use the word soul. They may say man became a living animal, or man became a living being. They use other words for soul. When I look at the Hebrew word God inspired to be used it's the word Nephesh. That's the same word used to describe all other forms of fleshly life, like animals, fish and birds. It was never meant to be used to describe immortality. In fact, when I checked the terms of usage in the Strong's Concordance, it specifically tells us it refers to mortality. That's the opposite to our church's doctrine."

Taken aback by Isaac's investigations, Matt sits up straighter and tries to digest the points made. He'd never dove deeply into these Bible verses before and felt a little over his head. "You have been busy, I'm afraid I'd have to look into this a bit more for myself. I couldn't comment intelligently on the subject right now."

"Well this is only the start!" Isaac says excitedly. "There is so much more. Like if mankind had immortality when they were created, then why did God keep them from returning to the garden of Eden?" Answering his own Question, Isaac blurts out. "So they couldn't eat from the tree of life! Had they already possessed immortality, which means they would live forever, God would've known that keeping them from the tree of eternal life would be a waste of time!"

"Maybe it's speaking metaphorically." Matt grasped for a quick answer. "I believe it says, 'become like us and live forever', which would allude to spiritual life, like God has. Not a physical life, where you don't die. God created them perfect, so they wouldn't have died if they hadn't sinned. The Bible is saying God kept man from spiritual immortality."

Isaac shakes his head in disagreement. "Immortal means you can't die. God is immortal, he can't die, he'll never die, that's what immortality means. Things that are mortal do die, no matter what they're made of. That's the meaning of being mortal. Our church's doctrine of an immortal soul tries to give mankind something extra, intangible, a spirit life that's immortal."

"You've obviously given this a lot more thought than I have. I find it hard to discuss it intelligently with you. It would help if I could look at your ideas written out." Matt squirmed uneasily in his chair as he spoke, looking for an exit from the conversation.

Oblivious to Matt's discomfort Isaac continued undaunted. "Like I said, the doctrine of the immortal soul is a conspiracy. Mankind was infected with it at the start by Satan. He told Eve, you shall not surely die, if she ate from the tree of knowledge. He wrapped this lie in the truth that she would have knowledge deciding good from evil like God in Genesis 3:4-5. The immortal soul doctrine even contradicts New Testament truth. Take John 3:16 for example."

"Now you're getting into my realm. I'm familiar with that verse, it's probably been the most quoted verse for the past fifty years. I've used it several times when preaching Jesus to the lost. But what does it have to do with the doctrine of the immortal soul?" Matt questions, reinvigorated in the conversation.

"Well it's more about what's not said." Isaac tries to explain. "Verse 16 tells us, 'For God so loved the world, that he gave his only begotten Son, that whosoever believeth in him should not perish, but have everlasting life.' This verse explains to us belief in Jesus is the only way to obtain eternal life. We are saved only through Jesus."

"Amen, thank you Jesus." Matt says, nodding his head.

Continuing, Isaac stresses. "What it doesn't say, but is just as true, is the opposite. Those who don't believe in Jesus, will not receive eternal life and will die. Therefore, mankind could not have received an immortal soul at creation. If we have immortality as part of us at birth, we wouldn't need Jesus to avoid death, we'd already have eternal life by having an immortal soul, making John 3:16 a lie."

"Well it's obvious, we need Jesus so our soul won't perish in hell. Without the salvation of Jesus, our souls are tortured forever in the fires of hell. There is no escape for the wicked people sent there." Matt is exuberant when sharing his faith. "You must know this, I taught this to you in Sunday school." Matt is shocked at Isaac's questioning of basic church beliefs.

Isaac presses his point. "In order to believe that, you'd have to rewrite the verse to say; will not suffer but have eternal bliss. Your misunderstanding the term soul. Not using it the same way it's used in Genesis. Your saying it's something immortal. As you'll see when you check, you'll find it's talking about anything made of living flesh, not of spirit.

That leads to another belief full of contradiction. How can evil people be tortured forever if they aren't immortal? According to verse 16, only the believers in Jesus will gain eternal life and live forever. Having a belief in Jesus keeps people out of hell, it doesn't give those inside Hell eternal life."

"Perhaps it would be best if we just agree to disagree, it makes it easier to remain on friendly terms if we do."

"Yes, it is easier to do that, however ignoring the facts won't make either of us any wiser. It'll only leave one, or both of us in our ignorance. I think we both want to know and live in Bible truth rather than believing things that aren't true."

"Well yes of course, following the Bible is the only way to live." Matt agrees heartily. "As I said, our denomination is founded on following Bible teaching in all aspects of life. We don't want to be wrong either. I just meant that rather than arguing about what the Bible says about peripheral things, we should see where we can agree on the essential topics of Christianity."

"I'm not trying to be argumentative. I think we both agree; the Bible is the word of God and will not contradict itself. If our church and you don't mind following doctrines not supported by the Bible then just say so, but that's not what I want. I wouldn't be discussing it with you if I thought you didn't care." Isaac candidly speaks with sincerity.

Matt recognizes Isaac's heart to follow God. "No, no, we, I care very much about following Bible scripture. I'm sure we can find the meaning together. Are there any other topics you have questions about? Let's get them all out in the open and see which ones we should tackle first."

"I suppose that would work. There are many doctrines affected by humans not having an immortal soul. One that comes to mind right away would be the resurrection of those who die. Rather than going to heaven or hell after the body dies: we do just that. We die and sleep until God resurrects us back to life. Christians are to be brought back to life at the return of Jesus. Jesus explained this thoroughly in John 6. Bible scholars tell us, the more a point gets repeated the more important it is. Jesus tells us four times during one conversation when he will come back to get his followers. Here, let me use your computer and I'll show you."

Matt turns his monitor around and passes Isaac the wireless keyboard. Isaac types in the search and soon gets his answer.

"Ya here they are.

6:39 Now this is the will of the one who sent me—that I should not lose one person of every one he has given me, but raise them all up at the last day.

6:40 For this is the will of my Father—for everyone who looks on the Son and believes in him to have eternal life, and I will raise him up at the last day.

6:44 No one can come to me unless the Father who sent me draws him, and I will raise him up at the last day.

6:54 The one who eats my flesh and drinks my blood has eternal life, and I will raise him up on the last day.

Christians are all raised up on the last day. Not having an immortal soul means we are dead, waiting in the grave, until we are raised on the last day when Jesus returns."

"So, your saying Christians don't go to heaven when they die? That's not from the Bible! Heaven is the hope of Christians, it's our true home, our reward for following Jesus." Matt's voice turns hard, as he looks intently at Isaac.

"I'm not saying that; the Bible is proclaiming it! Following Bible teachings is what we both want. If I'm misinterpreting the scripture, then please show me where. I don't want to be wrong." Isaac's heart pleads through his voice.

"OK, I'll try." Matt says, then clears his throat. "How about where Paul says he would rather die and be at home with Jesus. He obviously is talking about being in heaven, or probably the most famous, Lazarus and the rich man. That parable shows Lazarus in heaven with Abraham and the rich man in Hell, how much more proof could you need? Perhaps the words of your savior will do it for you. You seem to forget about Jesus telling the thief on the cross that he would be in paradise that very day, not after some resurrection in the future." Matt sits up straight at his desk, his face reddening.

"Like I've been saying, the satanic conspiratorial lie leads all who believe it astray. For those examples to prove we go to heaven or hell immediately after death, we would need to have an immortal soul. When did we get that? Where is the verse saying humans possess immortality?" Isaac continues to push for Bible proof.

"Why would I need a proof verse? Those examples circumstantially prove we're immortal."

"Well let's look at those examples." Isaac calmly replies. "Circumstantial evidence alone isn't enough to convict someone of murder and it's not enough to base my beliefs on. First, Paul is saying he would rather die than continue to be tortured. Knowing about the resurrections, we know that Paul's next conscious thought would be one of rising from his grave and meeting Jesus as he returns to earth. Once Paul died, he would be free from the torments of this world, which would be better for him. The verse doesn't say he would be in heaven. People only presume he's in heaven, if they believe Satan's immortal soul lie."

"I'll have to look more into your opinions. What about my other examples? Matt seemed interested in Isaac's point of view, pulling out a pen and paper, he starts to take notes.

"OK, let's look at the next one, the parable of Lazarus and the rich man. First off, we should remember that it is a parable. It wasn't given as a description of heaven and hell; any more than the parable of the mustard seed explains the Kingdom of God to be a giant garden. The meaning of this parable comes at the end, where Abraham tells the rich man that if his brothers wouldn't believe the words of the prophets, neither would they believe someone who came back from the dead. Jesus was predicting the religious leader's contempt for the resurrection of his friend Lazarus. This final miracle performed by Jesus, fulfilled all the messianic miracles the Jewish leaders set out for their messiah to fulfill, proving his authenticity as their messiah.

Abraham is said to be alive and in charge in this parable, yet at the end of Hebrews 11 we're told Abraham has yet to receive all his promises. He must wait in his grave for eternal life, until all believers gain perfection together at the same time. When they are resurrected on the last day."

"I've read Hebrews 11 often and I don't remember reading that. Let me look it up right now." Matt says, taking back the keyboard and typing. "Here it is,

'39And these all, having obtained a good report through faith, received not the promise: 40 God having provided some better thing for us, that they without us should not be made perfect.'

Huh, I've never paid much attention to those verses before. I'll have to study more about that later. There must be an explanation." Matt takes more notes on his pad of paper.

Encouraged by Matt's attentiveness, Isaac goes on to the last example. "The thief on the cross story is usually misunderstood because of a translation error."

"What? Are you going to say the words got mixed up, or misinterpreted, like you think happened in Genesis?" Matt was incredulous.

"No, it's not the words that got misunderstood, it's the punctuation. Greek has no punctuation, when the translators added punctuation to the sentence spoken by Jesus, they misplaced one of the commas." Isaac takes over the keyboard and types in a search. Reading the reply off the screen he makes his point. "For Jesus to be our savior it should read,

42 And he said, "Jesus, remember me when you come into your kingdom." 43 And he said to him, "Truly, I say to you today, you will be with me in paradise." Rather than, 42 And he said, "Jesus, remember me when you come into your kingdom." 43 And he said to him, "Truly, I say to you, today you will be with me in paradise."

Isaac reads the words off the screen, following the words with his finger so Matt could follow along.

"Jesus proved he was our savior by coming back to life after being dead and in the grave for three days and nights. Being in paradise with the thief that same day he died would make it impossible for him to be dead in his grave for three days. That would eliminate Jesus as being our savior wouldn't it?" Isaac asked Matt, hoping for an answer.

"I've never thought of that verse like that before. I've only used it to teach about going to heaven, not about Jesus being dead in the grave for three days." Matt was thoughtfully quiet after he spoke.

"Like we agreed at the start, the Bible isn't contradictory. Each verse must jive with what the rest of the Bible says. If it doesn't, then we are misunderstanding it." Isaac passionately speaks his heart. "Words and their meanings are important. God never inspired one word to have opposite meanings. When we are told Jesus was dead for three days and nights, he wasn't just mostly dead, or just extremely physically handy capped, alive in some spirit form somewhere else. He was completely and totally dead. To teach that Jesus wasn't dead for three days, denies his divinity. It rejects the proof he gave to demonstrate he was our savior.

Jesus was fully man. Believing mankind is born with an immortal soul demands that Jesus possessed an immortal soul as well. Having possession of an immortal soul would make it impossible for Jesus to be completely dead, as his soul would remain alive and conscious, making it impossible for him to die for our sins. The most he could have done would be tortured for us, as he couldn't be completely dead. Supporting the doctrine of the immortal soul ultimately denies the proof Jesus gave as our savior. What's more essential than that? We need to make sure what we teach others is accurate, not contradicting Bible truth."

"It's not like our denomination has antichrist tendencies. We do our best to teach the gospel of Jesus to the lost." Matt countered, stinging a bit from Isaac's comments.

"I didn't mean to say it's done intentionally." Isaac's tone was conciliatory. "It just feels like denominationally we speak before we have all of the facts. We don't seem to think through our beliefs, seeing where they lead before teaching them as truth to others. All I'm asking for is some Bible supported discussion on these topics."

"What do you mean? You make it sound like we jump to conclusions and don't think our beliefs through. We prayerfully look at all the facts." Matt was trying to remain calm in what seemed like a steady barrage against his cherished beliefs.

"Well, besides the points I just made showing our doctrine of the immortal soul isn't completely accurate, take our understanding of what the gospel of Jesus is." Isaac hesitantly brings up another bone of contention. He had been hoping to keep the conversation to one topic at a time.

"What about it?" Came Matt's terse reply. "We proclaim the Gospel of Jesus, just like he commanded his church to do before he left. It's the great commission."

"We teach the gospel, the good news, about Jesus and the salvation he alone brings. But that's not the Gospel Jesus taught." Isaac states confidently. "They are very different. The Bible defines the Gospel Jesus taught as the Gospel of the Kingdom of God. Jesus proclaimed the coming Kingdom of God. It's even embedded in how he taught us to pray. He taught us to pray for it to come, it's our focus for the future. It's what we're to seek first in our lives. Jesus didn't go around Israel encouraging people to repent and accept him as their personal savior. He didn't preach salvation to the masses in an effort to save them from damnation. We incorrectly define what the Gospel is, we make it a gospel of salvation, a gospel about Jesus and what he did for us. That's not the Gospel Jesus preached. It's not the Gospel he told us to take to the world. Jesus told us to preach the Gospel of the Kingdom of God, that's what he taught for three and a half years. Paul continued taking that Gospel to the world by teaching the Kingdom of God specifically. They're recorded nineteen different times in his letters to the churches and yet our church never even mentions the Kingdom of God today."

"Your confusion seems to be as layered as Donte's inferno." Matt replies, wiping his brow. "I'm not sure how to answer your deceptions. The Kingdom of God is not something that is coming. My Bible tells me it's already here, in my heart, all I need to do is spread it out to others, so it can fill the world with God's love. I do that by teaching people about Jesus and his salvation."

"I'm not saying we shouldn't teach others about Jesus and salvation, but by limiting our message to that, we've lost the true Gospel Jesus told us to preach, the gospel about the coming Kingdom of God. The Kingdom message is good news because God's Kingdom gives hope to everyone who ever lived. God has made a way that all men might know him, no matter where or when they lived. God wants everyone to come to him so that none should perish."

Matt breaks in excitedly. "That's what I preach, those exact words! Everyone needs to come to God through Jesus, so they don't perish!"

"What about those who couldn't come to Jesus because they didn't understand, God didn't draw them? What about those who didn't because there was no one to teach them about Jesus where or when they lived? It seems to me that the gospel of salvation alone leaves them outside of God's love. They had no way to accept Jesus as their savior."

"Oh, I'm confident God's love will work it out for them. Maybe Jesus comes to the good ones before they die so they can accept him. We can't know all the mysteries of God."

"No, we don't know all of God's mysteries." Isaac agrees. "But we can know the ones he reveals to us through the Bible. Understanding his coming Kingdom explains what happens to those who don't accept Jesus during this life. Knowing the limits of our physical mortal nature, is key to understanding God's Kingdom and how it's coming. It started with Jesus, but it's coming in stages. First Jesus paid for our sins, then the Holy Spirit came to comfort and guide his disciples. Next Jesus will return, this is when his followers are resurrected, then he fights…" Isaac is cut off short by Matt's abrupt interjection.

"You talk about being faithful to the Bible! All your resurrection talk contradicts Hebrews nine. That chapter tells us clearly that man is once to die, then comes the judgement. Here, I'll look it up for you since you seem to like reading scripture so much." Matt types hard on the keyboard searching for the verse he wants. "Here it is,

Hebrews 9:27 And as it is appointed unto men once to die, but after this the judgment:

See, the Bible tells us that man only lives once. It's right there, no conspiracy, no bad grammar or punctuation, just the plain Bible truth you're looking for." Matt sits back in his chair, confident with the lesson he's just taught Isaac.

Isaac is slow to answer but finally speaks. "If you are understanding that verse correctly, then no one who has ever lived would have come back to physical life after they died, as that would make them have to die more than once."

"Physically, yes I suppose that would be correct. Their souls would always be alive as they are immortal. Like our doctrine of the immortal soul teaches." Matt spoke confidently about his long-time belief.

"But the Bible tells us about several people being resurrected back to physical life in the Old Testament. They would have died more than once because there's no one alive on this world over one hundred and twenty-five. There are several more people in the New testament who came back to a physical life, like those who came out of their graves after the crucifixion of Jesus. Here let me look it up." Isaac reaches for the keyboard and types. The verse he wanted soon appeared on the monitor. "Here read this." He said, pointing to the monitor and passing the keyboard across the desk to Matt.

"OK." Matt said, turning his chair so he could see the screen better.

"Matthew 27:51-53

51 And behold, the curtain of the temple was torn in two, from top to bottom. And the earth shook, and the rocks were split. 52 The tombs also were opened. And many bodies of the saints who had fallen asleep were raised, 53 and coming out of the tombs after his

resurrection they went into the holy city and appeared to many."

"See, these people lived twice and would have died twice, not just once. Hebrews nine is talking about Jesus living once perfectly, becoming an unblemished sacrifice for our sins." Isaac tries to explain.

"No, no. They were resurrected into immortality, then went to heaven with Jesus, becoming the twenty elders at the throne of God." Matt passionately defends his beliefs.

"How could that be possible? We are told Jesus is the first to be born of many brethren. Being the first means, no one can come before him and he wasn't raised from the dead until three days later. They were at least three days too soon to be raised as spirit beings, they would've had to be raised as mortals. Unless you don't believe the Bible when it tells us Jesus is the first to be raised to glory. Your belief in them being raised to spirit life contradicts the immortal soul doctrine. Why would they need to come back to life, glorified in spirit form, as you have said, if they already had that spirit life innately inside of them? It would be pointless. Your arguments and beliefs are contradictory." Isaac tries to help Matt see his point.

Matt thinks for a moment then with a snap of his fingers he replies. "Jesus said I am a child of God and that I will never die."

"Yes, that will happen in the future. The followers of Jesus will become the children of God and will never die. But we're told that right now we are heirs of God. Heirs to a fortune do not possess it right away. It's something they get in the future." Isaac countered.

"I told your mom I'd try to help you sort out your strange new beliefs. I don't know how you came up with them. You certainly didn't get them from our Bible school. I went there after I graduated from high school. It was the first term for the new dean. I was a new student and he was a new educator; I suppose you could say we learned a lot together during those years. We explored many different Bible teachings, but none as strange as the ones you have. You've really got the scriptures twisted into knots. I can barely follow your logic in conversation. I've tried making notes to help make sense out of them, but it's no use." Matt gestures towards the yellow pad of paper with the pen in his fingers. "It's getting late and I have some morning appointments. Why don't you write out your ideas for me to read over, I'm sure I can find some Bible scriptures that would be helpful to you if I had time to study your questions logically.

Isaac was unsure of the idea. "It would take a while to get all of the verses organized. It's like a game of pick up sticks, one doctrinal change influences another one, until they all seem to shift."

"I can help you out with that." Matt said brightly. "You aren't the only one to have gone to Bible school, only I graduated. You won't have to use your proof scriptures, I know the Bible, I'll recognize your references. You know, sometimes you come across as a bit of a righteous showoff when you quote, or read, all your Bible verse references. Just write out your ideas and I'll study them and get back to you. If I have any questions, I know where to find you."

Isaac gives the proposal some consideration for a moment, then responds to Matt. "Ya, I think I could make that work out. I don't mean to show off, I just don't want there to be any misunderstandings between what we think the Bible says and what it actually does say. If you have any misunderstandings or need help finding a reference, you'll call me right."

"Of course I'll call. It would make no sense to spend my time reading your ideas if I couldn't understand them. I'll get a hold of you for any required authenticating."

"OK. I'll get to work on it. It may take a couple of weeks as I've started a few new college courses this semester."

"Well take your time to get it right. I don't have a lot of time to go over this stuff with you. I'm spending my time with you as a favor to your mom, because of the close family bonds we've developed over the past years. I won't have time to do it more than once, so let's make it count the first time."

"Ya, I can agree with that. I don't want to waste my time either."

"One other thing. I'll have to ask you to not see Becky until we can get these matters straightened out. I won't have her exposed to any misleading or dangerous doctrine. She's had some struggles while you were away. I don't want to risk her turning away from her faith due to misleading or inaccurate beliefs causing her confusion. I'm sure you wouldn't want that. You know how it doesn't take long for someone to question their lifelong beliefs.

"If people place their faith in Jesus and the truth of the Bible, rather than the doctrine of man, they can't go wrong. Becky needs to make up her own mind and not have others deciding her future. If her faith is anchored firmly in Christ, no storm can tear her from him." Isaac is firm in his resolve.

"I could sure use your support on this. You know, I've always thought of you like a son and Becky has always been sweet on you, we can't risk her future by cluttering her mind with falsehoods. I've raised Becky to be obedient. She'll listen to me, if I have to forbid her from seeing you I will. I'd rather you both keep your Bible studies separate. I'm not saying you can't talk to each other at school or church, just keep your conversations light and off questionable topics. I think it would be foolish for you both to pursue a deeper, personal relationship, if you aren't on the same page spiritually. A house divided will not stand, don't be unequally yoked.

It won't be for long, just till you write out your beliefs and we go over them. You said it wouldn't take you too long, this will encourage you to finish as quickly as possible." Matt was encouraging and made his request sound reasonable, knowing Isaac would try to protect Becky whenever possible.

"I don't know how you expect me to put my feelings for Becky on hold. We want to move our relationship forward, not put it on hold, like we were talked into doing before." Isaac's feelings were still stinging from when he left for Bible school. "I could never explain that to Becky."

Matt's tone goes strict and his face hardens in an instant. "I wasn't asking for your agreement, or endorsement. I was asking for your cooperation. I'm telling you what will happen, whether you like it or not. It will be easier for the both of you if you're on board and don't fight me. It won't be for long. It may not seem like it to you now, but I'm on your side son." Matt put his hand on Isaac's shoulder, giving it a squeeze. "If your beliefs weren't of concern, your mom wouldn't have been worried enough to ask me for help. Becky's told me about your ride home from Bible school and that old trucker guy. Quite frankly, I'm surprised that you, of all people, would have been swayed from your traditional upbringing."

"I was swayed, because my belief in the Bible was stronger than my faith in unproven doctrine. That trucker showed me how Bible verses I thought I knew said something different than I was taught. He gave me the understanding to freely let the Bible speak for itself, with all its verses speaking in harmony, not contradicting themselves. The fundamental understanding he gave me was the true mortal nature of man."

"I don't have time to debate or study this with you now. That's why you need to write it out for me. The sooner you get it done, the quicker we can get you straight on your doctrinal understanding and the sooner you and Becky can start building your relationship again. You go home and pray about it, talk to your mom. I know that after you think about it, you'll see the wisdom of my plan. No good will come from getting Becky confused by your false doctrines."

"But you're assuming your doctrines are accurate!" Isaac protests.

"That's why you need to get busy." Matt urges "Get your ideas down on paper so we can go through them. It's the best way forward. Our denomination has been around for over a hundred years. I find it unlikely your new ideas will topple any of our long-standing doctrine."

"I need to talk to Becky. This is a big decision for both of us, it's not one I could leave her out of."

"I told you, I will stop her from seeing you if I have to. It'll be better if you cooperate. I'll tell Becky of your concerns, but you will stop seeing her. You better go home now. I'm sure you'll see it my way tomorrow after a good sleep. I'll say goodnight to Becky for you." Matt stands up and firmly helps Isaac to the door, handing him his coat and pushing him and his boots outside into the cold night air. "Don't say anything now that we may regret later. Go home, have a sleep and write out your ideas like we talked about. Things will work out for the best, you'll see." With that Matt turned and abruptly closed the door behind himself.

Realizing that now wasn't the time to argue, Isaac compliantly put on his coat and boots outside, then walked home. He did not want to cause any more trouble with Matt. As he walked in the dark, Isaac planned what he would say to Becky at school. When he arrived home the house was dark. He quietly gave Rosy some attention and a treat. Peaking in on Mum, he found her snoring rhythmically. Turning silently, Isaac slipped up to his room and went to bed.

Quietly praying, wrapped in his blankets, Isaac pours his heart out to his Lord. "Papa, please help me to boldly tell others about your coming Kingdom and the good news it brings for the lost of this world. Thank you for calling me into your family. Please help Mum as she learns to adjust without Pa. I know you care for me and can see the path I need to take to make it safely to you. Please guide me in the paths you have laid out for me to walk, I want to follow you. I am yours for whatever you want. Lead me in your ways and your will all my life. Please help Matt work things out with Becky.

Father, I want to follow you in all that I do. Help me uncover the truths you reveal in your word. Where I'm wrong, please set me straight. I only want to support your truths. If it's your will, please work things out for Becky and me. You know my feelings for her. But my love for her or anything else in this world comes second to you. Guide me, I pray, in the name of your son Jesus, my savior. I rest secure in your love. Amen."

Chapter 3

"As Jesus rose from the tomb, most autonomous nations, cities, or tribes of the world were governed by some form of absolute monarchy. One where the ruler is vested with absolute power. The monarch is the head of state as well as the civil government. Their rule was absolute. Two thousand years later, at the turn of the twenty first century, this form of governance had all but been abandoned by mankind leaving only five small enclaves of it to be found worldwide. Of these five, only two claimed Christianity as a national religion, one was a city state, the other was land locked in southern Africa.

The sun from the southern quarter of the African continent had bleached the outer stucco walls of the royal household bright white. It was an abnormally cool afternoon for early January as the sky was filled with clouds, threatening a summer shower.

"The car is just pulling up now ma'am." Nomba's aid said to her. Finishing off her letter with a signature, an elegantly dressed woman straightens in her chair. The vibrant colors in her dress are nicely contrasted by her rich black skin. Nomba puts down her pen just as a bright eyed, exuberant twelve-year-old boy rushes into her welcoming arms. Out of the King's 70 wives, she had the possibility of becoming the 'Great Wife' after the death of the elderly King. Being the 'Great Wife' meant her only son, out of the King's 180 surviving children, would automatically become King.

"Mom!" Mark whooped, as he ran into his mother's arms. "I missed you. It's so good to see you again."

"Ah my boy. It's good to have you home." She rubs her hand over his short-cropped black nappy curls and down his back as she tenderly embraces him. "How was your excursion, did you see any new animals?"

"Oh yes, many animals. But no new ones. The migration was over but there were still so many of them. I'm glad I got to go, it was a great way to start the school break." Mark could hardly contain his exuberance.

"I'm glad you had a good time. I hope you enjoy the next adventure I have planned for you just as much."

"What is it? Came Mark's excited response. "Can you and sisters come too?" Mark pleaded, having missed being cared for by his sisters and mom.

"No, we'll have to stay home again, but you can take a friend with you, how about Musa. I could talk to his mom if you'd like." Nomba was pleased that the summer plans for her young prince were being received with such enthusiastic approval.

"Sure. He's probably my best friend. But where will we be going? Cadet camp, hiking Cathedral Peak in the Transvaal Drakensberg? Musa and I can survive anywhere."

"No, it's none of those, although those sound like very challenging activities for such a fine pair of young men.

What I have planned for you is more educational and long lasting."

"Oh mommy, I don't want to go to summer school! My grades were good. Why do I have to go back during my break? If you send me back for the summer, I don't think I'll survive!" Mark makes exaggerated dramatic gestures with his arms. "The whole reason for having a summer break is to get away from school." Mark whined pleadingly, desperately trying to get his mom to understand.

"I didn't say I was going to send you to summer school." His mom scolded. "I said it would be more educational than hiking in the mountains." Nomba held Mark at arm's length, looking intently into his deep dark eyes. "Don't worry, there will be plenty of fun outdoor activities, football, archery, canoeing. The camp director said he keeps young, wild boys like you exhausted with lots of physical activities."

"That sounds better already." Mark quickly switched off his whiny voice and was back to normal.

"Yes, I thought it might." Nomba said with the wisdom of motherhood. "You've spent a lot of your young life with the royal guard, training and learning regimentation. As your mother, I'm responsible for your spiritual education. It's time to put more effort into the spiritual aspects of your life. I'm sending you and Musa to church summer camp. It's time you learned more about Jesus, there's more to life than the physical things you can see."

"Oh, that's awesome! Mark's reply took his Mom by surprise. "I didn't get to go last year, thank you mom. Musa and I will have a great time. The cousins told us how much fun they had there when they got to go."

"It's not all about fun." Nomba warned. "I want you to grow spiritually while you're there. You need to learn more about Jesus."

"Of course, mommy. Don't worry, I'll tell you all about Jesus when I get back. Do you think they'll have crossbows?"

It had been a week jam-packed with actives. The two friends came back to their bunks each night after evening chapel physically drained and ready for sleep. They looked forward to winding down the day with the singing and instruction chapel provided them. On the last night of camp an evangelist from South Africa, Mike Kasy, came to the camp with a compelling and graphic message of repentance for the young campers. Lying on their beds that night Mark talks quietly with Musa about Mr. Kasy's appeal for them to accept Jesus as their personal savior.

"Mom has taught me about Jesus since I was a little boy. I've already accepted Jesus as my savior, keeping me safely out of Hell. But tonight, when Mr. Kasy was talking about our need to love Jesus, I kept thinking about my grandfathers. They never heard about Jesus. They were good rulers, who sacrificed greatly for their people. I fear they didn't have Jesus as their savior. That means they are lost. Doomed for all eternity, burning in Hell."

Even in the inky darkness Mark's anxiety is apparent to a young Musa, who tries to reason with his friend. "I'm a Christian as well. But I must admit, I've never thought about those who died not learning about Jesus. I've only thought that I must accept Jesus for my salvation. I have been self-centered, thinking only about my own salvation."

"That's what most people do. It's only normal to think about saving your own life." Mark tried to help Musa rationalize his selfishness. "I've been training with the Royal Guard now since I was four, working to become a good future ruler and king. I need to consider the lives of others. Dad told me many stories about my forefathers, what they went through in building our nation, the struggles they had, battles won and lost. He's never said they were believers. I worry, not only for them, but for all our past countrymen. Did they have an opportunity to accept Jesus before they died? If not, they are all lost. It gives me such pain in my heart, the subject is hard to think about."

"You think far more deeply than I do Mark. I don't know what will happen to people who don't get the opportunity to accept Jesus. All that I've heard from pastors and church people is, it doesn't sound very good."

"That's what troubles me. It seems wrong to say mankind can only be saved if they accept Jesus but offer no hope for those who never got to hear about or come to know about Jesus and his sacrifice. Preachers tell us God loves everyone and doesn't want anyone to perish and that accepting Jesus is the only path to salvation. Then they say that those who don't accept Jesus, even though they didn't get to learn about Jesus, are lost forever. It just seems unfair to me. Can God truly be so mean?" Mark's voice cracks, on the verge of tears. "Torturing people eternally for not doing what they don't know about?"

"I have no answers for you my friend. I don't know if anyone will. The most likely answer you'll get is, 'you need to trust Jesus in all things.' Grownups seem to use that answer a lot when they don't know." Musa confidently speaks from experience.

"That's what I'm afraid of. I think this question will haunt me all my life and I'll never find a satisfying answer." Mark's voice fills with regret.

"I promise you my friend, if I ever find your answer, I won't hesitate in bringing it to you." Musa is solemn with his vow.

"I appreciate that, though I won't expect your discovery to come any time soon. If those who study Jesus every day can't tell me, I don't expect the answer will come to you very quickly. It's the kind of answer that will only come through God's providence."

"Well if that's true, I pray God will shine his providence on me so I can bring you his good news. Good night Mark. I hope together we can find answers for all your questions."

"You're a good friend Musa. I too pray we find those answers together. Goodnight."

The sweet sleep of youth comes quickly to the two friends. Both exhausted from the week's activities, they don't stir until morning bells wake them for breakfast

Chapter 4

The hallway cleared quickly with the ringing of the school's bells. Students murmur with trepidation as they take their seats. Mr. Speckle enters the class, his pointer tucked under his right arm making him resemble a dominatrix. Striding confidently, taking his position behind the desk, the class comes to an intimidated hush. He eyes the students intently, finally fixing his gaze on Isaac. Addressing the class, his voice ringing with a tone of delight, a rare smile starts to break across his face.

"Last class I informed you that you will be working mostly in small groups. In the spirit of full disclosure, we will now take time to address the source of your beliefs. This will give each of you a stage from which you can defend your convictions in open debate. I trust you have all come prepared for a vigorous, intelligent exchange of ideas. I did however, neglect to mention that your participation and logical arguments will be graded as part of your final mark." When speaking the word logical, Speckle locked eyes with Isaac who submissively looked away. Confident in his intellectual superiority, Speckle continues.

"I want the class to split into two groups." Gesturing to a wall with his right arm. "Everyone who believes in the proven facts of the universe and man's evolution, please move to this side of the class. Those who believe in some sort of a creator responsible for the existence of all there is, please move to the other side of the room."

Commotion breaks out as the students pick up their books and shuffle themselves to the appropriate sides of the class. Moving desks, they make sure there is a wide gap between the two groups.

"Good! Now that each of you have self-identified, it will be easier for your classmates to make informed decisions when they choose their small group teams. For the logic and reasoning part of today's studies," turning to his right, Speckle rubs his hands together joyfully as he lays out the game rules. "this side of the class can explain why and how the scientific method is best for explaining the world and life around us. While this other side of the class," gesturing to his left, "get the task of defending why they believe and support the unsubstantiated teachings of men to explain the physical world around us."

At this point in Speckle's oratory, a vibrating sound cuts loudly across the classroom. Isaac proceeds to drag his chair and desk towards the other side of the room. Finding a convenient space for himself, he ends up sitting near the center of the class, in no-man's land, facing squarely towards Speckle's throne.

Speckle was surprised by this uninvited activity. Looking down his nose at Isaac he mocked. "So, did the prospects of having to defend your beliefs logically prove to be too much for you? I was hoping for a better showing than this, your reputation has preceded you."

"Ya, Bible Boy. Did you lose your faith, along with your girlfriend? Bob called out. "We don't want or need you on our side. We've got science, we don't have time for your superstitious blind faith!"

"That's exactly why I thought we should take the time to explore the beliefs of this class' students." Speckle added swiftly, taking control of the conversation.

Isaac politely raises his hand, waiting for permission to speak. Speckle gives him a nod of approval. All eyes were on Isaac as he started to speak.

Isaac's eyes don't leave Mr. Speckle as he addresses him directly. "I felt compelled to move my position in the room, as I found your directions contradictory. First you instructed all those in favor of the evolutionary theory to sit on that side and those in favor of creation to sit on the other side of the room. Then you confused the issue by saying the scientific method supported evolution and having a belief in creation was nothing but superstitious blind faith in the fables of man. Your statements are opposite to each other and the truth. So, I believe the best place to be during this debate is in the middle, as that seems to be the place closest to the truth."

"I'm glad to hear you're eager to find the truth, that is after all, what science and the scientific method has been designed to do. Scientists pursue truth. It should be easy for us to find common ground as we look at the marvels of the universe and the origins of life. If truth is indeed what you want to find." Speckles voice is heavily laden with sarcasm.

"I agree. The truth should be as easy to discern as proving two plus two equals four." Isaac's demeanor is genuine.

"You Christians can't be right." Came a comment from the evolutionists side of the room. "I gave up my belief in God when I learned about dinosaurs. There's no way the earth was created only seven thousand years ago. I chose evolution. I could see the dinosaur bones; I couldn't see God."

Speckle added to the comment. "Yes, what about the Christian belief of the universe's age being limited to a mere six to ten thousand years? If that was its true age, most of the starlight wouldn't have reached us yet because the stars are too far away."

Saying a silent prayer for direction, Isaac takes a deep breath then starts to explain his beliefs. "It is true that most vocal Christians believe the age of the universe to be around six thousand years, they might be referred to as young earthers. But not all Christians believe that. Some, like me, believe the age of the universe to be much older, possibly more in line to what most scientists believe. We're often referred to as old earthers. Either way Genesis is understood, Christians believe God created everything."

"No way! You'd be ignoring the Bible if you believed that." Came a curt reply from the creationist side of the room. "I'm glad you moved; you obviously don't support the authority of the Bible as God's inspired word to mankind. Genesis specifically tells us of a seven-day creation period when God created everything, and no more than seven thousand years ago."

Speckle's smile widened at the growing fracture in the creationist's side of the room. 'they're unravelling already', he thought to himself.

"I believe Genesis is explaining creation from the perspective of being on the world as it takes place. That's why we have light on day one. Then after the waters separate and the clouds part, things get clearer. The planets and stars don't become visible until day four. If they weren't created until then, how was there light on day one?" Isaac answers his own question. "They were already there, you just couldn't see them with all the dark water." Going on with his explanation, "The world found in Genesis was waste and decay, without form and void. That isn't how God created it. He made it so beautiful that the angels sang for joy. Satan rebelled and was cast down to the earth with his demons. They destroyed the beautiful world God had originally created. I believe the Genesis account to be a recreation of the world, not the birth of the universe."

"That's not what I've been taught at church." The response comes from a different voice. "If you're going to ignore the plain Bible teaching of Genesis, what other Bible truths will you ignore because they don't suit your fancy?"

"For in six days the Lord made heaven and earth, the sea, and all that is in them, and rested on the seventh day. Exodus 20:11" Yet another creationist chimed in from memory.

"That's what a lot of Christians believe." Isaac agreed. "But let's read what the Bible tells us. Is that alright?" Isaac asked, looking for Speckle's approval.

Amused at how quickly the creationists were falling apart, Speckle couldn't keep the smile from off his face. "Well I suppose it wouldn't hurt." He said with a chuckle. "This once."

"Let's start with the seventh day when God was done and work backwards." Isaac directed. "Day six we have man and land animals."

"Day five are the sea creatures, fish and birds." Shouted a creationist.

"Sun, moon and stars. Day four." Shouted another.

"Day three, land and vegetation." Another said confidently.

"Land and sea on day two." An evolutionist joined in, followed by a hasty explanation. "My mom took me to church when I was little."

"Night and day on day one." Isaac ended the count. "Is that how the Bible starts? With night and day?

"No. You're at verse three." Came a reply from a creationist.

"But we've just counted seven days back from the day of rest. Was there eight days of creation? Isaac looked puzzled. "What do the first two verses of Genesis 1 say?"

"In the beginning God created heaven and the earth. And the earth was without form, and void; and darkness was upon the face of the deep. And the Spirit of God moved upon the face of the waters." A creationist recited off by heart.

"Exactly my point." Isaac replied. "God gave mankind time by using how the sun relates to the earth on the first day at verse three. All of mankind still uses that same way to count time today. It's called daylight standard time. Verse one tells us, in the beginning God created heaven and earth. But God didn't give us time to count when that beginning was until verse three. There's no way of Biblically proving when the beginning was, as the Bible gives us no time reference to establish it."

"You're twisting the scriptures around." Came another loud complaint. "We need to follow what the Bible clearly states as fact, not look at it from some crazy perspective."

"I'm not surprised you haven't looked at the subject from my point of view." Isaac counters. "But tell me," Isaac addresses the entire class, "all those who believe the world revolves around the sun, raise your hand."

Everyone in the class, Mr. Speckle included, raised a hand high in the air.

"Exactly!" Isaac continued passionately, looking around the room. "We all agree on that scientifically proven fact. We can see the pictures brought back from space demonstrating it." Turning to his fellow creationists he asks. "So why do you disbelieve clear Bible teaching? The Bible describes the earth as stationary. It tells us several times that the earth does not move, therefore the sun revolves around it. The Bible also describes the sun moving and even standing still." Pulling out his new phone, Isaac googles it. "Here I'll read them to you."

Speckle quickly interjects looking directly at the creationists. "Reading from the Bible isn't what we do in this class! But if it will help bring enlightenment, to those less scientifically inclined, then I suppose we could tolerate it just once more. You may proceed." He was delighting in the creationist's decomposition.

Having received Speckle's blessing, Isaac starts to read out loud from his new phone.

"Psalm 93:1 **The Lord reigneth, he is clothed with majesty; the Lord is clothed with strength, wherewith he hath girded himself: the world also is stablished, that it cannot be moved.**

Psalm 96:10 **Say among the heathen that the Lord reigneth: the world also shall be established that it** shall not be moved: he shall judge the people righteously.

1 Chronicles 16:30 **Fear before him, all the earth: the world also shall be stable, that it be not moved.**

Psalm 104:5 **Who laid the foundations of the earth, that it should not be removed for ever.**

Ecclesiastes 1:5 **The sun also ariseth, and the sun goeth down, and hasteth to his place where he arose.**

Joshua 10:12-14 **Then spake Joshua to the Lord in the day when the Lord delivered up the Amorites before the children of Israel, and he said in the sight of Israel, Sun, stand thou still upon Gibeon; and thou, Moon, in the valley of Ajalon.**
13 And the sun stood still, and the moon stayed, until the people had avenged themselves upon their enemies. Is not this written in the book of Jasher? So the sun stood still in the midst of heaven, and hasted not to go down about a whole day.
14 And there was no day like that before it or after it, that the Lord hearkened unto the voice of a man: for the Lord fought for Israel.

These verses were foundational in supporting the ancient belief that the earth is the center of the universe. For centuries Christians violently enforced the belief these verses had to be taken literally, until the weight of scientific evidence demanded a new understanding of them. Now, most Christians don't give them a second thought when defending the accuracy of the Bible. They read them metaphorically, not as literal truth."

"Your logic is unorthodox; we'll have to check out your history." One of the creationist's replied cautiously.

"The history is correct." A student from the evolutionary side confirmed. "I did a research paper on Galileo and how he was persecuted by the Catholic Church for his beliefs on how the galaxy works. They wanted to put him to death but ended up letting him die in house arrest instead."

"Yes! That's how fanatical Christians were over the validity of the Bible in the 1600's, they understood those sections literally. But now, not even the most ardent Bible follower would argue in support of the earth being the center of the universe. Because of scientific proof we now understand the Bible differently, yet it's still revered as the inspired word of God." Isaac said, continuing to support his position. "What's truly important is that God is the creator, not when he did his creating."

"So, you're saying the world isn't only seven thousand years old, like other Christians do? Yet you claim the Bible is the inspired word of God, the same as them? You are a conundrum." Speckle comments to Isaac, while shaking his head and pointing to the creationist side of the room. "Do you believe in the scientifically proven facts of evolution in demonstrating how your God created life as well?

Isaac responds to Speckle's questions. "No, I don't believe God used the evolutionary model to create life. He may have used species adaptation to suit different areas of the world. Take the different kinds of Finches or ants. Each has a different family within their kind. Lions,

Leopards and Tigers are different families within the feline kind which break down into different, smaller family groups. There was a family of dark coloured lions that grew up to twenty feet long from north eastern Africa. They were distinctly different from the smaller, lighter coloured lions found in southern Africa. Animals can make local adaptations as needed rather than be created as separate families. The very structure of DNA molecules, created by God, allow, and encourage these adaptations to take place within each kind of creature. What we don't see is a shark becoming a turtle. Or mutations intermixing the kinds between creatures, as we might expect, if the random selection belief of evolution was in charge." Continuing with his thoughts, Isaac doesn't pause.

"The Bible tells us God created. It doesn't tell us specifically how, other than by his word. Then God said, "Let there be light"; and the light appeared. Later in the Bible we're more specifically told about the 'word' from creation. In the beginning was the Word, and the Word was with God, and the Word was God. The same was in the beginning with God. All things were made by him; and without him was not anything made that was made. When God spoke, the word created everything. For by him were all things created, that are in heaven, and that are in earth, visible and invisible, whether they be thrones, or dominions, or principalities, or powers: all things were created by him, and for him. That word became flesh and dwelt among us as Jesus."

"I told you, we don't normally read or quote from the Bible in this class! We follow the scientific method of discovery here! You're getting carried away with fables now." Speckle angrily stopped Isaac from continuing.

"I'm sorry." Isaac sincerely apologized. "I was only doing it to help bring enlightenment to those 'less scientifically inclined'. After all, this class follows the scientific method of discovery, right? We don't want to follow the fables of man into false beliefs, we want to follow the truth."

"Exactly!" Mr. Speckle seemed frustrated with Isaac's approach. Over the years he had dealt with several Christian students insisting that God was the creator of everything and denouncing anything scientific. But he never had one who didn't insist on the world being only seven thousand years old. All of his rehearsed arguments were based on the short timeline the creationists clung too. He wasn't comfortable having to venture into new debates unprepared. "The scientific method of discovery is the only tried and true method for discovering how the world around us works. 'Truth' is what science is after, not fables." Speckle felt comfortable rooting his classroom lectures in his deeply held personal beliefs. "Science has proven beyond any doubt that mankind is the result of evolution."

"Then why is it called the theory of evolution?" Isaac questioned. "If it's accurate, beyond any doubt, shouldn't it be called the science of evolution?

"It's called evolutionary science, rigorously rooted in the scientific method." Bob called out not wanting to take a backseat in adding to Isaac's misery.

"Like a lot of things in life, the name used to describe something, doesn't always reflect the truth about them. They're oxymorons. To be sure we all know what we're talking about, let's look up an explanation for the scientific method." Isaac suggested.

Taking Isaac's que, an eager evolutionist types a google search on her tablet. "Got it." She shouts, surprising the class with her speed. "It may be a bit longer than we were looking for, but it explains it well. It's from Live Science." She starts to read to the class, looking to Speckle for his tacit approval, he gives her a nod.

"Pure Science
Reference:
What Is Science?
By Alina Bradford, Live Science Contributor | August 4, 2017 07:49pm ET

Science is a systematic and logical approach to discovering how things in the universe work. It is also the body of knowledge accumulated through the discoveries about all the things in the universe.

The word science is derived from the Latin word scientia, which is knowledge based on demonstrable and reproducible data, according to the Merriam-Webster Dictionary. True to this definition, science aims for measurable results through testing and analysis. Science is based on fact, not opinion or preferences. The process of science is designed to challenge ideas through research. One important aspect of the scientific process is that it focuses only on the natural world, according to the University of California. Anything that is considered supernatural does not fit into the definition of science."

"That's interesting to take note of." Mr. Speckle spoke out authoritatively. "Science deals with the natural, tangible, world. Not the world of fairytales and make believe." Pleased with his student's findings Speckle adds. "You may continue."

Picking up where she left off, the student continues.

"The scientific method

When conducting research, scientists use the scientific method to collect measurable, empirical evidence in an experiment related to a hypothesis (often in the form of an if/then statement), the results aiming to support or contradict a theory.

"As a field biologist, my favorite part of the scientific method is being in the field collecting the data," Jaime Tanner, a professor of biology at Marlboro College, told Live Science. "But what really makes that fun is knowing that you are trying to answer an interesting question. So, the first step in identifying questions and generating possible answers (hypotheses) is also very important and is a creative process. Then once you collect the data you analyze it to see if your hypothesis is supported or not."

Interrupting again, Speckle adds his two cents worth. "As I had pointed out earlier, good science always pursues the truth." Giving the girl another nod of approval, she carries on reading to the class.

"The steps of the scientific method go something like this:
1. Make an observation or observations.

2. Ask questions about the observations and gather information.

3. Form a hypothesis — a tentative description of what's been observed, and make predictions based on that hypothesis.

4. Test the hypothesis and predictions in an experiment that can be reproduced.

5. Analyze the data and draw conclusions; accept or reject the hypothesis or modify the hypothesis if necessary.

6. Reproduce the experiment until there are no discrepancies between observations and theory. "Replication of methods and results is my favorite step in the scientific method," Moshe Pritsker, a former post-doctoral researcher at Harvard Medical School and CEO of JoVE, told Live Science. "The reproducibility of published experiments is the foundation of science. No reproducibility – no science."

Some key underpinnings to the scientific method:

* The hypothesis must be testable and falsifiable, according to North Carolina State University. Falsifiable means that there must be a possible negative answer to the hypothesis.

* Research must involve deductive reasoning and inductive reasoning. Deductive reasoning is the process of using true premises to reach a logical true conclusion while inductive reasoning takes the opposite approach.

* An experiment should include a dependent variable (which does not change) and an independent variable (which does change).

* An experiment should include an experimental group and a control group. The control group is what the experimental group is compared against.

Scientific theories and laws:

The scientific method and science in general can be frustrating. A theory is almost never proven, though a few theories do become scientific laws. One example would be the laws of conservation of energy, which is the first law of thermodynamics. Dr. Linda Boland, a neurobiologist and chairperson of the biology department at the University of Richmond, Virginia, told Live Science that this is her favorite scientific law. "This is one that guides much of my research on cellular electrical activity and it states that energy cannot be created nor destroyed, only changed in form. This law continually reminds me of the many forms of energy," she said.

A law just describes an observed phenomenon, but it doesn't explain why the phenomenon exists or what causes it. "In science, laws are a starting place," said Peter Coppinger, an associate professor of biology and biomedical engineering at the Rose-Hulman Institute of Technology. "From there, scientists can then ask the questions, 'Why and how?'"

Laws are generally considered to be without exception, though some laws have been modified over time after further testing found discrepancies. This does not mean theories are not meaningful. For a hypothesis to become a theory, rigorous testing must occur, typically across multiple disciplines by separate groups of scientists. Saying something is "just a theory" is a layperson's term that has no relationship to science. To most people a theory is a hunch. In science, a theory is the framework for observations and facts, Tanner told Live Science."

"So according to this article Isaac, when it comes to science you have a lay person's understanding of the theory of evolution. When in fact, it is the framework on which observation and fact are laid." Speckle was snide with his remark.

"That's what the article says." Isaac replied coolly. "Doesn't evolution tell us that all life evolved from the simplest of life forms. Single celled creatures found in the muck of a newly formed earth?"

"Yes, that would be where it all started, if you go back far enough." Bob retorted aggravatedly. "Life had to start somewhere, then over time it grew more developed until we get to the present day."

"Well where's your reproducible experiments for that?" A creationist asked from their side of the room. "There's been a lot of time for evolutionary scientists to create a simple life form, where is it? For the scientific method to be followed properly, there has to be a reproducible experiment."

Speckle wades into the conversation. "Observations, the observations of multi-disciplined scientists from separate groups are laid onto the evolutionary theory."

Isaac has his phone out and is quoting from the article just read. "That's only part of what it says. The entire thought says, for a hypothesis to become a theory, rigorous testing must occur, typically across multiple disciplines by separate groups of scientists. So, where's the successful, rigorous test results for creating life. If there are none, then evolution should be downgraded to a hypothesis."

The evolution supporting side of the class perks up. "There's lots of proof." They shout. "Look at all the fossil evidence that's been dug up! Skeletal evidence of early man as they evolve from apes. You creationists just don't want to see the evidence." The responses came so fast and overlapped they couldn't all be heard or understood.

Isaac defends his opinion when he finds a break in the melee. "The scientific method must be adhered to if we want to keep evolution in the realm of science and out of the fables of man. There may have been early Hominids, but that doesn't prove humans evolved from them. Where are the transition skeletons? There's only jumps, from one family to another, like a horse and a donkey are from the same kind, but different. Regardless of the fossil record, for evolution to work, you must get life to spontaneously spring from a soup of ingredients void of life. Where are the scientific experiments for that? Until there are verifiable, reproducible experiments, then the theory of evolution, according to the scientific method, should be referred to as a hypothesis."

With Isaac's arguments in favor of biblical fidelity and the scientific method, a few students from both sides, drag their desks into the middle of the room to join him.

"As Winston Churchill once said 'The only instance of a rat swimming toward a sinking ship...'" Speckle said disdainfully referring to the evolutionary students joining Isaac. "Don't forget you'll be graded on the choices you make and how logical your arguments are." He warned the class with a grimace.

As Mr. Speckle spoke, a student anarchist, looking intently at Speckle, noisily slid his desk into the center of the classroom joining the small group, just on principle.

Clearly agitated, Bob lashes out at those sitting in the center of the room while focusing on Isaac. "If it's experiments you want, are you aware of the reproducible experiments made by scientists in the field of Quantum physics? From a vacuum, using a magnetic field and mirrors, they can get virtual particles to wink, or pop in and out of existence, producing flashes of light. They create this phenomenon from nothing. We don't need a creator; science can reproduce the very beginning of the universe. What more proof do you need?"

Isaac starts his defense. "Yes, those experiments are reproducible, however your using those experiments to simulate a time before the universe began, pre-big bang. That's a time before anything existed. There was nothing anywhere, no vacuum, no light, no magnetic fields, no virtual particles to pop in and out of existence."

"Ya." Chimed in one of Isaac's new compatriots. "The University of California said an important aspect of the scientific process was that it only focused on the natural world. Do you remember Mr. Speckle? You told us to take note of it. Science didn't deal with the supernatural, only the tangible, physical nature."

"Scientists tell us everything started with the Big Bang and before that there wasn't anything, meaning there was no physical matter. We just heard that the first law of science is energy can't be created or destroyed, it can only change forms. So, where did the universe building energy come from before physical matter was created? This is a time when there is nothing for the scientific method to experiment on or study." Isaac drove the point home further, as a couple more desks were moved into the growing group of desks near the center of the class. "There is no physical for the scientific method to explore. It's in the spiritual realm, a place where science is out of its league. To find out about spiritual matters, you need to study into the Godly realm."

Bob brakes in, loudly voicing his opinion. "Oh! I knew this was coming. Any excuse to talk about your precious Jesus. Next thing you'll be telling us is Jesus is the answer to everything. How everything we have, know and need comes from him." Making quotation mark gestures in the air with his fingers, he adds in a mocking tone. "Jesus, our great savior."

Isaac is quick to respond. "Evolutionists believe people of faith are blindly following the ideas of man. You think science alone has brought enlightenment to the world."

"That's because it has!" came a loud comment from the evolutionists.

Bob looks to Speckle for support as he continues his argument. "Science and the scientific method have been the real savior for mankind. Look at all the developments it's made in health and medicine, insulin and penicillin alone have saved millions. If God wanted to help mankind so much, why didn't he give us science sooner?"

"God does want to help." a creationist spoke out. "But he doesn't only want to give humans physical life. He wants to cleanse them from sin, giving them eternal life. That's what Jesus came to do."

Mr. Speckle speaks up in defense of his beliefs. "Throughout the entire history of mankind, humans have always felt like they had to please some all-powerful, life controlling God. Whenever something went wrong, we got sick, the crops were bad, the house burned down, humans would look for what they did to displease their deity. Then do whatever they had to do to get back into their god's good graces. As a species, man has always looked to please a higher power. We never collectively broke free from multiple millions of years of superstition until we developed science and learned to analyze our world through the lens of the scientific method. Science has set us free from fables developed by other men. Now we can put our faith in the truths of our scientific discoveries."

"That's true." Isaac takes Mr. Speckle by surprise with his agreement.

"Well, I'm glad to see you've seen the light, furnished by science." Speckle was unsure where this was going.

"Humans have always tried to please their man-made gods. Like you said, from our earliest beginnings. Now science can break us free from the fables of men." Isaac continues to startle Mr. Speckle. "Your faith in science is just that, faith. Evolution is your religion as it requires your faith, as we have seen, it's free of the scientific method of discovery. So tell me, what happened in our global collective history to cause such a worldwide, mind-altering shift toward science, freeing us of slavery to man-made god's? Let's look into our collective world history and find out what it was and when it happened."

"It didn't happen all at once, it was a process. Starting out small, with perhaps one idea. It has developed through other like minded people and it's still increasing ever larger, with free thinking scientists from every discipline adding their research to it. Deepening my faith in science." Speckle's voice takes on a majestic tone.

"Well that's OK." Isaac insists. "When did this process start?"

"It started in Europe with the renaissance, around thirteen hundred, but it probably had thinkers using it's reasoning before that." An evolutionist blurted out.

"Can we think of any major, collective mind shift that happened back then, leading humans to believe they didn't have to make sacrifices to please their gods in order to gain their favor?" The room was quiet in thought. Isaac pressed for an answer. "Is there nothing in history to release humanity from offering sacrifices to gain god's favour? Nothing that said, now you can come freely to your true creator, proving your creator loves you?"

"Jesus did that." Someone from the creationist side said. "That's what Jesus did for us. He opened a free path for us to access God, without fear of rejection. He demonstrated God's love for us, proving God loves and cares for us."

"Exactly and when did that take place?" Isaac asked excitedly.

"That's where we divided our counting of time. Earth's history before Jesus is called BC, or now BCE. After he died it was AD, after death. Now it's called CE. Evolutionists want to remove Jesus from history." another voice from the same side of the room comments.

"That's circumstantial." someone from the opposite side of the room objects.

"Is it?" Isaac said demandingly. "You're the ones who say humans have been around for millions of years. Why is it, after all that time of trying to please a god, did humans suddenly change? Going from fearing some god, to living in scientific enlightenment in just over seventeen hundred years. What happened after those millions of years to make us change. Is it just coincidental that this enlightenment happened just after Jesus came, literally altering how we count time and our understanding of God? Jesus proved that God loves us, freeing us from the god-fearing fables of man."

"Like you just pointed out, your Jesus came over a thousand years before the scientific method started to take root and it's been growing now for more than eight hundred years, getting stronger by the day. Why did it take so long for the ideas of science to take off if Jesus was responsible for them?" Bob was loud and angry.

"Just like Mr. Speckle said about science, it takes time for mankind's collective conscience to change." Isaac was slowly winning more students to his position in the class. "The knowledge of Jesus had to reverse our history of living in fear of gods that wanted to punish us for our mistakes, to understanding a God who loves us and is on our side. Not until humans stopped fearing punishing gods, could we develop thoughts that illnesses were caused, not because the angry gods were punishing us, but because we caught a virus and that virus could be destroyed, leaving us healthy again. Jesus gave mankind that collective mind change about God through his sacrifice."

Mr. Speckle returns to the conversation with a question. "Are you saying we only have science and the scientific method because of Jesus? You'll have a struggle to substantiate that position logically. Remember your logical arguments will be counted towards your grade."

"Bible Boy doesn't care about marks! He only cares about his Bible and Jesus. That's all he's ever cared about. Even girls don't interest him much." Bob's comments were delivered bitingly mean. "He's been spouting off about Jesus since kindergarten. But these ideas are grandiose, even for him."

"Look at the history and use your reasoning. Jesus came and gave us free access to God. His teachings were so revolutionary, that four hundred years later the pagan religions around the Mediterranean had been abandoned. Gradually, as people came to understand our world wasn't controlled by fickle gods and we didn't have to worry about making them mad, that's when the salvation Jesus brought us left us free to think scientifically. After the millions of years, you say mankind preceded Jesus, we only start to analyze the world around us using the scientific method, a short twelve to thirteen hundred years after Jesus came. Other than the world changing life and message of Jesus, nothing had changed in the world, or in the minds of the people living on it. It took more than twelve hundred years before some of those freed minds would begin to develop a scientific outlook." Isaac sets out a challenge. "If it wasn't because of Jesus, then you tell me, why did the scientific method start? After the millions of years, you say humans lived under superstitious fables, nothing else mind altering or God understanding in history had changed."

"This class studies science, not man's fables!" Speckle growls at Isaac. "We don't have to justify our reasons for believing it."

"Not for believing in science, but for believing in your man-made superstitious fables of evolution and in the total expanse of the universe developing from absolutely nothing, neither of which are supported by the scientific method of discovery." Isaac shot back. "Or are your beliefs 'not worthy of logical', scientific, defense?"

Speckle and the shrinking evolutionist side of the class were just about to respond to Isaac's challenge when the bell rang, marking the end of the class.

"Well, this has been interesting." Speckle said, breathing a sigh of relief. "Unfortunately, our time has come to an end. I trust you all will have a better understanding of your fellow student's beliefs and who you might want to be partnered with in your small groups. I'd love to continue this discussion in our next class but I'm afraid our class schedule will not permit the time expenditure. We'll be starting right into our geography studies when we meet next, so be sure you come prepared." Speckle turns, wiping his brow of forming beads of sweat. Clearing his desk, he closes his briefcase.

The classroom is quickly straightened up a bit before the students hurry off to their next class. Isaac pushes through the crowd. Catching up to Bob, he takes hold of his arm spinning him around, so they stand face to face.

"What did you mean when you said, 'Maybe I lost my faith and my girlfriend'?"

Bob's grin covers his face as he speaks. "Oh yeah, I forgot. She didn't want to tell you."

"Tell me what?" Isaac demanded.

"When you left last year, to go to your 'Bible school', Becky was feeling left out and unsure of you. The way you and her dad planned out her future, without even consulting her. That really ticked her off. I offered her somewhere to vent. I always liked her. I could never understand what she saw in you though. You never appreciated what you had right at your fingertips. We got to know each other all winter, until you came back early. She wanted to give you one more try. Lucky for me, you and her dad messed that up the other night, by once again leaving her out of the decision-making process."

"I wanted to talk to her about it right then. Matt wouldn't let me! He practically pushed me out of the house. Same as last year, I didn't get to talk to her like I wanted to. I've been trying to call her for two days now. I even got a new phone like she wanted!"

Bob pretended to wipe tears from his eyes while playing an imaginary violin mockingly as Isaac explained his actions.

"Oh, poor Isaac." Bob said in mock sympathy. "Woulda, coulda, shoulda!" His voice turned cold and hard. "I don't care! And judging from what Becky told me last night, she won't care either. Oh, and I tell you this purely out of spite." Bob leans his head in close to Isaac's. "I was a comfort to her, all night. She wasn't sure what to do, 'so I filled her in' on how to respond." Bob's grin turned into a full toothy smile as he enlightened Isaac about his relationship with Becky. Pulling his elbow free from Isaac's hand, Bob turns to go to his next class. Then stopping briefly, Bob turns back and looks squarely into Isaac's eyes, "The next time you touch me, you better expect more than a verbal response. I'll rip your head off." Bob threatens before he spins to leave.

Chapter 5

As Israel crosses through the Red Sea fleeing the Egyptians onto the Sinai Peninsula, God keeps them safe with many miracles as he leads them south into the wilderness. When they reached Rephidim the Amalekites cowardly attacked the tail end of the group where the weak and sick were traveling.

Deuteronomy 25:**17 Remember what Amalek did to you on the way as you were coming out of Egypt, 18 how he met you on the way and attacked your rear ranks, all the stragglers at your rear, when you were tired and weary; and he did not fear God.**

Through the Israelite army led by Joshua, God defeats Amalek as Aaron and Hur hold up the weary arms of Moses.

Exodus 17:8-13 New International Version
The Amalekites Defeated
8 The Amalekites came and attacked the Israelites at Rephidim. 9 Moses said to Joshua, "Choose some of our men and go out to fight the Amalekites. Tomorrow I will stand on top of the hill with the staff of God in my hands."
10 So Joshua fought the Amalekites as Moses had ordered, and Moses, Aaron and Hur went to the top of the hill. 11 As long as Moses held up his hands, the

Israelites were winning, but whenever he lowered his hands, the Amalekites were winning. 12 When Moses' hands grew tired, they took a stone and put it under him and he sat on it. Aaron and Hur held his hands up—one on one side, one on the other—so that his hands remained steady till sunset. 13 So Joshua overcame the Amalekite army with the sword.

Deep seated animosities held by the Amalekites against Israel had been developed over multiple generations. It started with the sibling rivalry between their forefathers Jacob and Esau. Even before they were born these brothers were at odds.

Genesis 25:22-26 New International Version

22 The babies jostled each other within her, and she said, "Why is this happening to me?" So she went to inquire of the Lord.

23 The Lord said to her, "Two nations are in your womb, and two peoples from within you will be separated; one people will be stronger than the other, and the older will serve the younger."

24 When the time came for her to give birth, there were twin boys in her womb.

25 The first to come out was red, and his whole body was like a hairy garment; so they named him Esau.

26 After this, his brother came out, with his hand grasping Esau's heel; so he was named Jacob. Isaac was sixty years old when Rebekah gave birth to them.

A lifetime of family unrest results in Esau losing his birthright to his younger brother Jacob, fulfilling God's prophecy and leaving Esau hateful of deceitful Jacob. A hatred that is passed on to all branches of Esau's family tree.

Genesis 27:41 King James Version
41 And Esau hated Jacob because of the blessing wherewith his father blessed him: and Esau said in his heart, The days of mourning for my father are at hand; then will I slay my brother Jacob.

Jacob's family becomes the nation of Israel while hatred toward them grows in Esau's family throughout their generations. Esau's descendants acted individually or as a group with allies whenever the opportunity arose to harm Jacob's family. The offspring of Esau joined Babylon when Jerusalem was taken into captivity. The family line of the Amalekites becomes the most aggressive against Israel and the God who blesses them. In the time of Esther, Haman, a descendant of Agag the king of the Amalekites, acted alone when trying to destroy the Persian Jews.

Judges 3:13-14 New King James Version
13 Then he gathered to himself the people of Ammon and Amalek, went and [a]defeated Israel, and took possession of the City of Palms. 14 So the children of Israel served Eglon king of Moab eighteen years.

Judges 6:3-6 New King James Version
3 So it was, whenever Israel had sown, Midianites would come up; also Amalekites and the people of the

East would come up against them. 4 Then they would encamp against them and destroy the produce of the earth as far as Gaza, and leave no sustenance for Israel, neither sheep nor ox nor donkey. 5 For they would come up with their livestock and their tents, coming in as numerous as locusts; both they and their camels were [a]without number; and they would enter the land to destroy it. 6 So Israel was greatly impoverished because of the Midianites, and the children of Israel cried out to the Lord.

Psalm 137:7-9 New International Version
**7 Remember, Lord, what the Edomites did
on the day Jerusalem fell.
"Tear it down," they cried,
"tear it down to its foundations!"
8 Daughter Babylon, doomed to destruction,
happy is the one who repays you
according to what you have done to us.
9 Happy is the one who seizes your infants
and dashes them against the rocks.**

Esther 3:1 New International Version
Haman's Plot to Destroy the Jews
1 After these events, King Xerxes honored Haman son of Hammedatha, the Agagite, elevating him and giving him a seat of honor higher than that of all the other nobles.

Although the exact lineages of Esau have been lost through passing generations, his national descendants through Amalek, can be seen as an archetype for all those who oppose the plans of God. No matter where your historical lineage comes from, no matter how you dress or what your stated beliefs are, if you oppose the will of God, you're joining yourself to the family of Amalek. Though evil people may try to undermine God's plans, he is in control and works things out for those who love him.

Romans 8:28 New International Version (NIV)
28 And we know that in all things God works for the good of those who love him, who[a] have been called according to his purpose.

God has a fearful future planned for those who refuse to follow him. Not having love towards others, God will destroy the house of Amalek.

Exodus 17:14-16 The Voice
Eternal One (to Moses): 14 Write down what I say on a scroll as a memorial record of these events, and read it aloud so Joshua can hear: "I will erase all traces of the memory of Amalek from under heaven."

15 Then Moses constructed an altar and called it, "The Eternal Is My Battle Flag."

Moses: 16 Because Amalek raised a defiant hand against the throne of the Eternal, He has promised to wage war against Amalek through future generations.

From a rocky ledge overlooking the Albanian Valbona Valley, a sentry stands guard, scanning the blue sky for aircraft. Deep beneath his boots inside the mountain's concrete shelter, an air traffic controller studies his monitor's flashing light tracking an inbound helicopter. Keying the mic, he speaks articulately, sending his message over the latest Motorola radio equipment of 1984.

"Home base calling. Home base calling three x-ray, two, two, two. Come in, three x-ray, two, two, two. Can you read me? Over."

"Three x-ray, two, two, two, I read you loud and clear home base. We'll be making our approach soon. Permission to use the main landing pad. Over." Came a crackling reply from the room's wall speaker.

"This is home base, three x-ray, two, two, two. You're clear to use the main landing pad. Opening the dome doors now in preparation for your arrival. Security will be on deck to receive your delegates. Over."

"Roger that home base, we are picking up your beacons now and will be looking forward to the escort. Over."

Wind whips violently as the helicopter loudly sinks slowly into the deep recess exposed by the open dome doors. It lightly touches down onto the bull's eye shaped landing pad. No sooner had it landed and started slowing its roaring engines than the large dome doors started to close again, concealing its location. Simultaneously the Heli-pad started to sink even deeper into the fortified bunker built into the rugged mountain top.

A tall, thin, well-dressed man stands looking out of what appears to be a wall sized window. He smiles as he watches crystal clear turquoise water lap onto a white sandy beach while palm trees sway in the light breeze against the backdrop of an endless blue sky. His personal secretary approaches respectfully.

"Your excellency, the Holy Father has arrived. I will show him in at your discretion."

"Good, thank you. Give me a moment, then show our Polish friend in."

The secretary turns and leaves, as his boss talks out loud to the large empty room.

"Hey! Show me mountain views from outside." The window wall flashes to a view of the Valbona Valley, as the tall man strides across the room sitting down in a large ornate chair behind an equally elaborate desk.

He no sooner sat down when the office door opened with the secretary ushering in a small group of dignitaries dressed in their ornate regalia. Getting up from his chair the tall man greets his guests warmly with practiced sincerity. Kneeling in front of the entourage, the tall man smiles as the exalted leader reaches out his hand. The kneeling tall man bows his head as he reverently kisses the leader's ring.

"Father, it's so good to have you here at last." The tall man says in impeccable Polish, getting to his feet, nodding with a large smile to the rest of the group he finishes in Italian. "It's an answer to an old prayer."

Speaking in English, Father replies, "Yes, you have been very persistent, I'm not sure why. Our interests don't appear to have any similarities. But the love of God is for all men and his mercy is most profoundly felt in the lives of the worst sinners. It is the sick, after all, who need a doctor."

"And I the chief sinner, am in need of that doctor." the tall man says humbly. "Despite what appearances may suggest, our respective organizations have had a long history of shared, behind the scenes collaboration."

"Yes, I am aware of the past. We've been striving to make our ministry more transparent and open, correcting our past errors. We seek to be relevant to the world's cultures and people."

"That's exactly what I'm trying to accomplish within my organizational family. We're trying to take a more socially responsible stance. It can be a daunting task to change attitudes."

"We all have to rely on our God of love for strength."

"That's for sure. Making positive changes is a task almost more than us mortals are capable of. I think you and I have that much in common."

"Yes, we seem to. And you are right, our organizations have worked together in the past. However, in this present political climate, I can't appear to be dealing with unsavory partners."

"I'm the head of a profiteering family, we're not all unsavory. Like businessmen, our job is to make money wherever we can. We have many legitimate businesses showing huge returns. We invest in everything. Are some of us drug traffickers? Yes, and proud of it. Our work developing new pharmaceutical wonder drugs allow doctors to help people worldwide. We move vast amounts of drugs. For full disclosure though, developing our hybrid strains of cannabis are illegal in most jurisdictions. But it's because of this research, we are now poised to make great strides in medication for those living with chronic pain; in the very countries where our cutting-edge research is illegal. It might not seem like it now, but one day those products will be accepted by governments who now so adamantly reject them only because they're made from cannabis."

"Yes, we do live in an ever-evolving world. That's why I need to tread carefully. We can't predict where things will end up." Father replies cautiously.

"Exactly! Laws change, societies find new ways to behave. What's unlawful one day can be legitimate another. We follow the money and make our profits from all sides. We helped in law enforcement during the US prohibition of alcohol, all while operating profitable distilleries in Canada. Bootlegging our product into the US, we profited off both sides. Create the demand, then supply the need. Gambling with us will get you a stint in a New York jail, while we own lawful gambling destinations in Las Vegas. Society will eventually catch up to us everywhere."

"Yes, I'm aware of how you operate, but it isn't appropriate for us at this time. The optics are bad. We want to elevate our image beyond reproach."

"That's our goal for you too. Let us' in some small way, elevate you to the stratosphere." pleaded the tall man. "We long to have just a bit of your purity shine on us. The American name Roosevelt is synonymous with great presidents, not the profiteering drug lord that bankrolled their family's dynasty. Let us help expand your greatness. Please, let us expunge away some of our sins. We have respectable, legitimate branches wanting to help in any way possible."

"You'd have me believe all things are just varying shades of grey." Father said grimly.

"I'm sure you can't guarantee the legitimacy of all your offering's origins. Not to mention the purity of all the leaders under you." The tall man pointed out.

"Yes. I'm afraid we've had our share of disappointing members."

"So, you might empathize with my problems which are exacerbated by the fact that most of my leaders have no aspirations to do good."

"I've dedicated my life to empathy. I can imagine the problems you must face as the leader of such a diverse group. Perhaps we might be able to explore some limited joint projects your 'legitimate' organizations could help us with."

"Oh, I'd be grateful for any crumb that you might toss us. There is virtually no area we wouldn't want to help."

Father is contemplatively quiet, then responds, "We run clinics in South America, helping sex trade workers, men and women, living with some new kind of virus. I was thinking, sponsorship from an upstanding drug company could be advantageous to both of us. There will be a lot of R and D needed, but if perfected a lot of marginalized unfortunates could be helped. The details would have to be worked out by our people."

The tall man is excited with the new possibilities. "But it could be the renewing of a working relationship. Our institutions have been estranged for far too long now, we haven't worked closely since the 1500's. It's time we started to get acquainted again. It may turn into a courtship, leading to the marriage of our ancient families, from where we can claim our ordained place in history."

"That may be true, but let's not get the cart before the horse. You will have to mend your ways if we're to have any real lasting connection. We won't be unequally yoked to any partner."

"True, we can't see what the future holds for us, but this will be a start. Thank you for your kindness father. We'll get the details worked out however you like. We need an ally who is willing to touch us in our leprous state. We seek healing from our trespasses and are reaching out to you for help from within our sins. We're desperate to do some good in this world." Bowing low on bended knee, the tall man gropes for the father's hand and repeatedly kisses his ring with tears of gratefulness falling from his eyes.

"Yes, yes, my son. All things work out for those who love the Lord." patting the tall man's head gently. Not sure what to make of the situation, Father looks awkwardly at those in his entourage.

"Their departure was successful, your excellency. We will be tracking them until they land." the secretary reports with a smile. "Things seemed to have turned out well for you, but I must say I was astonished by your groveling at his feet. It was beneath your greatness and the kissing of his ring was almost too much for me to watch without gagging."

"That's why you're the secretary. You're far too worried about appearances. I'd gladly lick the belly of a snake if it gets me what I want. I'm working on long range plans for this family of ours. Plans laid by my predecessors; plans we will never live to see come to fruition. We're laying the groundwork for those who follow behind us and working with that lot is a key stone for that foundation. With respectability comes acceptability and they will supply both to us through association. Then we can exploit profitability."

"You are a great leader excellency. I marvel at your insight." the secretary turns to leave.

"Have the fresh supplies arrived yet? I have cravings to fill."

"Yes. We are fully stocked for any desire. What would you like your excellency? I'll arrange it personally."

Licking his lips, the tall man decides. "How about a dozen tender delectables before the general staff get into them. Add some ginger to the mix for a treat."

Knowing how to fulfill his leader's desires, the personal secretary smiles proudly at being able to serve. Before exiting, the secretary playfully turns and says. "I'll make it a baker's dozen."

"Good! In that case make sure one of them is a boy," the tall man hollers. Turning to the window wall, the tall thin man commands, "Hey! Show me strippers from Vietnam." The wall flashes.

After living in sinful depravity his entire life, the tall man had developed hungers that he could only keep satisfied from the unsavory corners of the globe. His favorite place to scratch his itch was in a back alley bar where the girls, after generations of raising families off patrons' tips, learned the only way to survive was to dive deep into debauchery. Walking over to the bar the tall man pours honey coloured liquid into a shot glass, eyes barely leaving the screen he knocks back several of them. Hearing the office door being opened, the tall man drops his suit jacket on the floor before grabbing a leather riding crop from behind the bar. Rolling up his sleeves he approaches the opening door, trembling with sadistic anticipation.

Chapter 6

Isaac's been busy with his two classes at school. He tried to see Becky, but she skillfully avoided him for the past few months, she would not even return his texts. He called her good friend Sherry, but she was clueless as to where Becky might be. Isaac put his mind to work at writing out his biblical thoughts for Matt. Keeping the supremacy of the Bible forefront in his mind, Isaac worked at unravelling the tangled beliefs he had been taught as a child. Staying held up in his room whenever possible, Isaac poured his thoughts out into his laptop.

He worked hard, crafting a story that would explain all his thoughts to Matt. It had occurred to him that he might be able to get school credits for his efforts and explain his controversial doctrinal ideas to Matt all at the same time. Since Matt practically demanded Isaac not include any Bible references, but rather just write out his ideas as a story, Isaac thought he'd write a play for his English class.

Matt assured Isaac he could find all the Bible references himself, but if he did need help, he'd consult Isaac. Anxious to get his thoughts to Matt, Isaac does only a quick editing before pulling the ruf draft out of the printer. Looking over the pages carefully, Isaac tucks them neatly into a large envelope before putting them into his backpack.

Approaching Matt's front porch in the dusk, Isaac retrieves the large brown envelope from his backpack.

With his hand outstretched, Matt is ready to receive it as he leans heavily on his front door ready to take it from Isaac.

"So, you've finally finished it. I'll start reading this tonight. Your timing is perfect. I tripped and fell this morning spraining my ankle. My doctor told me to keep it raised and rest for a few days. I'll devote the time to reading this and then I'll get back to you."

"I wrote it as a play for my composition class so it has a story line, but all my biblical ideas are in there. If you have any questions about it, just call me and I can clarify my points. How's Becky? I haven't seen her since we talked last. She won't even return my texts."

"That was part of our deal. I told you I'd take care of things. You're not to have contact with her until we get this sorted out. I'm on your side son." Matt firmly grips Isaac's shoulder. "I told you, she was raised to do as she was told." Smiling warmly Matt leans close to Isaac. "Things will work out the way God wants them to, you just need to have faith."

"I do have faith. I know God's in charge."

"Well then, you better turn that faith into patient action. I need to get back to bed and get off this ankle. You should go back home. The sooner I can get this read, the sooner you and Becky can get back together."

Taking Matt at his word, Isaac politely says goodnight. Turning from the doorway, Isaac walks home in the cool darkness. Matt gets into his bed awkwardly, turning restlessly and arranging pillows until he finds a comfortable position. With his head and his leg propped up with pillows, he opens Isaac's envelope. Taking out the first page, he starts to read as his wife softly snores beside him.

FAMILY PLAN

This play begins with God's first desire to have family, and follows his resurrection plans for humanity, where all will receive an opportunity to follow Jesus.

THOUGHT

Where and how this story begins is hard to describe. It's really not in a time or place anyone could describe to you so that you'd instantly say to yourself, "Oh yes, I know just what you mean. I can see it so clearly in my mind."

In fact, most of this story is like that because there are no experiences, places, or times that any of us could use for a common reference point. There are commonalities that run through the whole story. Threads we can all relate to. Courage, daring, deceit, loyalty, greed, envy, pride, but most of all, above all, love.

Yes, the threads we can all understand and relate to, are the ones that are at our very core. They transcend time, nationality, culture, colour, or creed. They are the roots that make us human. They are also the roots that connect us to our Creator, the giver of life. And this is how the story begins.

In the beginning.

Now I know what some of you are thinking. "Oh, I've read that before. The nerve, starting his story the same way as the most popular book in history." Well that "In the Beginning", isn't this, "In the beginning". This one's way, way, before the famous, "In the beginning". So here goes.

In the beginning there was ONE, and ONE was alone. There was only one ONE to be found. ONE existed not in a place or a time for place and time did not exist. Perhaps we should say that ONE lived in thought, for how else could we understand a place that was real but did not exist in any time, or place and is indescribable? So, we'll say that ONE lived in thought. Not in our thought, but their thought.

Yes, that's right. It's not a type-o. It's supposed to be their thought. It's probably best if I introduce you to ONE. You see, ONE was alone and there was only one ONE, but ONE is made up of three parts.

It's kind of like Canada having provinces and... no wait. Silly me. I need to remember royalties. You know, braces for the kid's teeth, house and clothes. Nowadays parents need to keep track of all the angles. Not miss any opportunity. "Remember where your largest market is." my publisher always says. Sorry, where was I? Oh yes.

It's kind of like the U.S. having many states within its union, separate, yet indivisible. That's much better.

As I was saying, ONE has three parts. #One part was the leader, not pushy, or bossy, like you may think of some leaders to be. #One always had #Two and #Three's best interest at heart. #One never did anything selfish for as long as ONE could remember, which was a very long time.

ONE couldn't remember their first thought, or even a beginning. They had just always been in thought together.

#Two was the most talkative of them all. But not in a bad way, it's just that #Two had an eye for detail and loved to elaborate on the ideas that #One had. You could say that #Two thought in technicolor, once a thought got started.

#Three is a bit harder to describe, doesn't verbalize much, if at all. Almost more of a power than an entity, but a personality, nonetheless. In fact, if you weren't careful you wouldn't notice #Three to be present in a thought and only recognize #One and #Two. #Three is the strong silent type. #Three's presence could be felt in a thought, not like a shove or push, but more like a soft warm glow on a cold night that you just naturally gravitate towards. But, if you wanted to go a different way, you could. It would be your choice.

But when #Three got excited, with #One and #Two basking in his warmth, uncontainable feelings of joy, love and contentment flooded over them. They could stay wrapped in the snuggly warmth of #Three, deep in thought. This is what they did, the 3 of them together as ONE.

#One had a new thought; it was a bit melancholy. Not that #One was unhappy or unsatisfied with existence, just the thought that there could be more and better came to mind. #Two picked up on it right away, for #One and #Two were so close in their thoughts that #Two would often finish the thought that #One had started. It would be the same thought only slightly different, in a good way. Like you might think, "pancakes would be great for breakfast" and before you know it you've got fruit and whipped cream on top. Different than just pancakes, but pancakes nonetheless.

#Two: Yes, I know exactly what you mean.

#One: Not that I'm unhappy, it's just...

#Two There could be more! Oh, what a wonderful thought. Just imagine, it wouldn't be just the three of us here as ONE. Why there could be billions of us.

#One: Yes, but we'll have to be careful.

#Two: I can see the details will have to be precise. Oh but the possibilities, the marvelous possibilities. What a thought! That's got to be the best one yet. How did you ever...

#One: ...Come up with it? I'm not sure. It was just there, a shadow at first and then, there it was. It's almost like I was...

#Two: ...Led to it, perhaps?

#One: Yes, or close enough to it so it would stick.

Just then #Three's presence could be felt strongly. Warm and familiar, like your own special blanket as a child.

#One: OK, so maybe all the great ideas haven't been mine alone.

#Two: Oh, let's not worry about how it got here. It's the best thought yet. I'm surprised it didn't come sooner. I love it! Just the thought of it', I can't stop imagining all the wonderful possibilities. More of us. We'll have family, brothers, sisters, children. ONE will be able to create so many and with such variety.

#One: Create yes, but they must choose to become part of us, to become one with us. Remember who we are.

#Two: Yes we are love and all the emotions that go into it.

#One: And as perfect love, we must control our emotions. We must let love have its perfect work in us.

#Two: And so must they. If they don't control their emotions and become like us, their future will be full of unhappiness, endless suffering and misery. The consequences for them are too painful to dwell on. Do you really think it's possible to reproduce ourselves? For there to be children of ONE?

#One: Well, it won't be without its difficulties, but I believe it's possible given the right circumstances. We are pure and perfect love.

#Two: We can't create that.

#One: Exactly. They must choose to become it.

#Two: Ya, if we created them that way...

#One: ...they would have no choice but to do it. We must love them enough to let them make their own choices. They will have to be free moral agents.

#Two: But if they choose wrong, they can't be with us. We can't live with anything that's not of love. There would be no place for them to go where we aren't? ONE is everywhere, ONE is omnipresent.

#Three stirred and brought the thought into sharp focus.

#One: Yes, that's it. If they weren't completely like us to start with, only seeds with great potential ahead of them, then if a wrong choice was made willfully, they wouldn't be eternal yet. If they start out mortal, then only those who choose wisely would receive immortality and become like us.

#Two: An informed decision of their free will, that clearly rejects or accepts our life of love, would have to be made. We will happily welcome them into our lives, or we would have no choice but to respect their decision and let them cease to exist.

#One: That would be our true expression of love.

#Two: And their true expression of free will. But if they are to have a choice, they'll need another option other than our love. ONE is all that exists, and we exude love, that's what we are. Where would anything not of love come from? We can't create it! Just the thought is repugnant to me.

#One: Well if they are to develop our character, learn to control their emotions and grow in love as we have, they'll need to work against something that is the opposite of us, our antithesis.

#Two: They wouldn't have to be perfect in their physical form, would they? I mean, that is a bit too much to expect from seeds, even with great potential. If they set their course down loves path, willingly choosing love, they may stumble, but they wouldn't stray far.

#Three: Not if they had a guide to follow.

#One: #Three! I'd almost forgotten what you sound like. You so rarely talk, but you're right, you could guide them along the path that leads to 1.

#Two: But what about the sins they commit after they choose the path of love, not to mention all the sins they will encounter en route? They'll be covered in it! They can't show up here like that.

#One: We'll just have to clean them off then, won't we.

#Two: But how? What atonement could be made for them?

#One's voice fills with sadness as it cracks hoarsely, barely audible to #Two and #Three.

#One: The greatest sacrifice possible. The sacrifice of pure unblemished love. Only that could make them clean and pay for their sins.

There was silence in thought as ONE pondered all the ramifications that #One had set into motion. The stillness was shattered with a joyous shout.

#Two: I'll do it! Yes, it could work, it will work! I can bring many sons and daughters to ONE. What an amazing plan! So intricate, and yet so simple. Who would ever guess that love would be the sacrifice for sin? But isn't that what true love would do?

#One: Without a doubt.

#Three envelopes them in an embrace that feels like a warm blanket after a cold day of tobogganing, including sipping on a mug of hot chocolate with those teeny little marshmallows. Lost in thoughts and plans for their future family to come, they basked in their love, relishing their ONEness.

Matt squirms in bed, his ankle throbbing. "Well I suppose that could all be plausible." Matt thinks to himself. "The Bible does tell us that Jesus is the word. That the Word made everything that was made through the power of the Spirit and they all dwelt together with God forever before anything was created." Struggling to get himself up, Matt swings his feet off the edge of the bed and tries to sit upright. Rising painfully to his feet he makes his way to the kitchen. Returning to his bed with a straw protruding out of the lid on his extra large cup, he sets it on his nightstand as he laboriously gets himself back into a comfortable position. "There. That should keep me going for another chapter or two," he thinks as he picks up another page of Isaac's story and settles into his bed.

ANTITHESIS

ONE had been busy. Their plans thought through again and again. Everything, from the minutest detail to the largest galaxy had been worked out to its end, ensuring all would have the desired outcome. ONE was ready to get creating, not only bringing to life a new host of spiritual beings, but putting into motion an ever-expanding physical universe to unfold as it should. ONE knew it was time to begin their master plan.

#One: We need to start with created beings, so they can witness the birth of the physical realm.

#Two: Yes, it is time. I'm pleased with the way our planning has turned out.

#One: These beings must have freedom of thought and intellect so they can choose their own destiny. We must show our consistent love to all of our created life forms.

#Two: This part makes me sad.

#One: I feel it to. #Three is grieving as well. We've been through all the possibilities, there is no other way, nothing else worked.

#Two: I know, but the facts don't keep my heart from breaking.

#One: We can only hope that not many will turn away. The power of evil will seem as strong as love.

#Two: Once they start down the path of perdition, it won't be easy to come back to love.

#One: We'll do all that we can for them.

#Two: Once their spirit is set they will not be able to come back to love. Banishment into isolation will be the only option for them.

#One: Yes, but it will be their choice to leave ONE. They'll be in control of their own will and destiny.

Two: And whether they realize it or not, they're going to be playing a crucial part of our plan. I hope you're right and not many turn away.

#Three echoes #Two's thoughts, with a burst of empathetic feelings.

#One: They won't all be created equally or exactly the same. Some will have different gifts and abilities in varying amounts. Diversity should cut down how many we lose. There'll be less chance of one sin affecting them all.

#Two: Let's get started then. The quicker this uncertainty is over, the better I'll feel. I'd just like to put this all to rest. I know the end goal is worth it, but getting there is going to be so painful.

#One: It's not too late to turn back. Our old existence has been great. We don't have to do this.

#Two: I know, but 1 wants family and relationship. That's where true love can grow and thrive.

#One: True, but will it be worth the cost?

#Two: Oh yes, most definitely yes! In all our planning, we've been careful with every detail. Thought things through to the end and back again. I feel bad that some will be locked up forever, but I know there'll be no other way. The character they choose to form will be set for eternity. Being spirit like us, they won't be subject to death. Their fate can only be imprisonment.

#One: Then let's get started.

#Three moved in closer with reassurance and comfort for all.

A throng of angels is assembled in precise rows on a sea of glass that surrounds a glorious white throne. Mighty cherubim with their outstretched wings are covering over #One who is sitting on the throne. #Two is there as well, at his right hand. #Three is nowhere to be seen. In fact, #Three had decided to never be seen by anything that was created. Though it was through #Three that all had been made. #Three could still be felt if you were in tune with ONE. #One and #Two often admonished those created to leave themselves open to #Three. Some only half heartedly tried, though there were many that tuned in and relied on #Three's influence for guidance, comfort and strength.

#One: Lucifer, that was another splendid concert. ONE truly enjoyed it. You've certainly outdone yourself.

#Two: Yes, it's wonderful what you angels can accomplish when you work together. The feelings of love and camaraderie that came from all the performers washed over me as much as the music did. Especially Gabriel, he certainly has come a long way with that trumpet of his. Music may not be his special talent like yours, but his heart is in the right place and he always does his best. I admire that about him.

Lucifer: I suppose he is admirable, if one was to admire the mundane. And he is such a good sport. Fortunately, he's very consistent and predictable. Since I was created the sum of beauty and perfection, not to mention musically talented beyond compare, I've been writing a special score for him to play. I know which notes he can't get no matter how he tries, but how it will sound when he does. So, I give him the wrong notes to play, so it'll sound right when it comes out. What makes it more hysterical, he thinks he's doing it properly. Lucifer leans against a pillar as he laughs uncontrollably.

#Two: It's not nice to make fun of him, he has such a good heart.

Lucifer: Oh yes he has a good heart, it's too bad he can't play the trumpet with it.

#One: Your pride may someday get the better of you. You're only better because you were given more talents than the others.

Lucifer: Yes I was, and I am better than the others. I thank you profoundly ONE for creating me better than the rest of this mediocre lot that I'm stuck with.

#Two: Lucifer, you were created perfect so that you can lead and help others do their best and grow into perfection.

Lucifer: Smugly chuckling. Yes, I'm their leader. They all adore me, almost as much as they do you; but I do go on. I really must be going, I have much preparation left for the upcoming celebration. You know the one. ONE said there was a great surprise in store for all of us. And I've been working on a special surprise, a small token, to reflect the gratitude and love that I have for ONE. With your permission, I'll be off.

#One: It should be a great celebration for us all. ONE looks forward to it.

Lucifer turns his back and strides confidently away before #One had finished talking. His head held high, looking down his nose he makes a show of reviewing the angels assembled neatly around the throne.

#Two: He's a long way down the wrong path. So arrogant and self-centered. There seems to be no way to reach him.

#One: He was the most spectacular of them all. If only he had used his brilliance to help raise others up to his level, but it only served to reinforce his superiority.

#Two: He would've been unstoppable, if only he had tried to tap into #Three's power. Always self-reliant and proud, he had no use for #Three from the start. He spurned ONE's guidance and friendship. Developed his own leadership style of competition, bringing stress and strife to the other angels. If he had only learned the ways of love from us. It's such a waste of talent and potential.

#One: He never did get to know ONE very well. Because we're all spirit, he thinks ONE is like him, with the same limitations, he's not all knowing or omnipresent. He thinks himself to be so smart and cunning. We know his thoughts as well as our own. I don't believe he's a waste of potential though. Those that come later and need to struggle against him will be stronger for it. He will help build strong character in all of ONE's children. He will make his move soon.

#Two: This phase of the plan is almost over. And the next, he can't even imagine.

High in his office tower, Lucifer gazes out over the vast expanse of the universe. It's not fair, he thinks to himself. To be stuck here taking care of rocks, nebula's and the occasional supernova. Mimicking ONE, Lucifer speaks out loud mockingly.

Lucifer: It will be good for you angels to have some responsibility and to take care of things.

Lucifer's rage is building as he starts to rant.

Lucifer: That's fine for ONE to say. I do all the work! ONE just leans back, relaxing on the throne. Meanwhile this stupid universe keeps birthing new galaxies that I have to take care of. I do all the heavy lifting in this relationship. ONE created me to be a slave and do their bidding!

Lucifer's fist is clenched as it swings violently in the direction of the sea of glass. Lucifer's voice becomes controlled and calculated, taking a cunning, sinister tone

Lucifer: It should be me sitting on that throne. I'm as good as ONE! My ways of competition and striving for more has built this kingdom, and keeps it going. If it wasn't for me, it'd still be run by those pathetic weak losers.

Lucifer mocks.

Lucifer: 'Oh just do your best. Love will conquer all'. Wussy's. Love, ha. I've proven that anger, hate and fear are superior motivators to love. It's time for my ascension! I will be the one reclining on the throne.

Lucifer turns and hollers loudly in anger.

Lucifer: Wormwood! Wormwood!! Get out here right now!

Groveling in complete subjection and trembling with fear, an angel appears before Lucifer, hunched over looking small and diminished in stature.

Wormwood: Yes master? I. I came as fast as I could. What may I do for you, my lord?

Lucifer: Well to start with, you might as well begin calling me, 'Your Majesty'. The old ONE has grown weak and frail. They spent their strength on creating all of this.

Waving his arm in a wide arch, gesturing towards the expanding universe.

Lucifer: #One tells us the greatest most spectacular creation is to be revealed at the upcoming celebration. As a special surprise for us, as if we need more things to look after. It's to be the finest gift the angels have ever received from ONE. That will clinch it. I have calculated the total energy needed to create all of this, and if my calculations are correct, they will have used up what is left of their power reserves. We will strike before ONE can replenish them.

Wormwood: It's true. The top achieving 30% of polled angels have not felt the presence of the spirit of ONE for eons. Rumor has it that it has died or has gone dormant for some unknown reason. Tradition has it, ONE receives power through the spirit and that everything is made by it.

Lucifer: You talk like the superstitious fool that you are. The spirit has never moved in us. I have never felt its presence. Just a lot of hocus, pocus, ghost stories. There's only #One and #Two. They always talk in the third person, as if there are more that make up ONE. I'm not so easily fooled by their smoke and mirrors as the rest of you.

What's important is what's real and that's my power, my wisdom. I was created perfect in every way. Probably to replace ONE on their terms, when ONE wanted. Well I'm not waiting around for them to decide when to step aside. I'll show ONE that I'm master of my own destiny and that I'll be the one deciding what I will do and when

I'll do it. And I choose now! If #One won't step aside on his own and take that sickly sweet #Two with him, I'll push them both out. I'll take my rightful place as ONE, and all the privileges that go with it.

Wormwood: I've spoken to legion, as you instructed. They are ready to do your bidding and have persuaded most of the upper echelon to join with them in service to you.

Lucifer: Good. I could always count on Legion. That team of misfits would cheat their way to the top of whatever they did. They never let anyone, or anything get in their way.

Wormwood: I have done all the preparations as you have commanded; your majesty.

A smile crosses Lucifer's lips at the sound of reverence towards him.

Lucifer: You do know how to put me in a good mood. Well done my good and faithful servant. I'll see to it that you are well rewarded in my kingdom. This will be our time to celebrate and a celebration for ONE to remember, if they can.

#One sits on the throne as the angels gather around on the sea of glass as ONE had directed them to. #One and #Two prepare to address the anxious throng.

#ONE: As you all know, ONE has been working on our latest act of creation.

#Two: We feel it will be a milestone within our physical realm. So far, our physical creations have been limited to large galaxies, celestial bodies and overlapping multilayered orbits of rock and ice.

#One: And you've all done a wonderful job, taking care that it all functions in order.

#Two: With our new creation we've taken the basic principles and condensed them into one neat package. Beyond a doubt, our best work yet in the physical realm.

#One: ONE is going to use this as a platform to launch the next phase of our overall plan. So, it gives me great pleasure to present this gift to you all. ONE gives it with all the love that is in our hearts.

#One gives a wave of his hand, rolling the heavens back like a scroll. All the angles turn to look in unison as if with one head. A great sigh of wonder is exhaled as all their eyes are filled with the wondrous sight. A single, tiny blue orb of a planet, encompassed by the blackness of space, dangling as if suspended by the group of stars known as the southern cross.

Spontaneous shouts of joy rang out from the throng of angels encompassing the throne. Some were dancing with joy unable to contain their excitement. It was so beautiful, so delicate, so fragile. As the excitement and joy was slowly contained back within the heavenly host, Lucifer begins to approach #One on the throne.

Lucifer: Oh mighty #One. Glorious and awesome is your creative power! May your reign never end for us, your humble subjects.

He bowed low and approached the throne prostrate. When he was as close to one as a whisper, he sprang ferociously at #One, calling to his underlings to follow his lead and rebel.

Lucifer: Now is the time to throw this dictator ONE off our backs. Freedom.

#Three responded to the attack like a lightning bolt, sending Lucifer to the sea of glass. He lay there stunned, in a smoking, convulsive heap. #Three fills the angels loyal to ONE with his power and the rebels are subdued. Rising from the throne #One calls out to the rebelling angels.

#One: Why have you rebelled? Has not ONE only shown you love? We love you and want the best for you all. But because we love you we will not force you to choose our ways of love. You will have freedom of choice. You will be masters of your own fate, but your fate will be set.

#Two: Once your spirit has set, it will be permanent. You'll not be able to alter your decision. ONE is Holiness and love, we will not live with sin and lawlessness. Your poor choices here will lead to eternal banishment from ONE.

Lucifer struggles to get up and stands amongst the rebels, smoking and twitching uncontrollably from the jolt of Holy Spirit. Pointing a charred smoldering finger at #One he croaks,

Lucifer: Anything is better than living under your tyranny!

#One: Lucifer, you were perfect until iniquity was found in you. You are the tyrant. Your own lies have ensnared you, for you are the father of lies. From now on you will be known as Satan.

Lucifer looking around at his fellow rebels makes his choice.

Satan: Fine! We choose banishment.

The rebels join in blind unison with their chosen leader, chanting mindlessly.

Rebels: Banishment, banishment, we want banishment! Banishment, banishment, we want banishment!

Thinking of another way to stab at ONE, Satan calls out above the din.

Satan: Yes, banishment. Banishment away from your Hooollyyy Preessannce. Banishment to that shiny blue ball you gave to us.

Satan points to the lovely blue orb that ONE had just presented to all the angels as his finest creation so far. #One nods his approval and Satan commands his followers.

Satan: Wormwood, Legion, the rest of you, let's go check out our new home.

Satan turns for one last sneer at #One as the defeated rebels slink off the sea of glass and head towards the bright blue orb. To his dismay he sees his trusted servant Wormwood on his knees at the throne receiving forgiveness from #One, forgiveness that could have been his. His jaw hardens along with his heart. He vows to foil ONE's plans and fight them at every opportunity. Satan and the demons fall like a lightning storm, descending onto the fresh, lovely blue planet.

"Well that's quite fancifull," Matt says, talking to himself quietly so as not to wake his wife. "We are told about Satan's rebellion and Isaac did say he wrote this in story form. I suppose he can be afforded a bit of artistic licence, but he's taken the creation of Genesis way out of context. That would conflict with our church's doctrines on the creation of the universe. Isaac's always going on

about mankind's mortality, maybe he'll get to that later."
Picking up his large cup he sucks the last of his drink
through the straw.

SEED

In the heavens, a great season of refreshing had come at
last. With Satan and a third of the angels that followed
him banished, the endless competition for position that
brought anxiety and strife to the angels was gone. No
longer were they endlessly pursuing status and power.
Those sin driven feelings were being replaced by the
calm assurance that you were loved by ONE for who you
were, not for what you've done or accomplished. ONE
had wanted them to faithfully believe, then achieve using
ONE's ways of love. Calm strength of character was
being produced within the remaining angels, making
room for #Three to be felt dwelling within them, drawing
them closer to ONE through his soft, gentle call to their
hearts.

For the angels, time had healed their many wounds and
bruises, They were busy and productive. Good had come
out of their trials. They knew well the vile, bitter taste
that came from not living in the ways of ONE. Their
senses were so acutely attuned to Satan's ways, that just
the memory of them would send shivers up their backs.
Sadly though, time had not been so kind to the once
perfectly formed, beautiful blue orb. The shining globe in
the sea of darkness had taken a terrible beating from
Satan and his demonic horde. Over time they had twisted

and distorted ONE's pinnacle of creative genius until it was a dark mass, indistinguishable from the sea of darkness that surrounded it. Destroying their habitation made the demons uncomfortable, all while giving them great pleasure knowing they were destroying what #One had said was his best work. Reveling in the misery of their destruction, they hadn't noticed their spirits were now set by their choices as #One had warned. They could not, nor would they want to come back from the great depth of sin they had sunk to.

#One: Well #Two, this has been a great time of rejuvenation. Everything here in our realm is going great.

#Two: Yes, it is. I've never felt #Three so happy. Spirit power has spread throughout creation, making it work harmoniously in sync with ONE. I could bask in the bliss of it forever.

#One: Being surrounded by our creations has been more enjoyable than I thought it'd be. Community is certainly in our nature.

#Two: Well it's an extension of love after all, and that is what we're all about.

#One: You said that creation was working in harmony.

#Two: I know. I try to push them out of my thoughts, but I can't ever do it. Thoughts of them are always there, like a nagging pain. We've lost a third. They will never feel love again. I've been trying to put it off, but we must go on with our plans and make their downfall lead to good.

#One: It will lead to great pain for ONE, but we're only part way down the path we've chosen. I'll always be here for you.

The conversation ends on a positive note, as #Three's reassuring presence comes on like a warm embrace engulfing them all.

#Two: I know that ONE will always be here for me. Nothing could ever break us apart. This time we've spent together with all the heavenly hosts, together in love, has been so enjoyable. I can't wait to have more family to share life with. My desires are so strong I don't want to suppress them any longer. I ache to complete the plans we have set into motion.

A deep sadness is felt as #Two's voice starts to crack.

#Two: Parts of the plan will be very hard to complete. I won't be able to finish them without the love and strength of ONE helping me, but the rewards of having a family are so great. Let's not wait any longer and get started now.

#Two's voice steadies now with firm resolve.

#Two: The sooner we get started, the sooner we can experience the joyous outcome.

#One: #Three, you heard #Two, let's get started. It'll take your spirit power to get this job done. We know it all ends in good, so stay focused on that. #Two, you'll need to go down with #Three and be the Word. I'm sure Satan will have questions.

#Two: His arrogance will have only grown worse since we talked to him last. He always thinks he knows everything, making assumptions on how things are, rather than finding out the truth.

#One: He's never been big on the truth.

#Two: No he hasn't and he's only gotten worse.

Far below the throne #Two and #Three descend to the now dark troubled globe that was once so spectacularly beautiful, that the heavens rang with the angelic joy over it.

Satan: What are you doing here #Two? We've all been banished to this place because your holiness can't abide with the likes of us. How is it you can tolerate our company now?

#Two: ONE will not dwell with sin, but is ONE here? I came here to be the word and to talk to you. #Three is here to do the work and #One is sitting on the throne. So, you see ONE is not here. Besides, is there anything that ONE cannot do? ONE chooses not to abide with sin, as it ultimately leads away from love and into pain and misery.

Satan: Just another one of your deceitful word games. And did you say that you brought along that power thing #Three? I could never understand it and I never liked it.

Satan looks around nervously as he rubs an old scar from the rebellion.

Satan: Is it here now? I don't sense it anywhere.

#Two: Yes it's here now. In fact, #Three is all around us recreating this planet. #Three is following the plans of ONE precisely. You and the demons destroyed what ONE built the first time and ONE let you. But this time you will not be permitted to harm our physical creation.

Satan: Who are you to tell me what I can or cannot do on my own planet? This is our place of banishment, we are the masters here. You said so yourself and you can't lie. Or have you changed since we last spoke?

Two: No, I haven't changed and neither have you. You're still assuming, still believing your own lies, caught up in your own propaganda. ONE never said you'd be in complete control of this planet. Yes, you are the masters, masters of your own destiny, masters of the fate you freely chose. This is your place of banishment, but ONE never said you'd have complete control over it forever. ONE let you control it, providing you stayed within the will of ONE. And as for who am I to tell you what to do? I Am! If you know me, you know ONE!

#Three's power becomes very present as #Two speaks of his deity. Satan starts to twitch uncontrollably, slight plumes of smoke can be seen rising from his form. Satan continues, choosing his words more carefully.

Satan: Yes, yes, I see! Please forgive me your grace! And, and please keep that power thing away from me, I beg of you. I feel much better unaware of its presence.

#Two: That's because you never got to know ONE in all our glory. There is so much more to ONE than you have ever imagined. You could've gotten to know ONE if you'd wanted to. Nothing would've been kept from you, ONE's wisdom, ONE's omnipr...

Satan cuts #Two off angrily.

Satan: Oh, enough about you already! You can be so narcissistic. Yes, we all know ONE is truly great. Well I'm pretty darn good too! Look let's get the rules straight. Us rebels can't destroy this new physical recreation that ghosty thing is making, but we're still spirit beings, emitting our influencing power. If this physical creation should happen to respond to it, that's not our fault. ONE would be bound by love to let creation choose their own path. Isn't that true?

#Two: Yes, free moral agency will reign within our creation. All that can choose will have their opportunity.

Satan: As the rebel leader, I should be able to have an audience with #One. But don't worry, I won't dirty up the throne or anything. I'll stay before the throne, just at the edge of the sea of glass.

#Two: That will be agreeable, but only you.

Satan: Good, good, then I understand the rules. ONE creates stuff out of physical matter; the demons and I can influence it all we want; this planet doesn't have to be our permanent place of banishment and I can have an audience with #One at the throne.

#Two: That would basically sum it up. ONE would still reserve total over all control as Lord and creator.

Satan: Yes, yes, of course. ONE is the creator after all, bound only by your divine laws of love.

#Two: Absolutely! ONE is love and we will never deviate from it or its precepts.

Satan: Great, this could really be good. Go ahead, create all you like. You know, I'd really like to stay and chat about old times, but I've got to be running along. The pressures of leadership and all. I'm always needed to help others, there never seems to be any me time. Well I don't need to be telling you about all that. You, being master of the cosmos and all. Tata, see you later. I gotta run.

Back at Demon H/Q Satan is quickly surrounded by his sycophants. They're all worried about what their fates will be now that #Three is rebuilding the world around them. Their worst fear is the unknown, as they have no greater power than their own to look to for help or support.

Satan: Great news! As your leader and representative, I've been in delicate negotiations with ONE for some time now. I've taken our concerns and demands about this planet, with its appalling state of decay, directly to

ONE. I've demanded, on behalf of us all, that ONE makes some overdue repairs. After all, it's ONE's creation and we're merely tenants here and not responsible for the upkeep. I was a very tough and shrewd negotiator and I feel, as I'm sure you all will, that I've won some very important concessions from ONE. Yes, I really held their feet to the fire. I pointed out to ONE that although this may be our place of banishment for now, as supreme ruler, they're still responsible for it. And they fell for it, yes (laughing heartily) old ONE bought it, hook, line and sinker. They're really just putty in my hands.

Joviality ran rampant through the demonic assembly as they playfully slapped each other's backs. They were in awe of their leader and how he played ONE like a violin. It made them proud to be on Satan's side, to once again rage at ONE and be part of foiling their plans.

Satan: Here are the details, limited as they are. ONE will be doing some rebuilding around here, but as any reasonable being would expect, ONE doesn't want to rebuild it only to have us destroy it again like the last time. So being the reasonable and dynamic leader that I am, I agreed. Caught ONE completely off guard. Then I said, 'we still can use our influence on creation and that, although we may be banished to this planet we don't always have to stay here, as long as we stay away from ONE'. And ONE agreed! Fell right into my trap. You see, now when this new physical realm destroys itself, under our influence, it can't be blamed on us! We didn't touch a thing. That way, later we aren't stuck here in the mess, we can move on to new places of banishment.

The demons think of endless possibilities where they could foil ONE's plans, while still clinging to plausible deniability for what the physical realm did to itself. They erupt in spontaneous praise for their glorious leader. If it were possible for them you could say they loved him, but adoration and reverence was the best they could do, which was fine as it was the best Satan could imagine.

It's been close to a millennium now since ONE planted the seed of his likeness with the creation of man. From the outset it was apparent Satan's influence over mankind would be strong, though some would try to follow ONE's ways of love instead of the enticing desires of society. None could come close to the perfection ONE longed for. Flesh's only desire was for sin and sin alone. ONE's disappointment was growing stronger than they had hoped it would. They had always known how things might turn out and they had contingency plans in place. Now it was clear that mankind was hopeless at defeating Satan on their own. Their contingency plan would have to be put into effect.

#One: Man's wickedness has become so great through Satan's influence. Their hearts always desire sin.

#Two: Man is truly no match for sin. Pushed by every breath Satan and the demons blow their way, they fall prey to his lies, choosing those lies over the truth of ONE. Even Adam, with my close personal contact, didn't put up much of a fight. My heart is heavy with sorrow for creating them. Perhaps we should wipe them out and start over again?

#One: We could do that, but there's one who I think may have a chance. He's shown himself open to ONE's laws of love and the influence of #Three.

#Two: I'll go visit him. If he's receptive we will make a covenant with him and the earth can have a fresh start. This time we will limit mankind by shortening their time on earth. That should slow down their descent into sin.

#One: We knew things might turn out this way.

#Two: So many variables for them to choose from. At every turn a new path. With free will in play, it's hard to predict how all the details will play out.

#One: Regardless of the path they choose, all will have the opportunity to know ONE. All will be able to decide if they want to become a child of ONE or reject the love of ONE, as Lucifer did.

#Two: Their potential is great, greater than that of the angels. They can become children of ONE. When given the opportunity, I'm sure most will embrace ONE's ways of love.

#One: Mankind needs to try their own ways to not sin. Their sins will come from their own will. Collectively, mankind will have to acknowledge that none of them could live a sinless life. Hopeless to free themselves from the grip of sin, they'll have to recognize their need for salvation and their need for a Savior.

#Two: They'll have the same conceit for their own strength as Satan does. They'll all have to recognize the need for ONE and my salvation. We'll work with those who respond to the calling of ONE. Mankind will come to see they can't defeat sin through their own wisdom and strength.

#One: Stories from the lives of the faithful will display ONE's majesty and glory for all to see.

#Two: After mankind's had time to try their own ways of living, we'll give them a codified set of rules to follow.

Rules to spell out what ONE expects from them so they can never say, ' ONE never told us what we had to do. If ONE had told us what was expected of us we would've been happy to comply'.

#One: First we'll work with a few, then we'll be working with many. Under the guidance of #Three, ONE will record our history with man, to guide and encourage those called to love and to follow ONE.

Satan: Yoo-who. Your Majesty, can you hear me?

#One: Of course we can hear you.

Satan: I just wanted to stop by and point out, it isn't my fault. You can't hold me responsible for what those pathetically weak mortals did, you allowed them to populate the planet. The demons and I didn't ask for them, though they are such fun to play with. Just being with them brings me and the demons such joy and fulfilment.

#One: You mean the pleasure you take influencing them into sin and rejecting ONE.

Satan: We can't help who we are. It's not our fault you made us this way! But since we are, we take advantage of life's few fleeting pleasures the best we can.

#Two: Your life choices were your own. You and the demons are self-made. ONE didn't want you to end up as you are. ONE gave you the freedom to choose and you did.

Satan: Yes, ONE is so loving. ONE would've never created us evil as we are, but we aren't completely void of compassion. That's why I stopped by. We all felt such profound sorrow when ONE drowned those poor humans in that horrific flood. How the little ones cried, and their parents desperately clung to their pathetic mortality. It was such a terrible, oh how should I put it, 'Act of God'? The demons and I know of your perfect love and just wanted to give you our deepest heartfelt sympathies. It must have been so hard for ONE. Such a heartache witnessing all that terror. Having to ignore those pleas for help and mercy coming collectively from all of humanity at the same time. It must have been almost more than ONE could bear. I say all of humanity but there are now, what is it, eight still alive? Only eight humans were worth saving? My, your perfect love certainly was popular, wasn't it. Popularity does seem to be my strength though. How they adored me! The demons and I do hope your plans include allowing mankind to repopulate. We feel so good when they're around. It would be such a shame to see them gone for good.

#Two: You don't need to worry about their future, ONE has a plan. ONE knew every human that has lived. ONE knows and remembers everything about them, even down to the number of hairs on their head. ONE will never forget them. ONE is following a plan and all will be revealed in ONE's time.

Satan: Well I do hope you take your time. We demons like the limitations ONE has implemented on humanity. I just need to reiterate our lack of responsibility for the choices humans make. ONE gave them free will. If anything it's ONE's fault. We're just being ourselves and they're just so weak and gullible.

#One: You're acting just as ONE knew you would and we do plan for a lot more human population. Like the sand on the seashore.

Satan: Well that's terrific. I'm glad we haven't disappointed you. The demons will rejoice with the news.

But I think I've kept you long enough, I better get going and give my underlings all the good news. I'm so glad I dropped by and had this little chat. Talk to you later, tata.

"If I don't get to the bathroom soon I'll explode!" Matt thought to himself as he frantically got himself out of bed. "That drink went right through me." Several minutes later as the ensuite toilet can be heard refilling, Matt makes his way back into bed. "He's started going off the rails of truth. I may need help finding references to dispute some of these thoughts. I wonder if my old dean would have any input for scripture? He knew Isaac from Bible School. I'll reach out to him for help later but now I need to get some sleep."

The next morning Matt was awoken by a sharp throbbing coming from his ankle. "I was hoping to go into the office this morning." Matt said to his wife as she was getting dressed. "My ankle is killing me! I'll stay off it till noon and see how it feels then."

"If you had been acting your age you would have never gotten hurt in the first place!" she said angrily. "You're always showing off to the girls. Have you forgotten you have a family?" asking as she turns to glare at Matt. "I'm glad you got hurt. Maybe this will give you time to examine your actions. I'm about done with them." she said, slamming the bedroom door as she left.

Matt was unable to get out of bed to pursue the argument. Hearing the kitchen door close hard and his wife's car roar out of the yard and down the street, Matt knew his opportunity for explanation had passed. Settling back into his bed Matt picks up another page from Isaac's book and reads to himself.

REDEMPTION

Satan is in a high-level meeting with his commanders at Demon H.Q. Attentive to his every word, the commanders are ready to act on his next plan to thwart ONE.

Satan: Look I don't understand it either. How am I supposed to know what ONE is up to? We only know they are up to something. Ever since ONE started working with those oddball losers, people have been harder to influence into our way of thinking. It's hurting our numbers and our quotas have been dropping. I've reviewed the statistics and a trend is forming and I don't like it. Increase all the surveillance, we must find out ONE's objectives.

It was all fun and games in the beginning. Even with the commandments of ONE, those humans are so easily swayed to our way of thinking. Some would go repenting back to ONE, like whimpering dogs, their tails between their legs. As if the sacrifice of animals could wash their hearts clean of us, saving them from their sins. We got most of them back the next day, some by the next thought. It's been so simple, just wave anything shiny under their noses or flash a bit of taboo skin for them to see and they'd be ours all over again. No matter what they do, they're still flesh, they're still mortal, prone to our influences. In the long run we win them all.

ONE has always been tricky with word games, using analogies and letting one thing represent another. ONE is up to something, I just know it. We've infiltrated his priesthood and know that ONE will be sending a savior king to deliver his people from their torment and sins. We've gotten it wrong before. Trying to destroy those who follow ONE, only to have our efforts work out for their good, making people love and worship ONE even more. But we would always get them back. They could never get it right with us to influence them. They mustn't yearn for ONE at all. We must snuff out all hope and leave them nothing. It's been four hundred years since the last prophet has spoken to the people of ONE. I don't like it, it's too quiet. ONE is up to something good, I can feel it. Now get to work!

Satan turns leaving the commanders talking amongst themselves in serious tones. As he does, he rubs his old scar that has started to irritate him again and mumbles to himself about crazy old ghost stories.

#One: It's been a challenge with all the changing circumstances, but #Three has managed to follow our schedule faithfully. All the loose ends have been tied up and it's time for us to proceed.

Speaking slowly, #Two's voice has a slight quiver to it.

#Two: You know it's funny. I've been longing for this moment to arrive and now that it has I feel so nervous and apprehensive.

#Three gives #Two a long reassuring emotional hug. #Two's voice steadies as he talks again.

#Two: Thank you #Three. I know that ONE will be vital to me through this part of the plan. I need to keep my eyes on the final goal and most of all stay in touch with the power of ONE. It's the most crucial part of the plan and needs to be completed. I won't fail in my mission. I won't let ONE down. I will fulfil, all that I must do.

#Three and #One embrace #Two in thought.

#One: We'll be here for you. No further than your thoughts. #Three will be your lifeline to ONE as you'll be fully human, leaving #Three as your only source to the power of ONE. Always stay close to #Three as we know the dangers that are down there waiting to destroy all we've worked for.

#Two: I'm nervous. I'll be leaving my divinity behind. For the first time we'll be separated, apart from ONE.

#One: It won't be for long, then we'll be reunited together again.

#Two: No, we won't be separated long, but an instant is too long. I know it must be done. We've been through it all and there's no other way. I'll bring them salvation, humbly and completely. My coming has been foretold by our prophets and now all is ready, waiting for my arrival. I've been preparing myself for this moment since before we formed our first creation. Through the plan of ONE, a bountiful harvest will soon be reaped.

At Demon H.Q. a frantic messenger rushes into Satan's presence. Groveling he prostrates himself low before his master.

Messenger: Your eminence, news is coming in from our scouts in Judea. They all claim to have seen angelic beings, singing praises to ONE and telling shepherds about the arrival of a new king, who will save them from their oppression and sins.

Satan: What's that you say? Telling shepherds? Surely we have reports from the scouts with the synagogue leaders and elders.

Messenger: No master, it was only proclaimed to children of humble families and lowly shepherds out in the fields. We've received no other reports about the event.

Satan: It must be a ruse by ONE, to divert our attention away from his priesthood. When ONE announces his coming king, saving his people from their Roman oppressors, freeing them from bondage and slavery, ONE will be working through his temple leaders.

It's a trick ONE thought I would fall for. But I'm too smart for that. Again I'm one step ahead of ONE, but just to be safe, put Harod's personal demon on yellow alert. I'm confident ONE will be working through his loyal priesthood. I've been grooming them for generations. Keeping my influence strong, but low key, so as not to raise any suspicions. With my special blend of pride, arrogance and superiority, look at how zealously the Pharisees keep the laws of ONE. They even add on more laws so they can be extra righteous in the eyes of ONE. ONE must be so proud of them.

Yes, we'll keep a close watch at the temple. Our best analysts have been studying the case for centuries. They assured me we're well prepared for ONE's next move. I've gone through their reports and I wholeheartedly agree with their conclusions and assessment of the situation.

Messenger: But your majesty, the Judean scouts are very reliable. They believe the reports of the angels and their message are true and came directly from the throne of ONE. Furthermore...

Satan: Who do you think you're talking to!! I am your leader! You were not asked for your input! I just told you that I was handling the situation with the advice from those at the very top. Minds much better than yours. We have better insights than those of some scouts from the backwater of the empire. If you didn't grovel so well, I'd have you assigned somewhere very uncomfortable! You'd do well to keep your inner thoughts private.

Stooping even closer to the floor, the messenger stammers with fear.

Messenger: Well said your exaltedness. I was wrong to appear to be questioning your wisdom. I humbly beg your forgiveness.

Satan appears to be playacted as the tension slowly drains from his face. Looking intently at the messenger, he speaks calmly with self-control.

Satan: A great leader can be measured by the love he receives from his minions. I will choose to overlook your shortcomings for now. ONE is sure to be sending a savior soon. We will have to patiently bide our time till he appears and then spring our trap. But rest assured, we'll be ready.

Then came a report from Herod's personal demon. Visiting magi from distant lands seeking to welcome and honor a new King had arrived at his court. Satan was still positive that the angelic host appearing at Bethlehem was a ploy from ONE to get him off the trail of the priesthood. These magi felt like yet another attempt. Not wanting to let anything escape his control, Satan influences King Herod to have all the male children under the age of two killed in the entire region of Judea.

Satan: That should put to rest any future kings causing us problems. Can't be too careful when dealing with ONE and that freaky power thing. My demonic spies are with all the powerful elite. When the Savior King comes, we'll be ready. Now it's a game of cat and mouse. Meeeeeyyyooooowwww!

#Two: Oh father. You have kept me safe from Satan and the power of evil since my conception. Through the power of #Three, I have kept my fleshly desires in check. My entire life has been lived in accordance with the loving laws of ONE. My will is that your will be done in my life and on earth. The carpenter trade that I was born into has honed my body well. I'm strong, healthy and without blemish. A perfect sacrifice. Thank you father for letting my cousin John go before me, preparing my way. Thank you for reassuring me with your open exaltation of pleasure.

As #Two is praying these words in his mind, #Three is sitting on his head in the form of a dove, as if anointing him with oil. #Ones voice could be heard proclaiming the true identity of #Two as the Christ, the savior of mankind. Satan was at the side of #Two in the wilderness as soon as the message of the redeemer's arrival and identity reached him. With a sneer, he scornfully addresses #Two.

Satan: You are the Messiah? The great ruler prophesied to save ONE's people? You're nothing but a peasant! Your hands are rough from labour, you smell like you've slept in a fishing boat and you have splinters like a carpenter. How could you be the coming King? The

Clayton Carlson

powerful, cunning world rulers won't give you the time
of day. You're supposed to save the people of ONE from
their Roman bondage?

#Two: Yes. I've come to save my people from bondage,
to set the captives free. Through me, mankind can be
saved from their sins. With ONE all things are possible.

Satan: Wait. I recognize you. Well if it isn't #Two
himself. Isn't this an interesting twist? The great I Am,
now here before me in the form of a mortal man. Tell me,
are you wholly mortal or did you retain your power of
ONE?

#Two: I have no more of ONE's power than any other
human has the opportunity to have. All my power comes
through #Three.

Satan: Just a mortal man? Well I like the sound of that!
I have lots of experience with mankind. Come, let's talk.
I think we can come to an amicable arrangement.

For forty days and nights in the wilderness, Satan
tempts a fasting #Two. Trying to entice #Two to sin with
every trick and scheme he could think of. Through the
unrelenting pressure #Two stays firm in his resolve,
keeping his eyes fixed on the ultimate prize that lay ahead
of him. Using the words of ONE preserved in sacred
texts, #Two rebuffs Satan and his twisted logic. After
Satan has finished with his tempting, #Two finally orders
Satan to leave and he slinks away. Finally, #Two has
proved that a man could resist the pull of sin and live an
unblemished life. Although great obstacles still had to be
overcome, the door was now unlocked for mankind's
redemption to come.

#Two: Father, the time for me to come out into the
public as your son is very near. May I start just a little

sooner? Mother says it would mean so much to them, saving them from ridicule on what should be such a happy occasion. They had no way of knowing the guests would be so thirsty on this unusually hot, dusty day. They planned for so long to make this day the highlight of their lives, only to have run out of wine. A small thing in the grand scheme of things but it means the world to them in this moment right now.

#Three's presence floods into Two's body with the reassuring approval of #One. #Two feels a power surge as #Three can hardly wait to be sent out to do #Two's first public miracle. What a joyous miracle #Three will make it, one that the guests will talk about for years and one that will leave the bride and groom scrambling to find leftovers to save for special occasions.

So, what should it be? A lively Gewurztraminer, or perhaps a Chardonnay. No, no, those wouldn't be suitable, thinks #Three. Lamb was served at the meal. Only the soft mellow notes of a Merlot will do. At #Two's direction, a Merlot it is. The best Merlot anyone had ever tasted. And not just a bottle or two, but huge water pots filled to the brim.

At Demon H.Q. Satan is furious, blindly raging at his subordinates.

Satan: You bunch of pathetic losers! You all failed completely, you all missed his coming! One minute I'm told everything is going along as planned and the next minute I get an urgent message telling me that #One himself is heralding in the new Messiah! To make matters worse, the new Messiah turns out to be #Two born into the flesh of a man. How could've you all missed that for the past thirty years! Do I have to do everything around here myself? How can I make good plans without good information? Not one of you gave me any inclination that things were going so badly. Why? Because all of you weren't doing your jobs! I have repeatedly asked for your input so I can make good decisions. I don't know how many times I've told you all that a good leader is a good listener and I'm a great leader surrounded by incompetence!

Demon 1: But master, we've proved ourselves more powerful than man.

Satan: Yes we have. But we can't kill him, we can only influence him. I've just come back from forty days in the wilderness trying to influence and tempt him. Not a chance.

Demon 2: Well if we can't influence him, we can still influence the others.

Legion: We've lived right inside some of them, they do our bidding. We could get them to kill him.

Demon 1: Hey, let's get the temple guards to kill him.

Satan: No. Better yet, let's use the elite to kill him. Oh, oh, oh, this is it. Let's get the Pharisees and the chief priest to condemn him to death. That'll be ironic! The leaders of ONE's chosen people killing the person who ONE sent to save them. Killing the one who made them in the first place. Killing their own creator and God.

Legion: Let's use the Romans to do the actual killing, that way the salvation of ONE will be destroyed by those ONE is trying to redeem his people from.

Demon 2: Ya, not just kill him but crucify him with some despicable reprobates, thieves and cut throats. That would be a fitting end for his hooooollyy Gooooodneesss.

Satan: Oh, I do like that plan. I just love the way a demonic mind thinks. After all the pain and trouble #Two has gone through to get humanity to choose him, then to be rejected by the leaders of his own chosen people and killed by those he came to save them from. The rejection and defeat will be complete. What a glorious way to mess up the plans of ONE. I'm so glad I'm here with you demons, you always know how to cheer me up when things look grim. It'll take a while to set up and plan but let's do it.

For three and a half years the demons follow and watch #Two carefully, always influencing the leaders towards jealousy and hatred towards him at every turn. They don't miss a trick or opportunity in their plans for #Two's demise. Time flies by as their plans come together and before they know it they are victorious over #Two and rejoice in his final words as a man, 'it is finished'. Now was their time to celebrate and boast about their achievements in destroying #Two and his plans for redeeming his people from their Roman oppressors. The demonic party had been going strong for three days and nights with Satan reveling in their midst, immersed in their adoration. He takes all the credit for their hard-won victory over #Two and for striking a solid blow against the plans of ONE.

None of the demons notice a messenger grimly approach Satan. He bows low in humble submission, then cautiously whispers into Satan's ear. Satan's smile vanishes and he excuses himself from the revelry. They quickly leave to a private location so their conversation can't be overheard.

Satan: Tell me the story again. Exactly what happened?

Messenger: Well like I said, I was about half way through my shift with the high priest in the temple when a group of centurion's barged in, demanding he listen to them. They were very scared. They tell the high priest that #Two's body is no longer in the tomb.

He asks them, 'how do you know, there's a bolder sealing the entrance'? They explain to him that just before light some ladies came with spices and linen cloth to prepare the body for burial. These ladies no sooner get there and there's an earthquake, then an angel from ONE appears, telling the ladies #Two isn't in the tomb but has been resurrected. To prove it, the angel rolled the stone back revealing only some rags where the body had lain. The centurions were afraid they would be killed because the body was stolen under their watch. They hightailed it, reporting to the high priest.

Satan: This is an unexpected twist. I had hoped to be rid of #Two for good. I should've known ONE would change the rules to suit himself. It's time I find out for myself what's going on. #Two is bound to come back to see those uncouth, cowardly, clods he called disciples. Just a bunch of unschooled, stinky fisherman. When he shows up I'll be waiting to talk to him.

Somewhere between heaven and earth, Satan finds #Two.

Satan: You lied to me #Two! You said you had no more power than any of the other mortal humans. Well I don't see any of those mortals flying around here. I had you killed. I dominated you. I was victorious over you. I kept you from saving your special nation of losers. They're still under the tyranny of Rome. You failed to redeem and free them, even in this year of jubilee.

#Two: I feel sad for you Satan. I talked openly to my disciples and others about the plans of ONE. None of you really understood. You all thought wrongly that ONE was only concerned with the nation of Israel. You thought I had come to physically free the captives from their bondage. The concern of ONE goes far beyond the nation of Israel or limited to only those who follow his laws. The national blessings given to Abraham, Isaac and Jacob will come about in this world when it's time. I came to redeem the captives yes, but the captives to sin. I came to free captive mankind from you.

Satan: Again with the word games. I have no shackles on mankind. They aren't my slaves, they want to follow me. My ways are more popular and fun. You're just jealous of their love for me.

#Two: I defeated you in the wilderness. I lived a perfect, blameless life. I became human for the sole purpose of becoming mankind's sacrifice for sin. The first man brought death and sin because of you, now I have brought salvation and life because of you. You thought you were clever having me crucified. Had you understood the prophecies, you would have known that was what I wanted. It was my display of love to humanity. Now with my resurrection to immortality, I show there is a hope and a future for others to follow and share in. Just as I take my place again with ONE, humanity will also be able to be with ONE as I am. Humanity's destiny is to become the children of ONE. Full heirs to the throne of ONE. To be joined with ONE as I am.

Satan: What! Those frail, mortal, humans? Become children and heirs of ONE? That would make them greater than the angels, greater than me!

Satan seems to be staggered by the prospect.

#Two: That is their potential, if they choose it. The choice will be theirs to make. They'll all be given the opportunity to choose life or death.

Satan: When? They have all chosen! They chose me, they followed me into sin, they chose death. Except for those alive now, all of mankind has died before your sacrifice came to rescue them. They're all lost to ONE through death, without the chance to accept you and your salvation.

#Two: Well if everyone died without hearing of my offer of redemption how could have they made an informed choice?

Satan: ONE gave laws to follow, sacrifices to cover their sins. If only a handful of humanity knew about them or followed them, that's just too bad for them.

#Two: Laws just teach them they are sinners needing saving. Daily, monthly and yearly sacrifices of animals only show the need for a perfect sacrifice, good for all time and everyone. A heart of love is what ONE desires.

Satan: Humph. Love! ONE never said anything about love. ONE gave laws to follow and sacrifices to make. ONE wanted zealots, righteous men dedicated to following his rules regardless of the cost. Take Saul for example, a Pharisee of the Pharisees. He embodies all that keeping the laws of ONE can achieve. He's not concerned with love.

#Two: Yes. As you well know he's full of rage, hatred and murder, all in the name of ONE, all coming from you. ONE wants a heart of love, pure, unselfish love. That's who we are, that's all we will live with. ONE can no more dwell with Saul the way he is now than we could abide with the sons of Eli the priest. Or you for that matter. Your hearts are far from ONE, far from love and mercy.

Satan: Then you've lost them all, just as you lost me. None of them received your salvation, none of them chose you to cover their sins. And unlike me, they were all mortal and died before they even knew of your sacrifice. I'm immortal. I'll never die and I will never choose you or your forgiveness!

#Two: Yes, they're dead, but so was I. I was resurrected. All of them will be brought back to life in a resurrection as well. ONE has a plan of redemption for all of humanity. All will have their opportunity to freely choose me and follow the love of ONE. If they do, they will have true life. If they don't, they will be choosing eternal death. Going forward, ONE will call out to some humans. Those who choose to answer that call and accept me, growing in the love of ONE, they'll be resurrected into the fullness of life as I have it now. Those who aren't called to ONE, will have their opportunity later.

Satan: You make no sense at all! Choices, resurrections, love. You were very cut and dry with the laws, do them or die. ONE wanted rule followers who kept the laws perfectly, not letting anything or anyone stand in their way. Now you say you want sinners who try their best as long as they have love. Claiming you'll clean them up through your sacrifice. Again ONE is changing the rules, playing word games, treating me and the demons deceitfully. What is it? ONE can't live with sin so you better be perfect. Or is it, accept your sacrifice and live in love as much as possible?

With a deep sigh of sadness #Two continues to explain.

#Two: Satan you still choose not to see. ONE has always accepted a humble and contrite heart. ONE has always forgiven those who asked, like Wormwood.

Satan: Don't talk to me about him! I'll fight those kinds of backstabbers and ONE with all my might. Go ahead, take all the weak and lame, those who need your crutch of support. The strong and proud will choose me. I'll gladly take the superior ones from ONE, they don't see the need for ONE or for your salvation. They'll join me in my fight against ONE right till the bitter end. We'll persecute those who follow ONE, crush them, abuse them. Extinguish their love and their lives.

#Two: You can try but you will fail. The church of ONE will prevail over all things and finally over death itself.

Satan: We'll see #Two. We'll see!

Putting Isaac's book to the side and with his ankle feeling slightly better, Matt forces himself out of bed, gets dressed and makes his way to his downtown office. Determined to finish off some open work files on his desk, Matt focuses his mind on work most of the day until his throbbing ankle forces him to retreat back home to his bed.

As Matt was recovering, Isaac stayed active with Speckle's class. Isaac not only had been busy working to get a good mark on his creative writing project with Val and flesh out his thoughts to Matt, but he also kept up his marks with Speckle. The collaborative student teams gave powerpoint reports to the rest of the class on Speckle's favorite topic, disasters that could wipe out North America. Speckle's students kept safely to the information they found mostly through online research. They had facts, figures, graphs and charts describing the size and shapes of the looming disasters. Speculation was rampant during classroom discussion on when these disasters might occur or what trigger mechanisms would cause them to awaken.

The class started with destruction through volcanic eruption. As it turns out, the US western states are home to three of the six-top super volcanoes of the world, not to mention the dozens of small regional ones like Mount St. Helens. Simple descriptions of the three by Analise Dubner were found on a quick website search, similar to the following information.

Unbeknownst to most, Yellowstone National Park sits on a subterranean chamber of molten rock and gas so vast that it is arguably one of the largest active volcanoes in the world. A magma chamber not far below the surface fuels all the volcanic attractions that Yellowstone is famous for. The last major eruption at Yellowstone, some 640,000 years ago, ejected 8,000 times the ash and lava of the 1980 Mount St. Helens eruption and it is alive and well today.

Second only to Yellowstone in North America is the Long Valley caldera, in east-central California. The 200-

square-mile caldera is just south of Mono Lake, near the Nevada state line. The biggest eruption from Long Valley was 760,000 years ago, which unleashed 2,000 to 3,000 times as much lava and ash as Mount St. Helens, after which the caldera floor dropped about a mile, according to the U.S. Geological Survey ash reached as far east as Nebraska.

What worries geologists today about Long Valley was a swarm of strong earthquakes in 1980 and a 10-inch rise of about 100 square miles of caldera floor. Then, in the early 1990s, large amounts of carbon dioxide gas from magma below began seeping up through the ground and killing trees in Mammoth Mountain part of the caldera. When these sorts of signs are present it could mean trouble is centuries, decades, or even years away say volcanologists.

The 175-square-mile Valles caldera forms a large park in the middle of northern New Mexico, west of Santa Fe. It last exploded 1.2 million and 1.6 million years ago, piling up 150 cubic miles of rock and blasting ash as far away as Iowa. As with other calderas, there are still signs of heat below: hot springs are still active around Valles. Geologists suspect the cause of the Valles caldera has something to do with how the western United States' portion of the North American tectonic plate is being pulled apart.

While Isaac was keeping up with his studies, Matt was making a speedy recovery as he kept his ankle elevated. Alone in bed, he picked up another page of Isaac's story and read to himself.

POWER

#Two: It's good to be back here as ONE. Things are familiar and yet it still feels a little strange.

#One: I know what you mean. It'd be wrong to say you've changed. Perhaps you're stronger in certain aspects of love than before. It was a totally new experience for you, as it was for me. We've never gone through anything like that before. Humans are a whole new ballgame, let alone becoming one. I felt the heights of joy and the depths of sorrow, more than I had expected. There was a time when you carried the sins of the world. I couldn't bear to look any longer, I had to turn away. But the dark times are behind us now, the hurdles of sin have been bound by love and love's victory is complete.

#Two: I can hardly wait to welcome those wonderful personalities I got to know as humans to their new home here with us and into their new bodies as one of us. It's going to be exciting expanding the scope of ONE with more family. I tried to tell them what it'll be like here, but how could I explain it so they'd understand?

#One: You did very well, considering their limited terms of reference. How can you explain to a dog what it's like to see in colour? You did all things well, nothing was left undone, you were perfect, and I am well pleased with the outcome.

#Two: Thank you #One. That means a lot to me. I missed being here with you and #Three, it's good to be back home.

ONE rejoices together, the angels can be heard expressing love and adoration for ONE with songs of hallelujah. The heavens rejoice at the triumphant return of #Two, but not all of creation was rejoicing. Deep within Demon H.Q. the satanic mob saw nothing to rejoice over. All they could see was their best laid plans dashed against the rocks of despair. #Two had slipped through their grasp and emerged victorious, completing the plans of ONE. They were looking for answers as to why their hard work had not paid off as promised. They wanted someone to blame for the failure and were starting to turn on themselves.

Satan: This bickering is not getting us anywhere! I've told you what #Two said, since he lived a perfect sinless life as a mortal, he wasn't subject to the death penalty of sin, like all other humans are. He's correct, he didn't sin. You all failed to get him to sin! You're all responsible for this mess we're in, not me. I tried my best. Can the rest of you say that?

Legion, what'd you say coming out of that crazy man? 'Oh, please, please send us into those pigs'. You didn't fight #Two. I've heard a lot of talk, but I haven't seen much action. You were all afraid of him. As your leader, I've done the best that I can.

Demon 1: Well maybe it's tyme we gets us a new leadar? One thatsa looking out fer us, an not his own self!

Satan: Good idea, and whom do you think that new leader should be? You?

Demon 1: Yah! I's gets a lot of good idears. Bettern yours sometimes.

Satan: Yes. Yes, you do. Sometimes! But so does he, and him over there. (Satan points out into the crowd). It takes more than a good idea to make a good leader. A good leader needs to be selfless, honest and humble. A good leader must be in control of the situations around them. Be decisive, responsible and respectful. They must have poise and eloquence. Do you possess these skills? Would you feel comfortable approaching the throne of ONE? More importantly, would the rest of us be comfortable with you as our leader, dealing with ONE on our behalf? I don't think so! We all know that I'm the only one who can be our leader. The heavy mantle of leadership has always rested upon me, and for that purpose I was created perfect in all my ways through the wisdom of ONE. No. I alone carry the heavy burden of leadership, humbly, without malice towards anyone.

Placated, the demons accept Satan's rule again without further dispute. They know that none of them would do any better than he had when dealing with ONE. With leadership concerns amongst the demons put to rest, Satan resumes his full control over demonic affairs. Forcing his best smile he bows humbly to the gathering before him. Turning to his trusted personal aid, Satan has a brief discreet conversation.

Satan: I know how we demons love hot, arid places. I'm sure an extended stay with the locals at Haida Gwaii on Turtle Island is in order for our friend who likes to speak his mind so freely and openly. Tell him it'll be a good career move, add something about paying ones does. Whatever you do, get rid of him! I don't want to hear from him for a very, very, long time.

Personal Aid: Yes, your Grace. I will see to it immediately.

Satan: Good, see that you do. Many uncomfortable places await those who cross me.

Personal Aid: My Lord and Master, whom else could I serve?

Satan: That's right. No one else would have you and don't you forget it! You serve me, at my pleasure.

Trembling with fear the aid kneels and kisses Satan's hand. With a shaky voice the aid can barely squeak out his response.

Personal Aid: As you say so shall it be, your exalted eminence.

With a broad smile of satisfaction Satan watches his Aid scurry away, then faces the demonic gathering and addresses them regally.

Satan: Friends, let's not sit around moping and feeling sorry for ourselves. We knew ONE couldn't be trusted to play by the rules fairly and not save the beloved #Two from eternal death. With all of ONE's talk about honesty and integrity I haven't seen any come from them. ONE's always playing those stupid word games. Never giving us a straight answer to our questions, but this time we may have a chance to really foul up ONE's master plan.

#Two slipped up and said something about his church, how it would grow and flourish. Let's not let that happen. We'll concentrate all our efforts on destroying it and those who belong to it. They claim to be ready to die, following their crucified king. Let's help them with that so they can join #Two in martyrdom. Once the fate of Christians is seen, others won't be so quick to take on the faith, as a painful death will be the only outcome.

Century's pass into history and Satan's good to his words of persecution, but the faithful led and powered by

#Three stand boldly for #Two and the truths of ONE. They persist like leaven inside dough. Always spreading the news about the kingdom's eternal life and the rewards awaiting those who are willing to accept the sacrifice of #Two, living in love and abiding with ONE.

It's a slow start, but those following ONE soon turn into a flood of converts willing to be punished even unto death. Their deaths only seem to embolden others to take up the promise filled faith. Even though faith, hope and love was strong in the people of ONE, ONE never asked more of them than they could give without breaking. The message of a loving father, reaching out to his children seemed to resonate with humans deep inside their psyche, for they were made in the image of ONE. It was as though humanity had a piece missing inside of them that could only be filled by having a personal relationship with ONE. Surrendering their lives to #Two and living through the guidance of #Three, they found that relationship and the promise of eternal life.

Personal testimonials of changed lives were good on an individual level but #Three led some to write about their personal experiences, trials and triumphs. Still others had prophecies flow out of them as if ONE was giving dictation. Soon the letters, stories and books were gathered and reproduced for the edification of the faithful and the new converts. #Three was the careful overseer, giving direction, keeping the efforts accurate. The writings proved very successful with masses of new converts who abandoned the once powerful satanic religions, leaving them to fade into oblivion. The power of #three living inside the converts, changing their lives for the better, was more than Satan had bargained for.

Things weren't going as well as the demons had hoped they would. By now they had thought humanity would've given up on a story told by outcasts shunned by societies' elite. The lack of social status and popularity seemed to somehow make the message all the more believable to people who were hungry for authenticity and ONE was glorified all the more because of it. Try as they might, plans of extinguishing the church through persecution wasn't working out for the demons.

Satan: I've called this special meeting, gathering all you demons together. We need a new plan of attack. The mark of a truly gifted leader, like myself, is the ability to change direction, set a new course when it's needed and to respect the wisdom of others' council. So, I'm asking all of you here for any insights that you might have in charting a new direction for us to follow.

There's a nervous silence in the crowd. No one wanted to incur the wrath of Satan for speaking out of place.

Satan: Come now! Surely there is at least one of you who can offer some small amount of advice. Doesn't anyone have an idea on how to mess with the plans of ONE?

The hushed silence of the crowd is broken by the halting stammer of one loan voice coming from the back of the gathering.

Demon 1: Well thar is won litl thang I'v lerned.

Satan: Oh, yes of course. Our friend from Haida Gwaii. How has Turtle Island been treating you? Pleasantly, I trust, despite the cold, wet weather. Has your time there given you opportunity for reflection and thought? Please tell us all, what is your, won litl thang? We're all dying to hear it!

Demon 1: Well it liak dis. I says yur de boss. An dat's goodnuf fur me. Wat yu say's is wat wees shuud beleeve.

Satan: I'm humbled by your public vote of confidence. You really should spend more time around here at Demon H.Q. I don't know why a talent like yours has been wasting away in some back water. We could use someone with your keen insights closer to the leadership team.

Demon 1: Tankyu, tankyu, yur greyse. My pleshur is to serv yu my Lowrd.

Satan: Now, back to the matter at hand. We need a new plan of attack, try something that will take ONE by complete surprise. There seems to be no torture so grievous that it can turn the devout from following ONE or keep them from making new converts. I've handpicked a team of innovators known for their cunning and wisdom when dealing with the humans. They've worked diligently under my guidance and leadership. We've decided to go with the flow. If you can't beat-em, join-em. Our new plan is to help deliver the gospel of ONE to humanity.

Outcry's of 'traitor to the cause' and 'deceiver' could be heard coming from the murder of demons. Satan outstretched his arms, hands patting down the discontent, until all are silent again.

Satan: You should know me better than that! Let me finish. ONE knew that humans wouldn't be scared off by death if they had the promise of eternal life to look forward to. #Two told me, 'the gates of hell couldn't prevail over his church', that we demons couldn't destroy it. But he didn't say the humans couldn't destroy it. We only need to get involved and help them do the work of ONE. I've figured out ONE's word game.

Legion: Do you mean to say I should help ONE build his church? That's more than we could bear!

Satan: Yes! Help ONE with his new church, just like we helped him with his old one. It only stands to reason. The first converts to One's new church came out of his old church, the one we were influencing. Now most of the converts to his new church come out of the very religions we started. The best way to get ahead of this curve is to get involved with the leadership. Be in on the ground floor and guide the progress of the new builders to suit our outcome, not the outcome of ONE.

Legion: But to help ONE goes against my values and beliefs. I don't know if we can do it.

Satan: You're not seeing the big picture. It's semantics. We aren't really helping ONE, we're helping like we helped the chief priest to condemn #Two. If we stop persecuting the converts, #Two will become irrelevant to them and they'll get busy with other things in life. If the wrath of Rome wasn't enough to kill the church, perhaps the blessings of Constantine will? He'll make people join whether they want to or not, make them claim to be followers no matter what their hearts want. This new church will kill those who claim they aren't followers. We'll help turn it into a social club where the attendees grow spiritually lazy, apathetic, prominent and prosperous. Without fear of persecution, they'll soon lose their need for a protector. The state and commerce will provide all they need and that will soon become the gods their hearts serve. Giving ONE's church prominence, wealth and power will attract those hungry for those things. They'll turn the ones who have pure hearts away from ONE in bitter disillusionment. Yes, we need to help ONE with his church all we can.

Legion: I'm starting to see the merits of your plan and it sounds better than what we're doing now.

Satan: I knew you'd see it my way once it was explained properly.

Legion: Truly you are a great and wise leader. Unafraid to implement bold new initiatives. That is why we hail you as our master and king.

Satan, glowing with pride, accepts the adulation of the demons. With their accolades still ringing in his ears, he prepares to set his new plans into action.

#One: This is new. What do you suppose they're up to?

#Two: No good I'm sure. Anything to fight against the cause of ONE anyway they can.

#One: Well, they'll help spread the gospel throughout the world to all people.

#Two: That it will. However, without opposition to joining the church the converts level of commitment will drop off sharply. If it comes free without personal cost, many won't put a high value on their salvation and will just join for the social status, not because they're interested in following ONE into love.

#One: No one can come to you from out of the world unless I call them. Having the whole world hear about our message of salvation will only enable us to draw the ones we want at this time from a larger pool of people. The ones we work with will grow strong against sin regardless if those sins come from brothers and sisters or from those openly following Satan. Many will claim to be our true followers, but the genuine will be known...

#Two: By their love.

#One: That's right. Love is the one thing Satan can't duplicate.

#Two: Pure love, the love of ONE.

#One: We'll let them all grow together. The good and the bad. We'll sort them out later after they show what type of fruit they'll produce.

Time speeds by and as in other times, we find Satan at the throne of ONE accusing the brethren, pointing out their weaknesses and sins to ONE.

Satan: Do you see what he's doing? He has a wife and children at home. Doesn't it break your laws for him to be having extramarital affairs? Not to mention the money he's been stealing from that do-gooder charity he runs. It seems like he's his own favorite charity. I don't mind telling you these things because he seemed to have been ONE's bright hope for his generation. He was your 'Golden Boy' when he graduated from seminary. You just can't count on anyone anymore, can you ONE?

#Two: There's still time, he can repent and be forgiven.

Satan: Yes, I suppose he may, but through his misdeeds he's made at least four hundred others run away from any talk of ONE. The way I see it, that's four hundred fewer following ONE. Four hundred more for me to enjoy.

#One: It's not like that Satan! It's not a numbers game to see who can get the most now.

Satan: Oh, that's too bad! If it were, I'd be winning big time!

#One: #Two told you before, all will have their opportunity to freely choose the ways of ONE. Free moral agency will be adhered to and respected.

Satan: But they've had their chance, they got to live a life, their redeemer paid their penalty of death. If they missed out on accepting or were put off the message by an untrustworthy messenger who had a taste for wine, women and song, too bad for them. They used their free moral agency by not accepting ONE. But they do love me.

#Two: Satan, there's no excuse for your ignorance of the rules. I spoke plainly to the disciples. You know that unless #One draws them no one can come to me, then those called must freely choose me. Those not called by ONE haven't had their time to exercise their free will yet, but they will when their time comes. Until then, my church will preach the gospel message like I told them to, so ONE can draw those wanted at this time.

#One: They will go to all nations with the good news about the coming Kingdom Of ONE, making disciples and baptizing them.

#Two: By teaching others what I've taught them, the love of ONE is getting out to humanity and will continue getting to those who need to experience it.

#One: ONE won't force people into accepting the love of ONE! We want love to be freely accepted by those who want to follow, not like your perversion, forcing a form of Christianity on people through sadistic torture and coercion.

#Two: Deceiving many into believing they were doing the work of ONE through torturing others into confessions of faith, perverting the love of ONE, making a mockery of our love for humanity.

Satan: Yes! That was some of my best work. I'm flattered you took note. It was rather good I thought. Using your own words, 'better to enter the kingdom blind and lame than not enter at all'. By adding my special 'brand of spin' for those zealous believers, they killed their fellow man to show how much they loved ONE and those they killed. My twisted logic showed them it was the most expedient way to have those infidels accept the love of ONE and forgiveness.

#One: No! It wasn't good! It was repulsive to ONE.

Cowering, Satan slinks back from the throne, defensively answering #One's strong rebuff.

Satan: I really can't take credit for all of it. The demons fed me the ideas, the concepts were theirs. I was forced to comply with their demands on how to deal with your people. I found the whole topic quite distasteful. To be perfectly honest, I'm pretty much just a figurehead for them, not what you'd call a hands-on leader. I mainly just rubber-stamp their ideas as they come along. I'm helpless to direct them in any way. You know how they won't take direction from anyone!

#Two: The point is, all of humanity at some point in their existence will get a genuine chance to know ONE and what true love is. A time and place where salvation will be available to those who want it and choose it.

Satan: Then why not end it all now? Why grind it down to the bitter end. The planet is groaning from all the devastation those humans have brought upon it.

#Two: You're no one to talk about others devastating the planet. I remember what it was like before I spoke mankind into existence.

#One: The time has not yet come, there is still much to happen, but more importantly there are still more people to make.

Satan: What! More people to be made? Don't you realize there is a species going extinct at a rate of over one hundred a day because of those humans? And you want more of them? I've given mankind the lust for power. In their minds power is how best to kill their enemies. They've gotten so good at it, they have the power to destroy all life from the earth a thousand times over and ONE wants to make more of them? Nothing good can come of it.

#Two: Yes there will! The thing ONE most desires is a strong, loving character that will turn into the love of ONE.

Satan: You're talking foolishness again! Love is for weaklings.

#One: Foolishness to you Satan. You don't know ONE or the true power of love. You never have.

#Two: You thought that by creating all those denominations within my church you could splinter its effects and focus. Instead you gave it a broader approach to relate to a multicultural humanity. From within all those denominations ONE has called to his chosen. Usually the weak and broken. ONE exalts them and through the power of #Three, makes them stronger than anyone would have imagined, bringing more praise to ONE. People gaze at them with astonishment, seeing the greatness of ONE made manifest through them.

Satan: What do you mean, I don't know ONE. ONE created me. My first memory is of ONE. Oh yes, I know ONE and your ways of love. Be giving you said. Give your time, give yourself to others, be more concerned for others than for yourself. Giving will make you stronger. Rubbish! Giving only makes you weaker and depleted. I found a better way, the way of take. Take what you want. Take all you can. Take all you can get, from whoever you can get it. Whenever you can get it. The strong don't give, they take from the weak. You say I don't know ONE or the power of ONE's, 'love of give'. I have known them intimately and have rejected them thoroughly. I reject the ways of ONE and proudly help others to see the errors of ONE's ways, guiding them to the paths of power and my ways of get.

#One: You've always thought yourself wise, putting your twisted ideas above the wisdom of ONE. You've also misrepresented the truth to all who would listen to you.

#Two: You thought by causing division within my church you'd get people to destroy it through legalism and endless lists of do's and don'ts. What's important and long lasting is the love they learn, practice and display. The true followers of ONE will be known by their love.

#One: The very love you've always rejected and actively try to destroy.

Satan: Hey now! Let's not start playing the blame game. I am what I am. You created me. I can't change now, remember?

#Two: You mean wouldn't change when you had the chance.

Satan: Whatever! It's still not my fault, I just played out the hand I was dealt. As for those humans, they've gone their own way. They are as strong willed as any demon. They willingly followed me and my ways of greed. ONE is just jealous of my popularity with them.

#One: ONE has called out the ones that ONE wants at this time. Those who respond to us will bring about much good.

Satan: Yes, you've called out the weak, broken and foolish. What a bunch of losers! I don't want them anyway. The strong and wise are all that I have time for. They will prove to be victorious in the end, securing my victory over you and ONE's plans for greatness.

#Two: Your time of influence on mankind is running out Satan. Soon you'll see ONE's plans unfolding, the plans you never took the time to understand or desired to be part of. You'll learn that ONE knew the end from the beginning. That ONE is all knowing and omnipres...

Cutting #Two off abruptly, Satan angrily responds.

Satan: Why do all our conversations have to end up about you? Yeeess, ONE is powerful, ONE is wise! But for once I want to talk about me, what I know, what I want, what I plan, what I can do! I want to talk about me! Me! I don't mind talking about you, you, you, you, you. But occasionally, I want to talk about ME!

In a huff Satan storms out of the presence of ONE. Returning to the place he truly feels superior and in control, back to his seat of prominence and power deep within Demon H.Q. There he basks in the adoration of the demonic horde where his power and authority are feared and obeyed.

"You're starting to get out into left field now, Isaac. I can't tell what is your made up story or supposed to be biblical. Good thing I've enlisted the help of my old dean. He'll help set you straight." Matt says sleepily rolling over onto his side with his leg propped up with pillows. Switching off the light, he's soon snoring.

With his ankle doing better, Matt didn't get to read Isaac's play as often as he had promised he would. Patiently waiting to hear that Matt was ready to discuss the points made in his play, Isaac kept up with his studies.

While one part of the class worked on volcanoes, other groups researched the sleeping peril of earthquakes. Reporting on the numerous earthquake zones in North America, the students discovered the one most likely to devastate the west coast was found in Alaska, rather than California. It produced a magnitude 9.2 quake in Prince William Sound in 1964, the largest in North American modern history.

Another prone area, stretches from British Columbia to Baja Mexico. This area spawns many active fault lines throughout California's coastline. This is caused by the Pacific plate rubbing against the North American plate. This friction leveled San Francisco in 1906 with a 7.7 magnitude earthquake. One of the more positive students added that fortunately these mega quakes only happen once every few hundred years. Unfortunately, the faults should be due for another big one any day now… according to the experts.

North America's east coast and its center aren't free of threat either. The largest quakes ever recorded occurred close to the middle of continent near New Madrin Missouri. Scientists can't explain why it happened there but they do know that in 1811 and 1812 at least three quakes over magnitude 8 shook over two million square miles, almost two thirds of the continental US. Lifting the ground by as much as thirty feet, they not only destroyed buildings and killed people, they caused the mighty Mississippi river to run backwards.

Moving westward, a 7.5 magnitude quake shook the 240-mile-long Wasatch Fault in 1847, one of the world's longest "normal" faults. It has a history of dropping as much as 10 feet during a single event. Located in the eastern foothills of the Rocky Mountains this fault underlies the densest populations in the area. Seismologists believe another big one is due anytime soon.

Remembering his promise and having already involved his old dean, Matt moves his reading downstairs into his home office where he could take notes better. He picks up Isaac's story where he had left off.

RETURN

When the demons started on their descent into the abyss of sin, they started out gradually. Before long however what would've once been repugnant to them became the ordinary, quiet scoffing at 1's love, turned into open scorn and disdain. Once they reached the point of rebellion they had decided they no longer wanted to live under ONE's rule of love. They were almost at point of no return. Some like Wormwood, managed to pull themselves out of this death spiral of sin, sensing it would be their last opportunity to do so. Sadly, the others did not recognize their peril in rejecting ONE and continued headlong in their race towards self-guided morality.

All the while their spiral into the depths of sin were getting tighter and quicker until it would become more recognizable as a gunshot than a spiral. Collectively they had become the opposite of ONE in every way. You can walk on freshly poured concrete in a day, build on it in four, but for it to be completely cured it can take over forty years. The time of demonic curing had arrived, they had completely hardened into sin.

#One: The time for your return has arrived #Two. We will begin the final chapter of Satan's control over mankind.

#Two: Good. Me and #Three have been faithfully working with those you've called out of the world to come to me. #Three has done many great works through them, even though Satan has done his best to confuse them and scare them off.

#One: He is like a roaring lion searching for prey.

#Two: Roaring and intimidating yes, but he has no power over them except for what they give him. His power has only ever come from one thing, the only power he can claim as his own, the power of the lie, for he is the father of all lies.

#One: Soon he will be exposed for the liar he is.

#Two: The martyrs voices are crying out to us from their spilled blood, they are awaiting the day of their Lord.

#One: The crop is almost fully ripe. Let's begin the preparations for the first harvest.

Leaving nothing to chance, back in his lair at Demon H.Q. Satan is repeatedly and meticulously going over his plans to fight ONE. He's determined to leave nothing to chance. H.Q. is a hub of frenzied activity as Satan bosses the demons around. Barking out orders like the power mad despot he had become.

Satan: Let me see that new report! It's out of date! How can I make accurate decisions based on old, out of date reports? LISTEN UP ALL OF YOU! I've just been handed a report that's way out of date, containing information that could affect our outcome in the war on ONE VERY NEGATIVELY! I will not tolerate any more of your sloppy work, it's already cost me plenty.

I've been grooming a powerful dynasty for over five thousand years, steeped in tradition, it's infiltrated all aspects of human endeavor. It has a proud military heritage and dominates international commerce. Securing control over this world's population has been no easy task but those mortal morons didn't know what hit them. Since mankind seems to have an empty spot for ONE, we built something to fill it. A spiritual organization that filled humanities emptiness for ONE rather nicely, full of ONE's piety and religious legalism. The majority of those who served within its ranks didn't recognize its hidden potential, they thought they were doing the work of ONE.

I've just had its new leader appointed, he's the opposite of #Two in every way, the anti #Two so to speak. As you all know he's joined forces with our beastly world controlling kingdom. Ruling over it, giving it the moral authority to subjugate the world, all in the name of peace. My scheme to wipe out the followers of ONE has been brilliant in its treachery. We're about to strike our killing blow at the followers of ONE. If any of you mess it up, you'll have my full wrath to answer too. DO I MAKE MYSELF CLEAR!

A din of groveling can be heard rising from the demons at H.Q. A demon clerk kneels at Satan's feet.

Demon clerk: My great and wise majesty, I have news that I just know you'll want to hear.

Satan: How would you know what I would want? You risk wasting my valuable time on something that you just know? You should have gone through the proper channels. My time is too valuable to be taken up by the likes of you, giving me some tid-bit of important news. Well you're here now, so you might as well tell me. What is it?

Demon clerk: It, it's about Wormwood sire.

Satan: I gave explicit instructions never to talk about him!

Cowering and afraid the clerk stammers.

Demon clerk: I beg your pardon my lord. It's just that I've seen him.

Satan: Where? When?

Demon clerk: By the water your excellency.

Without another word Satan rushes out of Demon H.Q. eager to see his old henchman Wormwood.

Satan: So, Wormwood. What brings you down here with the likes of us? Has your new master tired of you so soon? Have you come to see about getting your old job back? I'd have to check, but I may have an opening coming up soon. I suppose I could fit you in somewhere till then. I knew you'd never last serving ONE, you really do belong at my side, serving me and my pleasure.

Wormwood: The answer to all your questions is no. I'm on an important mission for ONE. The first two trumpets have sounded and I am the third.

Satan: Du tell. Well, I wouldn't have taken you back anyway, you treacherous leach. I'm glad to be rid of you. ONE seems to enjoy your clingy ways and he's trusted you with a solo mission. My, you must be so proud of yourself.

Wormwood: ONE is the best master an angel could hope to have. I'm ashamed of all the time I wasted serving you. ONE has been loving and kind, helping me in ways I never thought possible.

Satan: Yes, ONE is such a gem of a friend to the poor and needy.

Wormwood: ONE is better than you'll ever know Satan.

Satan: So, Mr. Third Trumpet. What've you got for us? Or should I say, for them? Humanity awaits your gift from their loving father. I'm sure it'll help win them over to ONE. ONE hasn't been very popular so far.

Wormwood: One third of the fresh water will become bitter and poisonous. Those who drink it will die. Mankind will be punished for their many sins.

Satan: Oh, that should do it. That's the way to show them the love of v. Kill off a few more then they'll flock to ONE with deep adoration and love. They're sure to see their errors better when they're thirsty or dead. Does ONE think that punishing humans will drive me out of their hearts? Anway, I don't care about them. I don't get thirsty.

Wormwood: It's not about you it's about them. They're what's important to ONE. They'll come to know the love and justice of ONE. There are for more trumpets to come, when the last one sounds your reign here will be through.

Satan: OOOUUGH I'm so scared. Well you can tell ONE that I still have a few tricks up my sleeve. Do what you've come to do then get out of here. Only a fool would count me out yet.

Wormwood: I'll relay your message. Nothing can stop me from serving ONE. You were wrong, I don't belong here with you, I was made for a relationship with ONE and so were you.

Satan: Run back to your good friend ONE. I have my own friends here to keep me company.

Enraged Satan storms back into the demonic may-lay at Demon H.Q. He gets the attention of the demons and announces.

Satan: ONE has made his biggest blunder yet, they sent a fool to do their bidding. Our old friend Wormwood was back, begging me to let him stay with us. I played him along until I got what I wanted. He spilled ONE's whole plan of attack to me, now there'll be no more surprises from ONE. Once I got the information I wanted, I discarded Wormwood like a used hanky. Poor broken hearted Wormwood was sent back to the farm team. How he begged me to let him stay but I explained how only the strong could play with us big boys. I sent him back to ONE who likes having weaklings around, making himself appear stronger. I know for sure that we're on track to destroy the plans of ONE, all we need to do is spring our trap. The time is right for us to strike out at the church of ONE. The supposed bride of white #Two's coming back for. Let's see if we can't give her a good soiling. For three and a half years now mankind has been adoring their new piece keeping leader and his beastly power, let's see if they'll worship him as their piece making dictator, wielding all-encompassing power. I'll personally direct him to launch a surprise attack on the church of ONE.

Satan personally speaks into this prodigy's ear, the antichrist pays close attention.

Satan: Your position as leader could be in peril. You've been a kind, merciful leader, some may interpret that as weakness. You need to give the world leaders a show of force they can respect. I've found a small, socially outcast, little group of people? You know the ones. They bother everyone, claiming to be the followers of #Two. They seem to be infected with a martyr complex. Making the piety of others look bad through their use of what they claim to be, the self-sacrificial love of ONE. You should use all your power against them for best effect. Crush them, destroy them, kill them all. The power and the might of all mankind is at your disposal, use your control to wipe them from the face of the earth. Their obliteration will be your finest hour, announcing to the world that you alone are in charge. Show no mercy, let all see who is the real boss, let all men know who should be feared.

Filled with pride the False Prophet heeds his masters sage words of advice. Perhaps he has been far too kind and the word should fear him and the power he controls. A lifetime of sacrificial work has gotten him into his position of power, he deserves to be the one ruling the world now at its most critical stage. He knows that he's the best and only leader capable of saving humanity.

Those self-proclaimed followers of #Two have been a pain in his side for as long as he could remember, not a progressive thinker among them, always spouting some Bible quotation on how things ought to be done. He feels good about giving the order to attack, knowing there would be no one who would be objecting. He was certain of a decisive and speedy victory for his forces.

The armies of the Beast plan to make the Church Of ONE look like terrorists by planting a wide array of contraband weaponry on the murdered church members. With the Beast's overpowering military might over the unarmed pacifist families of the church, the leadership is self-assured of a stunning victory resulting in a large civilian body count. Kill them all, was their battle cry.

The False Prophet sits in stunned silence as he's briefed by aides. Satan flies into a rage after he hears how the earth opened, swallowing the armies of the Beast pursuing the Church Of ONE who escaped to safety, as if on eagle's wings.

#One: Just as we thought they went after our church.

#Two: #Three got them to safety just in time.

#One: #Three had to wait until the chase was on and the army had fully committed themselves.

#Two: We are on time. Can't spring a trap prematurely and expect to catch your prey. There was no turning back once the army was in full pursuit.

#One: Satan is certainly upset, I can hear his thoughts now. Accusing ONE of being a lyre and cheat.

#Two: I told him from the start, ONE reserved the right to have total overall control. He never listens to anyone, his voice is all he hears. Things could have been so different had he made better choices. It pains me to see the misery he brings to those under his control.

#One: Me too, but it was their free choice, we had to give them that.

#Two: The Beast and the False Prophet will demand revenge, they'll go after the remnant of the church, it's late sprouting seeds. Those who didn't commit to ONE before but finally do come to us over the next three and a half years. They'll have their faith in ONE tested through all the fire and fury Satan can inspire.

#One: Fire is what they'll need to purify their hearts. #Three will empower them through it all to the astonishment of their tormentors. As before, martyrdom will spread the word of ONE to those weary of Satan's corrupting influence.

#Two: Their fiery trials will cleanse them of character flaws, only love will be left.

#One: We'll have our two witnesses prominently speaking to the world, giving instruction, correction and discipline when needed. Always pointing to the way of ONE and our love.

#Two: The times of great tribulation will only last for three and a half years, then Satan will be bound when I return as King of Kings and Lord of Lords.

#One: Yes he will, but it won't be without a fight. He won't go easily into the night, that's for sure.

At Demon H.Q. things seem to be going from bad to worse for a brooding Satan.

Demon Aid: Your majesty, the guards and tormentors are starting to lose heart, every day more people are added to their ranks of ONE's followers scheduled for martyrdom. Many of those new converts are coming from their own ranks, converted by the testimony of the condemned. They're having to torture their old comrades, friends and even family.

Satan: I know! I've seen the lost time stats from stress related illnesses skyrocket. If only we had some way of silencing ONE's two witnesses. People would forget about ONE and settle into complacency.

Messenger: Your grace, an urgent message from the Two Witness think tank.

Satan: What is it? Good news I trust.

Messenger: Yes sire. They seem to have found a way to neutralize them despite ONE's protection.

Satan: A silver bullet?

Messenger: Yes my lord, it was there all along. It was so simple we never thought to try it before. Like breaking into a house through a window when the front door is unlocked.

Satan: We've lost a lot of time but the important thing is we've found it. How soon can we move on this? It's been practically three and a half years now. With those two droning on and on about ONE I'm anxious to see the last of them.

The whole world rejoices as they watch the bodies of the Two Witnesses lying in the street where they fell dead. For three and a half days the earth's inhabitants rejoice, exchanging presents in a festive, carnival atmosphere. A day for every year the Two Witnesses had pestered the weary world's inhabitants. Heaping condemnation and plagues on mankind as they go through a time of great tribulation. The Two Witnesses continually point out mankind's sins, endlessly teaching about the virtuous ways of ONE.

Satan personally scrutinized all the incoming reports of plagues and devastation brought onto the earth and humanity by ONE. He was ecstatic that the divine punishment hardened mankind into rebelling against ONE as he had done. Then the sky was rolled back as a scroll and all people, including Satan's handpicked leaders trembled in fear of the most high ONE.

Satan anticipated the arrival of the moment Gabriel blew the seventh trumpet, sounding a blast that was heard around the world as #Two descends from the clouds. Graves of the saints are opened, those who responded to the call of ONE rise with freshly minted spiritual bodies like #Two's. Members of 1's Church, hidden in the wilderness are changed at the same time, in the twinkling of an eye. All of them adorned as a bride about to marry her beloved. The week and outcast of the word that had been rejected by Satan were now being exalted, coming with #Two as the ruling family of ONE.

It was now that Satan strikes out at ONE with all-out war. This was going to be a showdown of winner take all. Satan influences the kings of the world to fight alongside the Beast and False Prophet, against the returning #Two and family. #Two's feet touch down on mount Zion triggering a massive earthquake, splitting the mountain in two, leaving a large valley running east and west. Into this valley the armies of the world pour ready to battle the newly arrived King of Kings. The armies have learned the ways of the Beast well, indoctrinated in the ways of war they mindlessly obey their orders without a thought for their own self-preservation. Onward they go, trying to destroy the one who came to save them. Wanting only to

Vanquish the one who gave himself as a ransom, freeing them from their sins.

They go forward like a human tide trying to wash the earth clean of its new King. Their own lifeblood, running like a river from the valley to the sea. As the last soldier sheds his blood in the battle the power of the mighty Beast disappears. There is no one left to follow orders, no one left to fight. The dreadful war-making machine that held the world in terror vanished, the great Babylon had fallen from its place of splendor, all in the space of a day.

Triumphantly #Two approaches the false prophet and the Beast commander.

#Two: You're no longer in charge here. A time of refreshing has arrived. I'll be ushering in ONE's Kingdom of love and of that Kingdom there shall be no end.

False Prophet: Who are you to usher in anything? We don't recognize your authority here. You're just some sort of space alien, coming to take over our planet. I personally know the god of this world and he's nothing like you.

Beast commander: You may have defeated our armies for now but we'll come back with the next generation of warriors. We'll always fight you, we will never surrender to you, your authority, or your ways of love.

False Prophet: Yes, with all our heart, soul and strength, we reject your rule over our lives. We'll pursue the freedom of our personal liberty with our last breath of life.

#Two: Are you sure about that? Do you completely reject my authority as your true and rightful King?

Before #Two, both leaders are kneeling and in unison, as if with one voice they say.

Beast commander and False Prophet: You may be our true King but yes, we reject you and all that you represent. We'll never accept you as Lord over our lives. Give us our freedom or give us death!

#Two looks at them sadly for a moment, then with a melancholy tone he says.

#Two: Then you leave me no choice. I'll have to give you what you want.

The pair of rebellious leaders rise to their feet with broadening, smug smiles of satisfaction growing on their faces. They were used to getting their own way and they'd be having it their way again. Motioning to an angel standing at the ready #Two gave the order.

#Two: Take these two esteemed leaders and cast them alive into the lake of fire burning with brimstone.

Surprised faces of hate replace the smiles of victory as the two leaders sneer and hurl cursing insults at #Two. They loudly reaffirm their desire for death over living within the loving ways of ONE in a Kingdom of peace not ruled by themselves. With their hearts hardened through Satan's influence they seem overjoyed at the prospect of death rather than submit to the love of ONE. Then it was Satan's turn to answer for his misdeeds. Defiantly he addresses #Two.

Satan: So, you've finally come back to save mankind. There's not much to come back to or many left to save after the plagues and destruction ONE brought down onto these poor people of mine. How I've struggled trying to help them improve their pitiful lives. Encouraging them in technological advances, I guided them as they explored their innately, inquisitive and inventive nature. All was in vain though with ONE coming along, indiscriminately destroying all our hard work whenever things weren't going ONE's way. Just like the flood, you haven't changed a bit.

#Two: ONE didn't come to destroy but to save. ONE's Kingdom has now arrived to take control of this world and its people. Those who are left and their children after them will see and enjoy all the love and peace that can be realized living in the Kingdom of ONE, without your influence around to distract them. They'll love ONE as a father and he'll love them as his children.

Satan: Sure, they'll love ONE. They'll have no other option without me around. But even if they should worship and love ONE for more than a thousand years, the vast majority would choose me and my ways over ONE when given a chance. As usual you underestimate me and you're self-deluded about your wonderful ways of love.

#Two: Do you think so? You only turned a third of the angels your way. Do you really believe the vast majority of mankind would choose you over ONE?

Satan: Absolutely! Even after more than a thousand years, they'd still choose me. I take great pride knowing I've destroyed something you've worked so hard to build. It must be heartbreaking for you to see all the death I've caused? All the needles pain. From the very start I held sway in the lives of man. You got but a mere handful to follow and love ONE."

#Two: "We got the ones we wanted, the ones who wanted us."

Satan: "Do you think I didn't know your plan from the start? You wanted family to recreate ONE and perfect love. ONE was foolish to use such frail creatures. All I had to do was play my pipe and they danced any jig that I wanted. I enticed them into all their sins. You killed off your own potential children because of me. Your sworn enemy. Ha, ha, ha, ha, ha, ha. I do love the irony. Now You'll have less family and I'll have more pleasure. The flood, the Philistines, you wiped out entire nations, man, woman, and child. You even had your zealots kill all their animals. Just because they didn't know ONE. How could they? They weren't the children of Abraham.

I had all humanity fooled. Even after your personal sacrifice #Two. I twisted your religion, I made so many religions mankind didn't know what to believe. And Your precious church, what a joke. I broke them into bickering factions. Divide and conquer, that's my strategy. Most people couldn't find you or your message through all my decoys.

Misleading your called-out ones gave me my greatest joy. I had my way with your beautiful bride, soiling her before your wedding day. Now that I look back on it, it seems to me like I haven't done too bad at all fighting the great all-powerful ONE. Judging by sheer numbers alone, I'd say you lost."

#Two: "Satan, again you are betrayed by your own arrogance and pride. You think you know the plans of ONE. You know nothing! And your ignorance has no excuse. You could have known ONE if you had chosen too. You could have known ONE is all knowing, all-powerful, omnipresent, omnipotent. You thought your plans were so smart and secret. ONE was there beside you the whole time. ONE can hear your very thoughts. ONE planned the beginning from the end. As for you winning over ONE, nothing could be further from the truth. To create the strong character needed for leadership, mankind needed to work against a force that was opposite to love. You willingly chose that role for yourself. You helped build our children's strong character. Without struggling against your pull towards sin, those who chose ONE during their lifetimes could've never developed such strong character."

Satan: "Well maybe that's all true but there's still so many lost to sin. Dead in their sins and lost to you.'

#Two: "Why is it so hard for you to see? You know that I was resurrected. I made a way for all mankind to follow.

Satan: Sinners deserve eternal punishing, they chose sin not your way of love. There's no atoning for them. They didn't choose you. They followed me.

#Two: "No Satan. You deserve eternal punishing. Those who don't choose ONE will receive eternal punishment. You said yourself the sins they committed came from you. If they choose to continue to walk in sin and reject ONE, along with my atoning sacrifice, then they will die, they are mortal. ONE kept them from the tree of life at the garden so they wouldn't have immortality. But mankind will have a chance to know ONE. There's a great harvest yet to come where they'll learn about ONE. It'll be their time for them to choose love and receive salvation and the forgiveness you rebels rejected. The sins of mankind are on your head as the originator of them, that's the part you'll play on the day of atonement. On that day you'll be cast out from mankind, imprisoned in a desert of despair.

Satan: You're confusing the issue as usual. You're just jealous of my influence over man and their love for me. I know what they crave the most, how they strive for the power and prestige that I give them. Mankind finds fulfilment with me and my ways, so don't try to frighten me with 'the desert of despair'. Oh it sounds so melodramatic.

#Two: The only way to know for sure is to try. Shall we find out.

Satan: By all means. If you can handle the rejection.

#Two: So be it. You and the demons will be bound and chained in the bottomless pit for over a thousand years. Separated from mankind. A seal will be set upon you, so you can't deceive the nations during that time. Then after the thousand years are over you'll be released for a short season.

And so it was done as #Two commanded. Satan is bound in the bottomless pit, unable to influence mankind for over a thousand years. A thousand years that he and his demons spend plotting, strategizing, on how best to fight and thwart the plans of ONE. The next time they strike, they'll be ready to destroy and extinguish all traces of love.

"Now that definitely goes against our beliefs in the rapture. I hope the dean can help sort out this mess. Where did Isaac get such crazy ideas?" Matt's still shaking his head and laughing confidently as he puts Isaac's book away in the desk drawer.

Back in college, Isaac's class is finishing up Speckel's triad of destruction. Rounding them off, another group provided information on Speckel's favorite, which highlighted the power of water. The Cascadia Subduction Zone is a 700-mile long, slow motion collision, as the Juan de Fuca plate is forced under the North American one. Colliding about 50 miles offshore from southern British Columbia to Northern California, the Cascadia Subduction Zone is capable of spawning magnitude 9 earthquakes, up to 30 times larger than those of the San Andreas fault line. Expected to shake for up to four minutes, it would not only devastate buildings along the coast but would soon be followed by a wall of water. Easily topping 150 feet high, the tsunami would rush over low-lying land, clawing what it can back out to sea. Although magnitude 9 episodes happen around every 530 years, with the last one occurring in 1700, smaller quakes in the range of magnitude 8 occur on an average of 270 years.

Although offshore quakes trigger devastating tsunamis, tsunamis are mostly produced by underwater landslides just offshore. This makes them harder to predict and leaves little time to react. These landslides can be triggered by small quakes, collapsing underwater volcanoes, or even heavy rainfall. Tsunamis like these have a history of occurring on the east and west coast. The vulnerability of the densely populated flat eastern seaboard was highlighted in 2012 by hurricane Sandy.

These topics kept Isaac busy in his studies. He had often tried to get a hold of Becky but with no luck.

Confident in the thought she was avoiding him as her dad had instructed, he chalked Bob's lurid comments about Becky up to Bob's ongoing harassment. Isaac was sure that once he could talk to Matt about his biblical findings, he and Becky would soon be back together as a couple and moving towards marriage. Isaac was expecting to hear from Matt anytime now and was apprehensive about how long it was taking him to respond. Focusing on his studies helped to keep his mind free of the doubts that would often wake him in the night.

Matt finally pulls out Isaac's book to read the last chapter. After microwaving a frozen bachelor's supper, Matt sits in his home office, his computer ready to look up any reference he can think of to set Isaac straight on Bible beliefs.

REBUILDING AND THE HARVESTS

On the throne ONE is discussing the events leading up to #Two's return to earth as King of Kings.

#One: #Three, you express the anxiety and tension everyone felt so vividly. I feel like I was one of the frightened saints there living it out. Fear mixed with patient faith in the face of urgent necessity brought me to tears.

#Two: Or the supreme joy of the wedding banquet. I'm so giddy at having all the new family members around. My cheeks are sore from smiling. It's fun helping them get used to their new bodies, discovering how to channel #Three through themselves.

#One: Peter certainly hasn't changed. He's still got the same zeal that made him jump overboard onto the water. It hasn't diminished one iota. Not used to his new powers, he zoomed out past Jupiter with his hair straight back and his tail on fire. Took him way past Neptune to get stopped.

#Two: He always did do things wholeheartedly. He exudes passion. He's a valued member of the family.

#One: That's right #Three, they're all valued members of our family. Each has a spot where they fit. I called humans to #Two who'd be best suited for our family at this time. They will make good kings and priests in the kingdom of ONE.

#Two: They have a big job ahead of them but they're only the first fruits of the spring harvest.

#One: There's plenty to do before the main harvest comes.

#Two: Yes. The main fall harvest is still to come. Your right #Three, we need to stay focused on our tasks at hand. One step at a time and all will get done. By the looks of things our family will soon be growing even bigger.

#One: No sense counting eggs when it's chickens we want. Our new children will only be born after they decide for themselves.

#Two: Our prime law of love at work. Free will. Humanity choosing to willingly follow our ways of love and become children of ONE, or to reject love and life, leaving death as their only remaining option.

#One: Those left alive from the old world have a lot of work to do. The earth desperately needs a makeover, healing it of its wounds. #Three's begun flowing the healing waters out of Jerusalem. Those waters will aid them with earth's restoration.

#Two: Now that the influence of satan has been removed, mankind will be able to achieve more than ever before. They must feel refreshed not having that ever present pull of sin being broadcast onto them. They can prosper with no war. Families can live in peace, spreading the healing waters throughout the earth and make it a beautiful garden once again.

#One: It was the pull of sin that built such strong character in our called-out ones, the first fruits. As the pull of gravity builds strong muscles, the pull of sin was necessary in building their character. It'll be good for them to get used to being in the family of ONE without Satan around. They're just baby ONE's now. The thousand years will give them time to grow fully into ONE's loving nature.

#Two: Yes, it'll take them some time to adjust. I'm glad Satan will be imprisoned for more than a thousand years. I'm still surprised he suggested he be removed from the world.

#One: Yes #Three, he is overly self-confident. Maybe he finally read some of our prophecies. His fate is clearly laid out in the book, but he still thinks he can beat us.

#Two: But to have him goad me into banishing him to the bottomless pit. I was just about to pronounce his fate when he claimed most of mankind would choose him over ONE, even after living for more than a thousand years in a loving kingdom.

#One: Of course, that's it #Three. He always had to be the leader. He's the epitome of controlling. He had to feel in charge, especially when it involved his personal incarceration.

#Two: That does make sense, but enough about him. Let's concentrate on the joy we're about to bring into the world. The gospel message about the coming Kingdom of ONE that I preached to the world when I lived there the first time, that coming Kingdom has arrived. It's now begun to rule the world.

Construction booms like never before. After being traumatized by Satan's pull into sin, mankind blossoms when they work in harmony towards the common goal of Earth's restoration. The new baby ONE's grow in wisdom as they fill their roles as kings and priests to the inhabitants of the world. They lead mortal mankind to the love of ONE through gentle guidance, counselling and love. Each new member of ONE has their own special talents and experiences. Looking back on their lives they empathize with those they lead. They're glad for the paths ONE took them on, getting them to where they are now and working within the expanded family of ONE. Now they're laborers in the Kingdom working to fulfil ONE's master plan. Work they were born to do as children in the family of ONE.

Years melt into memories, turning the bad old days into stories told by parents, then grandparents. After several generations the stories become common folklore passed down to the following generations. Wounds on people's emotions and the environment, caused by man's rule, are slowly healed. Washed away by the cleansing waters of ONE. When the people turn to the right or left they are shepherded back to ONE's ways by their kings and priests.

#One: Mankind has lived in peace and tranquility now for many generations.

#Two: The world has been peaceful for so long now, people are forgetting what the world was like before I came back to bring love and heal creation. After living so long without Satan, humans are beginning to think there is no other way, was no other way to live. Some are naively beginning to take our family for granted and are displaying indifference to our love.

#One: Beginning to doubt that ONE's ways are best.

#Two: They have no fear of sin, or its consequences.

#One: They have no experiences with Satan. Some believe the stories about him are only parables to be rationalized away.

#Two: Those who think that way will never fully embrace ONE's ways of love.

#One: They think they know best and are not willing to test their beliefs against the truth of ONE.

Those who trust in ONE notice the lack of faith displayed by those doubters who only seek their own pleasure. ONE's ways of love and give have no relevance in their lives. Withdrawing emotionally from the congregation of ONE, rejecting the love of ONE, they rebuff #Two's sacrifice for their salvation. When they die of old age they go back to the soil they came from, unlike their peers who gladly accept #Two as Lord over their lives. They are resurrected into the family of ONE as children when they die. Finally, the last generation of millennials has lived their lifetime and have chosen their fate.

#One: It's harvest time.

#Two: Yes, it's been a thousand years now since I returned at the Feast of Trumpets. The world has grown lush, healing from the wounds left by carnal man. The millennium of rebuilding has all its infrastructure in place. Houses, farms, cities, now stand empty. Crops are ready to plant, barns are full of food, void of human habitation. The Earth will now welcome all its previously dead inhabitants. Food and shelter won't be a problem.

#One: This'll be the largest of the resurrections. With Satan and the demons chained in prison, finally all who ever drew the breath of life with Satan around will get their opportunity to live ONE's way of love without being led astray.

#Two: They'll be resurrected back into healed mortal bodies, like the ones they died in. They'll still have themselves and their addictions to overcome, old habits die hard. Who they truly are and want to become will be shown by their choices, revealing their true colours.

#One: Our family will help them become the best people they can. Our ways will be freely available to everyone, those who want to follow them will be able too. We'll offer help when asked, but we must not force ourselves on them. Everyone must willingly want to live in the ways of love and accept your sacrifice to cleanse them of the sins they will inevitably commit.

#Two: I'll be glad to greet all those personalities when they become reanimated into new bodies. ONE remembers each of them, as a hen remembers her chicks. We'll recreate their personality and emotions exactly as they were when they died, resurrected back into new physical bodies similar to their original ones.

#One: This will be the greatest time of family growth. Everyone who has ever breathed and died not being drawn to you, #Two, will now have their opportunity to receive you and live in the love of ONE as a family member.

With a word from ONE, the ground gives up its dead. The seas and waters of the world release the people they held entombed. Anywhere there was a human in the sleep of death, unaware of the passage of time, they are now expelled at the command of ONE. ONE remembers them all, recognizes every individual and reproduces them down to every hair. The mighty and the weak, all who had taken the breath of life, now stand before their maker.

Any conscious thoughts they may have had are restored back into their minds. Their character in tact, the way they developed it, is now replenished through the perfect memory of ONE and ONE's creative genius. The bulk of mankind is now reanimated with their full mental capacities as they left them, as ONE gently blows the breath of life back into them.

There are many questions to be asked. Before they are, ONE speaks with authoritative reassurance. Every heart instantly recognizes their maker. The empty spot inside them is filled so perfectly by ONE's presence.

#One addresses the sea of humanity.

#One: Many of your fellow brothers and sisters have already entered the family of ONE. Their names were written in the book of life.

#Two: That means they willingly embraced ONE's way of love during their first lives. They claimed it for themselves as the free gift of salvation from their sins, brought to them through my redemptive sacrifice. They made this choice of their own free will."

#One: Your free moral agency will always be respected by ONE. ONE will not force you to join the life of love.

#Two: But the choices are final. The history of mankind clearly demonstrates, beyond any doubt, that all humanity has sinned and is incapable of living free of sin on its own.

#One: The choices before you are to accept #Two as your Lord and Master and to repent and accept his sacrifice to blot out your sins.

#Two: Or you can reject all that ONE has to offer you and die. You will cease to exist, even the memory of you will vanish.

#One: ONE knows that many of you are thinking that your sins aren't your fault. That you had no chance to know ONE or what ONE required of you. Perhaps you were never told of #Two's sacrifice and the redemption that he brought. These are true and valid points.

Most of you had no way of knowing ONE or about the ways of love. More importantly you never learned of #Two or his sacrifice which brings life. Some of you did learn of #Two, but it never made sense. You were never drawn by ONE to Him."

#Two: Now you'll all have that opportunity to come to know ONE without Satan's pervasive message of sin. You can freely choose the salvation of #Two for yourself. You'll all be able to choose the path you'd like to take. Your choice will be irrevocable once it's taken.

#One: Some of you died before you really got to live. Others had some inkling of a creator somewhere but had no teacher to show you the way.

#Two: Now's your time. Come, drink in all the fascists of ONE and love. You'll have a lifetime if you need it. The earth will sustain you. There are cities to live in with fine accommodations, orchards and gardens to feed you in abundance. The family of ONE will be at your side, helping you as friends and guides, kings and priests.

#One: You'll have time to make an informed choice. Again, let me stress to you that ONE will not force any choice on you. ONE wants you to joyfully, wholeheartedly and freely choose love.

#Two: Remember your past lives of sin, get to know each other, seek out your families and friends to see where their sins brought them. If you didn't have a long life before, as you mature in this one ask yourself, would I have been any better on my own at resisting sin than anyone else was? You'll come to see that all humans succumb to sin without exception. That's why there had to be a sacrifice made on your behalf. Sin only leads to misery and ruin. The only chance for mankind's happiness and individual growth...

#One: ...is to accept salvation, made possible through the great sacrifice of #Two.

The world is alive with every nationality, color and background of people. Every size from the very tiny to the giants of old. Every age, from newborn to those who died with their days fulfilled. They were all brought back in this, the largest resurrection. As they lived out their new life in a peaceful prosperous world, they shared their stories of personal struggle. All coming to recognize their old sin or how they would have sinned just the same as the rest had they lived long enough. Everyone finally came to recognize that humans were destined to sin and the only possibility for salvation was to accept #Two's sacrifice for themselves.

Sadly though ,some wouldn't join with ONE and the family. They didn't want anything to do with love or it's purity. The incorrigible who hardened their hearts wouldn't let the healing power of ONE do its redemptive work in their new lives. They held onto their pride and hate as tightly as they could, refusing to let go of it. Holding onto the past they were unwilling to grasp hold of the marvelous future before them.

#Two: Our family has truly blossomed. Having a lifetime to decide if they would accept us, most people have made better choices than the Angels did.

#One: Those with love in their hearts did. Being pure love, we couldn't force the others to choose our ways. Just as the Angels before them, mankind must be free to decide their own fate.

At the prison gates the demons are impatiently awaiting their release when #Two comes to set them free.

Satan: You're late! The thousand years were up long ago, I was beginning to think you were going back on your word.

#Two: I'm not late, I'm right on time. As was agreed, you've been imprisoned for more than a thousand years. We never established how much longer. I thought a tithe of time would be appropriate. The extra hundred years are now over. You're free to go.

Satan: Did you manage to get many to follow in your ways of love and self-sacrifice?

#Two: Those who chose to follow ONE are faithful followers.

Satan: Faithful now, but we'll see how true they stay to ONE. Once humanity feels the power of my influence, they'll turn on ONE like wild animals. We've been planning this for more than a millennium. Now it's our turn.

As the locks are removed the unshackled demons, led by Satan, flee their restraining chains and head for a naive mankind. Having experienced sin, those who had a thirst for righteousness found strength in #Three and the family of ONE. They were willing to work at overcoming their sins through ONE's forgiveness and love. Those who chose not to follow ONE succumbed quickly to the demonic influences on them.

Having lived in peace as neighbors and friends, the opposing cultures of give and get now clash head on. With the way of love not penetrating their stony hearts, those only concerned for themselves and their own, despise the seemingly weaker, unenlightened and giving followers of ONE. Plans for eradication of the presumed weaker culture of love are made. Led by satanic influences, the takers plan a full-scale attack on the followers of ONE who live without fear of others. Having no walls or fortifications, their cities and towns were as open to all as they had ever been. They were easy to enter, accessible from every angle, friendly and inviting. The followers of ONE are ripe for plundering.

Satan: Doesn't it feel great to be free again Legion?

Legion: Yes master. It's good to be out influencing and indwelling gullible humans once more.

Satan: You certainly haven't lost your touch with humans.

Legion: This is my true passion and gift. Influencing with evil, fighting ONE and His love.

Satan: Now this time you demons stick to our game plan. We want the humans to attack swiftly and as soon as possible. We'll take ONE and His extended family by surprise.

Demon one: We've infiltrated all the leadership that was open to us. They're ready to attack.

Satan: Good, let's swoop down upon the unprotected before they think to mount any kind of defense.

Influenced by Satan and the demons, sinful mankind, led by Gog and Magog, attack those living in peace with the love of ONE. ONE comes to the defense of his people and, as it was in the valley of Megiddo, the fighting is ferocious. Just as before, the dead pile up on the side of evil. The victory goes to those who weren't afraid to lose their lives for love. For in the losing, they knew they'd gain them.

This time though, the end of this battle would mark the end of all wars. For this was the famed war to end all wars. The time mankind had dreamed would someday come. Those who were on ONE's side and had chosen to willingly follow in the ways of love, persevering through the temptations of sin brought back by Satan. These people are now resurrected into new immortal bodies, delivering them into ONE's spiritual family.

Those people who died fighting against ONE, who willingly chose not to follow ONE, their deaths were now permanent. They lived a lifetime with the love of ONE, free of Satan's influence, yet in the end they rejected love to follow Satan back into sin. Being resurrected as mortals over a hundred years earlier, their deaths were now final. Their free choice between life and death will be honored. They'll never again be resurrected back to life. ONE will respect them and their choice to not receive the gift of eternal life by letting them stay dead.

Now the satanic hoard must be dealt with. They'd never change, wanting only to hate and destroy. Their looming fate weighs heavy on their minds.

#Two: Now you Satan, you and your demons will be locked away for all eternity. Banished into the lake of fire to be tormented day and night forever and ever. You wanted to be masters of your own destiny, now you'll reap your rewards. Sin is on your heads, not on the heads of tricked and lied to humanity."

Satan: No. Wait. No! That wasn't part of the bargain. We don't deserve this. We have culpable deniability. Humanity chose for themselves to willfully sin. You tricked us. You used us. You lied to us. It's not fair!

#Two: Silence Satan. ONE is righteous and true. You are the father of lies. As the source of its origin, sin will go to Hades with you, as sin is your responsibility.

By the power of #Two's words, Satan and the demons are cast into the lake of fire. Where they will endure punishing that will last for the rest of eternity.

#One: Now we need to deal with all those who were called to you, #Two. Those who accepted your sacrifice of salvation, then turned their backs on you returning to their sins. They tasted forgiveness and then willingly rejected you. It leaves them no other possibility for salvation.

#Two: They proved themselves untrustworthy, unfit for eternal life. The final resurrection is reserved for them, the resurrection of the damned.

#One: Some have fooled themselves into thinking they were doing the will of ONE, even casting demons out of people in the name of ONE. Still we will have to send them away, telling them we never knew them.

#Two: Being resurrected back into their familiar mortal bodies and not having their names found written in the book of life, they'll be burned up like chaff in the lake of fire. There they'll suffer the second death, from which there's no return.

#One: I called them all to you. Giving them their opportunity to accept you as their personal savior. They did, then they willingly rejected you. Their fate was sealed. They can't change their minds and accept you twice. It would be like crucifying you all over again. There can be only one opportunity to accept the free gift of salvation. Through the resurrections we have made sure everyone who's ever lived has received their one and only opportunity to accept salvation.

#Two: It will never be said I didn't get a chance to know ONE. All have now had their opportunity to accept love and my sacrifice. They've spurned it or are living in new immortal bodies as children of ONE. This will be the final resurrection for humanity. Soon our family plan will come to its conclusion.

The final resurrection now takes place for those who rejected ONE's love after accepting the salvation of #Two. There's weeping and gnashing of teeth as each one of them cannot be found written in the book of life. Each pay for their own choices with their lives as they're cast into the fiery lake and die.

Being mortal, they're burned up. Never to have thought, consciousness, or life of any kind again. Satan, who is made of immortal spirit and cannot die, will be tormented for the rest of eternity. For mortal's, punishment comes to a swift end in the flames. Their punishment will last for all eternity as they will never again have life. Death and the grave are now thrown into the lake of fire as all mortals have passed through them, leaving none to endure them again. ONE now prepares for the exciting, grand culmination of their plan that had been set into motion so long ago.

#Two: Well #One, the harvests are now completed. Our seeds have produced well for us. We now have a bountiful crop of family.

#One: Things have turned out tremendously well, haven't they? Our plans worked out great.

#Two: Of course #Three, just as we anticipated.

#One: There's just one more thing to do and then we're done.

#Two: Your right. I told them all when I was on earth as a man that my father had a large house with many rooms waiting for them. Since there is no more sin on earth to contaminate ONE, it's time we showed the kids the new family home.

#One: #Three, if you would be so kind as to usher in the new and splendid city of ONE. The New Jerusalem, where each member of the family has their own room.

#Two: Not that they'll have to stay in it.

#One: No, of course not. They'll have to be out and about doing ONE's business. Can't do that stuck in your room.

#Two: ONE seems to have gotten into the planning and construction business.

#One: Well you must admit it's been productive for us, and what better work could there be where the whole family can pitch in and be together? I love building stuff when the whole family is involved. Why, the possibilities are endless!

#Two: Let's enjoy the fruits of our labors for a while before we start any new projects. Three, you keep your ideas to yourself would you.

#One: It's time for a rest. No new plans just yet. Besides we have new babies in the house to take care of, but they'll grow up soon enough. Then we'll see about more plans.

#Two: Speaking of the new babies, who's up for a walk'?

A shattering YES erupts from the family that shakes the throne on the sea of glass. #One looks at #Two with love in his eyes as he holds hundreds of babies in his arms. What ONE had only dreamed of so long ago had now finally come to pass. Now instead of ONE being just one, there was an entire family. ONE's quiver was full and ONE was happy. As #One and #Two bask in mutual admiration and love, they feel #Three shouting to them.

#Three: Last one around Andromeda and back is a rotten egg.

They turn to see #Three with most of the family, babies and all, streaking across the sky like a comet, the slower family members making up the tail trailing behind.

"Well that's quite the story. Good luck finding scriptural support for all that," Matt says out loud. "I'm glad he didn't get Becky mixed up in all that foolishness! He'll be sleeping for sure at this hour. Maybe I'll call him later." He puts the envelope containing Isaac's story in his desk drawer. Turning off the lamp, he leans back into his big office chair and falls asleep.

Chapter 7

Laying on his sheepskin mattress, Jacob knows he is close to death. Coming in and out of focus his memory replays hazy, random scenes from the past. "Can these all be real?" he thought to himself. "Did all this happen to me or is death closer than I know?" Rolling onto his side he goes to tuck his arm under his head. His hand hits a large hard rock bringing him into full consciousness.

"Oh yes," speaking to the rock out loud. "How could I doubt you? I've been sleeping on you to remind me of the promises God made to me. I did see Angels going up to heaven that night." Getting a reminder from God, Jacob responds. "Yes, yes Lord, the blessings, pass on the blessings." Jacob is muttering incoherently to those nursing him, but inside his head the words and thoughts are focused, crystal clear, as he talks to God silently in his mind.

"Thank you for reminding me. I must pass the blessings you gave me onto my favorite son. You used him to save my family from starvation when I was powerless to do so. You must have seen something good in him like I did. Looking back now I see how you've been working through him since his youth, turning calamity into great power. I'll give all your blessings to him just as my father gave them to me and grandpa gave them to him. Going forward your blessings will flow in my family throughout all our generations." Jacob's face is wet with sweat even though the night is cool, his body twitches randomly without restraint.

"What? Don't give them to Joseph? No Lord. I don't want to pass your divine blessings on to his brothers. I'll give them my blessings, but now I need to pass on your blessings to Joseph. Oh, yes. I understand now, a double blessing. Yes. Joseph will receive a double blessing from you. A nation and a company of nations, just like you said will come from me. Through Joseph, kings shall come forth from me as well. My descendants will be like the dust of the earth you said and they will spread out to the west and to the east, to the north and to the south. They shall possess the gates of their enemies. From my seed all nations will be blessed." With his mind at ease, Jacob's mumbling fades to silence. He begins to snore as his twitching slows and then stops, leaving him in sleep's sweet embrace.

Joseph is told by an aid, "your father is ill." Saddened, he goes to see his dad for the last time. He takes his two sons, Manasseh and Ephraim with him. When Jacob heard Joseph had arrived, he summoned all his strength to sit up in bed and speak softly to Joseph.

"God Almighty appeared to me at Luz in the land of Canaan and blessed me. He said to me, 'Behold, I will make you fruitful and multiply you, and I will make of you a great company of peoples and will give this land to your offspring after you, for an everlasting possession.' Now your two sons, who were born to you in the land of Egypt, before I came to you here, are mine; Ephraim and Manasseh shall be mine, just as Reuben and Simeon are. The children that you fathered after them shall be yours, but these shall be called by the name of their brothers in their inheritance. When I came from Paddan, to my sorrow, your mother Rachel died in the land of Canaan on the way to Ephrath. I buried her there on the way to Ephrath."

Joseph comforts his dad as Jacob recounts one of his greatest sorrows. Looking past Joseph who was leaning close to him, Jacob sees Joseph's two sons. He said, "Who are these?"

Joseph replied to his father, "They are my sons, whom God has given me here in Egypt."

"Bring them to me, please, so I can bless them." Jacob's voice was choked with emotion, making it hard to talk, his eyes were dim with age, making it hard to see. Joseph brought them near his father. Kissing them and hugging them, Jacob said to Joseph through his tears,

"I never expected to see your face; and behold, God has let me see your offspring also."

Joseph took them both, Ephraim in his right hand toward Jacob's left hand, and Manasseh in his left hand toward Jacob's right hand and brought them near to his father. Jacob stretched out his right hand and laid it on the head of Ephraim, who was the younger, and his left hand on the head of Manasseh, crossing his hands. Then he blessed Joseph through his two sons saying.

"The God before whom my fathers Abraham and Isaac walked, the God who has been my shepherd all my life to this day, the angel who has redeemed me from all evil, bless these boys; and in them let my name be carried on, and the name of my fathers Abraham and Isaac; let them grow into a multitude in the midst of the earth."

Looking down, Joseph saw that his father laid his right hand on the head of Ephraim, it surprised him and he took hold of his father's hand to move it from Ephraim's head to Manasseh's head saying.

"Not like that father; since this one is the firstborn, put your right hand on his head."

Jacob refused and said, "I know, my son, I know. He also shall become a people, and he also shall be great. Nevertheless, his younger brother shall be greater than he, and his offspring shall become a multitude of nations."

Jacob further blessed Joseph's two boys that day by proclaiming, "By you the rest of Israel will pronounce blessings on each other by saying, 'God make you as Ephraim and Manasseh.'"

Through God's guidance, Jacob put Ephraim before Manasseh when he blessed them, then he said to Joseph,

"I know I am about to die, but God will be with you and will bring you again to the land of your fathers. When you get there, I have given to you, rather than to your brothers, one mountain slope that I took from the hand of the Amorites with my sword and with my bow."

Jacob looks contentedly at his beloved son Joseph and his two new sons, Ephraim and Manasseh. Giving out a sigh, with his strength dwindling, Jacob drifts begrudgingly back into sleep, still holding his three sons in a tight embrace.

Through many trials, Jacob's family, the Israelites, made their way back to the land God had promised Jacob. In their travels, the tribes of Ephraim and Manasseh grow in strength and stature within Israel. After many centuries, the leaders and Kings of Israel turn their backs on the God of their father Jacob, leading Israel into sin. In a civil war the nation of Israel splits over taxation. The northern tribes, including Ephraim and Manasseh, follow a new god and King, splitting from the southern two tribes who stay outwardly loyal to the God of Jacob and their appointed king.

Abandoning the worship of their true God, the northern Kingdom of Israel started to worship Baal, descending into the debauchery of the people around them. After repeated warnings from God to repent, the northern Israelite Kingdom is taken into captivity by other nations and are scattered throughout the world. The southern Israelite Kingdom doesn't fare much better at staying true to the God of Jacob and is taken captive by the Babylonians less than a hundred and fifty years later.

God sent several prophets urging the Israelites to stay true to him but the warnings went unheeded. The last prophet God sent was Jeramiah. God sent him with a message for both Kingdoms, north and south. With the northern tribes already gone, Jeramiah personally proclaims his message to the southern Kingdom for forty years. After the southern King was killed following a rebellion, the nation's new leaders ignore Jeramiah's warning not to flee Jerusalem. Instead they take him and the daughters of the slain King off to Egypt.

Jeramiah goes on to give several more prophecies from God while in Egypt, then he and the princesses are lost within the annals of time. Jeramiah was sent to both Kingdoms of Israel, yet the Bible only records him spending time in the south. This leaves some Bible students to wonder if Jeramiah left Egypt to continue his work with the tribes of the northern kingdom of Israel.

Where this Bible speculation ends is where ancient secular Irish legend and folklore begins. It tells us about a great prophet arriving around 583 B.C., approximately the time when Jeramiah disappears from Egypt. Legend tells us the ancient prophet comes with his scribe, a princess and a large rock, reportedly the one Jacob slept on when he had his vision of angels from God. The princess marries into the Irish royalty, ultimately extending into the British Monarchy, as well as the extended interrelated aristocracy of Europe. Jacob's pillow is said to have gone on to become the Stone of Scone or the coronation stone. It was sat on when English Royalty were crowned, last used for the coronation of Elizabeth II in 1953.

World history is rife with nations struggling for dominance and power. However, history doesn't record any nation with true global domination, possessing the gates of their enemies, until the rise of the British Empire, a company of nations. At one time they controlled every strategic sea gate on the globe. Their rise to power started slowly. Winning individual battles like the Battle of Cadiz in 1587, led to greater victories such as the victory over the Spanish armada, propelling them into world greatness. God's favour seemed to follow England for the next three hundred and thirty years.

While England was still firmly in control, another great nation rose to power alongside her, literally splitting out of her. Like ancient Israel did, they split over a taxation dispute. Taking over the mantle of worldwide control after helping to rescue the British Empire for the second time from its enemies, this kindred nation came to dominate the world. Only these two nations, the United States of America and Great Britain, have been blessed with the world dominating promises passed on to Ephraim and Manasseh by a dying Jacob.

The blessings they received came directly from God. All of the combined promised blessings given to Abraham, Isaac and Jacob, have been heaped onto Joseph's two offspring nations. Recognizing their shared family history as well as the source of their greatness will help reveal where these nations' futures will lead them. The British and American rise to power has more to do with the faithfulness of God in fulfilling his promises to Abraham, Isaac and Jacob, than it does with the worthiness or virtue of those nations.

Chapter 8

Rosy sat up on the bed whining, her eyes fixed on the open bedroom door.

"What is it girl?" Isaac said looking over from his desk where he was doing schoolwork. He had no sooner spoken when he heard the kitchen door being opened downstairs.

"Isaac," Mum hollered from the bottom of the stairs. "Come help me bring the groceries in from the car."

"OK, I'll be right down," came his reply. Mum was lifting a bag from the trunk when Isaac got there, and Rosy was excitedly spinning in circles banging into them with her tail as it whipped back and forth.

"Yes, I'm glad to see you too and yes I did get you treats," Mum told her.

"I'll put these right into the freezer," Isaac said. Lifting an insulated bag from the car, he started for the open kitchen door.

Rosy calmly chews on a newly awarded treat as Mum and Isaac sort the rest of the groceries on the kitchen counter.

"I saw Matt at the store," Mum said nonchalantly. "He said he had finished reading your story and could discuss it with you tonight if you're available. He's really going out of his way for you."

"Oh good. I've been waiting to hear from him about it. Did he say anything else?" Isaac was hoping for news about Becky.

"No, just some chit chat." Mum carefully chooses her words while looking intently at Isaac. "I hope he can help bring closure to some of these wacky ideas of yours. I can't debate with you about them."

"I don't want to argue Mum. I have tried to discuss them with you and get the biblical reasons for why you believe what you do, but you tell me what you believe and then just stop talking. I want the Biblical proof for your beliefs."

"Well I give them to you and you reject them as inaccurate," Mum replies exasperatedly. "You dismiss my scriptures, saying they don't say what I believe them to say."

"That's because they don't. God wouldn't use black to describe white. One word can't effectively describe opposites."

"There you see, you're doing it again. Your tone! I just can't talk to you about this stuff." Mum wipes her eyes with the hand towel. "Since you've come back from Bible College, nothing I say to you is good enough. That's why I asked Matt to help you, maybe he can set you right again. Pa's heart will be breaking, watching you from heaven behave like this, turning your back on what we've taught you from infancy."

"Mum. You taught me to always follow where the Bible and its teachings lead. You taught me the Bible is the word of God, non-contradictory truth and that if I did find a contradiction, I needed to look further into the Bible to find the answer because I misunderstood something. Well I have found several contradictions in our denominations interpretation of what the Bible says. I am doing what you taught me, seeking a correct understanding from the Bible."

"Justifying your insistence that Pa isn't in heaven with Jesus by saying you're looking for the Bible proof astounds me. It goes against my Christian faith. I pray Matt can bring you back to the fold. He said he'd be free to see you at six if you can make it. I can't talk to you anymore about this. I just don't know what to say." Mum's voice is cracking as she again wipes her tears with the hand towel.

Silence hangs heavy over the kitchen as the two put away the rest of the things and get ready for supper. Rosy breaks the tension between them with her antics and they eat with light conversation and a few jokes. At 5:45 Isaac gets his laptop and heads out the door for Matt's, leaving Mum with a hug and a goodbye kiss on the cheek.

Matt ushers Isaac into a dark, empty house and down the hall to a disheveled study.

"You'll have to excuse the mess; things have been hectic for the last week." Matt looked weary and sad as he rubbed his forehead.

"No problem, what's up. Looks like you're reorganizing the house."

"More like reorganizing my life. Becky and her mom moved out. They said they couldn't live with me, 'constantly controlling their lives'. I just want things to be right." Matt's voice becomes unsteady. "It really came to a head over you and Becky not seeing each other. Becky was mad at me for telling her she had to stop seeing you and at you for agreeing. I didn't want to be the one to tell you, but she ran wild with some boy after you left for Bible school. I finally convinced her to settle down and live right just before you came home early last spring. This time she said she was fed up being told what to do and was going to control her own affairs. She wanted to experience life her own way, not mine or anyone else's. Her mom took Becky's side the whole way, saying she never experienced personal freedom either. They both left together."

Isaac was stunned at this unexpected news. "Well did Becky say anything about me?" He asked hopefully. "I haven't heard from her at all."

"She's as mad at you as she is at me," came Matt's reply. "She said we were both out to control her and tell her what to do. She moved in with the guy she had been seeing last winter. Her mom went to her sisters."

"I wish you had told me all this sooner! I could've talked to her, explained how things were out of my control," Isaac was starting to choke up.

"It wouldn't have done any good. In her mind you were at fault for not fighting hard enough for her. Hell has no fury like a woman scorned. Your sin was being compliant, always trying to do the right thing. She wanted a bad boy and that's what she's got now," Matt pauses thoughtfully. "That's why I didn't want you to challenge any of her religious teaching. I was afraid she'd reject everything, saying it's all up to interpretation. Trying to justify her actions and lifestyle."

"Well she's rejected everything anyway," Isaac pointed out. "At least she would have known how I feel." Isaac wipes the tears from his eyes with the back of his hand.

"Yes, well speaking of your ideas," Matt's voice hardens. "I've read your story and I must admit, I had a hard time finding any references to support your ideas.

Were you using the Bible as a reference? If you were, your assertions are farcical. For your ideas to have any validity you needed to include your Bible references. As it is, it's just a bunch of unsubstantiated nonsense. I even went over it with the dean from my Bible school days. We both agreed your conclusions are pure fantasy. Certainly not grounded in the Bible like our denomination's doctrines are. Right from the start, with your inaccurate interpretation of creation, all the way to that ridiculous ending. You miss the rapture completely and don't have the believers going to heaven, or sinners suffering eternally in hell."

"You didn't want references!" Isaac protests. "You said you'd find them yourself!"

"I could have if there were any to find. Your ideas are just ridiculous, bordering on heretical," Matt's voice is loud and angry. "I'm glad I managed to keep them from Becky for as long as I did. She didn't need any help from you to reject her faith in the Bible. I'm just glad she heard the gospel and accepted Jesus when she was a child, now nothing can take her away from salvation and having an eventual home in heaven." Matt spoke earnestly from his heart, his voice cracking when he talked about his little girl.

"You say I don't understand. You don't even know what the Gospel is!" Isaac was angered by Matt's refusal to ask him for his Bible references.

"The gospel is the good news that Jesus died for mankind's sin. Bringing salvation to all who will accept him as Lord of their lives," Matt responded loudly.

"No. that would be the gospel of salvation." Isaac replied, trying to calm himself down. "The Gospel Jesus taught was the Gospel of the Kingdom of Heaven. The Gospel Christians were told to preach to the world was the same Gospel Jesus taught about the Kingdom. Jesus seldom taught the gospel of salvation. The Gospel of the Kingdom includes the good news that Jesus brought salvation, but it's not limited to salvation alone. Understanding the good news of the Gospel explains the Kingdom of God and how all humanity will have the chance to be saved from their sins. It's no wonder you and the dean couldn't find any of my references." Isaac put a lot of work writing out his thoughts for Matt, not being consulted for his Bible references really annoyed him.

"Exactly!" Matt exclaims red faced with excitement, ignoring Isaac's anger. "Anyone who wants to receive the salvation Jesus provides, can be saved. We need to preach the salvation message so they will want to be saved. Now is their only chance, that's why it's imperative we preach Jesus to the lost of the world. They need to accept Jesus now, before they die and go to hell."

"That's not what Jesus taught," Isaac was quick to jump in. "Jesus taught in parables, deliberately obscuring the truth from those who heard it." Reaching for Matt's keyboard on the desk he says, "Let me show you." Isaac pecks on the keys with a finger. "Read this," he turns the monitor towards Matt. "Here Jesus has just taught a large crowd his doctrine of the Kingdom of God. The deeper meanings Jesus taught were only for his disciples to understand."

Mark 4

11 And he said unto them, Unto you it is given to know the mystery of the kingdom of God: but unto them that are without, all these things are done in parables:

12 That seeing they may see, and not perceive; and hearing they may hear, and not understand; lest at any time they should be converted, and their sins should be forgiven them.

13 And he said unto them, Know ye not this parable? and how then will ye know all parables?

"Again Jesus teaches with parables," Isaac shows Matt more scripture on the monitor.

Mark 4:**2 And he taught them many things by parables, and said unto them in his doctrine,**

"Jesus wasn't offering salvation to the people of his day. Instead, he tells us that we have to be drawn to him by God." Isaac is quick to find his next reference. "Here read this," the monitor flashes with a new verse.

John 6:44 New Life Version (NLV)
The Father sent Me. No man can come to Me unless the Father gives him the desire to come to Me. Then I will raise him to life on the last day.

"Or this one."

John 6

64 But there are some of you that believe not. For Jesus knew from the beginning who they were that believed not, and who should betray him.

65 And he said, Therefore said I unto you, that no man can come unto me, except it were given unto him of my Father.

66 From that time many of his disciples went back, and walked no more with him.

67 Then said Jesus unto the twelve, Will ye also go away?

"For those who continued to follow Jesus, that God given desire is referred to repeatedly in the New Testament as a calling. These verses also tell us we will be brought back to life on the last day, when Jesus returns. We don't go to heaven or hell directly after we die like you teach. Understanding the Kingdom of God and our mortality is key to knowing how God's plan of salvation arrives."

"Oh yes, the plan of God that you made up. Jesus gave his disciples the job of taking his Gospel to the world. Here let me show you," Matt said, taking control of the keyboard. "I can find scripture too you know. You need to read this."

Math 28

18 And Jesus came and spake unto them, saying, All power is given unto me in heaven and in earth.

19 Go ye therefore, and teach all nations, baptizing them in the name of the Father, and of the Son, and of the Holy Ghost:

20 Teaching them to observe all things whatsoever I have commanded you: and, lo, I am with you always, even unto the end of the world. Amen.

"See, baptize new converts, teaching them all that Jesus taught," Matt stressed his point.

"Yes!" Isaac agreed. "But Jesus continually taught the Kingdom."

Matt types and different scriptures appear on the monitor. "What about this?" He says.

Mark 16

14 Afterward he appeared unto the eleven as they sat at meat, and upbraided them with their unbelief and hardness of heart, because they believed not them which had seen him after he was risen.

15 And he said unto them, Go ye into all the world, and preach the gospel to every creature.

16 He that believeth and is baptized shall be saved; but he that believeth not shall be damned.

"See, those who don't believe will be damned," Matt says, continuing to defend his belief.

"Ultimately that will happen to all who don't accept Jesus." Isaac agrees.

"Ultimately! What's that supposed to mean? Keep reading. Jesus expressly tells his disciples to preach repentance and remission of sin through his name." Isaac reads the scriptures off the screen as Matt instructed.

Luke 24:47 And that repentance and remission of sins should be preached in his name among all nations, beginning at Jerusalem.

"Yes, he did instruct his followers to preach repentance and salvation. That was part of his teaching, not the sum total of it. The thrust of his teaching was about the Kingdom like in Mathew 13." Taking control of the keyboard Isaac searches for other scripture. "Like this one."

Luke 8:1 And it came to pass afterward, that he went throughout every city and village, preaching and shewing the glad tidings of the kingdom of God: and the twelve were with him,

"Here again he teaches his disciples to preach the kingdom."

Luke 4

42 And when it was day, he departed and went into a desert place: and the people sought him, and came unto him, and stayed him, that he should not depart from them.

43 And he said unto them, I must preach the kingdom of God to other cities also: for therefore am I sent.

44 And he preached in the synagogues of Galilee.

"It was urgent to Jesus to preach the kingdom because that was what he came to do."

Mark 1:**38 And he said unto them, Let us go into the next towns, that I may preach there also: for therefore came I forth.**

"Jesus taught what his father instructed him to teach," Isaac continued.

John 12:**49 For I have not spoken of myself; but the Father which sent me, he gave me a commandment, what I should say, and what I should speak.**

"Jesus taught his disciples to preach the Kingdom of God, not about himself. Why should modern Christians stop doing the work Jesus started?" Isaac continues with more scripture.

Luke 9
1 Then he called his twelve disciples together, and gave them power and authority over all devils, and to cure diseases.
2 And he sent them to preach the kingdom of God, and to heal the sick.

"Jesus instructs Christians to seek God's Kingdom before anything else, proclaiming it should also be our priority."

Luke 12
30 For all these things do the nations of the world seek after: and your Father knoweth that ye have need of these things.

31 But rather seek ye the kingdom of God; and all these things shall be added unto you.

"Your right Matt, Christians do need to preach salvation through Jesus, but not exclusively. It needs to be combined with Kingdom knowledge so we can understand God's salvation plan. When the kingdom is taught, those who are called by God will want to find out about salvation. We should teach both as if it comes from one breath."

"You keep searching the Bible until you find a verse that says what you want, don't you?" Matt observes sarcastically.

"No. At least I don't ignore the scriptures that contradict my beliefs. When there's a scripture I can't fit into my beliefs, then my beliefs are wrong or I'm not understanding the scripture properly," Isaac counters. "Jesus taught about the kingdom because people didn't understand it." Bringing up more scripture onto the screen, Isaac reads out loud.

Luke 19
9 And Jesus said unto him, This day is salvation come to this house, forsomuch as he also is a son of Abraham.

10 For the Son of man is come to seek and to save that which was lost.

11 And as they heard these things, he added and spake a parable, because he was nigh to Jerusalem, and because they thought that the kingdom of God should immediately appear.

"People still don't understand the coming kingdom. Those who aren't called by God to Jesus now, those who hear the good news but don't understand it, or those who never get to hear it, they all need a chance to come to know Jesus and receive salvation. Most Christians don't give people like that any chance for salvation. But God has a plan where everyone will have an opportunity to come to Jesus. It starts by understanding mankind's true mortal nature," Isaac speaks passionately.

"So you say! Why should I believe a young guy who dropped out of Bible school? As I said, I went over your ideas with respected leaders of our church and we couldn't find any biblical support for them. If they existed, why didn't you include them in your writings? Then I could have seen them. Now all we have is your unsubstantiated claims."

"You shouldn't believe me!" Isaac insisted. "You taught me in Sunday school the only way to get the whole story from the gospels was to compare them, as each book had its own information about a story. The same holds true for the entire Bible. Leaving out any biblical information on a topic only diminishes our understanding of it. Don't believe me, believe all of what the Bible has to say. The references are there in the Bible. You told me not to include them," Isaac was exasperated with Matt.

"I don't have the time to spend reading your story all over again, inserting Bible references. I spent time reading it the first time as a favor to your mum. I have no desire to dedicate any more of my time to your delusions. I already know the truth. I need to somehow put my life back together. I'm sorry, but I need to help myself before I can help anyone else." Matt reclines back into his office chair. "Maybe it would be best if you just go now. Looking at you makes me see all that I've lost. I thought you and Becky would make a good couple but it seems like everything has fallen apart. I need to be alone now and immerse myself in prayer."

Seeing that he would get no more Bible references from Matt, Isaac replies. "I'm sorry things have turned out badly. I need to find Becky. I need to talk with her and see if we can work this thing through. I've lost out as well you know." Rising from his chair Isaac turns towards the office door. "I'll let myself out," he mumbled.

"So how did things go with Matt?" Mom questions Isaac as soon as he is in the house. "Did he set you straight? It certainly didn't take him long. That man sure knows his Bible," she says confidently.

Isaac explains to Mum how Becky and her mom had left Matt, leaving his family in ruins.

"I'm so sorry for you and Becky." Mum said as she put her arms around Isaac. "But it doesn't surprise me one bit about Matt's tramp of a wife. I never did have much use for her or her deceitful ways. Sounds like Becky didn't fall far from the tree. Running around on you behind your back. While you were at Bible school of all things. You'll be better off without her. God knows what's best, you can count on that," she said assertively.

"Yes he does, but it still hurts." Isaac replies through the tears he could no longer restrain.

"I know dear." Mum said sympathetically as she gave him a tighter squeeze. "Don't lose heart. Why don't you take Rosy for a good long walk and a ball throwing session? You know how she can always cheer you up. I think I should go over and check on Matt. That poor man shouldn't be left alone, brokenhearted in that big empty house. I'll probably be back home before you are." Mom goes to put on her shoes.

"Ya, ok Mum. He did seem pretty upset when I left. I guess I was only thinking of myself. He could probably use a friendly ear."

When Isaac got home the house was as dark as the yard. He left the kitchen light on for Mum as he and Rosy made their way upstairs to his room. Flopping down on his bed fully clothed, God granted him the sweet peaceful sleep he had been praying for, with Rosy curled tightly beside him.

Chapter 9

When Isaac got to class the next morning, the room was
abuzz with chatter. He was in no mood for conversation
as he sat at his desk deep in his own thoughts. Speckle
came briskly walking in through the open door with an
unusual, chipper smile on his face. The chatter of the
students quickly came to an end as he stood at his desk
sorting his papers.

"It appears as though this institution, as part of the
National Association of Post-secondary Educators, has
just ratified a new policy on inclusiveness. Anyone who
has transferred credits from an institution, other than one
within the National Association, are to report to the
human resources office immediately for further
processing. They assure me it's just a formality. Nothing
to worry about." Speckle said with deep satisfaction,
looking intently at Isaac.

A few of the students, including Isaac, pick up their
books and head out the door and down the hall. When
they reach the HR office, they are each given a form and
are herded into a meeting room to join other curious
students. When the Human Resources manager arrived
she addressed them collectively.

"In our efforts to be inclusive on our campus, we strive
to give equality to all people, regardless of race, faith,
gender, or sexual preference. We simply will not tolerate
discrimination or bullying of any kind. We uphold the
charter of, um, rights and freedoms in our country and the

spirit of the rulings, um, handed down by our supreme court. Some time ago that, um, court ruled, um, that private religious based colleges could not, um, demand their student's sign a code of conduct based on religious, um, beliefs if they were to train lawyers. In the spirit of that ruling, the, um, National Association of Post-secondary Educators, um, will no longer accept course credits from any, um, institution that has similar religious, um, based codes of conduct. These codes, um, contradict the inclusiveness that our institutions promote. Effective immediately, um, we will no longer recognize course credits from, um, any discriminatory institutions."
Having read from her prepared notes, the HR manager quickly left the conference room, leaving her subordinates to answer any questions the students may have had.

When Isaac finally got his turn to see a counselor he was eager to find out how the new policy would affect him.

"Yes, I attended a college funded by my church's denomination," Isaac responded. "I willingly supported my church's code of conduct banning immoral lifestyle choices. I believe the Bible denounces those lifestyles as sinful. There are lots of moral choices that I believe to be sinful. Not only those who are fornicators, idolaters, adulterers, effeminate, abusers of themselves with mankind, thieves, covetous, drunkards, revilers, or extortioners. Those who choose any sin over the salvation of Jesus will not be in the kingdom of God."

The counselor squirms nervously in her chair as Isaac openly and honestly speaks of sin, salvation and Jesus.

"Only those who believe in Jesus can be saved and have everlasting life." Isaac continued.

"And you count yourself as a member of that exclusive club?" She snidely responds. "And those of us who aren't in your elite group are relegated to the fires of hell I suppose. Not worthy of the love of your Jesus because of our choices? Christians don't have the market cornered on morality you know. The way some of you carry on is disgusting, even I have better morals than those Christians."

Isaac tries to explain his faith to her. "As humans we're all sinners and as Christians we all start at different levels of sinfulness. Christians strive to be perfect like our savior, we should continually strive towards that perfection. It's a lifelong journey of overcoming the sin that so easily besets us. Some of us get closer to perfection than others. Even though we may fall short, the important thing is that we have accepted the covering sacrifice of Jesus and we never stop trying to overcome sin."

"That's convenient for letting you off sins hook," the HR girl huffs. "If believing in Jesus is the only way to eternal life then everyone from the other world religions, regardless of how good they are, will never have eternal life with God. They're all doomed, along with everyone who never got to hear about your loving Jesus. I don't find condemning people who never heard the truth to be all that loving."

"That does seem to be the prevailing Christian belief, but it's not mine. The Bible reveals a different future for them. A future where everyone who has ever lived will have the chance to know Jesus and accept him," Isaac explains cheerily.

"I've never heard that one before and I've looked into many different religions in my comparative religions class. I've come to believe we all just need to live our lives the best we can, in peace with those around us. Live and let live. Christians haven't cornered the market on God or the universe's higher power, depending on how you understand them, him or her. We're all equal in the sight of God. They love us no matter how we try to follow them. Like you said, it's a lifetime journey of trying."

"Your right about that," Isaac agrees eagerly. "God loves us so much that he made it possible for everyone to come to know him. All aren't called to Jesus in this life though. Through resurrections, God has planned a way for all who accept Jesus to get to him."

"Resurrections? Why should we need to come back to life? Our souls are eternal! We go on to live with our creator once we die. Our energies, merging with the cosmos, when we're worthy." The HR girl smiles, twirling her long blond hair with a pen as she talks.

"That's the point. As humans we can never be worthy. That's why we need the covering blood of Jesus. He did for us what we're incapable of doing. That's also why we can only find salvation through him."

"I don't believe that. I don't need saving. I don't need Jesus. I'm fine just as I am. I don't need a savior! Why hasn't God been calling me to your beliefs? Am I substandard or something? It seems to me like your ideas are just as exclusive as other Christians. I've heard nothing that would make your discriminatory beliefs compatible with our institution's policies of inclusion."

"I don't discriminate against anyone," Isaac protests.

"You judge others through your beliefs and convictions. Your Godly superiority is an affront to those of us who are tolerant of others, living in nonjudgmental harmony with the lifestyle choices of others. Your adoption of an archaic virtuous lifestyle speaks louder than any words of condemnation you could utter."

Isaac defends himself vigorously. "What? I'm being punished because I try to live a good life. We all make judgments every day between good and evil, right or wrong. If others are doing something evil I have to judge whether it's something I want to do or not. But I'm not judging the people doing it just because I don't want to participate in their bad choices."

"Who's to say what's good or evil? Your Bible? I don't recognize its authority over my life." Getting down to the business at hand, the HR girl turns the conversation back to the matter of course credits. "Our new policy excludes the incomplete course credits from your previous college, however we will allow you to fast track, make up classes that could catch you up by the end of the school year. What high school did you graduate from? I don't seem to have your official transcripts. They aren't here in your file. You'll have to get your high school to send them over right away."

"Except for kindergarten, I was homeschooled all my life. My parents used a curriculum from our church that was approved by the province."

"Oh, I see! Did this faith-based curriculum require you to adhere to any lifestyle restrictions or pledges?" the HR girls asked in amazement.

"Well yes, I was a child," Isaac said. Shocked by the question. "I was raised to live a Christian life and to have the same Christian values as our church. I dedicated my life to Jesus and to those values at a young age."

"Is that the same values your post-secondary institution espoused?"

"Yes. Our church denomination sponsors the Bible college I attended. The beliefs of one are also the beliefs of the other. They seamlessly transitioned from homeschool to college."

"That's what I thought. You're the only student so far that was homeschooled," the HR girl explained. "Public schools don't have such stringent restrictions on personal freedoms. However, if we can't accept the credits from your college, due to its discriminatory policies, I don't see how we can accept the credits from your home schooling. They seem to share the same intolerant, discriminatory policies. I won't be able to recognize any of your schooling credits for our institution. You're basically completely uneducated! There's nothing more I can do for you. Even if I wanted to! You're a victim of your own narrowmindedness. I would advise you to adjust your beliefs to reflect the society you live in. Continuing to maintain those lofty principles of yours will cost you dearly."

"Not maintaining them will cost me more. It would cost me my eternal life," Isaac replied somberly.

"No, not true!" the HR girl said with a big perky smile. "According to you, God will simply resurrect you to try again. A second chance is just waiting for you," she added tauntingly.

"We each only get one chance. If called, your chance is in this present life. If you're blind to Jesus now, your eyes will be opened to him at another time later on through a resurrection," Isaac corrects patiently.

"Ya well, good luck with that. I have other students to process now. If you want to contest my ruling there is a process to follow, it's on the back of your form. I've heard they might start processing complaints by the end of fall or winter as the adjudicator is on maternity leave and due to the lack of trained adjudicators, we only have one. Have a good day."

With that she closed Isaac's file and turned to motion another student to come over to her desk. Isaac got up from his chair as if in a daze, making his way down the hall and out of the building he silently prayed to God for direction and help in all that he did. Thankful that all things worked out for the good for those who loved the Lord.

I will praise you through the storm by Casting Crowns was the background music playing in Isaac's head. As he walked down the Greenway pedestrian path to his home, he prayed for guidance through his current schooling troubles. After walking in the shade along the creek to the park, he turned south using a footbridge to cross the creek, then followed trails through the park woods leading to his subdivision. Walking through the trees calmed him as the stresses of school and the loss of Becky diminished with each breath's exhale. He sings out loud with the soundtrack that's been playing on repeat since he left the college forty five minutes earlier.

"And I'll praise you in this storm
And I will lift my hands
That you are who you are
No matter where I am
And every tear I've cried
You hold in your hand
You never left my side
And though my heart is torn
I will praise you in this storm
I lift my eyes unto the hills
Where does my help come from?
My help comes from the Lord
The maker of heaven and earth."

Isaac's heart is bolstered by his praise as the sun filters through the tree canopy. It leaves a patchwork of shade and light on the forest floor of weeds and wildflowers pushing through what was left of the snow. Jumping over the back fence, Isaac crosses the lawn and enters the house through the kitchen door.

"What are you doing home?" Mum asked, surprised to see Isaac home so early in the day. "You're not normally home until the afternoon. Are you feeling sick? You look a bit clammy and peaked." Mum places her hand on Isaac's forehead to feel his temperature.

"No, I'm fine Mum." Isaac turns his head away from her hand. "It's school that's the problem." Isaac recounts his morning and all the calamity that has befallen him. "It seems like last year has been the worst ever. My life feels as though it's been unravelling since I graduated from homeschool. You, Pa, everyone, have always said that education and schooling was the key to success. That seems to have been all taken away from me. Now I'm not sure what I should do."

"Oh sweetheart, we can register a dispute. They can't say you're completely uneducated and refuse to accept your provincially accredited grades." Mom tries to put an upbeat spin on the situation.

"But they won't even look at those disputes until fall or later, when the adjudicator gets back. What am I going to do until then? Even if I do get back in, I'll still be behind on credits. We're in a deepening recession with all the Trump trade wars unravelling the world economy. Education seemed like the only path to having a secure future."

"I don't have all the answers honey, but I know the one who does. We'll have to trust and wait for him." Mum reaches up giving Isaac a tight hug like he was still the little boy in her mind's eye.

"Ya, I suppose we will. Until then maybe I'll clean up the yard and old shop. I could get the old truck working. That should take a week or so," Isaac said dis-heartedly. "Maybe the neighbors have junk they need cleaned up too. I might be able to earn some money that way."

"There you go dear. Keep yourself busy! A watched kettle is slow to boil. God will make a way for you somewhere." Mum was back to her cheery self again. "Widow Miller could probably use help cleaning her yard up of all that rusty old machinery her late husband had collected. You should go talk to her about it."

"You're right Mum. I'll go see her right now." Isaac was excited with the possibilities.

"That's good dear, see how things work better when you stay positive. Do you want some soup and a sandwich before you go? I just made some to take over to Matt. We had such a good talk last night. He really needs the support of his friends right now; he's very vulnerable." Mum said, flipping her hair through her fingers.

Oblivious to his mother's feelings, Isaac absentmindedly turns down the food and the opportunity to build a deeper relationship with her. She was still mourning the loss of her husband and would have enjoyed the talk with her only child. With his thoughts fixated on his own immediate problems, Isaac goes out the kitchen door to check over the old Ford flat deck. It was rusting into the ground beside the garage. After the inspection he heads to the Millers in search of new possibilities. Having gained old widow Miller's approval to clean up her yard by taking away the old rusty scrap iron, Isaac returns home and quickly gets dirty repairing his grandpa's old work truck.

"What the &$#@ have we got here? I haven't seen this &$#@in old truck for &$#@in ever." A short, grizzled, twisted, old man yells as he hobbles across the driveway from the scrapyard office. "I liked that &$#@in old %@$#@&%! He was a good friend to me. His &$#@in damn family never even told his friends when he died. They were probably afraid we'd actually show up and spoil their ceremony. &$#@ I still miss him."

"I'm his grandson. Grandma had already died and we didn't know all his friends. We put notices in the papers. We had no other way to let everyone know."

"I'm sure you did your best. Such as it was. I probably wouldn't have gone anyway. I'm not fussy about all that &$#@in touchy feely $#&@. I won't hold it against ya. You probably took the opportunity to have a 'call to repentance' anyway. Telling all us &$#@in sinners we're going to hell. He was never condemning like that," the bent old man said, tenderly stroking the truck's cab. "He liked me because of who I was, not what I said I believed."

"I'm sure he did. Grampa was like that. He liked people for their character. I'm sorry you didn't get to say goodbye at his funeral. Your right though, we did have a talk about repentance and the saving grace of Jesus. I've since learned how God's plan of salvation has a time of repentance for everyone, not just those who come to know Jesus during this life."

Ya! that's what the &$#@ I've been saying all along. My mom took me to church until I was old enough to say I wouldn't go. They'd love you on Sunday, and %$#@ you on Monday! I got away from there as fast as I could. All that holly roller, mumbo jumbo $#&@ never made any sense to me. &$#@. I didn't get it then and I still don't &$#@in get it now. The Jesus and God I learned about when I was little wouldn't torture a dog for ever for not doing something it didn't understand, let alone a &$#@in person! &$#@, the Big Man upstairs knows my heart, that's all that matters," the crude old man points and looks skyward earnestly.

Isaac is thoughtful for a moment then responds to the gruff old man's statement. "Your absolutely right. God will make sure everyone has the chance to understand and accept Jesus as their savior. Those who do, will have life eternal. Those who decide not to will be choosing death. God will respect their freely made decision and let them die. Their decision will be final and they will remain dead forever. Even the memory of them will die. Jesus told us only those drawn by his father could come to him. If you're not called now your opportunity will come later after a resurrection back to life. Only you can know if God is calling you now."

"Hu. You don't sound like most &$#@in Christians I've ever met. All they want to do is shove their &$#@in beliefs down my throat."

"I'm sorry to say I used to be like that, before I truly understood God's plan of salvation." Isaac looked down ashamedly, away from the old man's gaze.

Whatever! Like I said I won't hold it against ya," the short, gruff, old man moves back to the deck of the truck. "Let's see, what've you got here? &$#@! You've got a load of highly prized collectables here. It's not every day I see vintage motor parts like that. Those heads there," he pushes on them with the end of his cane, "those &$#@in things will fetch a couple hundred dollars each."

"Wow! I had no idea this stuff was worth so much!" Isaac was overjoyed with the news. "My neighbor gave it all to me for cleaning up her yard. I thought I'd only get a scrap iron price for it," Isaac explained.

"Well isn't this your &$#@in lucky day. You could probably fall into a bucket of $#&@ and still come out smelling like a &$#@in rose. Just like your grandpa,

someone was watching over him for f$#@in sure. The
f$#@in way things worked out for him. &$#@, he'd
never lose!"

"I must admit." Isaac said shyly. "When you first
started talking to me, I didn't expect to be treated very
honestly. But you don't seem to be out to cheat me."

"Well &$#@. You don't know how much I'll get for
those &$#@in parts now do ya?" The old man said with a
grin. "I got to make a &$#@in living too. But I'll treat
you fairlyish." Sucking hard he clears his sinus cavity and
throat of yard dust, then turns and spits on the dry
ground. "Auh &$#@, I don't need to make a living off
your back! Why don't you stick around? I could use some
help getting scrap from the more &$#@in politically
correct customers. You seem to talk their language."

"Well, I could use the money," Isaac admits.

"&$#@ kid, I can show you how to make plenty of
&$#@in money. I'm awash in cash," the old man leans
close to the driver's window and whispers. "But the best
profits are made trading commodities that aren't taxed.
Bartering," he whispers even softer with a wink and a
nod. "That's where the &$#@in real wealth is gained."

"Sure. If you say so. I've got nothing to lose." Isaac
replied with an apathetic smile.

"&$#@! That's the spirit kid," the bent old man was
back to his loud, boisterous self. "We'll get along just
fine once you learn &$#@ off is a term of endearment.
It's all in the tone. The words don't mean &$#@ all."

With that, the dirty, grizzled, bent, old man showed
Isaac where to drop off the prized items and how to sort
the rest of the salvage. In time they made a formidable
business team as well as amassing a sizable fortune.

Isaac's career path took a sharp turn to the redneck side of life and he never looked back or worried about the lack of recognition for knowledge he had already acquired. He just kept looking for God's open window when life closed the doors.

Through the contacts he made picking up scrap and salvage, he was building a career and a new life for himself. Mum was spending more time with Matt than just good friends would have. Isaac was beginning to feel alienated from her and doubted Matt's integrity. Matt always seemed to be playing a character rather than be himself. Although Isaac offered several times to supply Matt with the scriptural proof for his ideas, Matt would always mockingly put him off, calling Isaac's notions 'unsubstantiated nonsense'. Not having any luck in talking to or finding Becky, his previous life's goals faded into distant memories.

"Good afternoon. Sunshine Salvage," Isaac calmly said into his cell phone.

"Good day Isaac," came the reply. "This is Jim Waverly, with Government Infrastructure and Development. We talked last month about some salvage I needed to have cleaned up from a forestry site."

"Yes, I remember. Are you ready to proceed with it now?" Isaac replied. Turning his back to the idling truck in the wrecking yard, he scrambles away to hear better.

"Yes. Yes, we are ready. There turned out to be more salvage than I had originally thought. In particular, there's one old truck and a fuel trailer full of fuel that I need to make disappear quickly. The fuel has the wrong additives and the truck is too old. Neither will meet the new stringent emissions standards adopted by my department. We've been mandated to lead industry into a higher state of accountability. The suits want me to lead by example, going above and beyond any current federal standards. I'm not allowed to have anything noncompliant on any of my sites. So, I need to dispose of them ASAP. Besides, the new hires can't drive that old truck anyway. They all want automatics; the two sticks scare them. A couple of them tried but they messed up royally. Those units have outlived their usefulness.

The driver of the truck was Rodrick. He babied it through his whole career and he retired a few years ago. It's been sitting ever since." Jim continues to explain. "Federal Bean counters will be conducting an audit in my area at the end of the month and there can't be a trace of noncompliant stuff around. Look, my budget is tight this quarter. You can have it all for cleaning up the site, but it must all be gone by next weekend. Can you do that for me?" came the desperate plea.

"Sure Jim. I can do that," came Isaac's cool assurance. "We'll really clean up. I still have a key for the bush yards. I'll need documentation and transfers for all the vehicles. Can't scrap a thing without the paperwork nowadays. I may have to surcharge you for the fuel though, if it can't be recycled."

"You pirate, I bet you'll clean up! Sure, run your fuel tests, we'll pay what you need to get rid of the fuel. You've always treated us fair." Jim's smile is translated through the phone.

"Glad to help Jim. Customer satisfaction is our main goal." Isaac said with a laugh.

"Ya right!" Jim replied sarcastically. "Thanks, I knew I could count on you. Oh, and be sure to tell Stubby I told him to &$#@ off." With that the phone went dead.

Isaac had a big smile as he entered the office. "We can go clean up that government infrastructure bush yard. Now Jim's in a big panic to get it done before some audit happens."

"&$#@ that'll be good! We'll start in the morning. Be loaded by midafternoon and back here before f$#@in dark. Did we get the old truck and trailer?"

"We sure did and the trailer is full of fuel. I checked last time I was out there and the EVAP vents were tight so that fuel should still be good to use. Gota love government regulations that help us for a change. It'll save us a bundle." Isaac was doing quick math in his head.

"If that &$#@in old truck starts we can bring it back with the repair plates." Stubby rubs his hands together with glee.

"Oh ya." Isaac said laughing. "Jim sends you his regards."

The cold gray of dawn was just starting to fade as Isaac unlocked the chain link gate. Small piles of scrap steel littered the fenced compound. A few large spools of wire sat cockeyed, partially sunk in the mud beside a neat pile of ten-inch pipe. In the center rear of the yard sat a five thousand-gallon, three axle pup fuel wagon. The front axle drawbar was jutting off to one side at an awkward angle like it had been parked by an amateur. Beside it sat a late 70's International Paystar 5000. The setback front axle gave the bush bumper and solid fenders a menacing, ready to bite you appearance. Moss was growing on both of them as they slowly sank into the yard's soft gravel.

Isaac went over to check out the equipment as Stubby hobbled around the compound estimating the metal's value. 'Rod' was neatly hand painted on the truck's driver's door under the window ledge. The door opened with a squeal, revealing a surprisingly tidy cab. After rummaging around, Isaac found the keys under the driver's seat. Flipping the night switches on he was surprised to find the volt gauge reading a strong 12.7. Climbing up onto the front fenders, Isaac wiped dirt off the windshield with an old rag he had found in the cab. He noticed the reason for the fully charged batteries when he wiped the dust off a small solar panel mounted on the roof.

Pulling hard on the hood panel handles he folded the driver's side open exposing a dusty 19-liter Cummins engine. The 600 KTA emblem proudly identified the engine's power. After checking the engine oil dipstick, other fluid levels were verified and the engine accessories were carefully inspected. With everything looking satisfactory under the hood Isaac sat in the driver's seat, scanning the gauges before he twisted the key. Pushing the start button the old dinosaur awakened, rumbling to life once again. Light grey smoke was soon swirling around the yard stinging Stubby's eyes as the old-school mechanical diesel warmed up.

Isaac took note of the twin shift levers protruding from the floor as the low air buzzer irritated his ears. Finding the shift pattern labels he learned the main box was an RTO12513 speed, with a four-speed OD auxiliary. "Well that's not so scary!" he thought to himself. Holding the handrail with his left hand he jumps out into space and slides smoothly to the ground, slowing his descent by tightening his grip on the handrail. No sooner had his work boots lightly touched down on the ground, as if in one motion Isaac was making his way around the truck.

Inspecting the tires, he gave them each several kicks. He found them all in good shape but most surprisingly, they were filled with foam, making them puncture proof. Then he checked the twenty-four-foot deck that had a live roller tail, making it easy to drag things onto it with the small crane or by using the power take off winch. Both crane and winch were mounted neatly behind the cab. The air cushioned pintle hitch was ready to be hooked up to the fuel trailer. Scraped paint and a few good-sized dents told the stories of previous inexperienced drivers trying to hook the two together.

"So can you drive that &$#@in thing?" came a shout from across the yard. "We can load all this &$#@in scrap onto the deck with that crane. We'll put the pipe and the wire reels on the shop truck and trailer. You'll not have a problem pulling that &$#@in fuel trailer with the weight of all the iron loaded on the deck. I'll be &$#@ed if we'll have to make two &$#@in trips." Stubby is gasping for breath as he approaches Isaac, red faced and wet with sweat.

"You don't look so good." Isaac says with a tone of mock concern. "Maybe you better sit down and have a rest, you're getting pretty old for this kind of work. Do you have the blessings from your geriatric doctor for this much activity?" Isaac was smiling broadly.

"Oh, &$#@ off," came the curt reply.

"Ha. You can't fool me. I've been around you long enough. Thanks, I love you too."

Stubby smiles as he rests. His breathing slows as he dries his brow with his shirt sleeve. "I told you from the start, term of &$#@in endearment."

"You were right about one other thing. The word does lose its sting when you use it indiscriminately all the time. Do you even remember what it means?" Isaac's voice is still playful.

Shaking his head with a laugh, Stubby replies gruffly. "What the &$#@. Of course I know the meaning of the &$#@in word. We better get started loading all this &$#@in $#&@ if we're going to make it back to town before &$#@in dark."

Isaac was impressed with the old 5000 binder. It had more power than he could use pulling the loaded pup trailer. If he wasn't careful, the fully loaded 5000 would spin the drives going uphill on dry pavement. He was eager to get it transferred and inspected. He didn't think it would take much work to get it ready for the road. Rod had taken good care of it.

Chapter 10

As the last faint rays of the sun fade from the Passover sky, Joseph of Arimathea, along with a few friends of Jesus, hastily seal the entrance of the new tomb with a bolder, safely encasing Jesus within its darkness. Ever since then, animosity has thrived between Christians and Jews. The Jews have borne the blame for crucifying Jesus, but is that blame fully justified? True, they actively sought to have Jesus killed and successfully used the Romans who were very adept at killing people to crucify him, but was it really their fault?

Near the start of the twenty-first century a new term was coined within law enforcement. 'Suicide by cop' had become a recognized phenomenon. This term describes an individual who actively tries to be killed by on duty police officers. The Bible describes Jesus as having a similar life plan. Prophecies foretold the violent death awaiting Jesus and he repeatedly told his disciples what his fate would be.

Mark 8:31-33 New International Version (NIV)
Jesus Predicts His Death
31 He then began to teach them that the Son of Man must suffer many things and be rejected by the elders, the chief priests and the teachers of the law, and that he must be killed and after three days rise again.32 He spoke plainly about this, and Peter took him aside and began to rebuke him.

33 But when Jesus turned and looked at his disciples, he rebuked Peter. "Get behind me, Satan!" he said. "You do not have in mind the concerns of God, but merely human concerns."

When questioned by the high priest, rather than continuing to remain silent, Jesus gives an answer that he knew would require capital punishment.

Mark 14:60-64 New International Version (NIV)
60 Then the high priest stood up before them and asked Jesus, "Are you not going to answer? What is this testimony that these men are bringing against you?" 61 But Jesus remained silent and gave no answer. Again the high priest asked him, "Are you the Messiah, the Son of the Blessed One?"

62 "I am," said Jesus. "And you will see the Son of Man sitting at the right hand of the Mighty One and coming on the clouds of heaven."

63 The high priest tore his clothes. "Why do we need any more witnesses?" he asked.

64 "You have heard the blasphemy. What do you think?" They all condemned him as worthy of death.

Jesus knew he would die at the hands of the religious authorities as the scriptures foretold.

Matthew 26:53-54 New Revised Standard Version (NRSV)
53 Do you think that I cannot appeal to my Father, and he will at once send me more than twelve legions of angels?

54 But how then would the scriptures be fulfilled, which say it must happen in this way?"

Jesus often said he wanted to do the will of his father, not his own.

John 6:38 King James Version (KJV)
38 For I came down from heaven, not to do mine own will, but the will of him that sent me.

Even in his darkest moments Jesus sought God's will over his life and death.

Mark 14:36 New International Version (NIV)
36 "Abba,[a] Father," he said, "everything is possible for you. Take this cupfrom me. Yet not what I will, but what you will."

His entire life was in preparation for his crucifixion. He actively sought it. Jesus knew sacrificing himself as a lamb without blemish was the only way to save mankind from their sins. Giving his body and blood for us all, taking bruises and stripes for our salvation.

Luke 22:18-20 King James Version (KJV)
18 For I say unto you, I will not drink of the fruit of the vine, until the kingdom of God shall come.
19 And he took bread, and gave thanks, and brake it, and gave unto them, saying, This is my body which is given for you: this do in remembrance of me.

20 Likewise also the cup after supper, saying, This cup is the new testament in my blood, which is shed for you.

Isaiah 53:4-5 King James Version (KJV)
4 Surely he hath borne our griefs, and carried our sorrows: yet we did esteem him stricken, smitten of God, and afflicted.
5 But he was wounded for our transgressions, he was bruised for our iniquities: the chastisement of our peace was upon him; and with his stripes we are healed.

Jesus went to his death willingly, no one did anything to him that he didn't want to happen or wasn't preplanned. He used the Jewish leaders as instruments for God's purpose. Having fulfilled all the Messianic miracles, yet still rejected by the religious authorities, Jesus gave the Rabbis proof of messiahship they hadn't thought of. He said he would return from the dead after three days and nights in the grave then show himself publicly, alive and well.

Leaving his divinity behind at birth he became our perfect sacrifice. He was crucified after living a perfect, fully human life. This proved a human, living in harmony with God could live without sin. After being dead for three days and nights, he was resurrected by his father, returning to the immortal spirit life he had abandoned to become human. Rejecting all his proofs, the Jews actively harassed and killed the followers of Jesus.

Christians were persecuted for their faith until Constantine declared religious tolerance in 313 AD.

Constantine promoted Christianity within the Roman Empire by giving it imperial favor, uniting the differing Christian factions together into one state approved church. At this point in history the Holy Roman Empire was born. The Emperor was no longer hailed as god, for he acknowledged his humanity, humbling himself below the true creator God.

Acknowledging God's rule over himself, Constantine started a relationship between church and state that would last for centuries. Wanting to break away from Jewish religious persecution and traditions, Constantine and church bishops introduced new days for Christian worship at the Council of Nicaea in the year 325. Those who refused to adhere to these new traditions fled or were put to death. The new days of worship further distanced the Christian church from Jewish religious interference.

Historically, Christian church leaders have not always been above reproach. At times it's been hard to distinguish between the actions of church leaders and the pagans they preached to. Not having a Godly leader at the helm however, doesn't reflect negatively on those who faithfully follow Jesus and worship God within those churches. Before 1500 AD there were no other church options for worshipers in most countries. There was only one sanctioned church to attend.

It is more important for people to stay faithful to Jesus and his father, than what church denomination they attend or who the leader of that church is. God has used many sinful rulers to do his will. Take Nebuchadnezzar of Babylon, Cyrus of the Median Empire, or the pharaoh of Egypt for example. God used them as he wanted, to accomplish his purposes. The same will be true for the prophesied last revival of the Roman Empire. God will use it in bringing his Kingdom to this earth and aid in delivering his plan of salvation to all of humanity.

The Bible describes the chaotic and dangerous world Jesus returns to in several places. At his return, humanity will have come to the end of their rope as far as governing themselves and the world. The only hope for life's survival will be the direct intervention of God.

Matthew 24:21-22 New King James Version (NKJV)

21 For then there will be great tribulation, such as has not been since the beginning of the world until this time, no, nor ever shall be. 22 And unless those days were shortened, no flesh would be saved; but for the[a]elect's sake those days will be shortened.

God has planned for this end time world to be ruled by an Empire led by an arrogant dictator.

Daniel 7:8 New International Version (NIV)

8 "While I was thinking about the horns, there before me was another horn, a little one, which came up among them; and three of the first horns were uprooted before it. This horn had eyes like the eyes of a human being and a mouth that spoke boastfully.

God has a plan for humanity. We need not be fearful, for God is in full control of how and when his Kingdom comes to rule the world. Jesus will return and destroy the evil emperor who beguiles the world through signs and wonders.

2 Thessalonians 2:3-12 New International Version (NIV)

3 Don't let anyone deceive you in any way, for that day will not come until the rebellion occurs and the man of lawlessness[a] is revealed, the man doomed to destruction. 4 He will oppose and will exalt himself over everything that is called God or is worshiped, so that he sets himself up in God's temple, proclaiming himself to be God. 5 Don't you remember that when I was with you I used to tell you these things? 6 And now you know what is holding him back, so that he may be revealed at the proper time. 7 For the secret power of lawlessness is already at work; but the one who now holds it back will continue to do so till he is taken out of the way. 8 And then the lawless one will be revealed, whom the Lord Jesus will overthrow with the breath of his mouth and destroy by the splendor of his coming. 9 The coming of the lawless one will be in accordance with how Satan works. He will use all sorts of displays of power through signs and wonders that serve the lie,10 and all the ways that wickedness deceives those who are perishing.They perish because they refused to love the truth and so be saved.11 For this reason God sends them a powerful delusion so that they will believe the lie 12 and so that all will be condemned who have not believed the truth but have delighted in wickedness.

God reveals this Empire will rule for 7 years. The Emperor makes a pact with many nations but then breaks it half way through the term.

Daniel 9:27 King James Version (KJV)

27 And he shall confirm the covenant with many for one week: and in the midst of the week he shall cause the sacrifice and the oblation to cease, and for the overspreading of abominations he shall make it desolate, even until the consummation, and that determined shall be poured upon the desolate.

The last three and a half years of this seven-year period is known as the great tribulation. During this time God will be preaching to the world through his two witnesses. Bringing divine plagues upon the world and punishing the wicked, God will call mankind to repent of their sins.

The Empire and its ruler will persecute Christians until the return of Jesus rescues them.

Daniel 7:21-22 New King James Version (NKJV)

21 "I was watching; and the same horn was making war against the saints, and prevailing against them, 22 until the Ancient of Days came, and a judgment was made in favor of the saints of the Most High, and the time came for the saints to possess the kingdom.

Jesus will rule the world from then on. Coming as King of Kings.

Daniel 7:13-14 New International Version (NIV)

13 "In my vision at night I looked, and there before me was one like a son of man,[a] coming with the clouds of heaven. He approached the Ancient of Days and was led into his presence. 14 He was given authority, glory and sovereign power; all nations and

peoples of every language worshiped him. His dominion is an everlasting dominion that will not pass away, and his kingdom is one that will never be destroyed.

In a well-appointed boardroom the current Pope and an ambitious European General are relaxing in overstuffed chairs as their personal aides wait silently, eager to assist whenever possible.

"Yes, you are right. I can't deny the good that's been accomplished since we started working with that unsavory organization. There are a lot of poor people who now have access to life giving, advanced antiretroviral drugs because of them. They are capable of doing good. However, I find it hard to discern how far they can be trusted. But what I don't understand is, what do they have to do with you?" The Holy Father asked, somewhat perplexed.

The General sat back in his chair, wrapping his moist lips around a large Cuban. He sucked back hard. Shining the cuff stars of his free hand on his pant leg, he talks in a relaxed manner. "As you know, since the collapse of the euro, I've been working to reunite the European continent under my vision of a revived Roman Empire. This vision has a lot of moving parts to bring together. I needed private contractors with a particular skill set in persuasion. Their organization has a passion and a natural talent for it. I've found them to be very useful on many levels.

The Bush presidents often talked about an envisioned new world order; a world order led by the United States. That dream thrived at the end of the cold war but unraveled with Trumpian isolation and protectionism.

Started by Roosevelt and the allies, the venue of choice had always been the United Nations. Over the years though, the UN proved itself impotent at resolving world conflicts, always bickering, with no authoritative leadership. The EU started falling apart after Brexit with the PIG nations dragging the economy into the red. With the western nations searching for leadership and with eastern powers rising, I knew the time was right to bring Europe back to its ancient, world dominating glory.

By appealing to common historic roots, I have secured nine strong European nations, ruled by strong populist leaders, all of whom share my world vision. We need a common uniting figure head. A spokesperson beyond reproach, one who will be heard and believed. With you coming on board as our leader, your city state will make ten nations united under God's banner. Revealing to the world the latest incarnation of the Holy Roman Empire. What a triumph that will be for the Church and you personally."

The Holy Father weighs his words carefully. "That does sound tempting, but my nation isn't democratic. I have, or whoever is voted in as leader by the cardinals, has full civil control for life. I have an absolute monarchy. How would we share power?" He asked the General, making a back and forth gesture with his hands. "I could never share my power with another human. I'm under the direct rule of God; my office dispenses his earthly directives. I declare the very word of God. If you truly want to appeal to our common, European historic roots, you will have to make some provision for my form of governance."

The General thinks silently as he blows smoke rings in the air. "Why don't we make that as one of our constitutional amendments. Any nation with a historic absolute monarchy, is free to keep it as long as that nation deems fit," the General makes grand sweeping movements with his arms. "There are only five small nations in the world with absolute monarchies. By being conciliatory, the world will perceive us to be benevolent," tapping his forehead in a gesture of forgetfulness the General adds. "Oh, I forgot to mention, I've invited the leader of 'The Organization' to come meet with us."

Holy Father seemed slightly perturbed with the news, thinking this to be a private audience. "What do we need him for? Three's a crowd! They are after all, only contractors."

"Yes, yes, you're right. But I wanted to extend to him a personal honor. He's very frail, getting to the end of his life. I just wanted to thank him personally and show him respect for all his help in bringing my vision of a revived Roman Empire to fruition. I believe you have already been introduced," the General is nonchalant with his reply.

"We have met on a few occasions. Like I said, we have worked together on a limited scale." Father downplays his connections with the organization.

"His organization is large, profitable and has respect within cartels that I could only dream of influencing!" the General emphasizes. "Having them on our side will be a heavenly blessing. It too, is run like an absolute monarchy. But unlike yourself, their leader is more of a despot potentate. His minions blindly follow orders without question."

"Well if you think we need him, I suppose it won't hurt to flatter him a bit," Father says trying to be conciliatory. "But if I'm going to be the beloved leader and you're going to be the muscle. What role does he play?"

"We'll see, I'll send for him," the General said with a broad smile, gesturing to an aid. Moments later a stooped over, tall, frail centenarian slowly shuffles into the room with a small entourage of officials. The General jumps up leaving his smoldering cigar in the ashtray. He reverently greets the once tall man with a gentle embrace. They share private words that the Holy Father could only hear faint murmurings of.

"He's not opposed to the idea," the General whispered softly into the tall man's ear.

"That's good. Our political timing is right. But I don't think he's our man. He's a self-thinker. We need someone more compliant. Our sleepers have been embedded within their church for years. They tell me they are grooming just the right one now. All they're waiting for is an unfortunate accident to befall this Holy Father. We have the votes and we'll have our mouthpiece." Contrary to the tall man's appearance, his hushed voice is strong and clear.

"It shall be done master," the General solemnly promises.

"Our organization has been waiting for this moment in time since its conception with Nimrod. We thought our empire ruled the world with Nero. We had no idea the size and scope of the planet," the tall man makes a coughing laugh. "Constantine got it right, blending the

Christian Church with our endeavors. It fell apart several times, but I'm proud to have witnessed the beginning of our greatest success under your control. I joyfully pass you the baton my eager apprentice. You're like a son to me," the tall man squeezes the arms of the General for emphasis.

"I don't want to do this. Is there no other way?" the General pleads close to tears.

"Don't lose heart now my child," came the tall man's comforting words. "It has to be this way, it's our tradition," he says, struggling to stand upright. "Live by the sword, die by the sword. Besides, I have more local anesthetic than I need. My chest is completely numb. I won't feel a thing! When you get to my age it's a blessing to have control over your own death. I have no appetites left," the Tall Man said remorsefully. "Even my desire for children is gone! I don't want to die in my sleep like some passive old man." Leaning back a bit exposing his chest, he nods his head. "Do it now," he mouths the words out of sight of the Holy Father.

Pulling out a small ornate dagger concealed in his coat sleeve, the General forcefully plunges it into the tall man's chest. Splitting his brittle sternum, the sharp blade penetrates his heart, severing his main artery. Slowing the tall man's collapse, the General tenderly lays him down on the floor. The tall man's heart continued pumping his life blood onto the white marble. The entourage made up of high-ranking officials aren't fazed by the tall man's demise. They make no attempt to save him. They just neatly walk around the growing pool of blood to pay homage to the General who was now their new lord and master. The mantle of authority had been passed.

"I wanted you to witness this," the General told Holy Father. Stopping him from performing last rights for the tall man, "he wouldn't have wanted that. He knew where he was going," he said coolly, wiping his hands clean on his handkerchief before discarding it on the floor. "You were right. We didn't need him, but we do need the organization. I'm its new Potentate now and I'll do whatever it takes to achieve my objectives! If you 'throw in with us' there is no turning back."

"Well," Father paused nervously. "That was just beastly!" Visibly shaken, he continues to stammer. "I, um, I'll have to consult with, um, the Cardinals before I can commit the Church to, um, any long-term commitments. I'm, um, I'm getting to the end, um, of my term. It would only be, um, prudent, um, to seek their wisdom in this matter." Beads of sweat were starting to form on his forehead and his eyes were searching for the door.

Laughing heartily as if the Holy Father was making a joke, the General slaps Holy Father on the back. "Perhaps that should be my moniker, 'The Beast'. It has a nice authoritative ring to it don't you think? This will be a big commitment for you, seeing how you're coming to the end of your mandate. You should consult with your Bishops," the General said with practiced sincerity and a friendly tone. Respectfully kissing the Holy Father's ring as he bows, he helps Father to the door, jovially patting him on the back. "We can continue this another time, when you're more prepared," he says with a warm friendly smile.

"Absolutely, we'll do that for sure." Father says with more composure, then hastily makes his escape.

Once they were alone, the General orders his Sargent. "Put operation 'Retirement' into effect immediately. We don't have time to waste. Also, have our contacts within the jihadists to get busy and start another terror campaign. The waves of fear will come just in time for our newly installed Holy Father. He can ride in and save the day. Right out of the gate we'll start him with success. Seen as their savior, the public will worship him as a god."

The weapons development branch of the organization had always invested in cutting edge technology, no matter how long it might take to come to fruition. Thorium fueled, nuclear powered, pulse energy weapons and Animal mind control, are two prime examples. Just before the year 2000 AD arrived, weapons development heard about new research where rats were used in search and rescue missions. Researchers were electronically stimulating rat's brains through implanted electrodes, manipulating the rat's movements via remote controlled low voltage inputs. Seeing the potential for future use, the organization started funding the research, discreetly expanding the technology to include larger animals.

For two days the world was fixated on the small chimney perched atop the Sistine Chapel. Both days black smoke poured out into the bright blue sky, but on the third morning, white smoke billowed from it to the cheers of the waiting crowd below in the courtyard. The Cardinals debates had been successful. As the organization had planned, their man took the vote. One of his first official moves was to join his sovereign nation into the newly forming tenth resurrection of the Holy Roman Empire. As the tenth and final country to join, he would also become its spokesman and head of state.

The new Holy Father had humanity's good will on his side after his predecessor died in such a freak accident. An accident some were calling an act of God. The press interviewed countless animal behaviorists for weeks in the endless news cycle leading up to his election by the cardinals. None of them had an explanation for why the herd of young bulls would stampede into the VIP viewing box at Pamplona, trampling not only the previous Holy Father to death, but many other dignitaries including the mayor and several parliamentarians.

Security guards were helpless to stop the raging bulls with their small caliber side arms. Most of them died in their attempts. Witnesses described the bulls as having gone mad on mass, frothing at the mouth, their eyes appeared glazed as their hooves thundered murderously into the scrambling officials. Focused only on obliterating the VIPs, the herd of bulls became as placid as usual, having gored the life out of all they could reach. They were immediately rounded up without incident and sent for slaughter as the dignitary families mourned the death of their loved ones.

New worries soon plagued world societies daily. With every fresh terrorist attack, civilians looked for a strong global leader to provide the peace and security they craved. In this void came the new Holy Roman Emperor. His edicts were cheerfully accepted by most. Backed by the armies of The Beast, those who don't share the enthusiasm begrudgingly followed. Most of the world fell into line. Through trade and monetary restrictions, the Roman Empire begins its stranglehold on the countries and inhabitants of the world.

After performing many supernatural signs and wonders, the new Emperor makes peace accords with the jihadists and the leading Ummah's and Ayatollah's. Uniting them together with Rabbis, he brings them together as the common sons of Jacob under his firm spiritual leadership. Other world religions follow, recognizing the revered Emperor as their primary earthly spiritual leader.

Eastern religions talk about him as a great leader, just a little lower in status than Brahma or Vishnu. Buddhists follow him as a most powerful Buddha. He's universally hailed as the world's greatest leader ever. After enforcing peace and prosperity, people joyfully obey the Holy Roman Emperor, loudly proclaiming him their supreme leader during large public rallies around the world.

With such international favor on his side, the new Emperor forms an elite squad of worldwide peacekeepers. Staffed by each country's own concerned citizens, they call on the resources and help of their entire global network if needed. They start out in disaster relief where they were credited with saving countless lives everywhere regardless of race, creed, or color. They are hailed as merciful angels.

Looked up to globally as agents of peace, the ranks of the Special Services soon swell as those looking for notoriety and adventure joined them. Bands of international criminals soon try to cash in on their popularity by posing as Special Services agents, terrorizing and robbing unsuspecting citizens. As a security measure and for easy identification, all SS members willingly have the Emperor's crest tattooed on the back of their hand. Some zealots even put it on their foreheads.

Their new tattoos used special bioluminescent ink that changed colors in soothing waves and glowed in the dark. Made from live, genetically modified living organisms, the newly developed ink proved impossible for the criminals to reproduce, putting an end to imposters. With the quick success of the SS in gaining world trust, countries granted more authority to the Special Services. They soon became an international police force with far reaching power and authority. The SS worked effortlessly across borders and jurisdictions, ridding the world of criminal cartels and terrorists. Welcomed as fair, global law enforcement by honest citizens, they were feared by criminal's worldwide.

As researchers are by nature inquisitive, Dr. Harland Pickett, a researcher in microbiology at MIT, was concerned and intrigued with the ink used for the SS members tattoos. He studied into it further. His fears were soon validated after analyzing results from his lab rats. His published paper outlined how the inks toxicity would cause escalating neurological damage to the recipient's limbic system located in the temporal lobe. He found the ink altered the way the amygdala in his live animal subjects processed information, making them extremely aggressive.

His research showed that the genetically modified chemiluminescent agents of luciferin and photoprotein, extracted from invertebrates and fungi, disrupted the neuron connectors from properly transmitting their messages. During his trials, his test animals demonstrated a high degree of aggression when stressed. He hypothesized the same result would soon occur within the ranks of the SS. Adding "It was foolish of the Empire to have rushed a new ink into production without following standard protocols requiring rigorous testing before human applications began."

His results were immediately discredited by government officials, along with his credentials. Aspects of his personal life were brought into disrepute. For a week, news outlets ran lurid interviews with his disgruntled ex-girlfriends, exposing extreme sexual fetishes they would perform with him. By the end of that first week his lifeless body washed up on the banks of the river Charles.

An inquest into his death was quickly held. Finding a remorseful note in his lab, the coroner ruled it a suicide brought on by deep regret for bringing the SS and the Emperor into disrepute. His lab tests were soon forgotten as the story quickly lost its sensationalism and fell from the headlines. No one made any connection to his results in the following months as the SS became more and more heavy handed in dealing with the citizens they had vowed to protect.

Pointing to inadequate training, the Empire cited PTSD as the blame for the ever-increasing acts of violence committed by the first wave of SS volunteers. Installing new training guidelines and protocols to ease public concerns, they pronounced those first SS members as heroes who should be held in high regard. Giving them a blanket Imperial pardon for all crimes they may have committed, they were slowly retired from the force. No mention was made of the new ink formulated for SS tattoos which lacked the luster of the original ones still worn proudly by the origilal SS members.

Commerce and banking laws are changed to eliminate rampant fraud. All electronic communication is monitored due to security concerns. Freedom of speech is curtailed to reduce social conflict. Proclamations of faith are restricted to only sanctioned, Empire approved versions, where all are made to feel included regardless of belief or lifestyle choice. Concepts of sin are determined by the Empire, rather than being imposed by an omnipotent creator. These restraints are gladly adopted universally for continued peace and prosperity worldwide.

For the first few years the Empire and its Emperor, who liked to be referred to as Prophet Father, ruled the word with kindness and respect for all peoples and cultures. As a frog will gladly stay in a pot of water which is slowly heated until it's boiled alive, most of humanity fail to recognize the danger they're in. It's in this honeymoon phase we find Isaac and Stubby aligning themselves with those who suspect something evil this way comes.

Chapter 11

Around the world small groups persist in rejecting Prophet Father as their spiritual leader. Among those who refuse to give up their personal freedoms in the temperate valley Isaac lives in is a collection of evangelical Christians and conspiracy theorists. The evangelicals continued their practice of personally spreading the salvation gospel to a fallen world. A pair of them walk into the dusty yard of Sunshine Salvage. Stubby sees them coming through the dirty office window. Hollering to Isaac, who was in the bathroom, he makes a hasty retreat through the back door.

"Isaac. Isaac! Get the &$#@ out here. There are some people here to &$#@in see you. I don't want to &$#@in talk to them. I don't speak their &$#@in language. &$#@, that's why you're here."

Hearing Stubby's distress, Isaac quickly finishes and comes out of the washroom just as Stubby exits the back door. It no sooner closes when a pair of neatly dressed men enter the front office door. Smiling friendly, they get right to the point of their visit. Isaac surmises the reason for Stubby's quick departure.

"Hello friend," the taller of the pair greats Isaac. "We've come here today to tell you about Jesus and how you can have eternal life with him in heaven. Wouldn't that be great?"

"Yes, that sounds nice," replies Isaac warmly.

"Have you accepted Jesus into your heart?" The taller man asks with a smile. "It's the only way to save your eternal soul from the fires of hell. God will punish the wicked in those fires for all eternity."

"The only way to avoid hell is to gain eternal life through the salvation of Jesus." The shorter man adds. "He alone holds the keys to salvation, for there is no other name by which we can be saved. Eternal life is only for those who accept Jesus. All others are lost to the fires of hell."

"Hm." Isaac replies with a frown. "I do believe in Jesus, but your message seems to be contradictory."

"How's that? We proclaim the true salvation message to all who will hear it," came the reply.

"Well to start with." Isaac begins, shifting his weight to his other leg while leaning on the counter. "You told me, the only way to gain eternal life is to accept Jesus as my savior."

"Amen brother. That's absolutely true," the taller man jumps in.

"But then I'm told, if I don't accept Jesus I would be in the torments of Hell for all eternity. So, which is it?"

"Which is what?" The shorter man asked, looking perplexed. "That's what the Bible explains will happen to us all. One or the other."

"Both of those statements can't be true!" Isaac explained. "If I only acquire eternal life by believing in Jesus and believing in Jesus keeps me out of hell, how can I be tormented in hell for all eternity if I reject Jesus? I wouldn't have the belief that is required to possess eternal life."

Isaac's point catches the pair off guard. They hadn't thought of it like that before.

"Well regardless. We're here to tell you about the love of Jesus," came the reply. "Jesus came to save, not condemn."

"For God so loved the world that he gave his only begotten son, that whosoever believed in him would not perish but have everlasting life," the tall man recited John 3:16 as a reference.

"I think that's the most quoted verse in the Bible." Isaac adds. "I believe it to be the truth, the whole truth and nothing but the truth. Do you?"

"Absolutely!" The pair answer in unison.

"Then those who don't believe in Jesus won't have everlasting life. Wouldn't that be true?"

"Uh. Yes, I suppose so. Only those who believe in Jesus will go to heaven," came a bewildered answer, unsure where Isaac was leading.

"So, you believe people aren't born with eternal life within them, they don't possess an immortal soul. Being immortal or having eternal life means you will never die and can't be killed. If you can die, you can't be immortal. The word immortal means you can't die. The opposite of mortals who do die."

"You misunderstand us. Your body is mortal, but your soul," the tall man makes a sweeping gesture with his hands and talks slower and in a lofty tone. "Your soul is immortal."

"You just told me I could only receive eternal life by believing in Jesus!" Isaac contends. "What tells you we have an immortal soul that will never die?"

"The Bible tells me so," the short man recites a childhood song in rhyme. "We get our knowledge about God from his written word. It's the only true source of Godly wisdom."

"Amen to that!" Isaac exclaims confidently. "We can agree on that much. But we can't believe something just because the Bible records it. We need to check that it's true before we believe it."

"What do you mean by that? If it's in the Bible, then it must be true. It's the inspired word of God," the tall man passionately defended the source of his beliefs. "The Bible is the true word of God and will not lie or contradict itself."

"Again, we wholeheartedly agree on another point." Isaac's smile widens. "But the Bible is made up of a lot of conversations, not just wisdom coming directly from God to us. We need to put the things that are recorded in their proper context."

"Like what? Give me an example," the shorter man demands.

"OK." Isaac quickly replies. "Your right, the Bible does tell us we will not die. That is recorded in the scripture."

"See. That's what we said!"

"But it's important that we understand who's talking. It's not God, or Jesus! The conversation is recorded in Genesis," turning to the computer keyboard on the counter, Isaac searches for the scripture. It only takes a moment before he's swiveling the monitor towards the pair. They read the account from the Bible app Isaac has on display.

Genesis 3:1-5 King James Version (KJV)

1 Now the serpent was more subtil than any beast of the field which the Lord God had made. And he said unto the woman, Yea, hath God said, Ye shall not eat of every tree of the garden?

2 And the woman said unto the serpent, We may eat of the fruit of the trees of the garden:

3 But of the fruit of the tree which is in the midst of the garden, God hath said, Ye shall not eat of it, neither shall ye touch it, lest ye die.

4 And the serpent said unto the woman, Ye shall not surely die:

5 For God doth know that in the day ye eat thereof, then your eyes shall be opened, and ye shall be as gods, knowing good and evil.

"There it is." Isaac said. "The idea that we won't die comes from Satan, not God. 'The Bible tells us so'," he sang. "Why would any Christian choose to believe what Satan tells them? Satan is the father of lies, he knew this one would cause the most amount of confusion, ultimately leading most of mankind away from God. That lie, is why virtually all societies and religions have the belief of an afterlife and that they possess an immortal soul, like you claim to have. It's not a Godly belief. Rather it comes from Satan. God tells us our soul can die."

Isaac searches for his other references. Finding them he lets the pair read.

Ezekiel 18:20 King James Version (KJV)
20 The soul that sinneth, it shall die. The son shall not bear the iniquity of the father, neither shall the

father bear the iniquity of the son: the righteousness of the righteous shall be upon him, and the wickedness of the wicked shall be upon him.

"This verse from the new testament is similar."

Romans 6:23 ESV
For the wages of sin is death, but the free gift of God is eternal life in Christ Jesus our Lord.

"We get the free gift of eternal life, like you've pointed out, by believing in Jesus. Just as John 3:16 tells us. Also here." Isaac searches for another verse, displaying it once it was found. "God himself tells us we're mortal."

Genesis 6:3 New International Version (NIV)
3 Then the Lord said, "My Spirit will not contend with humans forever, for they are mortal; their days will be a hundred and twenty years."

"But most telling of all is after Adam was banished from the garden, God had it guarded to keep mankind away from the tree of life so we couldn't have immortality." Doing one last search, Isaac lets the two men read his last proof scripture.

Genesis 3:22-24 English Standard Version (ESV)
22 Then the Lord God said, "Behold, the man has become like one of us in knowing good and evil. Now, lest he reach out his hand and take also of the tree of life and eat, and live forever—" 23 therefore the Lord God sent him out from the garden of Eden to work

the ground from which he was taken. 24 He drove out the man, and at the east of the garden of Eden he placed the cherubim and a flaming sword that turned every way to guard the way to the tree of life.

"These verses may suggest what you think they say, but God created us with a soul at creation. That fact is definitely recorded in the Bible. Here, let us find it for you." Taking control, the short man types on the keyboard, then Isaac reads it.

Genesis 2:7 King James Version (KJV)
7 And the Lord God formed man of the dust of the ground, and breathed into his nostrils the breath of life; and man became a living soul.

"There, that should settle it. Man is a living soul. Our soul is an immortal spirit. That's what the Bible tells us," the two men step back a bit and look intently at Isaac with their arms crossed.

Isaac responds with an agreement and a correction. "We are a living soul, yes, that's exactly what the Bible tells us. But, that soul is not immortal. People only believe in an immortal soul because of Satan. What we believe to be true isn't important. What God tells us is."

"Now we can agree with you," the tall man said. "What God tells us is the important thing."

"Then we have even more to agree on. We all want to follow God to the best of our abilities. We agree the Bible is the inspired word of God," Isaac stressed.

"Yes, that's all true. So why don't you agree with what it says?" the short man asks.

"I do agree with what it says. Have you ever looked to see what word God inspired to be used for soul, or how the King James Bible translators said it should be used and what the word soul means? I agree with them completely," Isaac assured. "Do you?"

"Like you said, we all want to follow God to the best of our ability, the Bible is the inspired word of God and should be followed. But I must admit," the short man paused, thinking for a moment, then gesturing to include his taller friend. "I don't believe we've ever looked into what the King James translators had to say about the word soul," the short man speaks for the both of them as the tall man nodded his agreement.

"Here, I'll find it for you. Luckily the hard work has been done by the Strong's concordance scholars. All we have to do is read it." Isaac does a short search before the verse is displayed on the office monitor.

Genesis 2:7
IHOT(i) (In English order)
7 H3335 וייצר formed H3068 יהוה And the LORD H430 אלהים God H853 את H120 האדם man H6083 עפר the dust H4480 מן of H127 האדמה the ground, H5301 ויפח and breathed H639 באפיו into his nostrils H5397 נשמת the breath H2416 חיים of life; H1961 ויהי became H120 האדם and man H5315 לנפש soul. H2416 חיה: a living

H5315 נפש – Strong's Hebrew Lexicon Number
Previous Strong's #H5314 Next Strong's #H5316

נפש
nephesh
neh'-fesh

From H5314; properly a breathing creature, that is, animal or (abstractly) vitality; used very widely in a literal, accommodated or figurative sense (bodily or mental)

KJV Usage: any, appetite, beast, body, breath, creature, X dead (-ly), desire, X [dis-] contented, X fish, ghost, + greedy, he, heart (-y), (hath, X jeopardy of) life (X in jeopardy), lust, man, me, mind, **mortality**, one, own, person, pleasure, (her-, him-, my-, thy-) self, them (your) -selves, + slay, soul, + tablet, they, thing, (X she) will, X would have it.

Brown-Driver-Briggs' Hebrew Definitions

נֶפֶשׁ

1. soul, self, life, creature, person, appetite, mind, living being, desire, emotion, passion
2. that which breathes, the breathing substance or being, soul, the inner being of man
3. living being
4. living being (with life in the blood)
5. the man himself, self, person or individual
6. seat of the appetites
7. seat of emotions and passions
8. activity of mind
9. dubious
10. activity of the will
11. dubious
12. activity of the character
13. dubious

"Do you see it? In the terms of usage. Mortal. I bolded the word for you. The Strong's scholars say the word used for soul, nephesh, means mortal. It pertains to our physical mind and body as well as any animal flesh. It's not immortal as most people believe." Isaac looks directly at the two men expectantly.

"Yes, we can read it. We're just not sure that your interpretation is the right one," the taller man said.

"What's to interpret? Did God inspire one word to have opposite meanings? The Strong's scholars didn't think so." Isaac pressed, "Our soul can't be immortal and mortal at the same time!"

"That's not part of our exegesis or hermeneutics. We both have studied at established Bible schools, respected by major evangelical denominations. What you're saying simply isn't taught there. Therefore it can't be the truth," the tall man said confidently.

Isaac was quiet, letting the tall man's words sink in. Then with a wry smile he said. "Regardless of what others believe or teach, it's been my experience that truth is like poetry."

"How's that? the tall man questioned. "Truth is like poetry?" Both men looked puzzled by Isaac's response.

"Well," replied Isaac casually. "Not everyone likes poetry."

"We didn't come to argue!" The short man said emphatically, starting to look exasperated by Isaac's questioning. "We came to proclaim the love of Jesus and his gospel message. Bringing the lost to Jesus so they may be saved."

"And I appreciate your efforts. I'm only trying to clarify what your message is. Preaching salvation through Jesus is great, but it's only part of the Gospel. You provide no hope for those who aren't drawn to Jesus by God now. By not understanding man's mortality and the coming Kingdom of God, how the resurrections work will be hidden from you. Your message will abandon most of mankind in the fires of hell due to your adherence to the Satan inspired immortal soul doctrine. I'm asking you to give me the biblical reason for your belief in an immortal soul. Not what your schooling has taught you, but what the Bible has."

"We've been trying, but the verses we give, you reject as incorrect," the short man complained.

"Yes, I have challenged them. Like the Bereans, we all should examine the scriptures daily to see if teachings are true. As I believe I've shown, the verses you use don't say what you say they do."

"Those verses we used aren't the only ones that reveal the truth about our immortal soul. It's best to look at them as a collective whole."

"I don't understand how reading a collection of verses that don't say we have an immortal soul will sway me into believing we do, but I'm willing to read them with you."

"Here, let me use your computer and I'll find some of them," the short man reaches for the keyboard. "Let's start at the beginning," he says as he types. "We were created in the image of God, immortal like him." Genesis 1:26-27 appears on the monitor.

New International Version (NIV)

26 Then God said, "Let us make mankind in our image, in our likeness, so that they may rule over the fish in the sea and the birds in the sky, over the livestock and all the wild animals,[a] and over all the creatures that move along the ground."

27 So God created mankind in his own image, in the image of God he created them; male and female he created them.

"Your reading into that scripture. It doesn't say man is immortal, only that we are created in the image of God. A sculptor may make an image of a person out of clay, but that clay won't be alive. God made man from the dust of the earth, mortal flesh." Isaac points out. "And you're forgetting about what the Strong's scholars said. Man's soul is mortal."

"There you go again!" the tall man says, throwing his hands in the air. "We have an immortal soul. Jesus clearly tells us that with the story of Lazarus and the rich man and when we die our spirit returns to God who gave it. Look those up for him," he directs his short friend who quickly has one verse up on the monitor.

Ecclesiastes 12:7 King James Version (KJV)

7 Then shall the dust return to the earth as it was: and the spirit shall return unto God who gave it.

"Who's spirit?" Isaac questions sharply. "The Spirit of God that he breathed into us giving us life? Why shouldn't God's spirit go back to him? It's his! We only borrow it while we're alive. When we die and turn back into the dust we came from, God's spirit that gave us life goes back to him. Nothing there says we have an immortal soul." Isaac commandeers the keyboard for a moment. "Like this says. It's the breath of God that provides the spirit."

Job 32:8ESV
But it is the spirit in man, the breath of the Almighty, that makes him understand.

Shaking his head, the short man takes back the keyboard, then pulls up the parable about Lazarus. "Jesus tells us we are alive after death. He gave us this parable describing heaven and hell proving it," he displays Luke 16:19-31 on the monitor. Isaac looks at it and suggests.

"Yes, I know this one, but let's start reading it at the beginning of the conversation." After making a quick adjustment, Isaac reads the account out loud before he responds.

"Luke 16:14-31 New International Version (NIV)
14 The Pharisees, who loved money, heard all this and were sneering at Jesus.

15 He said to them, "You are the ones who justify yourselves in the eyes of others, but God knows your hearts. What people value highly is detestable in God's sight.

Additional Teachings
16 "The Law and the Prophets were proclaimed until John. Since that time, the good news of the

kingdom of God is being preached, and everyone is forcing their way into it.

17 It is easier for heaven and earth to disappear than for the least stroke of a pen to drop out of the Law.

18 "Anyone who divorces his wife and marries another woman commits adultery, and the man who marries a divorced woman commits adultery.

"It's important to understand, Jesus tells the parable to the Pharisees and the Jewish leaders, he's not instructing his followers about heaven and hell!" Isaac gives a running commentary.

"The Rich Man and Lazarus

19 "There was a rich man who was dressed in purple and fine linen and lived in luxury every day. **20** At his gate was laid a beggar named Lazarus, covered with sores **21** and longing to eat what fell from the rich man's table. Even the dogs came and licked his sores.

22 "The time came when the beggar died and the angels carried him to Abraham's side. The rich man also died and was buried. **23** In Hades, where he was in torment, he looked up and saw Abraham far away, with Lazarus by his side. **24** So he called to him, 'Father Abraham, have pity on me and send Lazarus to dip the tip of his finger in water and cool my tongue, because I am in agony in this fire.'

25 "But Abraham replied, 'Son, remember that in your lifetime you received your good things, while

Lazarus received bad things, but now he is comforted here and you are in agony. 26 And besides all this, between us and you a great chasm has been set in place, so that those who want to go from here to you cannot, nor can anyone cross over from there to us.'

27 "He answered, 'Then I beg you, father, send Lazarus to my family,28 for I have five brothers. Let him warn them, so that they will not also come to this place of torment.'

29 "Abraham replied, 'They have Moses and the Prophets; let them listen to them.'

30 "'No, father Abraham,' he said, 'but if someone from the dead goes to them, they will repent.'

31 "He said to him, 'If they do not listen to Moses and the Prophets, they will not be convinced even if someone rises from the dead.'"

"Yes, that's the parable Jesus told," Isaac agreed, nodding his head. "It's a story of good and bad told in a classic Hebrew style. As with the rest of the parables, it's meaning or lesson is revealed at the end. After rejecting the messianic miracles already performed, Jesus was describing how the Jewish leaders would also reject his final miracle. Proving he was their true messiah by bringing his friend, also named Lazarus, back to life after being dead for over three days and nights, this was the final messianic test left for Jesus to complete. At the completion of this last miracle, the Jews not only rejected Jesus, they actively sought a way to put him to death, happily paying Judas for his help."

"Jesus tells us Lazarus is in heaven and the rich man's in torment. He's describing where we go when we die. Jesus is literally describing heaven and hell to us," the tall man insists.

"This parable isn't meant to be taken literally to describe heaven or hell any more than other parables explain the kingdom of God is literally buried treasure, or a fisherman's net."

"No! It is literal," they protested.

"OK." Isaac says. "Let's look at this parable as literal Bible truth. As you pointed out and we agreed earlier, the Bible will not contradict itself, as it is the inspired word of God."

The short man steps up. "Agreed, let's do that. Let the Bible interpret itself. That's what we did at college, it's the best way to understand the word of God, we've dedicated our lives to understanding the Bible," he motions to himself and the taller man.

"In this parable Abraham is referred to as someone of responsibility in heaven."

"Ya, that's correct, the rich man and Lazarus refer to Abraham as someone in charge. They ask for his permission," the tall man agrees with Isaac.

"So then, it would be fair to say that Abraham is also alive and well with them in heaven?" Isaac surmised.

"Absolutely, along with a great host of others I'm sure," the shorter man agreed enthusiastically.

"Does the Bible support that belief? Does the Bible have anything to say on the whereabouts of Abraham?"

"I've never looked," came the unanimous reply. "But of course he's in heaven."

"Ya," the tall man said as a thought came to him. "We're told Abraham's faith was credited to him as righteousness, so obviously he's in heaven. Where else could he be?"

"Have you read Hebrews 11?" Isaac queried.

"The faith chapter? Yes, several times," the tall man said.

"Well let's read it again." Isaac said reaching for the keyboard. "We'll be scrutinizing the last two verses," the scriptures flash onto the screen.

Hebrews 11:39-40 New International Version (NIV)
39 These were all commended for their faith, yet none of them received what had been promised, 40 since God had planned something better for us so that only together with us would they be made perfect.

"According to these verses no Christian is in heaven. God has something better planned. The faithful will be made perfect at the same time as all the rest of the Christians. All together at the same event."

"According to you. So, when do you think we'll all experience this, better plan?" The short man scoffs.

"People have been asking that question for a long time." Isaac confirms. "Let's see what the Bible tells us," he does yet another search. They all read off the monitor as John 6 is displayed.

39 This is the will of the Father who sent Me, that of all He has given Me I should lose nothing, but should raise it up at the last day.

40 And this is the will of Him who sent Me, that everyone who sees the Son and believes in Him may have everlasting life; and I will raise him up at the last day.

44 No one can come to Me unless the Father who sent Me draws him; and I will raise him up at the last day.

54 Whoever eats My flesh and drinks My blood has eternal life, and I will raise him up at the last day.

"On the last day. That's what Jesus told us. It's not what I say, we want to let the Bible interpret itself, right?" Isaac questions the two men. "It seems to me we're being told that we all receive perfection at the same time, on the last day, when Jesus returns. We're also told this in 1 Thessalonians," he reads his next scripture off the screen out loud.

4:13-18 New American Standard Bible (NASB)
Those Who Died in Christ
13 But we do not want you to be uninformed, brethren, about those who are asleep, so that you will not grieve as do the rest who have no hope.14 For if we believe that Jesus died and rose again, even so God will bring with Him those who have fallen asleep [a]in Jesus.

"See! Right there. The Bible tells us, those who are dead return with Jesus. They must be in Heaven now to come back with Jesus later," the tall man said confidently.

"Let's not be too hasty. We'll keep reading the whole section. They arise with the sound of the trumpet." Isaac admonishes.

15 For this we say to you by the word of the Lord, that we who are alive [b]and remain until the coming of the Lord, will not precede those who have fallen asleep.16 For the Lord Himself will descend from heaven with a [c]shout, with the voice of the archangel and with the trumpet of God, and the dead in Christ will rise first. 17 Then we who are alive [d]and remain will be caught up together with them in the clouds to meet the Lord in the air, and so we shall always be with the Lord.

"We're all changed into our new bodies at the same event, when Jesus returns. Those who are already dead first, then quickly followed by those who are alive. The dead are said to be asleep, they get resurrected back to life just like Jesus was." Isaac pauses, waiting for a reply. A thought comes to him and he types in another search. They all read it together in silence.

1 Corinthians 15:51-58 ESV
Behold! I tell you a mystery. We shall not all sleep, but we shall all be changed, in a moment, in the twinkling of an eye, at the last trumpet. For the trumpet will sound, and the dead will be raised

imperishable, and we shall be changed. For this perishable body must put on the imperishable, and this mortal body must put on immortality. When the perishable puts on the imperishable, and the mortal puts on immortality, then shall come to pass the saying that is written: "Death is swallowed up in victory." "O death, where is your victory? O death, where is your sting?"

"We're mortal right now! We don't put on immortality until we're changed at the last trumpet, on the last day, when Jesus returns to rule the world." Isaac ties the verses together.

"Well Jesus told the thief on the cross he would be in heaven that same day. Not later at his second coming! They were changed that very day," the short man stammered.

"Exactly what I was thinking," the tall man added. "The Bible clearly records the words of Jesus as, 'today you will be with me in paradise'."

"Yes, those are the words Jesus spoke," Isaac agreed. "I'll give you that. It's the punctuation that's wrong."

"What do you mean? The punctuation is wrong?"

"The original text was written in Greek. Greek doesn't use punctuation marks," Isaac explains. "The translators, who believed in the immortal soul doctrine, put a comma in the wrong spot. To best match the rest of the Bible, it should read. 'Jesus answered him, 'Truly I tell you today, you will be with me in paradise'. Moving the comma one word to the right lets this verse agree with the rest of the Bible. Otherwise it's contradictory."

"You have an answer for everything that you don't agree with don't you?" the short man snorts disgruntledly.

"Does the bible contradict itself? I don't believe it does! If a verse appears to be contradictory, then we must not be understanding it properly. What's your explanation? Or are those other Bible verses wrong?"

"That's not what we've been taught. Our professors were all highly educated, faithful men of God. How is it you should know better than them?"

"Oh for sure, your right. I'm not the sharpest tool in the shed. Why, I'm the living embodiment of 1 Corinthians 1:27. I'm only upholding what the Bible tells me, not what I've been taught by others. 'Let God be true and every man a liar'. But please, give me your explanation for all my verses. How do you fit them in with your proof scriptures?" Isaac pleads.

"Brothers!" The tall man interjects. "Let's not bicker amongst ourselves. In these troubled times we're living, we can't afford to be divided internally. We have a bigger, common enemy. The way the New Roman Empire is restricting our economy and trampling our freedoms. The Emperor is even demanding our churches report all our activities and sermons to his SS agents. We're under constant surveillance, there's nowhere we can have privacy, our every move is being tracked as enemies of his religious doctrines."

"Your right," Isaac agrees, clearing his throat. "I do get passionate about what the Bible tells me."

"I know exactly how you feel," the short man says, extending his right hand towards Isaac. "We need a united front to stand against the Empire. Would you come to a meeting tonight? We're organizing local Christians into a resistance force."

"Yes, I would like to find out about some sort of resistance. If we don't stand together, we'll be picked off easily one at a time for not following the Empires dictates. My business partner and I have already been preparing for when things get worse." Isaac smiles shaking, the man's hand firmly.

"Good! Glad to have you with us. We're confirming a new leader for this area tonight. Brother Matias is truly a Godly man of deep conviction. He's been working with the grass roots, building up our movement. He's a born leader of quality. I can't wait for you to meet him." Bubbling over with excitement, the tall man puts his arm over Isaac's shoulder.

"Where and when is this meeting? My partner and I would like to come, we have no love for the Empire. It's going to destroy our country and kill us all. There's a storm coming. Our best chance for survival is to find a place to hide."

"Not us! Our resistance is going to send the Empire packing. We're not going to crawl into a hole and hide. This is our country; we'll fight to the death to keep it. 'For whoever seeks to save their life will lose it'," the short man says as a warning.

Isaac sincerely replies. "If I need to lose my life for Jesus, I will do it gladly. But this country is not my home. It's not what we should be fighting for. Christians are vagabonds, following Jesus to our true home. He tells us to overcome evil with love, not violence."

"God gave this country to us. He planted our forefathers here, building our nations into global powers because we followed him. I'll defend my nation from any foreign invader and those who would dare dictate to us how it should be run. We have a proud military history to uphold. I won't be slinking away like a coward! I thought you said you wanted to be part of the resistance?" The short man's passion showed in his red face.

"Yes, I will be active in the resistance, but I won't be an armed combatant. Like the stretcher bearers from World War 1, my partner and I will give assistance to any who need it, all the while causing as much trouble for the Empire as possible."

The tall man speaks up, temporing the short man's fiery response. "I'm sure there will be room in the resistance for whatever help you and your partner can provide. We'll all need to do our part in fighting for our rites." The tall man writes out the meeting details on a paper form off the counter then hands it to Isaac. "Hope to see you there. We'll all need to pull together if we want to keep our freedoms." With parting handshakes all around, the pair leave through the front door. Making their way across the salvage yard the two men get into their car parked on the street and drive off. Isaac watches them until they are out of sight, then goes to the back door, retrieving Stubby who was snoozing on the back-porch chair.

"It's safe to come in now. They're gone."

"%$#@. You know how I hate talking to those people. Always %$#@in telling me I'm %$#@in headed for Hell. There's only so much of that $%*# I can %$#@in take. That's your %$#@in job. Talking to %$#@in people I don't want to. Besides, I think you enjoy a good argument." Stubby rubs his stiff back as he hobbles clumsily into the office.

"You'll have to learn how to play nicer with people. They're organizing a resistance force we might want to join."

"Well I could pretend to be a %$#@in mute."

"That would work! But you'll likely mumble offensively. Maybe I should leave you in the truck when people are around."

"%$#@ no. I'll just be the %$#@in silent one, who's perceived to be wise."

"OK, you can try it out tonight at our first rebel meeting."

Stubby manages to hold his tongue through several meetings. Due to Isaac's extensive knowledge of back roads and Stubby's keen eye for salvage, Sunshine Salvage quickly becomes the go to people for providing transportation and supplying specialty items to the local resistance.

Chapter 12

A giant jewel bedazzled banner welcomes the leaders and dignitaries of, 'The Beast and Prophet Father'. The opulence of the ancient Roman Empire as displayed by Caligula and Nero paled in comparison to how Emperor, Prophet Father indulged those in power. Having the world's riches at his disposal, he showered those at the top with every kind of luxury. Quarterly meetings for top executives were not only a time to plan strategy and deal with problems, but were also a time for conspicuous opulence and consumption. The Empire took every opportunity to demonstrate their superiority over those they ruled. Enjoying a gaudily, lavish, lifestyle unattainable to the commoner, was only one of them. Those who sought upward mobility recognized the clear path for success and let nothing stand in their way of getting it. A constant competition for top positions kept those seeking the VP level ever vigilant and wary, doing anything they could to protect and advance their position.

Just off stage before being introduced to their assembled executives, the Beast and Prophet Father are having a private conversation as they wait in the wings.

"I'm just not satisfied with the way things have turned out!" Prophet Father complains to the Beast, the leader of the organization who provided him with his position of authority. "This will be our third quarterly meeting and I'm still not getting the respect I deserve. The VP's treat me as if I was one of them. They don't give me the reverence I deserve! Most don't even bow as they should, let alone kiss my ring hand as protocol demands."

"You're making a mountain out of a molehill," the Beast replies dismissively. "We hold all the power and wealth. We don't need their respect or love. They fear us unconditionally, that's what's important."

"That's all that's important to you! Money, power and being feared is all you've ever wanted. You don't understand true power. To be worshipped is the ultimate sign of success. That is why I joined you, I was born to be worshipped. You thought you chose me, but I chose you so I could fulfill my divine greatness. I will be worshipped by mankind as I see fit and you will make them do it." Prophet Father speaks darkly, pointing his finger in the Beast's face.

"You're forgetting how you got to where you are," the Beast struggles to keep his anger at bay, not used to being talked to so disrespectfully. "There could be another accident if you're not careful." His threat was real and calculated.

"I think not!" came a slow methodical reply. "You need me. There is no one else alive who can provide you with the legitimacy you need for worldwide dominance. The world recognizes me as the broker of peace, bringing warring factions together. I provide the stability and moral authority your organization needs to thrive unhindered." Father's eyes narrowed. "No, there will be no accidents for me, in fact, I think you better keep me as safe and happy as possible. You stand to lose all you've ever wanted if I'm not kept satisfied. And I'm not satisfied, not by a long shot! From now on I get top billing, Beast and Prophet Father no longer!" Prophet Father spits on the marble floor in disgust. "From now on the signage better read 'Prophet Father and the Beast'!"

Having his bluff called, the Beast nervously avoids eye contact and silently looks at the waiting crowd.

They stride to the podium arm in arm like best friends after being introduced. "Keep me happy." Father says just loud enough for the Beast to hear. "It's time to lead by example. Reverence starts from the top. Set a good example they can follow."

Before addressing the crowd, Prophet Father faces the Beast and extends his right hand out to receive the Beast's kiss. "Suck it up buttercup." Father says, barely moving his lips. The Beast gives father a deadly look as he kneels dutifully and humbly kisses Father's hand displaying his submission to the assembly of leaders. After an awkwardly long time kneeling, Father bends slightly and guides the Beast to his feet with a broad smile.

"Well done my son, that should work nicely. You've made me very happy."

The Beast leans forward giving Father a hug. Whispering in Prophet Father's ear the Beast warns. "If I didn't need you. I'd kill you with my bare hands."

"I'm sure you would. But you do need me," came Father's smiling, wispy reply.

Later in meetings Father was given more respect from the executives than he had ever received before. Following the Beast's example, they kowtowed to his eminence completely.

"My sector needs more SS officers to control the civilian population. The local insurgents are growing stronger," one VP reported later on at a large conference table.

"Yes," spoke up another. "It seems like the entire country is fighting our governance. They are an unruly nation," a VP from a neighboring district added.

"We are aware of your difficulties and have set plans in motion for addressing them," the Beast replied from his chair at the head of the table. "Our spies have infiltrated the rebels at the highest levels but we need to wait until the entire population shows their true loyalties. Then we will crush all those who would rebel against us without mercy."

"The historical roots of these rouge nations need to be understood." Prophet Father states from his chair to the left, slightly elevated higher than the Beast's. "As with others in many countries around the world, these rebels only trace their formal religious denominational roots back to the reformation. Some don't even go that far back, for they rejected the protestant church's authority over themselves, as well as ours. For the most part, they ignore my religious decrees. They claim to use the Bible as the sole source for their religious beliefs. Treason runs in their blood. They come from rebellious, stiff necked tribes that can only be dealt with by God or guns."

"Fortunately, we have plenty of the latter," the Beast adds with a laugh.

The rest of the delegates find humor in the comment and soon the entire room is roaring with laughter.

The Beast clarifies his orders. "Until the Empire is ready to spring our trap, each VP is free to only monitor the rebels however they see fit. I'll be personally directing the extermination strategy from headquarters. You're not to scare them off, only slow them down a bit and monitor."

Back in his regional office, the VP for Isaac's district is meeting with his SS officials. "It doesn't matter what you all think is best! I got my orders directly from the Beast himself. We are not to engage the insurgents in combat. Our job is to observe and record, gather intelligence."

"But Prefect," one of the generals urged, "we've tracked down a spy. She's one of our own, an original SS volunteer. She was going by the moniker of the Moth. It took time for us to find her. Our behavioral profiler gave us our big break by figuring out the riddles of her name. That's how we knew it was someone who worked the night shift and was morphing into a new person. Like a caterpillar that turns into a moth. We carefully started coding our dispatches separately and waited to see how the resistance would react. Eventually she was the only one to have seen the information that got passed on to the rebels. We've put plans in motion to deal with her. They will soon be finalized."

"Hmm," the Prefect considered the information carefully as he stroked his beard. "If she's one of ours, then she's not one of the rebels and our hands aren't tied.

We are free to deal with her as I see fit. Carry out your extermination plans and keep me posted."

When Isaac and Stubby went to the first rebel meeting, he didn't recall Brother Matias. It took several meetings before Isaac recognized him as Becky's dad Matt. He'd lost about a third of his weight, had a long ponytail and was sporting full scraggly facial hair. Add in his new attire of sandals and toga, it's doubtful Matt's own mother would have recognized him. Isaac hadn't seen Matt for several years, as he had stopped coming over to see Mum once he realized there was no life insurance money to be had. Mum was heartbroken at first, but upon further consideration of Matt's actions, Mum soon came to realize she was better off without him.

Needing an outlet where she could put her faith into action, Isaac encouraged her to volunteer with an international child and family supporting NGO. Being retired and using her meager government pension for funding, she was posted to several third world countries where her family skills were put to good use. She especially liked working with orphaned children where she felt she could effectively put her love for God into action by displaying that love to them. She missed spending time with Isaac but felt drawn by God to help those who needed to feel his healing love. Her and Isaac stayed in touch through regular personal electronic communication and her sporadic trips back home.

Visiting every dump site within a two-hundred-mile radius of Sunshine Salvage, Isaac had seen almost every vehicle wreck around the area. One day when picking up some copper and brass from a local scrapper, he recognized the side wall of a heavily damaged reefer van being used as a storage shed. The front right quarter was torn off and if it hadn't been for the faded mural of a naked lady relaxing under a tree with flowers and leaves covering her private parts, he would have paid it little attention. Remembering it as the trailer belonging to a generous old trucker who had once given him a ride, Isaac inquires how it became wrecked.

"Oh. That's all that's left from Adam's rig," the owner said. "Hauling food south from the connector junction, on the old number 5 highway, he took the ditch off a steep hill when a loaded school bus was forced into his lane by an oncoming, out of control bulk tanker truck. His old blue Western Star came out of that ravine in pieces. Adam and his wife Lilith never survived the crash, but they saved forty-two kids." Having known Adam as a friend, the owner choked up when relating the story of Adam's demise, even now, years after the fact.

Remembering Adam as well, Isaac wiped his eyes with the back of his gloved hand. "Oh. Sorry," the scrap yard owner said sympathetically. "You knew him too?" Isaac could only nod. Seeing a star shaped hood emblem on the ground under the van, Isaac bends and picks it up. Showing it to the scrap dealer he gestures, "How much?"

"Since you knew Adam too, you take it."

Clearing his throat, Isaac manages to respond. "Thanks. I'll screw it to the dash of the Paystar. It'll go with my eclectic motif." Isaac jokes, breaking the emotional tension.

Drawing on his extensive knowledge of the back roads up and down the valley, Isaac skillfully avoids the Imperial checkpoints set up by SS as he delivers first aid supplies and materials to the rebels. The Paystar 5000 proves to be a very reliable and useful vehicle for Isaac on the back roads and trails. Although being a large intimidating truck, it was surprisingly nimble and could climb like a Billy goat, often blazing through light bush or the asphalt jungle's debris. The large, puncture proof gripper tires proved very useful when forging new trails.

The 19-liter Cummins intercooled, turbo charged engine, had great power stock, but it was phenomenal after Isaac changed the fuel pump spring and button. Even when overloaded Isaac had to be careful not to spin the tires going up steep hills on dry pavement. He outfitted the deck with six-foot stake sides. Covered over with a light tarp, even the most inquisitive eyes couldn't see what was loaded on the deck.

Isaac was pop riveting placard holders onto the Paystar one sunny afternoon when Stubby shuffled across the dusty yard. "You only need one of those %$#@in things on every side you know. You've got three times too %$#@in many."

"Ya I know. I wouldn't want anyone to miss seeing my Infectious Biohazard waste decals. I'd feel terrible if anyone got accidently infected." Isaac's reply is dripping with false sincerity. "I want everyone to know they need to approach this truck carefully, if they approach it at all."

"Won't that put off our scrap clients? %$#@, they won't want you in their yards. They'll be %$#@in afraid to let you in."

"Maybe. I can take the placards off when I get scrap, I don't usually see anyone when I'm making pickups anyway."

"I still don't know why you bid that %$#@in health authority job. You bid it way too low! %$#@, I thought I taught you better than that. %$#@!" Stubby says, shaking his head in disgust. "We'll probably lose money on that %$#@in job."

"I didn't bid it to make money." Isaac replies. "But we'll at least break even."

"If not for the money, then what the %$#@ did you bid it for? We don't do favors for the %$#@in Empire!" Stubby leans close to Isaac and whispers as if they could be overheard. "We're part of the %$#@in resistance! Remember?"

"I know! That's why we're letting everyone know this particular truck carries dangerous cargo. Highly infectious, biohazardous waste. People shouldn't come too close if they want to stay healthy."

"%$#@ if I know what you're getting at."

"Last month I saw a couple of SS officers loading a drone into their pickup." Isaac explained. "They're starting to monitor the bush roads. It'll soon be harder to bypass the check points with rebel contraband. I'm going to need another edge."

This is the World at Six, the announcer's voice crackled the radio speaker in the repair shop at Sunshine Salvage. Isaac wasn't really paying attention as he was up to his elbows in servicing the Paystar. He hears bits of news about the state of the worsening economy and crippling sanctions the Empire had placed on nations who dared to defy their policies. News of another mass shooting by a first wave SS Peacekeeper suffering from PTSD made Isaac shake his head in dismay. "There's more to it than PTSD!" Isaac replies to the radio out loud. "They're all going crazy, you're just not telling us why." Isaac finishes working on the truck and is cleaned up by the end of the news.

Finishing the supper dishes, he relaxes in his chair with a sigh to watch some TV. A buzzing in his pocket accompanied by a melody makes him twist awkwardly as he retrieves the phone from his front pants pocket. "Hi Sunshine Salvage," Isaac's voice is jovial.

All forms of electronic communication were routed through biometric software intended to monitor and gather intel for the Empire's big data analysis systems. Due to this, the caller's words are carefully chosen. "Hello Isaac," came a familiar female voice from the past. "I need you to look at some old iron with me and give me a price for it."

Isaac recognized the voice instantaneously as Becky's. "I'm glad you called! Where is this old iron, I'd love to see it. When would be good?" His heart immediately reset to how he felt about her years before.

"I, I need to take you to it in person," she whispered into the phone.

"Anytime would be good, I'm free right now if you want!" After a long winter of separation his heart was blooming in the warmth of her voice and he was eager for the springtime of their reunion to arrive.

"I couldn't do it that soon. I can't see you for a day or two," her voice was filled with concern and fear.

"Ya. I could be free in a day and a half if that would work for you. Where could we meet to go look at the iron." Isaac asks cryptically.

"What do you pay for old scrap iron? I should find out first before I waste your time."

"The going rate is around five to eight cents per pound, minus the fee for pick up."

"Oh. I was expecting more than that! I'll have to make a u turn in my plans if that's all I can get. I was hoping for more."

"That's the rate. I need to make a living too. I don't have much wiggle room."

"Well, forget about meeting me. I'll do something else."

"I'm sorry I can't help you. Why don't you check around for better pricing? If you change your mind give us another call."

"I'll do that. Thanks for your help." The line went dead, and Becky was gone.

Isaac puts his phone away and distractedly watches the rest of his show as old thoughts of Becky race through his mind. Then he gets ready to go out. Putting on a long, dark, raincoat over his black hoodie, he scans a row of masks on the ledge above the coat rack. "Who will I be tonight?" he says to himself out loud. "Nixon, Reagan, Chairman Mao?" Making his choice, he fits a silicone mask onto his face and pulls his hood loosely over his head. "Come, come, comrade. Ve go for a little ride," he says with a heavy Russian accent. Looking like Vladimir Putin, he steps out into the night.

Isaac gets into his car and heads west towards the coast. With the Empire having CCTV surveillance on all major highway routes, he's outfitted his old car for covert travel. The car has headlights and taillights that change in position, color and intensity and flexible exterior body panels that change shape with air pressure. This makes his car virtually impossible for the computers to track him in traffic, especially on a rainy dark night. However, he still takes precautions as he drives to his destination. He doesn't want to take any chances of being tracked. It's a moonless night with low clouds and heavy rain, making the dark roads hard to navigate.

As he drives his mind replays the happy times he spent with Becky, the love of his life. He hopes he read her signals properly, a day for an hour was easy, but her doing a u-turn in thinking made him ponder. It must have meant she wanted to meet where they went to be out of cell phone range back when they were dating. Mat would track her through her phone but there was an underpass at the u turn on the connector highway that was out of cell range. The highway hugged the mountainside of the narrow valley and with the uturn going under the steep roadway, it was the perfect place to hide from any form of surveillance. It wouldn't take him long to get there, not that it mattered, he would have driven anywhere to see Becky again.

Power outages due to decaying infrastructure made travelling the roads at night fraught with danger. After forty minutes Isaac turns up the old connector, ten minutes later he pulls onto the off ramp of the uturn route. Turning off the headlights he parks his car just inside the underpass tunnel. At the far end another car's silhouette was barely visible.

Isaac gets out of his car and tentatively makes his way into the darkness on foot, removing his mask within the safety of the tunnel. Twenty paces into the abyss he stops short at the sound of Becky's voice coming from the shadows.

"Hello Isaac. It's good to see you again," a dim flashlight beam illuminates Isaac's face.

"I'd say the same, but I can't see you. Come over here so I can see you better."

"No. Not yet. We need to talk first. I owe you an explanation. A lot has changed."

"OK, so explain. We're alone, we can talk here. This tunnel is out of cell range, there'll be no electronic eavesdropping. What do you need to tell me Beck?"

"When mom and I left Matt." Becky started tenderly. "I just had to get away from everything. It felt like my whole life had been out of my control and I had to make it mine. For good or bad, I couldn't let Matt control it any longer. I was mad at you for not rescuing me from home and him. You've always done the proper thing. I wanted to rebel. So I ran off with Bob. It didn't take long for him to be bored with me though. I was so empty, confused and stubborn. I changed into whoever he wanted me to be. Convincing myself it was what I wanted, I traded Matt's control over my life for his. When I finally got it together and woke up to reality, I didn't recognize myself anymore."

"Oh Becky, I'm so sorry I wasn't more assertive. I wish you had talked to me earlier." Isaac almost sobbed into the darkness. "We can make a new start if you want. I still love you."

"I'd love to. But I don't have much time left, it's all I can do to daily battle back the darkness."

"Why Beck? What's wrong? Let me fight it with you."

"No! It's too late for that. I just had to see you one last time. I've loved you since I was little, I just didn't fully understand it then. But I do now. Now that I can't have it."

Her voice cracking, Becky starts to softly cry. Isaac is quick to be at her side, holding her close. As he squeezes her tight he can feel her thick, well pronounced back muscles bulge under her light jacket. She reciprocates his affection with her own strong hug that took him by surprise. She wasn't the skinny, girly girl he remembered.

Feeling Isaac's hands on her back and shoulder muscles she whispers. "This is me now." Her voice several octaves lower than just a moment ago, almost unrecognizable to Isaac, taking him by surprise. "Bob wanted us to join the SS when it first started. I thought it would be exciting," continuing in her comfortable lower register. "We were given genetically modified steroids to bulk up, they worked very well. I'm not the Becky you once knew." Laughing sadly, she flexes her arm and shoulder muscles constricting Isaac momentarily, driving home her point. "The cost of taking those pills was our gender. Male and female, we're all eunuchs' now. We were the heroes, rescuing people from danger, sending them home to families that we could never have. The public adored us. We proudly wore our vibrant tattoos for all to see," she pulled the glove off her right hand and the tunnel was bathed in a kaleidoscope of changing colors emitting softly from the back of her hand. "Now I'm ashamed of it. People only see me as a potential bomb, ready to explode unexpectedly.

"It's beautiful! I've never seen one from this close before." Isaac was spellbound by her tattoo.

"Yes, it is beautiful and deadly. It's turning me into a self-destructive psychopath. I'm ready to kill people and then myself at the slightest provocation. That's why I've been fighting back against the Empire that cursed me with it. I've been supplying inside information to the local resistance. I know your part of it."

"That's how brother Matias got his information. You were feeding it to him," Isaac said in sudden realization.

"Ya, dad profited off me as much as he could. I didn't care. I hate the Empire more than him. I live only to destroy it with what little life I have left. I'm worth a lot to the rebellion as a spy inside the SS."

"You've supplied us with a great deal of information. They must be getting suspicious?"

"Yes. I'm sure they are. That's why this is my last installment." Becky puts a thumb drive into Isaac's coat breast pocket. "It's time for you to be the hero. This tattoo is going to get the best of me very soon. I just wish it could be used for good and the destruction of the Empire. I'd gladly give my life for that cause."

"Oh Becky!" Isaac's voice is softly sympathetic. "Don't be quick to give up your life. God works all things out for the good for those who love him."

Tenderly cradling Isaac's cheek in the palm of her hand Becky looks him in the eye, her voice back to where Isaac recognized it. "I never knew Jesus like you do. I did and said what I was expected too. It was never really from my heart but I hope that someday you can introduce me to the Jesus you know. I'd like to have a faithful relationship with your God. A God that's loving and faithful." Taking in a deep breath, Becky stands straight and smooths out her SS uniform against her firm contours. Turning off her feelings of love like a switch, her voice goes comfortably deep and as cold as her emotions.

"It's late. I've got to finish my patrol before I'm missed. I'm glad you made it here, this needs to be closure for us. I have no future to give you. I've chosen a different path than you and I'll walk mine to the end." Straining her voice back up to her old pitch, she squeezes Isaac's hand tightly. With a tear in her eye she says, "Becky is gone now. She won't be back! Goodbye my love."

"Becky don't go," Isaac pleads as she walks back to her car. "We can work it out. I have a place we can go to. The Empire won't find us. God will supply our needs. I love you!" Isaac pours out his heart to a retreating figure disappearing into the darkness.

Becky turns with her cruiser door open and before getting in she hollers to Isaac, her voice deep and commanding, "Give me three minutes lead time before you head back to town. I can't be traced to you or we're both dead."

"Becky..." Isaac starts to reply but is cut off.

"Three minutes!" came a loud angry response. Then the slam of a car door followed by the roar of her overpowered pursuit cruiser's engine as she speeds away.

Isaac slowly heads to his car to wait out the appropriate time when he hears the unmistakable muffled sound of an Empire surveillance drone passing overhead. He runs to the tunnel entrance for a better look. Standing stealthily beside a tree at the edge of the highway he watches as the drone fires a rocket into Becky's car about a tenth of a mile away. Engulfed in flames, the cruiser cartwheels and slides upside down along the concrete barrier, before finally coming to a crumpled rest at the side of the road. Isaac sprints to the crash site. There was no surviving the devastation. Drenched by the falling rain Isaac tries to get to Becky's side but is blocked by the flames. Staggering in mental anguish, he breaks down in tears along the median barricade. After a few minutes, he realizes his peril. The fire would surely draw the SS and if he was caught out on the highway without the proper passes he would be aggressively interrogated. Isaac reluctantly tears himself away from Becky's funeral pyre.

Walking back to his car, he notices a soft glow in the ditch. It was Becky's ungloved right hand. It had been severed cleanly off at the forearm in the crash, it's tattoo's living organisms glow brightly, still thriving off her dead body. Picking it up gently he makes a promise to Becky, "I'll make sure this is put to good use in fighting the Empire. Just like you wanted." Hearing no trace of the drone, Isaac hurries to his car and hastily makes his way back to Sunshine Salvage as the rain continues to fall out of the inky black sky.

In the south-central part of Africa, the Empire's presence has hardly been felt. Insulated from the Empire's crippling edicts because of his absolute monarchy, Mark, now Sovereign King, has been able to keep his small country free of Prophet Father's tyranny by granting small requests. Mark has just received another one that he will reluctantly fulfill.

"Musa, my trusted old friend." Mark welcomed his boyhood companion, into his royal presence warmly. "I have been requested to send ambassadors overseas to represent our nation within a joint multinational SS task force. We'll be overseeing the humane treatment of combatants who are rebelling against the Empire," Mark continued to explain. "Prophet Father is anxious to have things appear humane and beyond reproach. He wants unbiased, impartial observers to be embedded within the SS security troupes. I would like to send you as head of our small contingent. Taking part in this mission will go a long way in keeping our country free of Imperial scrutiny. Will you go?" Giving his trusted confidant the ability to bow out, Mark hoped he wouldn't.

"From our childhood I have served at your pleasure," Musa humbly responded. "It would be an honor to represent you and our country. Do you have any special instructions that I should carry out while on this assignment?" wondering if the King had any ulterior reasons for sending him.

"No. Nothing special. Only keep in mind the difficulties we have here at home. The rampant HIV rates and all the resulting orphans. You have always shown great wisdom in your judgements!" Mark praised his friend. "I will back you and all your decisions," the King assured. "Go do your best and may God be with you."

With that brief conversation, Musa prepares his team to leave. He was almost ready to depart a week later when news of a natural disaster of unprecedented proportions was broadcast around the world. It appears the guns of the Beast wouldn't be needed to tame the troublesome nations after all. After fulfilling an ancient promise to their forefathers by blessing their nations for the past multiple centuries, God has seen fit to punish them himself through a series of natural disasters.

Prophet Father was correct in identifying the troublesome nations as coming from stiff-necked and rebellious tribes. The descendants from the split tribe of Joseph, Ephraim and Manasseh, arrogantly assumed God was blessing them as a result of their own righteousness and virtue. The question now was, how many disasters would it take to break their pride, turning them from their sins and to him in repentance? Only time would tell what kind of disaster would be needed to wake them from their slumber. They had strayed so far from God's truths that their nations resembled Sodom and Gomorrah more than societies where the people loved and followed God. We are reminded in Genesis 19 what it was like in those two notorious towns of old.

1-11 New International Version

1 The two angels arrived at Sodom in the evening, and Lot was sitting in the gateway of the city. When he saw them, he got up to meet them and bowed down with his face to the ground.

2 "My lords," he said, "please turn aside to your servant's house. You can wash your feet and spend the night and then go on your way early in the morning."

"No," they answered, "we will spend the night in the square."

3 But he insisted so strongly that they did go with him and entered his house. He prepared a meal for them, baking bread without yeast, and they ate.

4 Before they had gone to bed, all the men from every part of the city of Sodom—both young and old—surrounded the house.

5 They called to Lot, "Where are the men who came to you tonight? Bring them out to us so that we can have sex with them."

6 Lot went outside to meet them and shut the door behind him

7 and said, "No, my friends. Don't do this wicked thing.

8 Look, I have two daughters who have never slept with a man. Let me bring them out to you, and you can do what you like with them. But don't do anything to these men, for they have come under the protection of my roof."

9 "Get out of our way," they replied. "This fellow came here as a foreigner, and now he wants to play the judge! We'll treat you worse than them." They kept bringing pressure on Lot and moved forward to break down the door.

10 But the men inside reached out and pulled Lot back into the house and shut the door.

11 Then they struck the men who were at the door of the house, young and old, with blindness so that they could not find the door.

Some readers may find it fanciful to think that a nation blessed by God would sink as low as those wicked towns of antiquity. The Bible records what it was like in parts of ancient Israel before it too was punished by God. Destroying them with foreign nations, God had to shake them to their core before they would turn back to him.

Judges 19:14-30 New International Version

14 So they went on, and the sun set as they neared Gibeah in Benjamin.

15 There they stopped to spend the night. They went and sat in the city square, but no one took them in for the night.

16 That evening an old man from the hill country of Ephraim, who was living in Gibeah (the inhabitants of the place were Benjamites), came in from his work in the fields.

17 When he looked and saw the traveler in the city square, the old man asked, "Where are you going? Where did you come from?"

18 He answered, "We are on our way from Bethlehem in Judah to a remote area in the hill country of Ephraim where I live. I have been to Bethlehem in Judah and now I am going to the house of the Lord.[a] No one has taken me in for the night.

19 We have both straw and fodder for our donkeys and bread and wine for ourselves your servants—me, the woman and the young man with us. We don't need anything."

20 "You are welcome at my house," the old man said. "Let me supply whatever you need. Only don't spend the night in the square."

21 So he took him into his house and fed his donkeys. After they had washed their feet, they had something to eat and drink.

22 While they were enjoying themselves, some of the wicked men of the city surrounded the house. Pounding on the door, they shouted to the old man

who owned the house, "Bring out the man who came to your house so we can have sex with him."

23 The owner of the house went outside and said to them, "No, my friends, don't be so vile. Since this man is my guest, don't do this outrageous thing.

24 Look, here is my virgin daughter, and his concubine. I will bring them out to you now, and you can use them and do to them whatever you wish. But as for this man, don't do such an outrageous thing."

25 But the men would not listen to him. So the man took his concubine and sent her outside to them, and they raped her and abused herthroughout the night, and at dawn they let her go.

26 At daybreak the woman went back to the house where her master was staying, fell down at the door and lay there until daylight.

27 When her master got up in the morning and opened the door of the house and stepped out to continue on his way, there lay his concubine, fallen in the doorway of the house, with her hands on the threshold.

28 He said to her, "Get up; let's go." But there was no answer. Then the man put her on his donkey and set out for home.

29 When he reached home, he took a knife and cut up his concubine, limb by limb, into twelve parts and sent them into all the areas of Israel.

30 Everyone who saw it was saying to one another, "Such a thing has never been seen or done, not since the day the Israelites came up out of Egypt. Just imagine! We must do something! So speak up!"

Leaders that follow worldly wisdom have always become corrupt like the world they get their wisdom from. Many Kings of ancient Israel became corrupt, leading their people away from God.

2 Kings 16:1-4 King James Version (KJV)
1 In the seventeenth year of Pekah the son of Remaliah Ahaz the son of Jotham king of Judah began to reign.
2 Twenty years old was Ahaz when he began to reign, and reigned sixteen years in Jerusalem, and did not that which was right in the sight of the Lord his God, like David his father.
3 But he walked in the way of the kings of Israel, yea, and made his son to pass through the fire, according to the abominations of the heathen, whom the Lord cast out from before the children of Israel.
4 And he sacrificed and burnt incense in the high places, and on the hills, and under every green tree.

The modern leaders and elite of these rebellious, blessed nations were similar to those ancient kings of Israel. Following the wisdom of their day, chasing worldly gods, they rejected Biblical morality. Succumbing to the will of society and abandoning their role as loving shepards, the leaders permitted their people to follow ancient Israel's evil paths such as the thoughtless discarding of children.

Hearing the news of natural disasters, Musa changed his plans. He now expected to be on a humanitarian relief mission.

"God please guide my paths. May I please you as I serve my country and king. Help me to be a blessing to those that I can and may I be an agent for accomplishing your will," Musa prayed earnestly as he organized paperwork for his assignment.

For decades, the weather had been growing more unpredictable. There had always been storms and flooding, that was a natural part of seasonal change, but over the previous decades the extremes in weather had been swinging further towards destruction. Now extreme weather seemed to be the norm. Hot tower storms reaching over 14 kilometers in height spawned the most devastating hurricanes. Forming over increasingly hotter ocean waters, in a matter of days, the moist air would rise to the top of the thunder head. At the cold top, moisture would collect and fall out as rain. The resulting cool air would descend rapidly, spiraling to the ground. These fast forming, unpredictable weather events became the norm, leaving residents of the southeastern coastlines of North America weary of their repeated devastation.

Super-sized weather didn't make these nations turn to God for help. Rather than acknowledging their blessings were from God, officials explained why the weather was becoming more extreme through science. Governments helped prepare the populations for worst case scenarios.

No one in leadership thought to seek the face of their benevolent heavenly father in repentance.

The news outlets reported the 9.3 magnitude earthquake occurred at 3:47 AM Pacific standard time. After building tension for nearly four centuries, the slow-moving Juan de Fuca tectonic plate violently forced its way seventy feet under the North American plate. Resulting in devastation from the gold fields of Eureka, to God's Pocket Provincial Park on northern Vancouver Island, towns and cities were razed up and down the Pacific Coast of North America. The resulting tsunamis around the Pacific Basin flooded and washed the shoreline clean for 100 feet above sea level. Again, the leaders were ignorant as to the reasons why they suffered. None bent their knee to God or led their people in repentance.

Costs for the cleanup and helping the survivors were staggering. The governments, strapped for cash, received credit from the Holy Roman Empire. The Emperor Prophet Father made sure the international bankers were generous lenders to the beleaguered nations in their time of need. In the face of security concerns like international banking scams, identity theft and widespread fraud the Emperor insisted the SS identification system be extended to include the general public.

To give the voluntary system a kickstart, he ordered relief money be paid out in Empire credits, demanding his mark be used for monetary transactions and as security passes to reduce crime. Happy to receive the newly introduced personal ID markings along with their Imperial credits, civilians willingly get their tattoos.

Isaac, Stubby and other resistance members hold out, reluctant to receive the Empire's mark.

Chapter 13

Unable to avoid roadblocks undetected by using back roads, Isaac discovered a new way through the Imperial security checks. He found that by keeping the severed end of Becky's hand wet with a sugar water solution, the tattoo's microorganisms thrived with brilliant iridescent colors as well as preserving the flesh from decay. He mounted the hand on a short, wooden handle that held the water solution. Holding it from inside his coat sleeve, he would wave the hand's iridescent tattoo from his truck window to the check point guards.

Recognizing the brilliant display as a first-generation SS tattoo, guards feared a potentially deadly, psychotic explosion. They were careful not to upset Isaac with any questions. Assuming Isaac had transitioned out of the SS into a semi-retired civilian job, they would only smile and nod their respect as they waved him through their checkpoints. Recognizing the source of their discomfort, Isaac grew his hair longer and teased it so it would stand up in a crazy, frizzy mess. He also grew his beard out scraggly, giving him the look of a deranged axe murderer.

Stubby's language had started to mellow the more he was around people. Making food and first aid drops to those in need gave him a good feeling inside. He especially enjoyed helping the kids who were hungry and needed his help. Often families of bottom rung Empire staff were in dire need. Both sides came to respect and appreciate Isaac and Stubby's help. Buying supplies on the black market wasn't that easy if you weren't using Imperial credits. Still collecting salvage, Stubby and Isaac found that precious metals and hard to find machine parts were easy to barter with, as those supplies were valued everywhere.

Most rebel members were actively engaging the Empire in armed guerilla warfare. Isaac and Stubby were busy in the humanitarian wing of the resistance. As they had declared at the start, they would not take up arms to fight the SS troops but helped those in need regardless of affiliation. When pressed as to why, Isaac would answer for them both. His talking points were around how they preferred to follow the example Jesus gave of loving those who hate you and how the best sermons were the ones where you didn't say anything but let your deeds speak for you. Stubby was always thought to be very wise, as he silently let Isaac eloquently do the talking. He would often look thoughtfully at the ground or prayerfully into the sky as he smiled shyly nodding his head, all the while not uttering one word.

At a packed strategy meeting held in a rebel HQ boardroom, Stubby and Isaac's loyalties are being angrily drawn into question.

"You're both cowards!" Brother Matias hollers red faced, slamming his fist on the table knocking over several glasses of water. "We must have a united, obedient force. You will follow our orders or we'll consider you both traitors to our cause. When we give you a shipment to move, you deliver it! Does this council make itself clear?" Showing his domineering, dictatorial side, Matias angrily denounces the pair of free thinkers in front of him.

"We both voluntarily joined as conscientious objectors," Isaac calmly replied. "We were up front and open with how we'd participate in the resistance. Our position has not changed. As members of the Humanitarian Medic Core we will not bear or transport arms and munitions."

"You'll follow orders or I'll have you court martialed for insurrection and confiscate your property," Brother Matias said so forcefully he couldn't contain his spittle. "Even our evangelists are required to go out on dangerous sorties. They actively preach the Gospel to the lost on their own time. Why should you get special treatment? You don't actively preach salvation to people on your time off."

"We explain the coming Kingdom of God to those who express an interest. God calls those he wants to Jesus. Those who are interested and called will ask for more information," Isaac responds passionately. "It's not as though everyone can come to Jesus now. They must be drawn to Jesus by God. Unlike what you teach, now isn't everyone's time to follow Jesus. But in the coming Kingdom all will have their opportunity to receive salvation."

"That's just another example of your stubbornness," Matias snaps. "You think you're right about everything, including the Gospel of Jesus. You ignore Godly wisdom from those of us who have spent lifetimes serving Jesus. Your lips condemn you. This will be your first and only warning! Next time we'll make an example of you for others who think they can do as they please and get away with it," Brother Matias glares at Isaac in disgust.

"This is a rebellion? We are the rebels? Right?" Isaac questions aggressively. "Well then," Isaac says shrugging his shoulders and gesturing with his hands palms up, "we rebel!" With those final words Isaac and Stubby turn and quickly leave the meeting. Brother Matias, along with the other leaders, are still shouting insults and threats at them as they exit the command bunker and climb into the Paystar.

"%$#@ that man is full of himself! What a %$#@in @$$ hole."

"I completely agree with you Stubby. I completely agree," Isaac says nodding his head while shifting gears, leaving the HQ parking lot in a black cloud of smoke. "We'll help in our own way. Independently."

It may have been several months later going by solar time, but it was the next moment after the big earthquake in geological time. Everyone in the country was hard at work cleaning up and repairing the devastation. People were happily employed and living off borrowed Empire money when the first rumblings started at Yellowstone. Isaac and Stubby were busy stockpiling food and supplies at their old mine-site when they saw the first bits of ash falling from the darkening sky. News on the Paystar's radio explained how volcanologists believed the recent west coast earthquake triggered the 60-kilometer-long, 25-kilometer-wide and 12-kilometer-deep, Yellowstone caldera to erupt. They explain how it was lucky for the world that it was a limited eruption and that only part of the caldera's estimated 1544-cubic-kilometer volume was ejected into the atmosphere of western North America. Life was about to get harder, but still there was no talk of appealing to God for help from the continent's leaders.

More earthquakes struck over the next two weeks, this time in southern California. The buildings were less affected as the building codes had become more stringent in those areas. Most of the damage and loss of life came from the localized tsunamis that suddenly thundered ashore. They destroyed the low-lying area around Santa Barbara and Santa Monica Bay. The tsunami with the greatest economic devastation was saved for the one generated by the localized Santa Catalina Island fault zone.

Most faults along the southern California coast are strike-slip faults, where tectonic plates slide past each other. However, these slip areas are not always straight. There are areas that have bends. Bends form a strike forcing one side of the fault upwards at the bend as the rest of the larger fault slides sideways. Areas where there is a bend will build up tension as the plates continue to slide. When a large earthquake occurs offshore relieving the restraining bends built up energy, the ocean floor is pushed up along the entire bends edge forming a tsunami. One such bend is directly below Santa Catalina Island, which was formed by being pushed up from the ocean's depths.

Facing Catalina, San Pedro Bay is home to the Los Angeles and Long Beach container ports where billions of dollars' worth of material pass daily. The largest stress release in centuries resulted in a 12-foot tsunami. It was amplified by the shallow San Pedro shelf to 18 feet by the time it slammed into the inside harbor of San Pedro Bay. Extensive damage to the port's infrastructure would have taken years to repair under normal circumstances, but in the stressed climate of the day, it was just one more nail in the North American coffin.

Satellites were still offline as Yellowstone ash spread its blinding dust layer across North America. Communications within the continent were poor at best as modern technologies proved vulnerable to the natural disasters. The true extent of the latest west coast disaster was hard to decipher amidst the conflicting reports. Another cluster of tornadoes ripping through the eastern plains didn't even make the evening news.

There was another disaster that did get the attention of the world though. A disaster Speckle hadn't covered in his class. With over four hundred and fifty dams over its two thousand kilometers, the Columbia River of western North America is the most dammed river in the world. The river was first harnessed for hydroelectricity production at Spokane in 1885. The last hydro dam, built near the top of the Colombia, was completed by BC Hydro in 1984 using a blend of concrete and earth fill design. Located sixty four kilometers upriver from the Revelstoke dam, on the west bank of the reservoir, sits the largest active unstable slope in the world. Measuring 2400 meters wide and running 3300 meters up the mountain side, the Downie Slide is steadily creeping towards the Revelstoke reservoir.

The Columbia River basin had been economically exploited throughout the twentieth century, but one development in particular has left an indelible stain. Established in 1943, the first full-scale plutonium production reactor in the world was built on the banks of the Columbia River. Known as the Hanford site, it covers 586 square miles. The Columbia runs down its eastern edge, turns westwards and then bends through the northern quarter of the site. Needing river water for cooling, the nine reactors were located conveniently close to the river. The rest of the site housed processing plants, support buildings, laboratories, underground tank farms and contaminated waste dumps. The site is recognized as the most contaminated place in the western hemisphere. Overwhelmed by the scale and complexity of the cleanup, as of 2020, officials say they have no projected clean-up date for the site.

The devastating earthquakes shook the bedrock of the Columbia's headwaters, shifting Mica dam's earth filled base. Damaged, it started to let Kim Basket Lake escape its hold. Filling the downstream earth fill portion of the Revelstoke dam beyond its high-water safety limits, the dam was unable to withhold the wall of water set in motion by the sudden drop of the Downie Slide. The uncontrolled water soon burst through the earth fill portion, draining the reservoir in a wild torrent. The resulting wall of water continued downstream taking out all the dams it encountered, growing in size and devastation every time it burst through another obstacle along the Columbia River.

Making its way down the river's basin towards the Pacific, the wall of water does in days, what government agencies couldn't even imagine doing in decades. It scrubbed clean all contaminated waste from the Hanford site, distributing it downstream and along the coastline as it was washed out to sea. Within weeks the death toll from radiation sickness across all species including humans, was epidemic along the continent's north west coast.

Seeing little chance the indebted nations would repay their debt and staggering under the economic burden of their own natural disasters, the Empire's bankers demanded an immediate foreclosure of North American assets be implemented. The transferable reserves are siphoned off first, then the precious metals and what was left of exportable natural resources.

Unexpectedly, the world is beset by a new plague coming out of the sky in the form of stinging, winged insects, the likes of which no one had ever seen before. Randomly attacking people whenever they were in the open, there seemed to be no outdoor space where you would be safe from them. Despite the new peril, the SS become looters rather than benevolent aid workers, scouring the once proud world leading nations for anything of value

Before long, the poorer classes of the population are seen in monetary terms and are sold off as indentured servants to wealthy foreigners, helping to repay the national debt. Forced labor camps are set up near natural resources, enabling quick processing and shipping of valued commodities back to creditor nations.

Musa and his team find it hard to temper the SS troops as they victimize and rob the beaten down populations of the rebellious nations. Having received orders to plunder anything of value, SS troops eagerly confiscate whatever they can carry. Expecting to be helping those in need, Musa is disturbed with how the local inhabitants are being treated. Many kind and loving people were brought to nothing. Remembering Mark's words to look for ways to help their own countrymen whenever possible, Musa sets up a migrant, volunteer worker program to help citizens escape their devastated country to his poor but safe African nation. Musa is determined to help all who would receive his offer and escape to freedom. Mark's royal aircraft were soon flying mercy flights, full of those volunteers, to their new lives of volunteer service in a safe new country.

Hearing of a way to escape the tyranny of Prophet Father, those refusing to accept the economic and security markings of the Beast worldwide are glad for any relief. Accepting King Mark's offer to join the volunteer worker program, those who cling to their Christian beliefs of love eagerly trade their labor for room, board, and religious freedom. They flock into Marks country through any means possible, some quickly on unregulated royal flights, others on slower ground transport. They lovingly minister to the king's subjects, laboriously providing the physical and emotional needs of the orphans left from the years of an ongoing HIV AIDS epidemic.

Through all this, Isaac and Stubby remain free as they continue to exist on the outskirts of legality. Empire control was nearly impossible to avoid. Seeing the need to help, Isaac and Stubby begin to smuggle vulnerable children to safe houses, keeping them out of sweatshops, or worse, sent off to service SS troops in Imperial brothels around the world.

It had been almost three and a half years since the Holy Roman Empire was revived for the tenth and final time under the co-leadership of the Beast and Prophet Father. From its conception, there were many internal tensions within their Empire. Political unions are usually formed out of necessity, rather than fondness of the partners, making the military colossus politically fragile. This unstable union is what God had foretold would take place thousands of years earlier in the book of Daniel. God predicted the Empire Jesus returns to battle and destroy at the end time, would be formed from a mixture of iron and clay. Prophet Father's world ruling Empire, held together by the military might of the Beast, was as fragile as a clay pot.

Daniel 2:31-35 King James Version (KJV)
31 Thou, O king, sawest, and behold a great image. This great image, whose brightness was excellent, stood before thee; and the form thereof was terrible.

32 This image's head was of fine gold, his breast and his arms of silver, his belly and his thighs of brass,

33 His legs of iron, his feet part of iron and part of clay.

34 Thou sawest till that a stone was cut out without hands, which smote the image upon his feet that were of iron and clay, and brake them to pieces.

35 Then was the iron, the clay, the brass, the silver, and the gold, broken to pieces together, and became like the chaff of the summer threshing floors; and the

wind carried them away, that no place was found for them: and the stone that smote the image became a great mountain, and filled the whole earth.

After establishing his control over the world's cultural, economic, military and faith institutions, Prophet Father felt he still wasn't receiving the adoration he deserved. His desire to be revered by others was unquenchable. Knowing the worldwide, loving respect he desired would only come to him if he did something spectacular, something the entire world would be grateful for, he kept his scientists and military weapons experts working on eliminating the large stinging insects that had been punishing the earth's inhabitants unchecked.

After his spectacular demonstration, he would move into a more prestigious office space. One he had always aspired to occupy, one more suited for God's representative on earth. Knowing, to break his pledge in keeping Jerusalem neutral for all faiths to enjoy he would have to be worshipped as a Caesar of old by all the leaders of the world. Emotionally fragile, requiring constant praise, Prophet Father started planning to move his office and residence onto the sacred temple mount once he could eliminate the stinging menace.

Until then he kept the world's nations in line through crippling trade sanctions and tariffs against those who dared not follow his imperial edicts. When economic intimidation didn't work, the blunt, brute force of the Beast was liberally used. Crushing the once divinely blessed and proud world leading nations hadn't been hard for the Beast after the natural disasters all but destroyed them. With the banker's loans still not paid back,

Imperial troops led by the now feared SS, started grinding the debtor nations bones, extracting anything and everything of value. It's within these national death throes of confusion we find Isaac and Stubby, along with a small band of conscientious objectors they've befriended, doing their best to stay alive.

"That's going to be my last trip!" Isaac exclaimed to Stubby as he came through the office door with a small crowd of children surrounding him. "The SS troops must have orders to check everything no matter what. I just barely got through a roadside check. The officers all but ignored the infectious biohazard decals. They almost pulled the tarps back to look inside the drums."

"You had kids hidden in those drums!" Stubby gestured towards the small group of discarded children entering the office with Isaac. "The SS would have detained all of you! What did you do to get away?" Stubby said deeply concerned, demonstrating remarkable verbal self-control in front of the orphans.

"I could see in the mirrors the SS were ignoring the warning placards. So, I opened an old package of ketchup and squeezed it onto my face mask, adding a bit of water made it runny. When I put the mask on, the ketchup looked like blood dripping down onto my chest and it formed a red hazy cloud around my face when I breathed out. I jumped out of the truck waving my arms frantically and yelling, plague, stay back, plague! They almost got up onto the deck before I managed to stop them. I had to stagger and look like I was ready to faint before they would buy it. Once a swarm of those stinging bugs attacked, they couldn't leave fast enough. I didn't even have to flash the tattoo. Good thing, as it was still in the truck."

"I think you're right. The fu..." Stubby stops himself from talking just as one of the newly arrived malnourished orphans nervously reaches out to hold his hand. Composing himself, he chooses his words more carefully. "The Empire has taken everything of value. Our small group isn't much help here anymore. We're at the end of our fuel reserves for the truck, there's just enough diesel to get us back to the mine. We better leave while we can still get out."

"Let's talk to the others. If we choose to go, we should leave before dawn."

Having decided to escape while they could was their best option, the small group was busy that evening and late into the night preparing to bug out. Most personal items were always packed, but the old Paystar and pup trailer needed to be outfitted to carry people. Isaac and Stubby would be collecting those leaving with them from safe houses around town with the old truck. They strapped the body of an old school bus onto the deck of the Paystar and another one onto the three-axle pup trailer after removing the large fuel tank from off its frame rails. Welding chunks of scrap iron inside the bus bodies to block the windows, it made it appear the old bus bodies were full of scrap going to be processed rather than human occupants.

By now the old Paystar was known by the local SS as the town's scrap and bio waste truck. The new unsightly mess fit the image the authorities had grown to expect from Isaac, who they believed to be one of their own forced into early retirement with PTSD. Thinking his psychopathy was due to work related chemical exposure, they pitied him. Doing their best not to provoke him into a violent rage, they avoided him whenever possible. Having won many a poker hand with a bluff, Isaac took full advantage of their ignorance.

This strategy had worked well for Isaac since he had started waving Becky's amputated, tattooed hand, but unbeknownst to him and his friends, today was the first day of an Imperial crack down. All dissidents, especially those with ethical contentions against the Empire, were to be forcefully detained. Prophet Father was now insisting the world idolize him along with giving him their full exuberant, religious devotion. If it wasn't freely offered, he was now prepared to demand it.

Early before dawn Isaac parked the Paystar and trailer unit on a side street next to a tree lined park. Those escaping from the safe houses would rendezvous there and clandestinely load into the bus bodies a few at a time. The plan was to be loaded and ready to leave by noon. At nine a.m. an SS commander, freshly in from headquarters, stopped to tell Isaac he had to clear the street. Not put off by Isaacs usual tattoo revealing wave, he insisted the truck be moved immediately. Isaac started the truck with a frown and slowly drove down the street and around the block, parking on the other side of the park.

Two hours later the same SS commander was barking orders at Isaac to again be on his way. He was offended by the sight of the old truck and demanded it be out of his precinct. Isaac again gave his normal salute with Becky's tattoo. By this time they were only waiting for one more safe house to arrive and load into the bus bodies. Isaac drove a few blocks towards that last safe house and parked at the crest of a small hill. Setting the truck spring brakes so the truck wouldn't roll away, Isaac's mind wanders, thinking about Mum and where she might be.

Having volunteered to go overseas with a humanitarian NGO, Isaac hadn't heard from her since the Empire took full control of social media. Having lost contact with her, he prayed she was somewhere safe. Silently beseeching God for his continued mercies, Isaac and his compatriots wait quietly in the truck for the last safe house residents to arrive.

The last child was just getting settled into the trailer when the same new SS commander pulled his patrol car alongside the Paystar cab where Isaac was outside stretching his legs. Hurriedly getting out of his cruiser the SS commander started yelling at Isaac for not following his orders to leave the area.

"I'll teach you to obey my orders!" the SS commander barked. Walking briskly towards Isaac he cocked his handgun. Pointing the pistol towards Isaac he fired repeatedly, emptying the clip into the battery box of the Paystar just behind where Isaac was standing. Battery acid was soon pouring from the destroyed batteries behind the light aluminum battery box cover, forming toxic puddles on the dusty ground. "I'll send over one of our wreckers to collect your sorry mess. The Empire will impound and scrap this old junk heap ourselves." Not saying another word the SS commander turned on his heel back to his squad car. With the engine roaring and tires spinning, he left Isaac in a spray of gravel and dust.

Stubby's head emerged out the driver's window. "Now what are we going to do without any batteries?

One of the noncombatants jumped down from the bus body. "We're dead in the water! We can't get the ECM to work without at least 8 volts let alone run the starter. We better get everyone back to their safe houses and try again later."

"There won't be a later. We have to go now or we'll all be caught!" Isaac insisted loudly. "We don't need the batteries." Isaac explains, "this is an old truck, completely mechanical." With that Isaac climbed up onto the driver's front fender and flipped the hood wing open. Reaching down to the fuel pump, behind the tachometer cable, he turns the thumb screw clockwise into the electric fuel shut off solenoid, locking it into manual mode. Closing the hood and doing up the latches he hollers to everyone, "Load up! We're gonna go."

After isolating the batteries by turning off the night switches with a quarter turn, Isaac bounds into the driver's seat. Once behind the steering wheel he puts the tranny into third gear and depresses the clutch as he releases the spring brakes and charges the trailer with air. It takes a moment but the pull of gravity slowly works on the Paystar and the wheels start to turn as they head down the hill. Before long they're going 20 km/h and Isaac pops the clutch. The KTA sparks to life with a rumble.

Unsure they were going to get the truck started, Stubby hollers from the passenger seat with a wide grin of relief, "I love this %$#@in old truck."

Nodding his head, Isaac smiles, "Me too! Technology isn't all it's cracked up to be."

Passing a coffee shop on their way out of town, they are spotted by the hot-tempered SS commander. His surprise and anger at seeing the Paystar rolling past was displayed on his face as he rushed out of the coffee shop door to his cruiser. He is soon on their tail with lights flashing and sirens blaring. Pulling alongside the driver's door he waves his pistol at Isaac, motioning for him to stop.

"I don't think there'll be any bluffing him!" Isaac hollers to Stubby.

"He'll search us for sure. %$#@! We can't get caught with all these people, we'll all be sent to the %$#@in detention work camps, or worse!"

"Well they haven't stopped us yet!" Isaac replies. He swerves hard to the left into the path of the cruiser.

The SS commander brakes hard, successfully avoiding the big old truck's duels but forgetting about the pup trailer it was dragging. The fully exposed trailer's lead axle tires slam the back end of the cruiser to the ground as they climb up onto its rear bumper and trunk. Treating the cruiser like a toy Hot Wheels car, the trailer tires continue to flatten the passenger side up to the front seat. Spitting it forcefully out from under its bulk, the cruiser spins half a turn before the tires on the tandem rear axles of the trailer slam into its front right fender, flattening the hood. The cruiser smolders in a cloud of dust and smoke at the edge of the road. Any fears of the SS commander being killed were alleviated when he was heard on the police monitor calling for a roadblock to be set up ahead of the old Paystar before it reaches the highway and escapes.

Light grey smoke pours out of the twin five-inch stacks as Isaac presses the throttle to the floor coming out of a corner. The RPM reaches the governor and Isaac shifts up another gear. Now on a straightaway, he can see the troopers setting up a hasty roadblock. More cruisers arrive, parking in diagonal rows two to three deep, blocking the road ahead.

"They're getting out their %$#@in EMP blasters and spike belts." Stubby yells as he squints through the windshield. "I've seen those %$#@in electromagnetic pulse blasters melt control modules down to nothing but a %$#@in blob of %$#@in plastic. Can we get through?"

"The belts and blasters won't bother us much." Isaac replies loudly. "Tires are no flats and everything else is fully mechanical. Remember? All we have to do is get through those cruisers." He says a silent prayer to God for help as he makes sure all his electric switches are off protecting each circuit from an electrical overload. Then he picks up two more gears, propelling the Paystar to its maximum speed.

Showing no sign of slowing down the SS troopers scatter as the old Paystar barrels towards them. Diving into the ditches, covering their heads with their arms, they lie prostrate on the ground. With the spike belts already in place, those who must, ready the EMP blasters and wait for the Paystar to come into range. Seconds later the SS EMP squad sends their concentrated, high powered EMP waves into the Paystar expecting it to catch on fire from melting electronic components and come to a quick stop as the failing ABS system makes a full brake application. They were bewildered when the only smoke the Paystar emitted was from the stacks as Isaac powered through the cruisers parked on the road, scattering them effortlessly into the ditches as crumpled heaps of tin.

As it turns out, the moose guard bush bar that was designed to protect the front end of the Paystar from any hazard it may encounter during off road operation, was equally effective at protecting it from any hazards the SS might put in front of it. Isaac and Stubby replaced the old original one with a heavily reinforced one made from High Specific Strength Steel they had salvaged from a decommissioned military base. The HSSS material was not only lighter than the original steel, but had the strength to rival titanium. Plowing through the SS cruisers and SUV's, barely put a scratch on it.

The bewildered SS battalion members gathered in the center of the road carefully avoiding broken bits of the shredded spike belt prongs as they watched the Paystar disappear onto the highway on ramp. Not able to give chase as they all had parked their cruisers on the road in the path of the old Paystar hoping to stop its progress, the SS now had no working vehicles in which to give chase or report their failure to headquarters from. Attracted by the cruiser's smoke, swarms of stinging insects start to descend on the exposed SS who had nowhere to take refuge.

Isaac, Stubby and their band of noncombatants seem to have made a clean getaway as the lingering atmospheric dust kept satellite surveillance blind. Isaac turns off the highway and hides on bush roads as he heads into the mountains towards their secret old mine sanctuary. Unable to stay on bush roads the whole way, Isaac was forced to travel for twelve kilometers on a main road after an hour or two of travelling on the bush roads. They had been on the blacktop for about eight klicks when they passed an SS cruiser parked on a side road.

"%$#@!" Stubby said impulsively while slapping his knee. "I hoped we might get away without being %$#@in seen."

"Ya. Me too." Isaac said sadly, checking the rearview mirrors. "Yup, here he comes. Not very fast though. He'll probably just bird dog us until backup arrives. Maybe we can lose him once we're back on the bush roads."

"Can you see what make of %$#@in cruiser he's driving? I think these %$#@in locals are using the %$#@in latest safety rated, semi-autonomous import models." Stubby has a sinister gleam in his eye. "Maybe there'll be something we can do to slow them down."

"You know. I've noticed you manage to not curse around the kids. If you tried, you could probably stop altogether." Isaac changes the subject with a positive tone.

"Ya, so what of it?" Stubby's replies seriously.

"Well, it would make you more approachable! You tend to scare people off with your language. Most people aren't used to that ruff talk of yours."

"%$#@, I know that. But it's like I have to say it. It's a %$#@in itch that I have to scratch. Sometimes once isn't enough. %$#@, I can make an entire sentence using %$#@. I just change the tone of my voice like this. %$#@? %$#@ %$#@ %$#@. %$#@, %$#@ %$#@ %$#@ %$#@ %$#@!" Stubby says earnestly with varying degrees of vocal inflection. "It just has to %$#@in come out."

"But you do manage to control yourself around the kids. It's the only time you don't swear. So it is possible. I just thought you might try to expand on your success. You limit yourself with your language." Isaac tries to explain his motives.

"Ya. I might try," Stubby replies. "But first we'll have to get away from the %$#@in SS or we won't be alive long enough to see any %$#@in results. I've got an idea. I'll get into the back and have the others work on it while we're %$#@in driving. Then later we'll put my plan into action."

"Sounds mysterious." Isaac replies as he checks on the cruiser using the door mirror.

While they're still rolling, Stubby pushes hard on the passenger door, opening it against the wind and sood on the cab step mounted onto the outside of the truck. While holding onto the handrail he swung himself around the back of the cab and stepped onto the fuel tank, barely getting up onto the deck and into the first school bus body. Stubby had thought several child sized mannequins might come in handy when they were loading the bus bodies onto the Paystar the previous night, so he stored them under the first few rows of seats. After getting them out he instructed the kids to dress them up in some extra old clothes they had, then he carefully made his way back into the truck cab.

"My diversion should be ready soon." Stubby said as he breathlessly sat in the passenger seat.

"Good, we'll need it! We've picked up two more cruisers. We'll be back on the dirt at the next corner. We should be able to put some distance on them as I know of some swampy roads those blacktop cruisers won't like," Isaac said, relieved to see Stubby safely back in the cab.

"Good! We'll need about ten minutes lead time to get my %$#@in trap set up. I'd like to do it along Crazy Creek, just after we enter the gorge. That first hair-pin corner should %$#@in work," Stubby shouts breathlessly.

The muddy swamp roads proved to be better at slowing the cruisers down than Isaac had imagined. The SS abandoned their lead cruiser after it got stuck in the mud, blocking the road and leaving it impassable. They had to turn the other cruisers around on the narrow goat trail and take a long detour before they got back onto a road they imagined Isaac to be on.

The police monitor in the Paystar was abuzz with frenzied chatter from the pursuing SS officers. Headquarters was frantically trying to send forestry road maps of possible routes the rebels could be taking to the cruiser's communication tablets. Not wanting the rebel truck to get away again, the SS were out for blood.

Chapter 14

After snaking along the Shuswap river for about five kilometers Isaac had to slow down for a ninety-degree hard right turn as the road narrowed and headed up Crazy Creek canyon.

"Pull over right here" Stubby instructed from the passenger seat.

The Paystar hadn't come to a stop before Stubby was out of the truck and swinging down to the ground from the handrail. Dircecting the people in the bus bodies to pass down the mannequins, he started carrying the first one towards the corner. Other rebels soon follow with the rest of the now dressed, childlike mannequins.

"Bring some shovels too!" Stubby yelled over his shoulder to one of the older kids.

He stands the first mannequins on the hill side of the gravel road, just out of the ditch before the road straightened coming out of the ninety-degree turn. Then, taking one long step towards the center of the road and one away from the inner ditch, he stood the next one heading in the same direction angling across the road towards the creek. He set the rest of them across the road until there was a diagonal line of childlike figures stretching completely across the narrow gravel road. Not visible before the blind corner, the most logical way to avoid hitting the mannequins crossing the road would be to steer to the left, leading off the road and over the sharp embankment into the fast-flowing Crazy Creek.

Not satisfied with his trap yet, Stubby and the rebels proceeded to spread loose gravel onto the roadway until there was about an inch of slippery rock on top of the hard-packed road surface. They did this on the corner and all around the mannequins making the curve even more treacherous for vehicles traveling on it.

"Ok. That should do it." Stubby said as he motioned for his helpers to get back to the truck. "We better get going before the SS get here."

After helping the last orphan back into a bus body, Stubby breathlessly climbs through the passenger door of the Paystar.

"That ought to slow those &@$% &#&$ down. Their %$#.." Stubby stops mid-sentence when he sees a wide-eyed orphan child sitting beside Isaac in the truck cab.

"What was that? I think you were saying something about Bass, fish poop and ducks? It's noisy in here, I can't figure out what you're talking about. You'll have to speak up." Isaac replies loudly with a big grin. "This is Sam." Isaac introduces the little boy to Stubby. "He wanted to ride up here with us. He's never been in a truck cab before."

Finally taking his eyes off the dash gauges Sam exclaims, "I want to drive a big truck like this when I grow up!" Only now being aware of Stubby's presence beside him, he slides his little bum closer to Isaac, making room for Stubby to sit on the bench seat beside him.

Stubby regains his composure. "We'll see how the SS like those automated assisted driving cruisers now. The algorithms are programmed for keeping pedestrians safe at all costs." Wiping sweat from his brow he adds loudly, "I was saying, I hope they'll soon be in the fish poop with the ducks."

"I think I see where this is going," Isaac replies as he puts the truck in gear and heads down the road. "Good restraint," he says to Stubby, trying not to laugh. "Just thought I'd help you in your efforts to improve your speaking habits."

Stubby glares at Isaac silently as Sam sits transfixed with all the goings on around him in the cab. They follow Crazy Creek for about a kilometer to where the gorge narrows. Crossing a short wooden bridge over the foaming water, the road made a hard-left switch back before leading down the opposite bank. They travel back towards the Shuswap river for about half a kilometer before turning right onto a narrow road that leads them steeply back into the bush. Several switchbacks later they are high above Crazy Creek gorge with a bird's eye view of the trap Stubby has set for the following SS. Hidden by trees, they park out of sight from the road below. Just before they drop over the ridge into the next valley, they stop to watch and see if their trap works.

Standing by the rear of the trailer on the side of the bush trail, Isaac, Stubby, and several of the other rebels don't have to wait long before the first SS cruiser came around the sharp corner entering Crazy Creek Canyon. Stumbling into Stubby's trap at a good speed, the autonomous driving, crash avoidance safety feature takes control of the cruiser just as Stubby had imagined it would. As soon as the on-board cameras identified children on the roadway, the safety automation took control of the car. Following its lightning fast preprogrammed analytics, the control module activates the hard brake application but has no effect on the cruiser's speed due to the slippery road conditions. The positronic brain directs the car to steer hard to the left to avoid the children at all costs. Recognizing there was a line of children across the traveled portion of the road, the microprocessor kept the front tires pointed hard to the left, launching the cruiser over the edge of the ditch and into the boiling water of Crazy Creek.

The first cruiser's hood had just started to follow the water's current downstream when it was joined by a second cruiser, pushing the first one further into the swift flowing water. Suffering from the same autonomous driving calamity, the SS members from both cruisers make a soggy retreat up the slippery, craggy bank and back onto the gravel road. They take great pleasure in punching, kicking and pushing the childlike mannequins over, then violently throw them into the ditch or Crazy Creek's turbulent flow.

"That worked great!" Isaac exclaimed, slapping Stubby's back with a laugh. "We better get going before reinforcements get here. Once we're over this hill we'll be into a labyrinth of interconnecting bush roads that have been used for resource extraction for decades. From those we'll be able to make our way into the Monashees and our old mine hideout undetected."

"Let's go then. Once we get this outfit hidden in the shop and us safely tucked into our mine shafts, I'll sure feel better," one of the other rebels says.

"Ya, that's the last I want to see of the SS," another one said as she made her way back to the truck mounted bus body. "I can't wait to be swallowed by the inky black of the mine's safety."

"We're stocked up for years to come if we need it. We've been organizing it for months now. We have fresh water from our underground creek, generating electricity by diverting it down one of the vertical shafts feeding the valley's ground water supply." Isaac's voice reflects the pride he has for the work the small group has put into the abandoned old mine site.

Stubby recalls an interview he had seen with Michelle Obama where she said she was very careful in choosing her words when she spoke. She stated that we normally only had one chance to connect with people, if we put them off at the start, we may never have another chance to influence them. With these thoughts in mind Stubby chooses his words carefully before he speaks. "We've carved out several secret escape routes, just feet from the surface. If we need to use them, we can easily open them up the rest of the way, accessing roads far from the entrance. One even comes out at a lake if we need to escape by water." Stubby smiles at his verbal restraint.

"Once inside we'll blow the main entrance shaft. After the dust settles the SS won't dare come in after us. They'll think we've all died in the cave-in or will soon starve to death with no chance of escape. Either way they'll leave us alone," Jennifer, a lady rebel states confidently.

"Well we have to get there first. Let's load up and go." Isaac directs those standing on the road by swinging his arm like a windmill towards the idling truck. "We don't want to get caught out here before we even get to the mine."

"You're right! Let's go," came the unanimous response as the small crowd of rebels hurriedly get themselves back into the bus bodies.

Isaac takes a circuitous route with several back-tracks getting to the mine, just in case he was still being followed. He swung down a driveway off a narrow trail, well posted with private property, do not enter, biohazardous and infectious waste signs. For years these signs had been successful at keeping inquisitive eyes, and most importantly the Empire's SS, from getting too close. Encompassed by a ten-foot-high chain linked fence topped with razor wire, the large compound was secure and foreboding. Secluded behind mountainous stacks of disheveled, dinted, rusty and leaking forty-five-gallon drums, stood a large dilapidated warehouse. The bowed roofline along with the slanting walls made the entire warehouse structure look like it could fall over with the slightest breeze, even the large barn doors closed crooked, overlapping awkwardly.

Despite all external appearances though, the building was very structurally sound. Stubby, Isaac and their group had taken special care in making it and the fenced compound look as uninviting as possible. Additional warning signs adorned the perimeter fence every twelve feet, making them impossible to miss. Inside the warehouse, a steel beam superstructure reinforced the out of square exterior framing. Clad in salvaged, rusty corrugated tin sheets, it made most people seeing it assume it was too far out in the boonies for the owners to worry about tearing it down, rather they were letting nature do the job for them.

The overgrown driveway opened into a small clearing at the gate entering the compound. Isaac stopped the truck allowing Stubby to swing out the passenger door and unlock the heavy gate. After sliding it sideways along the inside of the fence, Stubby waited until the Paystar and trailer rolled past him. Pulling the gate closed again, he locked it securely. Isaac stopped in front of the warehouse bay door and waited for Stubby to make his way across the darkening yard to open it. Stubby walked up to the keypad to unlock the warehouse door, but rather than punching in the proper code, he grabbed the keypad box and twisted it clockwise. After numerous complete clockwise revolutions, the keypad box came off its mounting, revealing a traditional key lock slot. Producing a key from his pocket, Stubby inserts it into the lock slot and unlocks the door. Pushing hard on the large door, he rolled it sideways out of the way, allowing the Paystar and trailer to enter a large dark void.

He turns to close the big bay door after the trailer entered the warehouse. Before he has the chance to grab the door handle, Stubby feels the barrel of a gun being poked into the back of his neck. Large strong hands grab him, pushing him towards the passenger side of the truck. The rebels and children are unloading as Stubby and his captors approach them in the dim light. SS officers with their guns at the ready, emerge from the shadows of the warehouse, securely surrounding the rebels just as Isaac comes around the front of the truck. He is startled to find such a dangerous greeting committee. Unaware of the present danger, the last rebel loudly announces that everyone has been unloaded as she climbs down from the trailer bus body, only to find her rebel group surrounded by the silent SS.

"Good! Now that you're all finally here we can start processing you," the SS commander addresses the rebel group. "We've been waiting for you to arrive. We were beginning to think you had some mechanical trouble and wouldn't make it to this surprise party we've planned for you. But now here you are, and all is well."

"This is a level 1 secured, Imperial Biohazardous waste dump site. Our workers are professionals, highly trained to work with dangerous pathogens. Do you and your troops have all your updated government approved courses?" Isaac tries a provocative bluff.

Stubby picks up on Isaac's bluff expanding on it. "Ya you %$#@in idiots! This is a %$#@in secured site. You can't be in here. There's %$#@in highly contagious pathogens on these premises! All of you just can't %$#@in come in here %$#@in unescorted. There are %$$@in strict Imperial laws and protocols to %$#@in follow."

The SS commander looks down his nose at Stubby in disgust. "Yes. The Empire does have stringent rules and protocols. However, there have been a few changes to the rules in how we SS interact with those rebellious to our great Empire. Most importantly, we're now allowed to deal with you as we see fit. I don't like your tone or the way you address your superiors! You need a lesson on how to properly address your betters."

"And who's going to %$#@in do that?"

"I will." As he replied, the commander calmly drew his side arm and fired a round from it into Stubby's head at point blank range. The back of Stubby's head exploded into fragments of hair and bone as the bullet mushrooms upon exit. A chunky cloud of bloody red grey matter rains down on those standing behind Stubby. His body slumps to the ground as those around him instinctively turn, recoiling away from the carnage.

"The SS may be despised, but you will respect us. Any Questions?" the commander asks loudly.

The group of rebels were shocked into silence by the violence they had just witnessed. They had been mistreated and abused by the SS before but had never experienced such wanton brutality.

"As I was explaining to your deceased friend here, our rules of engagement have been altered. You will do as you are told or suffer his fate. Do I make myself clear?

"Perfectly!" Isaac says, his voice choked with emotion stepping forward out of the crowd. "We're all peaceful noncombatants here. We aren't out to kill anyone," Isaac addresses the SS with sincerity.

"Oh ya! Like you didn't want to kill me when you made my cruiser drive into the river," an SS member replied, shivering in his soggy wet uniform. "I could have drowned! You're more dangerous than those flying Scorpion bugs."

"But you didn't drown. We only intended to keep you from following us. We didn't want you dead," Isaac explained sympathetically.

"It doesn't matter now," the commander barked, "you'll all be taken to the Central Valley Detention Centre to be processed. Any further escape attempts will be dealt with harshly. Like what your short friend here received. We have lots of bullets, but not much time to spare."

Without further incident, the bewildered group of rebels compliantly boarded Imperial busses that arrived at the compound's gate. They rode in silence back into the heart of the valley they had just earlier escaped from, each of them wondering how the Empire had tracked them down and what was to become of them now that the Empire had them securely within its grip. Exhausted from their escape ordeals and loaded into the busses well after dark, they all soon fell into a deep slumber, helped along by the knockout gas being fed into the bus's passenger HVAC system. In the pre-dawn grey they disembark disoriented and groggy, going directly into holding cells at the valleys' main detention center.

The Empire was ready to process them quickly as their group trial was scheduled for later that morning. Sensitive to bad publicity, Prophet Father is eager to show the world the rule of law was still being followed despite the stories of imperial abuse in the disaster ravaged nations.

Not yet ready to show his true colors, Prophet Father demanded independent international observers be present in the courtroom to verify everything proceeded lawfully. Musa and his small team keep a watchful eye on the proceedings from the front row behind the group of rebel defendants as the trial starts. The Empire had a large dossier chronicling several years' worth of the rebel group's activities. Documenting everything from larceny to murder, most charges came with video evidence from the many imperial CCTV cameras that monitored every aspect of civilian life.

The public defender put up an impressive defense against the barrage of incriminating evidence coming from the prosecution, even getting some charges dismissed, but it was a show trial for the world's media. Like in a professional wrestling match, even though both opponents throw good punches making for a dramatic seesaw battle, both sides know what the outcome will be. This is a well choreographed dance intended to keep the audience enthralled as they head towards the predetermined outcome. Still not free of the paralyzing gas, the rebel defendants watched through glazed eyes not fully comprehending their peril. Most of them don't come to their senses until they hear the death sentence being read out.

Giving their testimony in open court and receiving amnesty for turning state's evidence, some in the rebel leadership, including Brother Matias, were praised by the judge for their months of undercover work. They were deemed essential in the Empire's victory, providing names, locations and attack plans. Rewarded with healthy pensions for their covert efforts in rounding up those who would terrorize the Empire, they were headed towards a carefree life in exotic locations with prestigious, director level accommodation. Their treacherous actions spared them from the capital punishment their former followers would soon suffer.

The judge acknowledged and commended the noncombatants for not taking up arms and killing Imperial personnel. But in the end, he found the passivists just as criminally responsible for Imperial casualties as the armed terrorists, even if their part in the struggle was supplying aid to those who did the fighting. Combatant and noncombatant alike, guilt by association, all were condemned for being participants with the same outlawed group. The judge said they all had the common goal of overthrowing the Empire and they would all receive the same lawfully imposed Imperial punishment for their actions. Death by beheading.

A razor wire topped fence surrounded the large inflatable compound built over a three-acre playing field to protect SS security forces from the scorpion-like stinging tails of the troubling locust plague. The compound was already crowded with those deemed to be terrorists against the Empire. The condemned prisoners were standing single file, like an airport check in line that snaked from the front to the back where Isaac's group entered through the guarded rear door. There was stifled murmuring as the newly condemned entered the killing field and took their place at the back of the line. Guided by the SS jailers, the prisoners at the front of the line were led away behind a wooden wall about ten feet high at the far end of the compound. Running from the left wall, it stopped about five feet short of the opposite wall on the other side of the yard. Prisoners reluctantly disappeared into this void in small groups of around fifteen. Muffled sobs and anguished cries were heard by Isaac at the back of the line coming from behind the wall, growing clearer as he followed those ahead of him towards the opening.

Most of the convicted stood silently looking at the ground, slowly shuffling ever closer to their fate. Recognizing a tall man and his short friend in the line ahead of him as they approached around a switch-back, Isaac gives them a nod and a shy smile.

"Being a noncombatant didn't help you did it?" The short man blurts out when he recognizes Isaac. "At least I got to take a few of the SS down before they caught me. We might have won if we'd had more fighters." The short man's voice was hardened and angry from his experiences endured in active combat. "All we needed was a few more patriots willing to fight for their country and freedom. Some who weren't so afraid of dying, willing to pick up a gun and fight!"

"We didn't fight and kill because we were afraid of being killed! We didn't fight because Jesus told us to overcome hate with love. We were afraid of who we'd become if we did kill." Isaac didn't expect he'd have to be defending his motives to his old comrades.

The tall man spoke up. "Where's your short, old friend? I saw him with you in town the other day. I don't see him here; did he decide to leave the rebellion and take the easy path joining the Empire? Afraid to die for his convictions?

Isaac replied sadly with determination. "No! He was never afraid. He chose to take his punishment earlier than the rest of us. He remained faithful to the end."

"Well it's too bad he wasn't more interested in accepting Jesus. That's the only way he'll escape his final punishment." The shorter man states confidently. "We only get one chance at accepting the salvation Jesus provides."

"True! We all only get one opportunity to accept Jesus, but Jesus himself told us no one could come to him until his father called them. People need to make the most of that calling when it comes." Isaac's faith in God's coming kingdom hadn't diminished despite his present circumstances. "The love of Jesus and his father goes beyond our present mortal lives and the grave. Everyone who has ever lived will receive God's call, in God's time."

"Well I wouldn't bet my eternal life on your imaginings," the tall man said. "Better to secure it while you can."

The SS guards pushed the line ahead bringing their conversation to an abrupt end. The three don't get another chance to communicate before it comes to their turn to go behind the wall. Their silent thoughts are troubled by the anguished sounds, becoming louder as they approach the high wooden wall. Isaac's group of fifteen included some of his fellow noncombatants, as well as the tall and short man. With backs against the wooden wall, Musa and his team stand in silent witness to the lawfulness of the rebel's fate up to the deadly end.

Once behind the wall, Isaac and the others are ordered to kneel in a row parallel to the wall, spaced so their hands wouldn't touch with outstretched arms. A large, dark, full bearded, SS officer wearing a decorative turban, addresses the convicted terrorists. His arms are crossed exposing massive well-developed biceps. From an official document he reads aloud the death sentence to those kneeling in front of him, informing them of how he will be conducting their impending decapitation.

The short man angrily rebuffs his large executioner, two defendants ahead of Isaac. "You might kill my body, but when you do, I'll be living in glory with my Lord. When you die, you'll be tormented in the fires of hell for the rest of eternity. You need to repent of your sins and accept Jesus before it's too late. No one can have eternal life and be spared the fires of hell unless they accept Jesus!"

The large turbaned executioner didn't respond, he only walked around behind the line of kneeling prisoners and picked up his saif leaning against a brace. Standing about a pace behind the tall man, he raises his long sword over his right shoulder, like he was using a baseball bat. Bringing the ornately decorated blade down and across the tall man's neck forcefully, the tall man's head was sliced cleanly from his body and fell into the bloody trough in front of him as his body slumped over sideways, its heart pumping his life blood onto the drain rock covered courtyard.

Stepping sideways behind the shorter man, the executioner carefully wipes the blood off his blade with a soft cotton towel. Positioning himself behind his next victim, he taps his sword gently on the short man's shoulder and calmly addresses him loudly.

"I was raised in a country free of Christianity and its fables, as was my father and grandfather. None of my family has ever heard about this Jesus of yours. They were simple, loving people, doing good works within their community. If they are destined for hell, why would I not want to be with them? Does your loving God punish those who don't know any better, those who have never heard of this Jesus of yours? I wouldn't want to be stuck in paradise with a savior like that!"

"Don't worry, you won't be. All who reject Jesus won't enjoy heaven's pleasures." Those were the last words the short man ever spoke. Seconds later his head laid in the trough.

"So tell me Christian, do you think your friend was right? The executioner asked the lady beside Isaac. "Are my ancestors in hell and will I be joining them there?"

"Only those who accept Jesus can join him in heaven. The wicked will suffer in hell forever," she replied, her voice barely audible through her sobs.

Laying in the trough moments later, blood matted brown hair partially covers her eyes as her head faces skyward, separated from her body.

Isaac was next in line. Again, the executioner asks his question. "Tell me Christian, do you believe my ancestors are in hell and will I be joining them there?"

Isaac had been praying for God's will to be done in all things. Preparing himself for certain death, he was comforted in the knowledge that all things worked out for the good for those who loved the Lord.

"Yes, it's true that only those who follow, and love Jesus will be saved. But that's not the whole story. Everyone who has ever lived will have a fair opportunity to know Jesus and decide if they want to follow him. God won't let evil thrive in heaven, nor will he force those who reject him to be with him. Once everyone has made their choice to accept Jesus or not, God will let those who reject salvation through Jesus, choose death instead. He doesn't sentence them to death, they willingly choose it." While he was talking, Isaac expected to be literally cut off at any moment.

"So, when do those people like my family and I receive our fair opportunity?"

"The Bible describes a time when people not called to Jesus will be resurrected back to physical life, into a world free of satanic influence. They will have a lifetime of at least a hundred years where they can make their decision."

"So, you're saying we'll all get a second chance?"

Isaac is emphatic. "No! You said you and your family never learned about Jesus. How could this be a second chance to know him if you've never got to hear about him during this life the first time? The next life will be the first opportunity for you and all of your family!"

"That's nothing like I've ever heard from a Christian before," the executioner said in amazement. "All they tell me is that I'm going to hell, like that vile little man before you. Are you sure you're a Christian?"

"Absolutely!" Isaac responded affirmatively. "Jesus is my savior. Salvation is found only through his sacrifice. I follow Jesus; hence I am a Christian."

"Then why are your beliefs about my fate so different from normal Christians?"

"I think Christians should use all of the Bible scriptures to form their beliefs, not just a few. I believe all the verses fit together to give us the whole story. If I'm abnormal, you'd have to ask the other Christians what scriptures they ignore or can't fit within their beliefs."

Laughter was the executioner's response. "People will say anything to escape death." the big turbaned man says, raising his sword.

"Those others didn't." Isaac gestures with his head towards the corpses beside him. "Why would I? I told you what the Bible describes will happen to your loved ones, not what church doctrine dictates. God has a life plan for everyone that will accept it."

Just before the blade starts to come down towards Isaac's neck, a muscular black hand firmly holds the wrist of the executioner, stopping him from completing his gruesome task.

"My King has need of this one," Musa said in a commanding deep voice. "He will be coming with me." Pulling the executioner off balance, Musa spins him around, so they are facing nose to nose behind the kneeling rebels. Musa's team quickly blocks the few death squad guards from interfering in the confrontation.

"I have my orders to follow and commanders to obey," the executioner protests.

"I have orders as well, along with diplomatic immunity. I serve an absolute monarch like you and your crew. There are only a few culturally relevant, absolute monarchies in the world, and they all have the blessings of the Empire. Their continuation is written into the Empire's constitution. Do you want to be the cause of an international incident, or would you rather exercise some diplomacy? I doubt your SS commanders will accept accountability for your actions. You and your men will be abandoned in the legal wilderness, like a sacrificial Azazel goat." Musa has the executioner and his men's attention, as they don't trust their sycophant commanders.

"I can't afford any witnesses or disturbances," the executioner says nodding towards the rest of the noncombatants.

"I have a royal plane fueled and ready to fly me and my party back to our homeland. We're scheduled to leave after witnessing these executions, we have room to take a few more with us. Once we've left the country there will be nothing your commanders can do." Musa can see his ideas are getting through to the large muscular man. "It's easier to get forgiveness than permission. My King might kill them anyway and save you the bother. Besides, you count the corpses that get thrown into the mass grave. No one will be digging them up for a recount. Who's to know or find out what really happens here? My plane is at the end of the airport. I'll take these prisoners with me now and we'll all be gone. It will be on my authority." The executioner was starting to subconsciously nod his head along with Musa. "I'm not leaving without him!" Musa puts his hand on Isaac's shoulder. "You decide how much trouble he's worth?"

Weighing his options, the executioner rubs his beard thoughtfully. Having no confidence in receiving his superiors support if he resists and not wanting to jeopardize his future, he could see the wisdom in Musa's idea. Recognizing Isaac as someone who had helped impoverished Imperial families by providing food and clothing, his men encourage him to agree, eager to see Isaac escape his death sentence. Knowing he could fudge the body counts and wanting his decision to go unnoticed, the executioner addresses those kneeling with Isaac.

"Do you want to peacefully go with him?" pointing towards Musa, "or stay and die?" He firmly grips his saif, twisting the handle in his muscular hands.

Getting ready to usher in the next group of condemned, the death squad hurriedly clean up the fresh cadavers. Rising to their feet, the remaining prisoners gather around Isaac, eagerly giving their tacit approval to the improvised escape plan. Isaac and the few noncombatants with him joyfully accompany Musa and his observer team through a rear exit to their diplomatic bus parked close by. Wasting no time in getting to the waiting royal plane in a private hangar, they all eagerly board as the jet's engines warm up and the pilots prepare to be airborne as soon as possible.

Safely airborne for forty-five minutes, the escapees start to relax and settle in for a long plane ride. Much later, when they were flying over the North Pacific Ocean, Isaac timidly approaches Musa as the jet airliner heads towards the African continent.

"Thank you for saving our lives back there. I don't know why you did, but we're all sure grateful. We'd certainly be dead now if you hadn't stepped in to save us."

"My mission was to be an observer, ensuring all interactions between the SS and civilian populations stayed within the legal boundaries set out by the Empire. Tired of seeing civilians taken advantage of, my team and I set up a humanitarian program designed to rescue

anyone who wanted to use it. Our King welcomes all who
will work diligently with love and compassion for the
welfare of my countryman. We are a small, unimportant
country by worldly standards, but we are peaceful and
law abiding by nature. My agrarian country has been
ravaged by an HIV epidemic, leaving countless orphans
in desperate need of foster moms and dads to take care of
them and help them work the farms."

"I heard something about that program. Participants
would receive free passage, room and board if they would
stay and work with those in need in your country. Even
with things being bad here in their homeland, I think only
those who had a deep compassion and love for their
fellow man would take advantage of your offer."

"Or they had no other viable options, like you," Musa
points to Isaac. "But yes, the program has only seen
limited success, however those who came have bonded
within our society and have even formed a new local
church denomination, one with the loving self-sacrifice of
Jesus at its core. With Prophet Father becoming more
tyrannical every day, it's not safe to continue our
immigration program any longer. This will be the last
mercy mission our jet will be making. I don't think world
politics will allow any more refugees to come volunteer
in my homeland."

"So why did you save us? You let those ahead of me
be executed. Why spare me and those few behind me?"

Musa thinks over his response carefully. "I hadn't
planned it that way. You and your fellow rebels were
found guilty under a legally binding court procedure. My
team was only there to observe. It was your answer to the

turbined executioner that compelled me to spare your life and demand you come with me. Your fellow noncombatants are just here for expediency sake, it was more the executioner's idea than it was mine. I didn't mind bringing them as well, as long as you came with me."

"What did I say that was so special?" Isaac asked inquisitively. "I only explained what I find the Bible to teach."

"And that's why I spared you. Your explanation was different from anything I've ever heard before. It made me think of a promise I made when I was a young boy. A promise you can help me keep. In order to do that, I need to take you back to my country. Don't worry, you and your friends will be safe."

"Oh I'm not worried. I've been alive for ten hours longer than I would have been if you hadn't stepped in when you did. Every minute of life from now on is an extra gift from God. He's in charge."

"That's a good attitude. Use this time to rest, we won't be landing for almost another twenty four hours."

Bringing the conversation to an end, Musa turns back to the open laptop on his seat back table and starts to type. Isaac returns to his seat, settles in and earnestly prays to God for wisdom and guidance for when he arrives in a strange new land.

A 24-hour TV news channel from a seatback screen cuts into Isaac's prayers as the announcer recaps the highlights from the seemingly unnatural disturbances that had taken place over the last few years. Interviewing a well-regarded scientist, she asks for the reasons why the world was experiencing such terrible calamity.

The professor answers her with an overview of the previous three years of large disasters. "The first wave of calamity was surely caused by the volcanic activity in North America. The iron rich ash caused red fall out, escalating hail and lightning storms to an unprecedented level, spawning fire storms that destroyed vegetation worldwide.

Next came the underwater volcanic eruptions. Leading scientists believe these eruptions released gasses trapped from deep within the earth's mantle. Changing the specific gravity of the ocean waters caused many ships to sink as they lost their buoyancy. This volcanic activity must have also disrupted Second World War chemical weapons dump sites in the Mariana Trench, releasing deadly toxins killing an enormous amount of sea life. The potassium and phosphorus rich volcanic ash falling into the oceans from the North American volcanoes caused a simultaneous worldwide Algae bloom turning the seas red as blood.

Then, as the volcanic ash settled to the ground worldwide the resulting seasonal rain runoff tainted the fresh water supply, making it poisonous and bitter tasting." The professor recapped the major catastrophes.

"So, you're saying these devastating events can be scientifically explained as natural occurrences and have no other cause."

"Of course! What other explanation could there be?"

"There have been many sceptics who claim these calamities are the result of extraterrestrial interference," she pushed for other possibilities.

"Throughout human history, there have always been wackos with unfounded opinions. Science can explain everything," the professor states confidently.

"How do you explain the changes in the sky's brightness? There's at least a third less light reaching the earth from the sun and moon. Lots of the stars have vanished, leading many to believe something other-worldly is happening. Supernatural even."

The professor snorted with disgust, "with all the dust in the atmosphere, it's only logical that solar light would be diminished. Our computer models show things returning to normal in no more than four or five years, once our atmosphere sheds all the volcanic debris."

"Well how do you explain the strange sounds emitted from the sky? Most people report it to sound like someone yelling woe, woe, woe. I've heard it myself and it's very unnerving?"

"Yes, I've heard it also. The scientific community isn't in full agreement yet but I believe it to be a unique phenomenon, like the sound produced by the aurora borealis. I believe the sounds are produced by charged dust particles. Suspended in the atmosphere, they are rapidly discharged and burst by space particles carried in the solar winds hitting the earth. The unusually high atmospheric dust content produces these strange sounds which coincide with increased solar flare activity."

"That sounds like a plausible explanation. But will it satisfy the critics who believe we're being revisited by the aliens who originally colonized our earth?"

"People will believe what they want but science will overcome mankind's problems in spite of themselves."

"Well how can science explain what happened nineteen weeks ago when we got the first reports of a meteorite striking the earth. The Imperial news outlets reported that it landed in the south Pacific striking the small Bikini Atoll in the Marshall Islands. They hadn't experienced such devastation since 1958. The Marshallese were all but wiped out by the celestial collision!"

"What do you mean? We have provided a scientifically plausible answer."

"Yes. You official scientific commentators attempted to soothe the public by touting the Imperial story. Trying to explain this strange new threat to mankind by theorizing where this new insect came from. First you described how insects can survive in an environment bathed in radiation at far greater levels than humans can. You pointed out that 10 sieverts of radiation will kill humans before a month, but some insects such as wasps, flies, scorpions, cockroaches and orthopods, frequently survive at levels 10, 100, even 300 times higher than that. The Hiroshima bomb, Little Boy, you told us, produced about 100 sieverts. And that some bacteria are known to survive 5000 times higher than humans can. That's more than even man's most powerful nuclear blast can produce."

"Yes, I still endorse those facts," the scientist replied. "All of us Imperial experts agreed this new hybrid species, growing up to four inches long, grew unabated since the first atomic test blast in 1946, deep within the Bikini Atoll's 229 square miles of radiation contaminated area. We still believe this new hybrid breed of aquatic-terrestrial winged insect was formed underground and apparently even below the shallow waters of the lagoon.

When the meteorite struck, this new hybrid insect rose high into the troposphere with the smoke of the blast, blocking out the sun. Propelled by the explosion, the strange new breed of insect quickly spread along with the dust, falling out worldwide. Carried by the winds they were soon tormenting humanity everywhere with their scorpion like sting. Those who are more susceptible to the non-deadly stings have filled the hospital wards. Desperate for relief, they frequently beg to be euthanized."

"Yes, that's what the Empire wants the world to believe. There are many counter theories running rampant, challenging the official experts," the independent reporter replied. "The unofficial theories describe these insects originating from outer space. Some say, aliens have been here before and are now planning to return in full force. They imagine this to be just the first wave of infestation, testing our defenses before the main onslaught arrives to finish off humanity. Others claim the aliens have been here all along, discreetly growing in strength until their time to attack arrived."

Rolling his eyes despairingly, the scientist commentator replies mockingly, "Disinformation always runs rampant in times of uncertainty. No one can conclusively prove where this new pestilence came from, or how to provide relief from it. Everyone is aggravated by these winged tormentors."

"Well. Thank you for your valuable input professor Speckle," the silicone beauty remarks contemptuously. Turning to face camera two, she smiles warmly, "Stay tuned for highlights from this year's Prophet Father's Day parade, right after these messages."

"It's all been predicted by God." Isaac rants back at the screen. "Professor Speckle hasn't noticed the small portion of the world's population, along with all green vegetation, that has been left unharmed by the winged tormentors. He believes their torment to be universal. Preoccupied with finding personal relief, he and everyone else never noticed that those who have self-sacrificial love for others aren't stung by those strange new insects. Speckle has never read what the Bible has to say. He should read Revelations 8 and 9." Isaac reads it again for himself from the pocket Bible he kept in the leg of his tattered cargo pants.

Revelation 8:6-13 English Standard Version

6 Now the seven angels who had the seven trumpets prepared to blow them.

7 The first angel blew his trumpet, and there followed hail and fire, mixed with blood, and these were thrown upon the earth. And a third of the earth was burned up, and a third of the trees were burned up, and all green grass was burned up.

8 The second angel blew his trumpet, and something like a great mountain, burning with fire, was thrown into the sea, and a third of the sea became blood.

9 A third of the living creatures in the sea died, and a third of the ships were destroyed.

10 The third angel blew his trumpet, and a great star fell from heaven, blazing like a torch, and it fell on a third of the rivers and on the springs of water.

11 The name of the star is Wormwood.[a] A third of the waters became wormwood, and many people died from the water, because it had been made bitter.

12 The fourth angel blew his trumpet, and a third of the sun was struck, and a third of the moon, and a third of the stars, so that a third of their light might be darkened, and a third of the day might be kept from shining, and likewise a third of the night.

13 Then I looked, and I heard an eagle crying with a loud voice as it flew directly overhead, "Woe, woe, woe to those who dwell on the earth, at the blasts of the other trumpets that the three angels are about to blow!"

Revelation 9:1-11 English Standard Version

1 And the fifth angel blew his trumpet, and I saw a star fallen from heaven to earth, and he was given the key to the shaft of the bottomless pit.[a]

2 He opened the shaft of the bottomless pit, and from the shaft rose smoke like the smoke of a great furnace, and the sun and the air were darkened with the smoke from the shaft.

3 Then from the smoke came locusts on the earth, and they were given power like the power of scorpions of the earth.

4 They were told not to harm the grass of the earth or any green plant or any tree, but only those people who do not have the seal of God on their foreheads.

5 They were allowed to torment them for five months, but not to kill them, and their torment was like the torment of a scorpion when it stings someone.

6 And in those days people will seek death and will not find it. They will long to die, but death will flee from them.

7 In appearance the locusts were like horses prepared for battle: on their heads were what looked like crowns of gold; their faces were like human faces,

8 their hair like women's hair, and their teeth like lions' teeth;

9 they had breastplates like breastplates of iron, and the noise of their wings was like the noise of many chariots with horses rushing into battle.

10 They have tails and stings like scorpions, and their power to hurt people for five months is in their tails.

11 They have as king over them the angel of the bottomless pit. His name in Hebrew is Abaddon, and in Greek he is called Apollyon.[b]

"The worst is still ahead, and you don't even see it coming," Isaac mumbled to himself as he tucks his Bible away. Rubbing his tired eyes with his knuckles, his head bobs twice and he's asleep.

Chapter 15

"Prophet Father, they're here to see you now," the personal aid reports over the office intercom. Moments later Prophet Father strides out through the office door.

"Professor." Prophet Father greets a small group of people in his lobby," he holds out his hand as the group kneels before him. Kissing his ring, the leader of the group waits for permission to rise. Nodding to the group, Prophet Father turns and retreats back into his office, the small group follows.

"I'm told you have good news for me. What breakthroughs has your team made? Did you find out how to eliminate those large stinging Locusts? I need to be the one who rids the world of this plague. When I do, all world leaders will bow before me, worshiping me as their Saviour. The inhabitants of the world will follow me as their God."

"We haven't discovered how to eliminate them but we do believe we know when they'll disappear," the leader reports.

"But I need to destroy them to be proclaimed the savior of the world! They just can't disappear on their own."

"If you knew when those Locusts would be disappearing, you could say you're getting rid of them for the world's sake and when they're gone, you'll receive the credit. No one would be the wiser," one of the researchers explained.

Not used to being addressed by an underling, Prophet Father looks to the group's leader for collaboration of what he was told.

"Yes, it is true. We don't know how to kill them; however, we've been studying them since they arrived. We've discovered some interesting facts about this winged menace."

"Go on, do tell."

"Well, for one thing they don't eat. None of the earth's plant life has been harmed by them and we've discovered why. They have an odd-looking face for an insect. That's because they don't have mouthparts capable of eating plant life at all. We suspect they evolved for life underground, where they probably fed on microscopic bacteria growing in the radioactive ocean waters of the Bikini lagoon."

"Well that's a start. But how does that tell us when they'll die?"

"We've measured the fat reserves of several thousand that were killed the first day they arrived. Every day since, we've collected dead ones sent in from around the world. Extrapolating the data of the diminishing fat reserves, we've predicted the majority of them will either die of starvation or head back home for more food by the end of this week. With the rest lasting no longer than the middle of next week. Those that return home for food will find nothing there but a crater filled with fresh sea water where they will die," the lead researcher assured.

"Well then, I better get started planning on how I will tell the world leaders that I've rescued them from this most torturous plague. They'll never suspect those locust were dying anyway. Are you sure about your data and when they'll start to disappear?"

"Absolutely! I'd bet our lives on it."

"Good? I would hate to get my timing wrong; it would look bad. Oh, and by the way, I'll take that bet."

The research group leaves Prophet Father's office nervously, fearing their lives were in jeopardy if their research was wrong.

"Stubby. Duck!" Isaac shouts, clutching his seat's armrest. Sitting bolt upright, his heart pounds hard in his temples. Isaac's eyes are wide as he wakes to the reality of his surroundings in an anxious sweat. Calming himself from his nightmare with controlled breaths, Isaac plays out the last 48 hours in his mind. Coming to terms with all he's lost and wondering where God would be leading him in the future. He's glad God is in control as he looks around the now familiar plane's passenger compartment.

Releasing his white-knuckle grip on the armrest he lifts the window blind and peers out into the darkness. Pushing his face against the cool glass, he strains to see any lights through the clouds below. His breath soon fogs over the porthole and blocks any light that might have been visible. Sitting back in his reclined chair he again is soon immersed into a twitch producing dream. Awakened by the chiming seatbelt light, he groggily buckles himself in.

The plane is buffeted and bounced by turbulence as it descends into the darkness. Runway lights flash past Isaac's window just before the plane sticks onto the tarmac. The engines roar as the pilots slow the plane to a manageable taxiing speed. Soon Isaac and his fellow noncombatants are disembarking into a strange new land, starting new adventures.

Taken to a shabby hostel in the downtown core about fifteen minutes from the airport, the noncombatants are left with a military liaison. Musa told Isaac he'd be back to get him in a couple of days after he talked to the king, giving Isaac time to recuperate. The others could rest up with him until they were found foster family placements. There they would begin their volunteer work of housing, feeding and parenting their young charges towards maturity.

Finally securing an audience with the King, Musa comes to collect Isaac after breakfast on the third morning. As they drive to the King's residence, Isaac questions Musa about his royal meeting.

"You never told me how I'm supposed to help fulfill your promise."

"I've already told the King about you. He will ask you some questions about your beliefs, just answer them in a manner that is faithful to those beliefs. If your answers are like what you told the executioner a few days ago, then you'll be solving an old riddle for the King and fulfilling my promise."

"I don't completely get it, but I'll be as forthright as I can. How should I address the King?"

"Your majesty will do. Giving him a small bow would be in order as well. Don't try to shake his hand unless he initiates the greeting. He is the absolute monarch of our country. One of a small group of absolute monarchs worldwide."

"Oh. I didn't know. I'll be on my best behavior and try not to offend. Thank you for the pointers."

"He realizes you come from a different culture and will tolerate some breaches of protocol, I'll try to help you out when I can. Just be open, honest and respectful. Above all, be genuine. Be yourself."

"Thank you, I'll do my best."

Isaac rides in silent prayer until he's stepping out of the car. Entering behind Musa through an ornately carved wooden door, Isaac waits a few paces away as Musa is warmly greeted by his King.

"This must be the man you've told me about, the one with the different ideas," the King says to Musa as he eyes Isaac up and down. "He doesn't look like the scholarly type. I was expecting someone pale and thin. Maybe with thick glasses."

"No, he doesn't look the part, but this is him. Your eminence, may I introduce you to Isaac," Musa encourages Isaac to approach closer.

"Your majesty," Isaac says with a small bow, his hands at his sides.

The King smiles and extends his hand to Isaac. "I hope you'll be able to answer an old question for us. Come, sit and talk with me."

Isaac shakes the King's hand and is led over to a couch and three chairs tastefully arranged around a large, tortoise based, glass coffee table. The King notices Isaac looking at the coffee table and nods towards it.

"That is Roger. He was my grandmother's childhood pet. Thirty-eight inches wide and twenty-seven inches high. The friendliest guy you could ever meet. He would follow us kids around the garden all day long. Slowly of course," the King chuckles at his own joke. Isaac smiles broadly and nods his head.

"So, you wouldn't say you were fast friends?" Isaac retorts.

They all chuckle light-heartedly relaxing on the comfortable furniture around Rodger's taxidermied remains.

"Musa tells me you have a fresh outlook on where my ancestors might be. I have been taught about Jesus, but I can't reconcile his teachings of love to where I'm told my ancestors are now. Where do you believe my forefathers are?" the King's eyes twinkle in the sunlight streaming into the room as he stares expectantly at Isaac.

Before Isaac can respond, a servant wheels in a cart with some refreshments for the three of them. After dutifully pouring the tea into cups and adding the requested cream and sugar, she leaves a plate of biscuits in the center of the table's oval glass top then leaves the room. Standing silently behind the butler's kitchen door she can hear everything but is safely out of sight.

Flustered by the tasty delay, the King again questions Isaac.

"So, where are the immortal souls of my dead ancestors? Are they in torment, or at peace?"

"To state the obvious, your dead ancestors are dead," Isaac replied hesitantly.

"Yes, I know they're dead! But where are their souls?"

"Their souls are dead. They are dead souls." Isaac says cautiously, letting his words resonate with the King.

The King takes a deep breath and exhales slowly with a sigh. Thinking Isaac to be a bit slow, he starts again, attempting to explain himself better.

"My extended family that has died. My kindly grandmother, her brave husband." The King gestures with his hands, almost spilling his tea. "The line of self-sacrificing kings that go back in my father's family for generations. They did their best for our people, they're all dead now. They never heard about Jesus. No missionaries preached to them when they were alive. So, I've always wondered. Where are they now? Are their souls being tormented in hell because they didn't have the opportunity to accept Jesus, or will their love for others save them?

Isaac sits forward in his chair, looking directly into the King's eyes. "In first Corinthians, Paul tells us the greatest virtue we can have is love. The first book of John is all about love. It tells us God is love and that's what he wants people to have for each other. The Beatles summed it up in their song, All You Need Is Love. Love is the building block God works with," Isaac oozes positivity as he speaks to the King.

"So, their love has saved them and they're in heaven," the King says with relief. "But how is that a fresh approach?" he says sternly looking at Musa.

"No!" Isaac breaks in. "They aren't in heaven."

The King looks sharply at Isaac. "You just said, all you need is love. Why aren't their souls in Heaven?"

"Because they're dead! They aren't alive anywhere."

"Their bodies are dead yes but their immortal souls have to be alive somewhere. You aren't making any sense," turning to Musa the King adds. "Are you sure about him? I don't think he knows much about the afterlife." Turning back to Isaac he asks bluntly, "what kind of Christian are you? Ignorant about people's eternal souls and where they end up. Shame on you for making people think you're a knowledgeable Bible follower."

"I try to be a disciple of Jesus and not only a Bible follower but a Bible believer. I believe the Bible is not contradictory, it's the true word of God. I'm not worried about humanity's' immortal souls, because they don't have one. We are all living souls, we don't have an immortal one."

"That's crazy! Everyone knows people are born with an immortal soul. Some say humans have one as soon as an egg is fertilized inside its mother's womb. Saying people don't have immortal souls goes against every religious faith in the world, Christian or not! Of course people are immortal!" the King was starting to raise his voice at Isaac. "I'm sure we're told that somewhere in the Bible as well."

"Yes, the Bible does say, you will not die."

"There, see. You testify against yourself."

"The Bible records it, but you can't believe it," Isaac replies dryly.

"You foolish man. You say you believe the Bible, now you say we shouldn't believe it. I think Musa should have left you to die in your own country rather than bring you and your double mindedness here to mine."

Isaac makes a silent prayer to God for inspiration. "I'm sorry. We seem to have gotten off to a bad start. I believe it stems from misunderstanding what words truly mean. There's been a lot of disinformation loaded onto the word soul. The word soul first appears in the Bible in Genesis. The Hebrew word it was translated from is nephesh. It means a fleshy breathing creature, or animal, like a cow, or bird. Genesis tells us man became a living animal, not an immortal soul."

"I suppose you might be right. I don't know. I've never looked into it," the King said, calming down.

"That's ok, most people haven't. I've gotten used to it but I have looked into it. You could too if you took the time. The Strong's concordance is a good tool to use. When you read the terms of usage for the word nephesh, you'll find it includes mortal, as in will die. It nowhere tells us that soul or nephesh, as it should be used, is immortal, as in cannot die. From the start, man has never had an immortal soul that won't die and we're still waiting to receive eternal life."

"But you just said the Bible tells us, you shall not surely die!"

"I said the Bible records that statement. The Bible records a lot of conversations, some true and some not. What we need to believe is the truth coming from God. The serpent, or Satan told Eve, you shall not surely die. He's the father of lies. I don't think we should believe him."

"If humans don't have an immortal soul, then why does virtually everyone believe we do? Are all those religions and spiritually minded people wrong? Christians have always believed they have immortal life through Jesus."

"Your words are expanding the scope of our conversation too fast. We need to stick to our first subject; do we have an immortal soul."

"I wasn't aware I had strayed from it."

"Yes. You brought in the Christian belief that Christians will gain eternal life. That's different from humans possessing an immortal soul from birth."

The King thinks for a moment and then nods his head. "Ok, I'll concede your point."

"If we want to believe the Bible then we need to believe what the Bible tells us, not make it say what we want or have always been led to believe. People from faiths predating Christianity believed they had an immortal soul, this alone shows the idea didn't come from Christianity. Satan's lie infected humanity at the very beginning as the Bible records. If we want to follow God's truth we can't believe Satan's lies. Believing we have an immortal soul takes us away from the knowledge of God and his plans for humanity."

"Well let's say I do believe you and agree that my ancestors are completely dead. That doesn't make me feel any better about their fate, or God. It just makes me sad and hopeless for them."

"That's because you think they're gone forever with no future." Isaac said in a positive tone.

"That's what you just said. They're dead, completely lifeless, without conscious thought."

"Yes, they are. But they don't stay that way. The Bible tells us about a series of resurrections where the dead are brought back to life. Abraham had faith that even if he killed his only son Isaac, God was able to resurrect him back to life. Jesus proved this fact by being the first to be raised from the dead into an incorruptible body. Christians know that it's possible to have eternal life because our big brother has it and has promised it to his disciples as well."

"That doesn't help my ancestors any. They weren't followers of Jesus. They never heard of him. Is it their fault no missionary came to them? Does God only want white European children? He was late telling his black, Africa children about Jesus. My ancestors didn't even get the chance to follow. And you said all we need is love. Typical double-talk. Why should I believe anything you say?"

"Because you haven't heard the whole story. Your ancestors will live again, in a resurrection to physical life where they will have their chance to follow Jesus. That's why love is all you need. If people have a kind and loving nature it'll be easy to follow Jesus when they get their chance. People that are hateful, arrogant and proud will have to retrain themselves to be loving. That'll make it harder to become a disciple of Jesus and gain eternal life. Ask anyone who has quit a bad habit how easy it is to change."

"So, your saying my ancestors will all get a second chance to follow Jesus. You say they'll have another life where they can choose Jesus and develop love. That is a strange belief."

"No! I'm not saying that, the Bible is. It tells us about a few resurrections of humanity, coming at different times as it suits God. One of those resurrections is a resurrection back to physical life for those who died not knowing Jesus. During this second life a baby will not die until it has lived a lifetime and those who die after living a full life of a hundred years and not accepted Jesus will be cursed. Those who choose to follow Jesus will gain eternal life, those who die not accepting Jesus will be cursed, remaining dead forever. I'm not saying or making anything up. I'm reading what the Bible states. But you're mistaken, humans don't get a second chance to accept Jesus, we all get only one opportunity."

"You say everyone will get another lifetime where they can accept Jesus. A second opportunity for salvation. Why should people choose to follow Jesus now, during this present life if they can do it later?"

"Jesus told us plainly, no one can get to God without going through him and we can't get to Jesus if God doesn't draw us to him. The apostles described being a follower of Jesus as a calling. God isn't calling everyone during this present life. He's drawing a few people out of this world now, the weak and foolish to shame the strong and wise. This life is the only opportunity for those who are called and choose to follow Jesus. People who aren't called by God have no chance to come to Jesus during this life.

You said your ancestors didn't get God's call during this life. I'm explaining how the Bible reveals they'll get their opportunity, during a life to come. That'll be their first chance to follow Jesus, not a second one. If they choose to follow him then they will gain eternal life. No one will gain eternal life without going through Jesus, so both beliefs are true. All you need is love, as that is what you need to follow Jesus and following Jesus is the only way to gain eternal life."

The King turns to Musa with a smile. "It appears you were correct in bringing this one home. He has a belief that is distinctive, providing salvation answers for all humanity. We may be on the cusp of answering my old question."

The King then turns back to Isaac. "You can say and believe anything. You can even find a few out of context scriptures to support those beliefs. The true test is having firm scriptural support for those ideas. Without that proof, you just have oddball beliefs."

"That's exactly what I believe. My beliefs may not be widely held but they are firmly rooted in the Bible. Furthermore, I can find those supporting scriptures for proof. My belief in the resurrections seem to be just as surprising to you as they are to most Christians. It saddens me that even though the resurrections are a common theme mentioned throughout the Bible, Christians know more about sports, comic book superheroes or the Greek gods than they do about the resurrections God has planned. Resurrection is the vehicle God uses in helping humans choose salvation."

Isaac explains his thoughts further. "Through a resurrection, God can transport humans from any time period of this present life, to a time far in the future. God can reanimate people back to life when the time suits him. He's not bound by the mortal frailties of our lives. Humans, being mortal souls, are completely dependent upon God for life. This allows God's love to save them beyond their graves. He'll resurrect humans back into a world where they're most likely to accept Jesus as their savior."

"Well I'm glad to hear your confident in your beliefs. I'll give you an opportunity to exercise that confidence. I don't have the time to do research but I'll make time to listen to a debate on the subject. The proof is tasting the pudding. I'll determine for myself if your ideas are able to stand up to the scrutiny of someone who disagrees with you and are also well versed in Bible scripture."

"That'll be great. Let God be true and every man a liar. As long as we let the Bible be the final authority, we can't go wrong. Like you said, if people can't support their beliefs through Bible scripture then all they have are some oddball ideas. If the Bible proves my beliefs wrong I don't want them and I'll gladly abandon them. I want to follow Jesus, not fables."

"Good! I'll arrange for a suitable debating opponent to be ready for the weekend, then we'll see how your beliefs stand up to a test," the King excitedly slaps his thigh. "I have just the man for the job. I've been supporting my boyhood camp evangelist in his retirement years. He's been living in a modest little house on one of my farms. I'll get him to prepare some Bible facts on the subject. He may be old but he's as sharp as a tack. I can't think of a better person to debate with you. I'll moderate and ask questions as we cover the subjects I'm interested in."

The King leans back on the couch and gestures for Isaac to leave. "Musa, get him any reference material he might need. Perhaps a laptop and password so he can surf the web for his scripture proof. I want this to be as definitive as possible. I've waited a long time for someone to reveal these mysteries to me, I won't be foiled this close to finding out."

Musa rises, giving the King his customary farewells and ushers Isaac out of the room. "Come with me this way. I'll put you in the guest wing where you can freshen up and change out of those dreadful clothes," he says, leading Isaac down a long corridor to the guest wing.

Later that evening, after Isaac has eaten his supper alone in his room, the house maid with the tea and biscuits from earlier that day delivers a box with a laptop. She picks up his empty dishes eyeing him discreetly. Paying her little notice except for saying hello when he opened the door and thank you and good night when she left, Isaac busily set up the laptop, getting it ready for the debate to come. Thanking God for his deliverance and mercies he was gladdened by the peace of mind knowing Jesus brought him.

Thinking about the debate he prays for the Holy Spirit to fill his mouth with the appropriate words at the right time. Surfing the web for news from home until late in the night his blinks get slower and longer until his head is resting on the keyboard, leaving a trail of g's across the screen.

Chapter 16

The weekend came quickly. Isaac was ushered into the side of a small banquet room with a short stage. The stage was just large enough for two lecterns sharing a large raised table, where a jug of water, glasses, a cup of pens, pads of writing paper and two laptops were set up. Scaffolding supported overhead lights, illuminating the lecterns and provided ample light for the table and stage. A pair of stools behind the lecterns gave the debaters a chance to sit. Audience seating was neatly set out, accommodating about fifty-five people. The King was already seated behind a decoratively carved wooden desk on a slightly higher stage off to the side of the main stage where he would moderate the debate.

Introducing the well-known local evangelist, the King heaps praise on a highly respected older but spry Mike Kasy. His tireless, lifelong work with local children had brought him favor with the elite of the country. He greets familiar benefactors as he makes his way to the stage, working the crowd of spectators like a seasoned politician. Once comfortably behind a lectern, he rests on the stool as Isaac is introduced.

"You may be wondering why I have arranged this gathering," the King starts to explain. "Ever since I was a preschooler, my mom has taught me about the love of Jesus. I would imagine how the self-sacrificial love of Jesus was demonstrated through the trials our kings of old endured as they guided their people through wars and famine. It is through the legacy of these ancient Kings that our nation has been able to survive independent, free of colonial masters. Jesus taught us having love towards others is important. The Bible describes love as being the most important trait people can develop and how having love will keep us safe.

When I was in my teens, I learned the importance of accepting Jesus as my personal savior. I've read where the Bible plainly describes the only way to be saved and gain eternal life is by personally accepting Jesus as my savior. This created a dichotomy in my mind. If I believe that personally accepting Jesus alone leads to salvation and eternal life, how can love be the most important thing? We are told anyone who never learned about, or accepted Jesus when they were alive are lost forever, no matter how much love they developed during their lives. Not knowing Jesus leaves all my loving forefathers without salvation or eternal life.

However, without possessing eternal life I could never understand the concept of them being tormented eternally in Hell. Never getting a satisfying answer, I distracted my mind with life's other concerns, believing the mysteries of God are unfathomable to us humans.

These questions have remained unanswered to me until recently. My boyhood companion Musa has found someone who claims to have the answers to these mysteries. Before believing his explanations, I want to test his answers against what the Bible says. I'm not qualified to delve into these subjects in depth, so I brought my old counselor Mr. Mike Kasy to debate the merits of these new beliefs. I hope we'll all find this debate enlightening and convincing. Later we can discuss the points knowledgeably amongst ourselves."

The King gestures for Isaac to take his place on stage. "So, I would like to welcome this new free thinker. Isaac, come take your place up on stage," at the King's direction Isaac briskly walks to the podium and stands behind his lectern.

"As I said in my introduction, Isaac believes people aren't lost until they decide not to follow Jesus. No matter where or when they lived, God will resurrect them into a new life, allowing everyone to freely choose to follow Jesus if they want to." Murmurs of disbelief rifle through the crowd. "I'll let him fill in more of the details," the King looks to Isaac for clarity.

After clearing his throat with a drink of water Isaac bends towards the microphone. "I'd like to thank Mr. Kasy for giving up his time to discuss these Biblical beliefs I have told his majesty about. You're looking very fit," Isaac says, trying to complement Mr. Kasy on his trim physique. "Do you do yoga in an exercise regime?"

"Certainly not!" Mr. Kasy replies offendedly. "Those exercises are steeped in pagan worship. I lead by setting good examples for others to follow. As a community leader, people look to me for spiritual guidance. I need to set the bar high and get it right in all aspects of my life. I would never taint myself by practicing those poses, profaning Jesus. I faithfully walk several miles every morning in prayer and meditation. God has rewarded my efforts with good health."

"I beg your pardon. I didn't mean to offend. I only meant to complement." Shaken by his miss step Isaac turns his attention to the audience. "As his Majesty has correctly stated. I believe the Bible tells us that everyone will have a fair opportunity to accept Jesus as their savior."

"There's nothing new about that!" Mr. Kasy cuts in abruptly. "The heavens declare the glory of God; the skies proclaim the work of his hands. Day after day they pour forth speech; night after night they display knowledge. There is no speech or language where their voice is not heard. Their voice goes out into all the earth, their words to the ends of the world. Psalm 19:1-4." Kasy recites by heart. "Creation has always declared God is the creator, people have never had an excuse for not knowing God." Still by memory he continues. "Ever since the creation of the world his eternal power and divine nature, invisible though they are, have been understood and seen through the things he has made. So they are without excuse. Romans 1:20. People have always had their opportunity to know God." Mr. Kasy is emphatic.

Isaac is intimidated by the tenacity of Mr. Kasy's early statements. He tries to collect his thoughts, not sure what to say. He feels a tingling in his hands and undirected by himself, they start to type on the laptops keyboard. Startled by scripture appearing on the audience's large display screen as well on his personal monitor, he hesitantly starts to speak.

"Those versus don't tell us that everyone has had an opportunity to accept Jesus as their savior" Isaac shakily points out. "Only that they should know there is a creator God. The leaders of the temple were without excuse only after personally being taught by Jesus," Isaac reads aloud the verse off his monitor.

John 15:22 NIV
22 If I had not come and spoken to them, they would not be guilty of sin; but now they have no excuse for their sin.

"If creation preaches Jesus," Isaac continues, "why do Christians send evangelists out to preach the gospel? Knowing there is a God who made us is very different than accepting Jesus as our savior. Knowing about God isn't enough, as salvation only comes through Jesus," Isaac states assertively. A new verse flashes up on the screen and he reads it to the audience.

Acts 4:12 New International Version (NIV)
12 Salvation is found in no one else, for there is no other name under heaven given to mankind by which we must be saved.

Unsure of what was happening with his hands, Isaac wipes them nervously on his pants and cracks his knuckles for good measure.

"Of course we need to preach the gospel. The great commission Jesus gave the church was to preach salvation to the world," Kasy replies. Fumbling with his laptop he brings up this verse to display on the big screen, then he reads it out loud.

Luke 24:47 King James Version (KJV)

47 And that repentance and remission of sins should be preached in his name among all nations, beginning at Jerusalem.

"Jesus told us to preach his gospel of the Kingdom of God," Isaac corrected, feeling supernaturally inspired. "Jesus was always preaching about the coming Kingdom of God, that was his gospel. He never appealed to the crowds to accept him as their savior. That's the gospel of salvation. That gospel tells us what Jesus can do for us. Preaching salvation alone preaches a gospel, or good news about the messenger, not his message. The message, teaching and gospel of Jesus was about the coming Kingdom of God." Isaac stresses.

"We can't enter the Kingdom of God without accepting Jesus," Kasy countered.

"True," Isaac agrees. "But salvation is only part of the gospel, not the entirety of the gospel."

"We should preach the gospel of the Kingdom and salvation, as if with the same breath," Mr. Kasy states.

"That would be great. But when have you ever done that? It seems to me most Christian evangelists run out of breath after talking about salvation. I believe we should first preach the Kingdom. That will lead our audience to ask how do we get into God's Kingdom? Then we can tell them how to receive salvation through Jesus. Ignoring the Kingdom message leaves out God's plan for saving mankind."

"We know what that is. His plan is Jesus!" Kasy is emphatic.

"Yes. Salvation comes only through Jesus but most humans will come to learn about Jesus in the coming Kingdom of God. The gospel of the Kingdom provides the answers that his Majesty has found so insightful and why we're here today," Isaac gestures towards the King and the audience. "The gospel of the Kingdom of God and how it arrives is what the world longs to know, but few have heard or understood."

"And you know this how? You make yourself out to be more knowledgeable than the giants of Christianity who've gone before you. None of the great reformers or revival evangelists preached what you claim as truth. You have no denominational support other than a few fringe cultish groups. I've done an extensive background check on you. You don't even have a record of elementary schooling and you're completely devoid of ecclesiastical training! Why should anyone believe what you have to say about the Bible? I'm only here indulging your delusional fantasies as a personal favor to the King. I led him to Jesus when he was a young teen and I won't have him led away from the Bible truth on my watch. Especially by the likes of you. An uneducated, rebellious scrap collector and convicted terrorist."

"I suppose that's what my record shows," Isaac says sadly. "As I told his Majesty, the important thing is what the Bible has to say, not what people want it to say. Don't believe me because I'm saying it, believe because the Bible says it. We need to trust the facts the Bible gives us."

"That's the truest thing I've heard yet this morning," Mr. Kasy smiles warmly from years of practice. "When would you like me to start correcting your errors?"

Isaac replies deliberately cautious. "I believe the gospel message of the Kingdom is founded on the resurrection of the dead. It's only through a resurrection that the bulk of humanity will have any hope of accepting Jesus."

"Yes. The resurrection of Jesus is humanity's only hope," Kasy again interrupts Isaac.

"No, I'm not talking about the resurrection of Jesus. I'm referring to the physical resurrection of most of humanity. It will be mankind's second mass resurrection."

"You do like speaking in riddles. Does using confusing biblical language help you bamboozle those you pretend to teach?" Kasy's tone is sarcastic and cold.

"I suppose it would be a riddle if you don't know about the resurrections taught in the Bible. Sadly, I find very few Christian teachers are aware of the resurrections God has planned for humanity."

"This should be good. Please enlighten us about these resurrections. We sit at your feet, anxiously awaiting your tutelage," Kasy's smile is broader than before.

"Resurrection back to a physical life is a recurring theme throughout the Bible. As you are probably aware, there were six resurrections before Jesus was crucified. Then after Jesus was resurrected, the Bible tells us of many saints that were resurrected back to life." Tingling as if being electrified, Isaac's hands fly over the computer keys, displaying scriptural proof on the screen which he reads.

Matthew 27:50-53 New International Version (NIV)
50 And when Jesus had cried out again in a loud voice, he gave up his spirit. 51 At that moment the curtain of the temple was torn in two from top to bottom. The earth shook, the rocks split 52 and the tombs broke open. The bodies of many holy people who had died were raised to life. 53 They came out of the tombs after Jesus' resurrection and[a] went into the holy city and appeared to many people.

"Jesus was the first to be resurrected into a glorified body. Later on there were a couple more resurrections back to a temporary physical life. Out of all the resurrections, Jesus was the only one to be raised back to immortality. All the others were resurrected back to mortality. They all died again later as mortals always do," Isaac explained.

"Nice Bible lesson but what about these mass resurrections you were talking about. The ones explaining the Kingdom of God. Your version of the gospel," Kasy's rolls his eyes derisively.

"The resurrections don't explain the Kingdom. They explain how mankind will have the opportunity to live in it eternally."

"That's easy. Every Christian knows they can only get into the Kingdom of God through the salvation of Jesus," Mr. Kasy was exuberant. "He came providing salvation for all who ever lived. Humans must accept the salvation of Jesus to have their sins forgiven. It's the one and only way to be saved," Kasy was alive with excitement.

"Exactly!" Isaac exclaims. "The only way to gain salvation is to accept the sacrifice of Jesus. That's why we need the resurrections, it's the only way most of humanity will ever have an opportunity to accept Jesus."

"What do you mean? Why would most of humanity need to be resurrected before they can accept Jesus. They had this life to accept Jesus, they don't get another chance."

"Those who never had a chance to hear about Jesus, those who died young, lived in a time or place where there were no Christians to tell them about Jesus, like the King's forefathers. They would've never had a chance during this life to accept Jesus. Another life, through a resurrection, will be their first chance," Isaac replies.

"We just read; creation declares God to humanity. They have no excuse," Kasy is adamant.

"I thought we said that would only let them know about God. Seeing creation explains nothing about Jesus. If it did, why do Christians worry about proclaiming the gospel to unbelievers?"

"You said that. I didn't agree with it," Kasy said bluntly.

"You quit discussing the point. I took that for agreement. But if you don't agree, how does seeing creation teach us about Jesus and why do Christians need to proclaim the gospel?"

Kasy coughs. "Well I don't know that I could give a reasoned explanation right now for those questions. I might be thinking you're right."

"Should I take that for agreement? Not only has most of humanity not heard about Jesus, they've been blocked from knowing him. Unless God draws them to Jesus they can't come to him."

"Not true! People from any background, or nationality can come to Jesus. The salvation of Jesus is open to everyone. That's why we need to proclaim him to the world. People must accept Jesus to go to heaven, otherwise they'll be condemned to hell."

"Yes, we need to proclaim the gospel to all the world, but Jesus made it plain that only those chosen by God can come to him." John 6:44 King James Version appears on Isaac's monitor and the big screen. He reads it out loud.

44 No man can come to me, except the Father which hath sent me draw him: and I will raise him up at the last day.

Isaac continues, "the New Testament has many verses about Christians being chosen or called. We preach the gospel to the world because we don't know who God wants to call at this time. As you pointed out, God might call someone from any nationality or belief. Not knowing who will respond, Christians proclaim the gospel to all people."

The King breaks in as moderator to try and steer the conversation. "We all know the traditional Christian beliefs about heaven and hell. Why don't we let Isaac tell us about these resurrections he's referring too? I'm sure the audience, as well as myself, would appreciate more information about them and how they work."

Mr. Kasy is reluctantly quiet as Isaac speaks.

"Sure," Isaac replies. "As I said, Jesus is the only person to have been resurrected back into a new glorified body. The first mass resurrection of humanity is for Christians when he returns." Isaac's hands pull up proof scripture on his laptop and the big screen for his belief. He reads them to the room.

1 Thessalonians 4:13-17 New King James Version (NKJV)

The Comfort of Christ's Coming

13 But I do not want you to be ignorant, brethren, concerning those who have fallen [a]asleep, lest you sorrow as others who have no hope. 14 For if we believe that Jesus died and rose again, even so God will bring with Him those who [b]sleep in Jesus. 15 For this we say to you by the word of the Lord, that we who are alive and remain until the coming of the Lord will by no means precede those who are [c]asleep. 16 For the Lord Himself will descend from heaven with a shout, with the voice of an archangel, and with the trumpet of God. And the dead in Christ will rise first. 17 Then we who are alive and remain shall be caught up together with them in the clouds to meet the Lord in the air. And thus we shall always be with the Lord.

"Here again we're told we'll be resurrected into a glorified, spiritual body like Jesus has when he returns for us. Until then the Bible tells us we are asleep. We need to wait for the return of Jesus to be resurrected back to life."

More scripture appears on the conference screen, without disrupting Isaac's speaking.

1 Corinthians 15:40-58 New International Version (NIV)

40 There are also heavenly bodies and there are earthly bodies; but the splendor of the heavenly bodies is one kind, and the splendor of the earthly bodies is another. 41 The sun has one kind of splendor, the moon another and the stars another; and star differs from star in splendor. 42 So will it be with the resurrection of the dead. The body that is sown is perishable, it is raised imperishable; 43 it is sown in dishonor, it is raised in glory; it is sown in weakness, it is raised in power; 44 it is sown a natural body, it is raised a spiritual body. If there is a natural body, there is also a spiritual body. 45 So it is written: "The first man Adam became a living being"[a]; the last Adam, a life-giving spirit. 46 The spiritual did not come first, but the natural, and after that the spiritual. 47 The first man was of the dust of the earth; the second man is of heaven. 48 As was the earthly man, so are those who are of the earth; and as is the heavenly man, so also are those who are of heaven. 49 And just as we have borne the image of the earthly man, so shall we[b] bear the image of the heavenly man. 50 I declare to you, brothers and

sisters, that flesh and blood cannot inherit the kingdom of God, nor does the perishable inherit the imperishable. 51 Listen, I tell you a mystery: We will not all sleep, but we will all be changed— 52 in a flash, in the twinkling of an eye, at the last trumpet. For the trumpet will sound, the dead will be raised imperishable, and we will be changed. 53 For the perishable must clothe itself with the imperishable, and the mortal with immortality. 54 When the perishable has been clothed with the imperishable, and the mortal with immortality, then the saying that is written will come true: "Death has been swallowed up in victory."[c] 55 "Where, O death, is your victory? Where, O death, is your sting?"

"You're interpreting those scriptures wrong!" Kasy insists angrily. "Our immortal souls don't sleep. They go to heaven to be with Jesus when we die. It's so lovely there, praising God for the rest of eternity, we wouldn't come back to this world even if we could. We only come back with Jesus when he raptures his bride, the church."

"That isn't what those verses said," Isaac contends. "They tell us that we're physical first and we don't become spirit until the resurrection." His hands take over and display verses that he dutifully reads aloud.

1 Corinthians 15:45-47 21st Century King James Version (KJ21)
45 And so it is written: "The first man Adam was made a living soul." The last Adam was made a quickening Spirit.

46 However that which is spiritual was not first, but that which is natural, and afterward that which is spiritual.
47 The first man is of the earth, earthy; the second Man is the Lord from Heaven.

These verses don't tell us that we're both at the same time. They tell us we're planted as a physical body and later we're resurrected as a spiritual body at the return of Jesus."

"No, that's wrong! When Christians die their souls go to be with Jesus in heaven," Mr. Kasy objected vigorously, wondering silently to himself how Isaac was able to find scripture and verbally defend his position all at the same time. After spending a minute finding them, he displays scripture on the screen as his proof.

Philippians 1:21-23 New International Version (NIV)
21 For to me, to live is Christ and to die is gain. 22 If I am to go on living in the body, this will mean fruitful labor for me. Yet what shall I choose? I do not know! 23 I am torn between the two: I desire to depart and be with Christ, which is better by far;

Pressing his point further, Mr. Kasy continued. "See, Paul knew he would be going to heaven to be with Jesus when he died. He doesn't think his immortal soul would be sleeping until Jesus returns."

"Those verses don't say that," Isaac insists. "They say Paul thought he'd be better off dead than being beaten all the time. They tell us Paul's desire was to die and be with Christ, which is far better than getting beaten up or stoned. They say nothing about when Paul would be with Jesus, or about possessing an immortal soul that goes to heaven when he died."

"Well we can only assume he would be with Jesus in heaven. Where else would we imagine him to be? We'll just have to agree to disagree," Mr. Kasy says with practiced humility.

"Agreeing to disagree will do nothing to help these people or the King to know what the Bible teaches on the subject," Isaac says forcefully, gesturing towards the audience, "and assumption, or imagining isn't proof! If I'm wrong, I want to change. I don't want to be left in my ignorance. Like the King, I want to know what the Bible really says. I'm not interested in following the fables of man or his assumptions."

"I don't preach fables!" Kasy stammers defensively. "I've preached the love of Jesus throughout my entire life. Jesus is love, as is his Father." After a long pause some scriptures flash to life on the screen that Kasy reads to the crowd.

1 John 4:7-10 King James Version (KJV)
7 Beloved, let us love one another: for love is of God; and every one that loveth is born of God, and knoweth God.

8 He that loveth not knoweth not God; for God is love.

9 In this was manifested the love of God toward us, because that God sent his only begotten Son into the world, that we might live through him.

10 Herein is love, not that we loved God, but that he loved us, and sent his Son to be the propitiation for our sins.

"God loves us so much, he sent his only son to save us by sacrificing himself for us," Mr. Kasy's voice quivers with emotion. "Accepting that sacrifice and Jesus as our savior is the only way mankind can gain salvation and eternal life in heaven. Those who fail to follow Jesus will be doomed to an eternity of torment in the fires of hell. We all must follow Jesus now while we can. Before it's too late!" Holding back tears of sincere sorrow, Kasy pleads to the audience, "Jesus is the only way to have your sins forgiven, he alone can blot them out." Eventually he displays more verses on the screen.

John 3:14-17 King James Version (KJV)
14 And as Moses lifted up the serpent in the wilderness, even so must the Son of man be lifted up:

15 That whosoever believeth in him should not perish, but have eternal life.

16 For God so loved the world, that he gave his only begotten Son, that whosoever believeth in him should not perish, but have everlasting life.

17 For God sent not his Son into the world to condemn the world; but that the world through him might be saved.

"We must all accept and do our best to follow Jesus now while we can in this life. It's the safest way to seal your place in heaven. When you die there are only two options for you and there's only one that you'll want," finishing his heartfelt plea, Kasy stands silently looking skyward, with his hands folded on his chest.

"Exactly!" Isaac agrees. "Jesus is the only path that leads to salvation. Without him, humans are lost. That's why everyone from before Jesus came to earth and those who haven't been called after he died, need to be resurrected so they can learn about him. They've had no opportunity to accept him."

"No, they've had opportunity. They can see creation; they have the laws of Moses and the prophets. They are without excuse for not having faith in God. Those from the Old Testament times were saved by faith, just like today," Mr. Kasy displays some scriptures and reads them to the audience.

Hebrews 11:17 New International Version (NIV)
17 By faith Abraham, when God tested him, offered Isaac as a sacrifice. He who had embraced the promises was about to sacrifice his one and only son,

Romans 4:18-25 New International Version (NIV)
18 Against all hope, Abraham in hope believed and so became the father of many nations, just as it had been said to him, "So shall your offspring be."[a] 19 Without weakening in his faith, he faced the fact that his body was as good as dead—since he was about a hundred years old—and that Sarah's womb was also

dead. 20 Yet he did not waver through unbelief regarding the promise of God, but was strengthened in his faith and gave glory to God, 21 being fully persuaded that God had power to do what he had promised. 22 This is why "it was credited to him as righteousness." 23 The words "it was credited to him" were written not for him alone, 24 but also for us, to whom God will credit righteousness—for us who believe in him who raised Jesus our Lord from the dead. 25 He was delivered over to death for our sins and was raised to life for our justification.

"Jesus taught us about heaven and hell in the rich man and Lazarus parable. There we find faithful Abraham in charge in heaven. By this we can be sure the rest of the Old Testament faithful are in heaven as well." Mr. Kasy expounds eloquently about the verses upon the screen as he reads them aloud.

Luke 16:19-31 New International Version (NIV)
The Rich Man and Lazarus
19 "There was a rich man who was dressed in purple and fine linen and lived in luxury every day. 20 At his gate was laid a beggar named Lazarus, covered with sores 21 and longing to eat what fell from the rich man's table. Even the dogs came and licked his sores. 22 "The time came when the beggar died and the angels carried him to Abraham's side. The rich man also died and was buried. 23 In Hades, where he was in torment, he looked up and saw Abraham far away, with Lazarus by his side. 24 So he called to him,

'Father Abraham, have pity on me and send Lazarus to dip the tip of his finger in water and cool my tongue, because I am in agony in this fire.'

Bothered in his spirit with Mr. Kasy's insistence that people could receive salvation without deliberately accepting Jesus, Isaac is compelled to step back from his microphone. A favorite old Sunday school song was forcing itself into his consciousness by growing louder and louder in his head. He wasn't sure why but he found himself singing it out loud, unobtrusively, yet loud enough for the audience to hear.

"What can wash away my sin?
Nothing but the blood of Jesus;
What can make me whole again?
Nothing but the blood of Jesus.
Oh! precious is the flow
That makes me white as snow;
No other fount I know,
Nothing but the blood of Jesus.
For my pardon, this I see,
Nothing but the blood of Jesus;
For my cleansing this my plea,
Nothing but the blood of Jesus."

As Mr. Kasy continues to talk, those in the front rows pick up on the well-known chorus and start to sing quietly along with Isaac.

"Oh! precious is the flow

That makes me white as snow;
No other fount I know,
Nothing but the blood of Jesus.
Nothing can for sin atone,
Nothing but the blood of Jesus;
Naught of good that I have done,
Nothing but the blood of Jesus."

Soon the entire audience is singing. Simultaneously reading off the screen, Mr. Kasy talks over them loudly as they continue in song.

25 "But Abraham replied, 'Son, remember that in your lifetime you received your good things, while Lazarus received bad things, but now he is comforted here and you are in agony. 26 And besides all this, between us and you a great chasm has been set in place, so that those who want to go from here to you cannot, nor can anyone cross over from there to us.'
27 "He answered, 'Then I beg you, father, send Lazarus to my family,28 for I have five brothers. Let him warn them, so that they will not also come to this place of torment.'

"Oh! precious is the flow
That makes me white as snow;
No other fount I know,
Nothing but the blood of Jesus.
This is all my hope and peace,
Nothing but the blood of Jesus;
This is all my righteousness,

Nothing but the blood of Jesus.
 "Oh! precious is the flow
That makes me white as snow;
No other fount I know,
Nothing but the blood of Jesus.
Now by this I'll overcome—
Nothing but the blood of Jesus;
Now by this I'll reach my home—
Nothing but the blood of Jesus.
 "Oh! precious is the flow
That makes me white as snow;
No other fount I know,
Nothing but the blood of Jesus.
Glory! Glory! This I sing—
Nothing but the blood of Jesus,
All my praise for this I bring—
Nothing but the blood of Jesus.

Mr. Kasy finished in time to hear the entire crowd sing the last chorus uninterrupted.

29 "Abraham replied, 'They have Moses and the Prophets; let them listen to them.'
30 "'No, father Abraham,' he said, 'but if someone from the dead goes to them, they will repent.'
31 "He said to him, 'If they do not listen to Moses and the Prophets, they will not be convinced even if someone rises from the dead.'"

 "Oh! precious is the flow
That makes me white as snow;

No other fount I know,
Nothing but the blood of Jesus.

"Christianity is exclusive!" Isaac begins. "What makes it that way is the truth of that song. One thing and one thing alone has the power to save us. Nothing but the blood of Jesus! There is no other way to gain salvation and eternal life," scriptures appear on the screen and he reads them to the audience.

Acts 4:12 King James Version (KJV)
12 Neither is there salvation in any other: for there is none other name under heaven given among men, whereby we must be saved.

1 Timothy 2:5 King James Version (KJV)
5 For there is one God, and one mediator between God and men, the man Christ Jesus;

John 3:36 New
International Version (NIV)
36 Whoever believes in the Son has eternal life, but whoever rejects the Son will not see life, for God's wrath remains on them.

1 John 5:11-12 New International Version (NIV)
11 And this is the testimony: God has given us eternal life, and this life is in his Son. 12 Whoever has the Son has life; whoever does not have the Son of God does not have life.

1 John 4:14 New International Version (NIV)
14 And we have seen and testify that the Father has sent his Son to be the Savior of the world.

"Not until the blood of Jesus was shed, making the way for our salvation to be possible, only then could people be saved. We're only saved through the blood of Jesus, there is no other way. Those who lived before Jesus died lived without access to that sacrifice. They had no opportunity to accept the sacrifice of Jesus as it hadn't been made yet."

Kasy broke in. "But I just read Jesus telling us that Abraham is in heaven with Lazarus. Their immortal souls are basking in heaven's joys this very minute."

"No. You're misunderstanding those verses. First off, Abraham's faith was credited to him as righteousness. The Bible doesn't say it gave him eternal life, or salvation. Furthermore, if we read to the end of Hebrews the Bible clarifies further," the verses are displayed instantly on the big screen.

Hebrews 11:35-40 New International Version (NIV)
35 Women received back their dead, raised to life again. There were others who were tortured, refusing to be released so that they might gain an even better resurrection. 36 Some faced jeers and flogging, and even chains and imprisonment. 37 They were put to death by stoning;[a]they were sawed in two; they were killed by the sword. They went about in sheepskins and goatskins, destitute, persecuted and mistreated— 38 the world was not worthy of them. They wandered

in deserts and mountains, living in caves and in holes in the ground. 39 These were all commended for their faith, yet none of them received what had been promised, 40 since God had planned something better for us so that only together with us would they be made perfect.

"As we read in verse thirty-five, the faithful rejected freedom from torture so they might gain an even better resurrection. They had faith that God would bring them back to life through a resurrection from the dead. It doesn't say their immortal souls would be whisked off to heaven after they died. Pay close attention to verses thirty-nine and forty. None of them received what had been promised because God has better plans for his faithful from all humanity, including Abraham. These verses show that Abraham is still waiting for all his promises from God. He doesn't gain eternal life until we're all made perfect. All together at the same resurrection event, when Jesus returns. Abraham isn't in charge in heaven, he's dead in his grave waiting.

Rather than describing heaven and hell, the parable of Lazarus and the rich man is predicting how the Jewish rulers would continue to reject Jesus as their messiah. Having completed most of the miracles the Jews considered only possible by God, Jesus was about to fulfill the last messianic miracle. Raising someone back to life after being dead for over three days was the last of the Jewish messianic miracles, proving his divinity beyond any doubt. Even after completing all their tests Jesus knew and was predicting through his parable that the Jews would still reject him and would want to kill him.

In John six Jesus told his disciples four times when this resurrection event would take place. He said he would come back for them and raise them up on the last day. This is the first mass resurrection of humanity, it includes all the faithful followers of God and Jesus. It's in this resurrection those from before Jesus was born will have their faith counted as righteousness." While Isaac talked more scriptural proof shows up with the appropriate verses out of John six displayed on the big screen. The room read along with Isaac.

39 And this is the will of him who sent me, that I shall lose none of all those he has given me, but raise them up at the last day.

40 For my Father's will is that everyone who looks to the Son and believes in him shall have eternal life, and I will raise them up at the last day.

44 "No one can come to me unless the Father who sent me draws them, and I will raise them up at the last day.

54 Whoever eats my flesh and drinks my blood has eternal life, and I will raise them up at the last day.

Chapter 17

"I've been a Christian all my life. I've dedicated my life to preaching the love of Jesus to the children of this country. You can believe me when I say, Christians go to heaven when they die. That's their Christian reward," Mr. Kasy adamantly defends his beliefs to the King and dignitaries. "Our immortal souls go to be with God when we die."

"No one is questioning your love of Jesus or your dedication to spreading the good news of salvation. The only way to validate your beliefs though, is through Bible scripture. Where are your proof scriptures?" Isaac tries to gently question. "I find the Bible explaining that no one goes to heaven," a verse flashes up on the screen.

John 3:13 New King James Version (NKJV)
13 No one has ascended to heaven but He who came down from heaven, that is, the Son of Man [a]who is in heaven.

Isaac continues further. "Believing that you will 'go to heaven', shows your starting point or fundamentals are wrong. Jesus alone is in heaven. None of his dead, faithful followers are there with him."

"What do you mean by that? My fundamentals are wrong? My starting point is the love of Jesus!" Mr. Kasy replies sharply.

"Let me explain my point," Isaac starts again. "How did you get here this morning?

"I took a taxi."

"Did the driver ask you where you wanted to go?"

"Of course he did. I gave him this address, then he drove me here. What's that got to do with going to heaven?"

"You say it the same. I'm going to a particular address or I'm going to go to heaven when I die. It involves you moving or traveling to a destination. You say you'll go to heaven when you die. That's not what the Bible describes. Why would you want to be dead in heaven? That would do you no good at all. Those in heaven will be very much alive. Jesus told his followers he would come back and raise them to life, as he brings the Kingdom with him. In the book of Revelation the Bible describes the new Jerusalem coming down to the earth. God brings the Kingdom of Heaven here, to the earth, to a resurrected humanity.

The Lord's prayer instructs us to pray for God's kingdom to come. It comes to us, here on the earth. We don't go anywhere. No one goes to heaven: heaven comes to us. The life, crucifixion and resurrection of Jesus started the process of the Kingdom's return by paying our death penalty for us. Before Jesus did that all were lost to sin. The debt of blood hadn't been paid yet. The next big milestone is the return of Jesus when his faithful are resurrected into eternal life with glorified bodies, like the body Jesus has," more proof scripture for the crowd is read aloud.

1 John 3:1-2 Easy-to-Read Version (ERV)
We Are God's Children
1 The Father has loved us so much! This shows how much he loved us: We are called children of God. And we really are his children. But the people in the world don't understand that we are God's children, because they have not known him. 2 Dear friends, now we are children of God. We have not yet been shown what we will be in the future. But we know that when Christ comes again, we will be like him. We will see him just as he is.

"I never thought of it that way before," Kasy admits. "I can see your point of view, even if I don't agree with it. I suppose what I really believe is I will spend eternity with Jesus, no matter where it is, or how I get there."

"On that we have common ground. It's the process of arriving into the kingdom that we differ on."

"But you said my fundamentals are wrong. Why do you think that if my fundamentals are the love of Jesus?" a bewildered Mr. Kasy asks.

"No. I didn't mean the fundamental love of Jesus is wrong," Isaac clarified. "Love is the best thing humans can cultivate as it's the only thing of lasting value. I meant your basic, fundamental concept of humans possessing an immortal soul is wrong. It leads you away from the plans God has for humanity. The immortal soul doctrine is the filter through which you understand Bible scripture.

Humans having an immortal soul dictates that when your physical body dies the soul must go somewhere, as it's immortal. Understanding that humans are physical mortal beings, completely dependent upon God for life, enables you to understand the plans God has for mankind's salvation through a series of resurrections."

"Yes. And I'd like to get back to those resurrections," the King again takes control of the debate. "We understand the first resurrection happens at the second coming of Jesus. We've seen the scriptures saying the followers of Jesus, the dead and living, will receive glorified bodies at the event of Jesus' return," the King sums up what he's learned from Isaac. "Then what happens?"

Isaac explains. "When Jesus returns to this earth he won't be welcomed by human governments. They make war against him and his rule over them. When the battle is over, the rulers of the world are defeated and their army's are dead. Satan is chained in the bottomless pit as Jesus, along with his saints', rule over the earth for a thousand years. The world is rebuilt and rejuvenated from devastation by the civilians who survive," Isaac reads aloud the verses his fingers have displayed.

Revelation 19:11-21 New King James Version (NKJV)
Christ on a White Horse
11 Now I saw heaven opened, and behold, a white horse. And He who sat on him was called Faithful and True, and in righteousness He judges and makes war. 12 His eyes were like a flame of fire, and on His head were many crowns. He [a]had a name written that no one knew except Himself. 13 He was clothed with a robe dipped in blood, and His name is called The

Word of God. 14 And the armies in heaven, clothed in [b]fine linen, white and clean, followed Him on white horses. 15 Now out of His mouth goes a [c]sharp sword, that with it He should strike the nations. And He Himself will rule them with a rod of iron. He Himself treads the winepress of the fierceness and wrath of Almighty God. 16 And He has on His robe and on His thigh a name written:

KING OF KINGS AND
LORD OF LORDS.

The Beast and His Armies Defeated

17 Then I saw an angel standing in the sun; and he cried with a loud voice, saying to all the birds that fly in the midst of heaven, "Come and gather together for the [d]supper of the great God, 18 that you may eat the flesh of kings, the flesh of captains, the flesh of mighty men, the flesh of horses and of those who sit on them, and the flesh of all people,[e]free and slave, both small and great."

19 And I saw the beast, the kings of the earth, and their armies, gathered together to make war against Him who sat on the horse and against His army. 20 Then the beast was captured, and with him the false prophet who worked signs in his presence, by which he deceived those who received the mark of the beast and those who worshiped his image. These two were cast alive into the lake of fire burning with brimstone. 21 And the rest were killed with the sword which proceeded from the mouth of Him who sat on the horse. And all the birds were filled with their flesh.

Revelation 20:1-4 New International Version (NIV)

The Thousand Years

1 And I saw an angel coming down out of heaven, having the key to the Abyss and holding in his hand a great chain. 2 He seized the dragon, that ancient serpent, who is the devil, or Satan, and bound him for a thousand years. 3 He threw him into the Abyss, and locked and sealed it over him, to keep him from deceiving the nations anymore until the thousand years were ended. After that, he must be set free for a short time.4 I saw thrones on which were seated those who had been given authority to judge. And I saw the souls of those who had been beheaded because of their testimony about Jesus and because of the word of God. They[a] had not worshiped the beast or its image and had not received its mark on their foreheads or their hands. They came to life and reigned with Christ a thousand years.

Zechariah 14:8-9 King James Version (KJV)

8 And it shall be in that day, that living waters shall go out from Jerusalem; half of them toward the former sea, and half of them toward the hinder sea: in summer and in winter shall it be.

9 And the Lord shall be king over all the earth: in that day shall there be one Lord, and his name one.

"Well I still don't see how all that helps those who haven't been called to Jesus during this life?" the King speaks impatiently. "When do they get their chance?"

"That comes at the end of the thousand years," Isaac replies. "I was trying to lay out the timeline in the proper sequence. We're told their resurrection takes place after the thousand years is over. They are welcomed back to a rejuvenated world in the second mass resurrection. Bigger than the first as it will include everyone who ever lived not called by God to the salvation of Jesus," scriptural proof shows up on the big screen.

Revelation 20:5-6 King James Version (KJV)
5 But the rest of the dead lived not again until the thousand years were finished. This is the first resurrection.
6 Blessed and holy is he that hath part in the first resurrection: on such the second death hath no power, but they shall be priests of God and of Christ, and shall reign with him a thousand years.

"Now you're the one who's not using a proper interpretation," Mr. Kasy breaks in. "Those verses are talking about the first resurrection. It says so at the end of verse Five. It doesn't mention anything about a second resurrection."

"No! Verse four was talking about the saints reigning with Jesus for a thousand years. Then the beginning of verse five tells us, the rest of the dead don't live again until the thousand years are over. Then the narrative goes back to telling us about those raised in the first resurrection, who became the priests of God and Jesus. The first sentence of verse five tells us the second mass resurrection of mankind takes place at the end of the first thousand years after Jesus returns to earth. All the resurrections take place here on the earth. Humanity stays here on the earth; they don't escape to somewhere else. The Kingdom of God is established here on earth, not in some distant heavenly place."

"So where does the Bible tell us about their new life and why aren't 'the rest of the dead' raised into glorified bodies like those in the first resurrection?" The King asks expectantly.

"Isaiah tells us about this time," Isaac replies looking at his monitor. His hands had the verses up on the screen before the King had finished talking.

Isaiah 65:19-21 New International Version (NIV)
19 I will rejoice over Jerusalem and take delight in my people; the sound of weeping and of crying will be heard in it no more. 20 "Never again will there be in it an infant who lives but a few days, or an old man who does not live out his years; the one who dies at a hundred will be thought a mere child; the one who fails to reach[a] a hundred will be considered accursed. 21 They will build houses and dwell in them; they will plant vineyards and eat their fruit.

"The rest of the dead come back to life, each one having a lifetime of one hundred years to learn About Jesus. They're raised back to a physical life like we have today, because they still haven't decided to accept Jesus. Eternal life is reserved only for those who willingly accept Jesus as their saviour. This resurrection will be their time to learn about Jesus and willingly follow him. Satan will be chained up, unable to influence them to sin.

Becoming immortal, being born of the spirit, means not only that you won't die but that you can't die. Rejecting Jesus as an immortal would mean you'd have to live for eternity apart from God. That's the future awaiting Satan and his demons, not mankind. God's plan is more merciful for humans as those who choose life and follow Jesus will gain immortality. Those who choose to reject Jesus are freely allowed to do so, ending in their death.

It will be their choice, made after having a full lifetime to decide. Their choice will be final. Life with Jesus or death without him. Not being resurrected into spiritual bodies like Jesus has, will allow them to die and not suffer in their sins for all eternity apart from God."

"That's not what my Bible teaches!" Mr. Kasy loudly protests. "What about all the New Testament scriptures telling us sinners will be punished? They're not shy about telling us the sinner will end up in hell." Fumbling with his keyboard, Kasy finds his proof scriptures and displays them for the audience to read.

Matthew 10:28 New International Version (NIV)
28 Do not be afraid of those who kill the body but cannot kill the soul. Rather, be afraid of the One who can destroy both soul and body in hell.

Mark 9:43 New International Version (NIV)
43 If your hand causes you to stumble, cut it off. It is better for you to enter life maimed than with two hands to go into hell, where the fire never goes out.

Kasy goes on, "this is only two of the many verses using the word Hell. It, along with Hades and Tartarus, are used in the New Testament to describe where the reprobates go. The Greek word Hades is a place of torture for our immortal souls. It's a place of eternal torment that I've been warning people about and helping them avoid my entire adult life."

"Yes, I know what those words mean in Greek." Isaac admits.

"Then what's all this nonsense you've been feeding the King. The meaning for the words God used to write the New Testament describe our eternal souls being tormented in flames for eternity by demons. If you know what these words mean, how can you stand before the King and ignore their meaning by teaching him something else as truth?" Turning to the King Mr. Kasy pleads. "He admits to his lies! Send this evil one from your presence before he causes any more doubt in your mind."

The King eyes Isaac suspiciously as Musa takes an aggressive stance.

Isaac doesn't take notice of his potential peril. His eyes are fixed on Mr. Kasy as he replies.

"Of course that's what those Greek words mean. Why should they mean anything different? They're Greek words that reflect Greek beliefs. The entirety of the new testament was written in that pagan belief filled language. Why would you think a Greek word would accurately reflect the truth of our creator God? Jesus spoke in Aramaic which was translated into the dominant language of the day, Greek. If it had been written in

Scandinavian the word used would've probably been Valhalla and would have all its associated meanings and myths.

To express where a person went when they died in Greek, you'd use Hades or Tarsus. No other Greek words would convey your meaning. But using those words didn't mean the god Hades ruled there with his three headed guard dog Cerberus and ushered the dead into his realm over the Acheron river with Charon as the ferryman.

Those Greek words were used to convey what was happening within a Godly, Hebrew understanding. We need to read the New Testament through an Old Testament understanding or filter," Isaac passionately expresses his belief. The King and Musa's moods change to ones of interest.

"Well that sounds reasonable, like I'd expect from a con man. But the Bible tells us that now is our time to follow Jesus," Kasy displays scripture on the screen.

2 Corinthians 6:1-2 New King James Version
1 We then, as workers together with Him also plead with you not to receive the grace of God in vain. 2 For He says: "In an acceptable time I have heard you, And in the day of salvation I have helped you."
Behold, now is the accepted time; behold, now is the day of salvation.

"See!" Mr. Kasy explains passionately. "Now is our time to follow Jesus. We shouldn't wait for some fantasy, maybe time in the future! It's the only safe and prudent thing to do. After all, we only have you telling us there'll be some other opportunity to repent. People need to follow now while they can."

"That might be the safest way to hedge your bet, if you're only interested in saving your own life. Jesus told us about people like that." Scripture appears.

Matthew 10:39 Good News Translation (GNT)
39 Those who try to gain their own life will lose it; but those who lose their life for my sake will gain it.

"Those who respond to the love of Jesus will want to follow him." Mr. Kasy is fervent.

"Exactly my point." Isaac replies.

"What do you mean? You've been teaching his Majesty people don't need to accept Jesus now while they can. You teach there's some other day of salvation waiting for people at some imagined time in the future, in this second resurrection you've been going on about. People need to follow Jesus now! 'For now, is the day of salvation.'"

"They absolutely do! Now is the day for those called. That verse is taken from a letter written to followers of Jesus in Corinth, right?" Isaac asks Mr. Kasy.

"Yes. The book is 2 Corinthians, it's the second letter Paul wrote to the church at Corinth."

"So, Paul is writing to converted Christians, encouraging them to stay strong in their faith as they follow Jesus," Isaac correctly points out. "For them, turning back into sin would be spiritual suicide 'for now' is 'their day of salvation'. Is that correct?" Isaac asked for clarity.

"Exactly!" Mr. Kasy replied, exacerbated. "Now is the day of salvation. How much planer could it be?"

"Well we're saying the same thing," Isaac replied scratching his head. "If you're called by God to Jesus during this life, then now is your day of salvation. Christians take on a great weight of accountability by accepting Jesus during this life. This life is the one and only opportunity Christians will receive to faithfully follow Jesus. If we don't get it right we will perish in the lake of fire." In a blaze of furry Isaac's fingers type on his lap-top displaying scripture to the audience.

Luke 9:62 New King James Version (NKJV)
62 But Jesus said to him, "No one, having put his hand to the plow, and looking back, is fit for the kingdom of God."

Hebrews 10:26-39 New International Version (NIV)
26 If we deliberately keep on sinning after we have received the knowledge of the truth, no sacrifice for sins is left, 27 but only a fearful expectation of judgment and of raging fire that will consume the enemies of God. 28 Anyone who rejected the law of Moses died without mercy on the testimony of two or three witnesses. 29 How much more severely do you think someone deserves to be punished who has trampled the Son of God underfoot, who has treated as an unholy thing the blood of the covenant that sanctified them, and who has insulted the Spirit of

grace? 30 For we know him who said, "It is mine to avenge; I will repay,"[a] and again, "The Lord will judge his people."[b] 31 It is a dreadful thing to fall into the hands of the living God. 32 Remember those earlier days after you had received the light, when you endured in a great conflict full of suffering. 33 Sometimes you were publicly exposed to insult and persecution; at other times you stood side by side with those who were so treated. 34 You suffered along with those in prison and joyfully accepted the confiscation of your property, because you knew that you yourselves had better and lasting possessions. 35 So do not throw away your confidence; it will be richly rewarded. 36 You need to persevere so that when you have done the will of God, you will receive what he has promised. 37 For, "In just a little while, he who is coming will come and will not delay."[c] 38 And, "But my righteous[d] one will live by faith. And I take no pleasure in the one who shrinks back."[e] 39 But we do not belong to those who shrink back and are destroyed, but to those who have faith and are saved.

"No! No," Mr. Kasy loudly complains. "Nothing can remove us from the hand of God. Jesus tells us he will lose none of those God gives him. Your perverting the message of Jesus. Once we're saved, we're saved." He displays scripture on the screen, reading it aloud to the audience.

Romans 8:31-39 New Living Translation (NLT)
Nothing Can Separate Us from God's Love

31 What shall we say about such wonderful things as these? If God is for us, who can ever be against us? 32 Since he did not spare even his own Son but gave him up for us all, won't he also give us everything else?33 Who dares accuse us whom God has chosen for his own? No one—for God himself has given us right standing with himself. 34 Who then will condemn us? No one—for Christ Jesus died for us and was raised to life for us, and he is sitting in the place of honor at God's right hand, pleading for us. 35 Can anything ever separate us from Christ's love? Does it mean he no longer loves us if we have trouble or calamity, or are persecuted, or hungry, or destitute, or in danger, or threatened with death? 36 (As the Scriptures say, "For your sake we are killed every day; we are being slaughtered like sheep."[a]) 37 No, despite all these things, overwhelming victory is ours through Christ, who loved us. 38 And I am convinced that nothing can ever separate us from God's love. Neither death nor life, neither angels nor demons,[b] neither our fears for today nor our worries about tomorrow—not even the powers of hell can separate us from God's love. 39 No power in the sky above or in the earth below—indeed, nothing in all creation will ever be able to separate us from the love of God that is revealed in Christ Jesus our Lord.

John 10:28-30 New International Version (NIV)
28 I give them eternal life, and they shall never perish; no one will snatch them out of my hand. 29 My Father, who has given them to me, is greater than

**all[a]; no one can snatch them out of my Father's
hand. 30 I and the Father are one."**

"That is true, nothing can take us from Jesus but we
can choose to turn our backs on him." Proof scriptures
appear up on the screen as Isaac speaks.

Hebrews 6:4-8 New International Version (NIV)
**4 It is impossible for those who have once been
enlightened, who have tasted the heavenly gift, who
have shared in the Holy Spirit, 5 who have tasted the
goodness of the word of God and the powers of the
coming age 6 and who have fallen[a] away, to be
brought back to repentance. To their loss they are
crucifying the Son of God all over again and
subjecting him to public disgrace. 7 Land that drinks
in the rain often falling on it and that produces a crop
useful to those for whom it is farmed receives the
blessing of God. 8 But land that produces thorns and
thistles is worthless and is in danger of being cursed.
In the end it will be burned.**

"We see a similar situation in Matthew," Isaac says,
reading from the display of more scriptural evidence on
the screen. "Not all who proclaim to follow Jesus do," he
reads aloud to the crowd.

Matthew 7:21-23 New International Version (NIV)
True and False Disciples
**21 "Not everyone who says to me, 'Lord, Lord,' will
enter the kingdom of heaven, but only the one who**

does the will of my Father who is in heaven. **22** Many will say to me on that day, 'Lord, Lord, did we not prophesy in your name and in your name drive out demons and in your name perform many miracles?' **23** Then I will tell them plainly, 'I never knew you. Away from me, you evildoers!'

With still more evidence being found, Isaac continues. "Even though we can't be taken from Jesus, we can be foolish and not be ready for him. Like the virgins Jesus told us about. The ones who didn't prepare for the returning bridegroom and got turned away from the wedding."

Matthew 25:1-13 New International Version (NIV)
The Parable of the Ten Virgins
1 "At that time the kingdom of heaven will be like ten virgins who took their lamps and went out to meet the bridegroom. **2** Five of them were foolish and five were wise. **3** The foolish ones took their lamps but did not take any oil with them. **4** The wise ones, however, took oil in jars along with their lamps. **5** The bridegroom was a long time in coming, and they all became drowsy and fell asleep. **6** "At midnight the cry rang out: 'Here's the bridegroom! Come out to meet him!' **7** "Then all the virgins woke up and trimmed their lamps. **8** The foolish ones said to the wise, 'Give us some of your oil; our lamps are going out.' **9** "'No,' they replied, 'there may not be enough for both us and you. Instead, go to those who sell oil and buy some for yourselves.' **10** "But while they were on their way to buy the oil, the bridegroom arrived. The virgins who

**were ready went in with him to the wedding banquet.
And the door was shut. 11 "Later the others also
came. 'Lord, Lord,' they said, 'open the door for us!'
12 "But he replied, 'Truly I tell you, I don't know
you.' 13 "Therefore keep watch, because you do not
know the day or the hour.**

"Gentleman! Gentleman!" the King again takes
control of the debate. "We're drifting off topic. Let's get
back to the resurrections. Those who are in this second
resurrection but don't accept Jesus during their new
hundred-year long lifetime, are they cast into the lake of
fire to be burned?"

"No. The Bible tells us they just die," Isaac replies.

"What? They die peacefully in their sleep I suppose,"
Kasy retorts sarcastically.

"No. Nothing that pleasant. God told John, after the
thousand years is over, at the end of the hundred-year
lifetime of the second resurrection, Satan will be released
from his chains. He goes out and deceives the nations,
turning mankind against those who accept Jesus during
this second life and are living peacefully. Sinful and
deceived, humanity again makes war against God. Only
this time will be the last. Being mortal, all those who
fight against God now will be brought to nothing and die
a second and final time. Rebuffing their opportunity to
follow Jesus and gain eternal life, had they wanted to,
God will respect their choice of not choosing life and let
them die. Having freely made their choice they will never
be resurrected back to life again and will remain dead for

the rest of eternity," Isaac's proof scriptures are shown on the screen.

Revelation 20:7-9 New International Version (NIV)
7 When the thousand years are over, Satan will be released from his prison 8 and will go out to deceive the nations in the four corners of the earth—Gog and Magog—and to gather them for battle. In number they are like the sand on the seashore. 9 They marched across the breadth of the earth and surrounded the camp of God's people, the city he loves. But fire came down from heaven and devoured them.

Kasy is indignant, "those not found in the book of life are thrown into the lake of fire at the final judgement. That's the fate of those who hate good and love evil. They're thrown into the lake of fire like thorns. Jesus said the evil doers will burn there forever. They'll be tortured in those flames eternally, never to escape," Mr. Kasy speaks with his evangelist's zeal.

"I find myself in partial agreement with you," Isaac said. Looking Mr. Kasy in the eyes. "However, his majesty the King didn't bring me here to perpetuate incomplete beliefs, but to bring clarity and understanding to the plans of God and that I will do. Some of those who choose evil will be thrown into the lake of fire. Humanity's third and final resurrection to physical life delivers them to judgement, at the great white throne. This will be some peoples second death, as this resurrection is their second life," Isaac reads the displayed scripture.

Revelation 20:11-15 King James Version (KJV)

11 And I saw a great white throne, and him that sat on it, from whose face the earth and the heaven fled away; and there was found no place for them.

12 And I saw the dead, small and great, stand before God; and the books were opened: and another book was opened, which is the book of life: and the dead were judged out of those things which were written in the books, according to their works.

13 And the sea gave up the dead which were in it; and death and hell delivered up the dead which were in them: and they were judged every man according to their works.

14 And death and hell were cast into the lake of fire. This is the second death.

15 And whosoever was not found written in the book of life was cast into the lake of fire.

"There, you see! You've got too many resurrections in your accounting. This is the one where the wicked must give account and be judged for their deeds. Your sins will find you out. Sinful humanity is judged by God and punished for those sins in the fires of hell for the rest of eternity," Mr. Kasy displays scripture to emphasize his point.

Numbers 32:23 King James Version (KJV)

23 But if ye will not do so, behold, ye have sinned against the Lord: and be sure your sin will find you out.

Revelation 14:9-11 New Living Translation (NLT)
9 Then a third angel followed them, shouting, "Anyone who worships the beast and his statue or who accepts his mark on the forehead or on the hand 10 must drink the wine of God's anger. It has been poured full strength into God's cup of wrath. And they will be tormented with fire and burning sulfur in the presence of the holy angels and the Lamb.11 The smoke of their torment will rise forever and ever, and they will have no relief day or night, for they have worshiped the beast and his statue and have accepted the mark of his name."

"But all have sinned," Isaac points out. "The only thing keeping everyone from punishment is the cleansing blood of Jesus. Their smoke of torment will rise forever, not 'they will be tormented forever'. They would need to be immortal to be tormented forever. The only way to be immortal and have eternal life is to accept Jesus, but accepting Jesus keeps them out of those fires.

That's how your immortal soul belief takes you away from the truth of God. Yes, evil people will have eternal punishment, not eternal punishing. Jesus told us the only way to gain eternal life through the cleansing of his blood is for God to call you out of this world and accept that cleansing. Leaving all those who didn't receive that call during this life excluded from salvation through no fault of their own. God didn't call them. He didn't send them teachers so that they might learn about Jesus. Those who lived before Jesus came had no chance to follow what wasn't available to them. Through the second resurrection everyone will have the opportunity to follow Jesus if they want to.

Just as God let the angels' rebel and choose their own way to live, he will let everyone make their own decision. He doesn't want robots that have no choice but to do what they're made to do. God wants children who actively chose to love him and want to be with him, following in his ways of love. In the second resurrection everyone will be free to follow if they want to. Those who reject his love will fight him and die for a second and final time at the close of the second resurrection.

The first resurrection was for those who follow Jesus during this life and are resurrected into immortal spirit bodies at the return of Jesus. That leaves only one segment of humanity left to be resurrected in the last, third resurrection. Those who had their opportunity to accept Jesus during this life. Those who were called but for some reason, perhaps through neglect or indifference, let the opportunity of eternal life slip out of their grasp. The New Testament is full of warnings to believers to make their election sure by developing love and kindness for others. Becoming more Christ-like every day. Taking every thought captive." His spirit guided fingers typing while he spoke, scripture is displayed and then read.

2 Corinthians 10:5 King James Version (KJV)
5 Casting down imaginations, and every high thing that exalteth itself against the knowledge of God, and

bringing into captivity every thought to the obedience of Christ;

Continuing, Isaac explains further as more scripture is projected to the audience. "Those who face the white throne are those who are called during this life, accept the salvation of Jesus and then throw it away. Those who reject salvation during the thousand years of worldwide restoration after Jesus returns and are ruled with his saints' will also be there. With Satan chained in the bottomless pit during that millennium, these people will have been taught free of Satan's influence during that life. After living in this loving kingdom, they'll only have themselves to blame if they decide not to accept Jesus and his atoning sacrifice. They'll have to answer to the righteous judge for deciding not to follow Jesus at that time.

Those who live their first physical life and wantonly shun Jesus will be thrown into the lake of fire as mortals. That completes the third and final resurrection. They don't suffer for the rest of eternity. These people will die and never live again. They will be done away with and become ashes under the feet of the saints," Isaac's hands display scripture on the monitor.

Malachi 4:1-3 New International Version (NIV)
Judgment and Covenant Renewal
1 [a]"Surely the day is coming; it will burn like a furnace. All the arrogant and every evildoer will be stubble, and the day that is coming will set them on fire," says the Lord Almighty. "Not a root or a branch will be left to them. 2 But for you who revere my

name, the sun of righteousness will rise with healing in its rays. And you will go out and frolic like well-fed calves. 3 Then you will trample on the wicked; they will be ashes under the soles of your feet on the day when I act," says the Lord Almighty.

"Now death and hell are destroyed. They will no longer be needed, as all humanity will have passed through them."

The King and audience are silent as they take in the information Isaac has provided about the resurrections. Not sure how he managed to find all his proof scriptures simultaneously as he skillfully argued his case, they mull over the information.

Mr. Kasy speaks up, "you tell a good story; I'll give you that. But there's no way that's what happens to people when they die."

"Yah-weh." Isaac replied dryly.

Chapter 18

"All that's a nice theory but the book of Revelation is a mysterious book, it has always been contentious. Bible scholars throughout history have deemed it a quagmire of allegory, pitting good against evil. Many have given up on completely understanding its true purpose, some don't even think it should be included in the canonical books. One needs to be careful when placing the weight of doctrine upon its scriptures," Kasy warns.

"Most of the confusion revolving around heaven and hell comes from a fundamental misunderstanding of the human condition," Isaac starts to explain.

"Hold it right there! I know where this is going," Kasy said. "But your disbelief in our immortal souls is unfounded. Having an immortal soul is not a new idea, even the Old Testament has many verses describing our immortal souls prophesying, talking and interacting with each other, even in Sheol."

"Let's read them and see what they say. I often find the Bible doesn't mean what people think it says," Isaac replies perkily.

Mr. Kasy looks up his first set of scriptures, "let's start with Saul talking to Samuel at Endor." Kasy starts to read the account out loud.

1 Samuel 28:5-19 King James Version (KJV)

5 And when Saul saw the host of the Philistines, he was afraid, and his heart greatly trembled.

6 And when Saul enquired of the Lord, the Lord answered him not, neither by dreams, nor by Urim, nor by prophets.

7 Then said Saul unto his servants, Seek me a woman that hath a familiar spirit, that I may go to her, and enquire of her. And his servants said to him, Behold, there is a woman that hath a familiar spirit at Endor.

8 And Saul disguised himself, and put on other raiment, and he went, and two men with him, and they came to the woman by night: and he said, I pray thee, divine unto me by the familiar spirit, and bring me him up, whom I shall name unto thee.

9 And the woman said unto him, Behold, thou knowest what Saul hath done, how he hath cut off those that have familiar spirits, and the wizards, out of the land: wherefore then layest thou a snare for my life, to cause me to die?

10 And Saul sware to her by the Lord, saying, As the Lord liveth, there shall no punishment happen to thee for this thing.

11 Then said the woman, Whom shall I bring up unto thee? And he said, Bring me up Samuel.

12 And when the woman saw Samuel, she cried with a loud voice: and the woman spake to Saul, saying, Why hast thou deceived me? for thou art Saul.

13 And the king said unto her, Be not afraid: for what sawest thou? And the woman said unto Saul, I saw gods ascending out of the earth.

Isaac interrupts the narrative, breaking into the story, "Saul never saw Samuel. He's relying on the witch to tell him what she saw. People think Samuel came back to life but God was ignoring Saul, he wouldn't talk to him through his own prophets. Why would God bring Samuel back to life through a despised median who he commanded to be killed? Unless you believe Satan has power to bring the dead back to life, snatching them from the splendor of your presumed heaven?" Isaac answers his own question. "No. God alone has the power to give life, he alone can raise the dead, not Satan!"

"Of course. God is the life creator. Satan only has the power of the lie, the power to kill and destroy," Kasy agrees.

"Exactly! Saul doesn't see Samuel brought back from heaven, delivering a message from God. The witch has a vision from her satanic familiar spirit. She describes to Saul what she sees. Saul repeatedly asks her what she's seeing and hearing. He converses with Samuel through her. She talks to her evil spirit, believing it to be Samuel. Delivering a debilitating message."

Kasy reads more of the account.

14 And he said unto her, What form is he of? And she said, An old man cometh up; and he is covered with a mantle. And Saul perceived that it was Samuel, and he stooped with his face to the ground, and bowed himself.

15 And Samuel said to Saul, Why hast thou disquieted me, to bring me up? And Saul answered, I am sore distressed; for the Philistines make war

against me, and God is departed from me, and answereth me no more, neither by prophets, nor by dreams: therefore I have called thee, that thou mayest make known unto me what I shall do.

"But here the scripture tells us that Saul is talking to Samuel! So, Samuel must have been brought back from the dead," Kasy says slyly.

"Saul was asking the witch what she saw. Saul perceived it was Samuel and bowed down. What's happening is the witch is translating what she is seeing in her vision, Saul bows down to her. The familiar spirit has a conversation with Saul through her. Saul never speaks directly with Samuel, or see's him. That's what mediums do. They're the go betweens with demonic forces. That's why God commanded they should be removed from the land."

Kasy just nods and continues to read, indifferent to Isaac's points.

16 Then said Samuel, Wherefore then dost thou ask of me, seeing the Lord is departed from thee, and is become thine enemy?

17 And the Lord hath done to him, as he spake by me: for the Lord hath rent the kingdom out of thine hand, and given it to thy neighbour, even to David:

18 Because thou obeyedst not the voice of the Lord, nor executedst his fierce wrath upon Amalek, therefore hath the Lord done this thing unto thee this day.

19 Moreover the Lord will also deliver Israel with thee into the hand of the Philistines: and to morrow shalt thou and thy sons be with me: the Lord also shall deliver the host of Israel into the hand of the Philistines.

"I've always believed along with most Christians, this is an account of someone returning from heaven, demonstrating their immortal souls are alive. However, I believe you make good points that I might look into later," Mr. Kasy reluctantly admits.

"When you do, I believe you'll see the validity of my position. Regardless, if you didn't already believe humanity possessed an immortal soul, this section of scripture wouldn't prove they did. At best, it would only prove Satan has the power to resurrect the dead."

"Well how about this section of scripture. It describes the dead actually talking to each other in Shilo. That must mean their immortal souls are alive." Mr. Kasy finds and reads the Bible verses aloud.

Isaiah 14:9-11 New International Version (NIV)
9 The realm of the dead below is all astir to meet you at your coming;
it rouses the spirits of the departed to greet you all those who were leaders in the world;
it makes them rise from their thrones all those who were kings over the nations.
10 They will all respond, they will say to you, "You also have become weak, as we are; you have become like us."

11 All your pomp has been brought down to the grave, along with the noise of your harps; maggots are spread out beneath you and worms cover you.

"See!" Kasy presses his point. "The souls of the dead are alive in the grave, conscious and talking. While their physical bodies are eaten by the worms and decay. It's only the physical body that dies. Our immortal souls live on."

"Those scriptures prove we have immortal souls about as much as it proves trees can talk," Isaac replies.

"You use sarcasm to mask your ineffectual arguments," Mr. Kasy says triumphantly.

"No. I wasn't being sarcastic. I was being scripturally relevant. Go back to the beginning of that passage and read it all."

Bewildered, Mr. Kasy starts at the beginning of the thought in verse three.

Isaiah 14:3-8 New International Version (NIV)
3 On the day the Lord gives you relief from your suffering and turmoil and from the harsh labor forced on you, 4 you will take up this taunt against the king of Babylon: How the oppressor has come to an end! How his fury[a] has ended! 5 The Lord has broken the rod of the wicked, the scepter of the rulers, 6 which in anger struck down peoples with unceasing blows, and in fury subdued nations with relentless aggression. 7 All the lands are at rest and at peace; they break into singing. 8 Even the junipers and the cedars of

Lebanon gloat over you and say, "Now that you have been laid low, no one comes to cut us down."

"That's what I meant." Isaac points out. "The scriptural passage you referred to is using allegory. It's no more explaining the souls of the dead are alive than it's teaching the trees of the forest talk and the peaceful lands sing. It's not intended to be taken literally."

"So you say."

"Are you telling the King and our audience this passage is teaching that the trees of the forest will start to speak? Or that it uses allegory and then two verses later in the same thought it's intended to be literal. Is that what you believe? Isaac asks Mr. Kasy incredulously.

"No, I wouldn't say that. I'd have to study this passage, check out some commentaries to see what other respected scholars have to say. Only then, after much thought and prayer would I be able to form an opinion on what is being said."

"So you don't know. You have to find out what others say first. I believe the Bible doesn't contradict itself. In order for people to be alive in the grave they must be more than just physical."

"Exactly! That's why the immortal soul doctrine is correct. Humanity has an immortal soul and these scriptures tell us our souls think and talk," Mr. Kasy is unrelenting.

"Those scriptures also tell us that the trees think and talk. Do they have immortal souls as well?"

"Now you're just being childish. This is a thoughtful discussion, try to treat it in an adult manner. Of course trees don't have immortal souls," Kasy replies contemptuously.

"Why do you say one verse is allegory and the very next verse is literal?" Isaac pressed.

"I already told you I'd have to do research into it. I couldn't intelligently comment. Afterall, God is all powerful, he can do anything he decides. If He wants to make the trees talk he will. He made Balaam's donkey talk."

"Yes, God could," Isaac admitted. "And he did. He's in charge."

"God talks about our physical bodies decaying but we all have an immortal soul. At the incarnation the disciples saw Elijah and Moses with Jesus. God brought their immortal souls down from heaven to talk to Jesus. The Bible makes that very clear."

"You assume they came down from heaven because that's where you believe they're residing. But the Bible doesn't tell us that. It just tells us the disciples saw who they thought were Abraham and Moses. Even if it was them, the Bible doesn't tell us they came back from heaven, only that they were there. God obviously resurrected them for a purpose. The same as he resurrected those believers from their graves after Jesus died on the cross. Or how he resurrected that young man who fell from a high window as Paul preached late into the night."

"When God resurrects someone back to physical life he needs their soul, their personality to do it. Who we are, our intellect, thoughts, emotions, likes and dislikes are contained within our souls. It houses our very essence. We wouldn't be us if God didn't reunite our immortal souls back into a body. If we just die completely with no record of who we were, we'd be lost forever as if we never were," Kasy presses his argument. "There needs to be something of us to resurrect."

"You're forgetting that God has a perfect memory. He'll never forget who we are. He created everything by speaking it into existence. Why do you doubt his ability to recreate us as we are?" Isaac reads the scripture that appears on the screen.

Isaiah 49:15-16 Easy-to-Read Version (ERV)
15 But the Lord says, "Can a woman forget her baby? Can she forget the child who came from her body?
Even if she can forget her children, I cannot forget you. 16 I drew a picture of you on my hand. You are always before my eyes.[a]

"God tells us he'll never forget us."

"Of course he won't forget us. But that's different than knowing what, or how we think. We're more than a collection of molecules," Mr. Kasy explains.

"Yes, we're more than that. However, God knew us before we were born. He's been planning a future for us for a long time. He knows everything about us and will have no problem recreating us." Scripture pops up miraculously on the monitor.

Ephesians 1:3-14 The Message (MSG)
The God of Glory

3-6 How blessed is God! And what a blessing he is! He's the Father of our Master, Jesus Christ, and takes us to the high places of blessing in him. Long before he laid down earth's foundations, he had us in mind, had settled on us as the focus of his love, to be made whole and holy by his love. Long, long ago he decided to adopt us into his family through Jesus Christ. (What pleasure he took in planning this!) He wanted us to enter into the celebration of his lavish gift-giving by the hand of his beloved Son.

7-10 Because of the sacrifice of the Messiah, his blood poured out on the altar of the Cross, we're a free people—free of penalties and punishments chalked up by all our misdeeds. And not just barely free, either. Abundantly free! He thought of everything, provided for everything we could possibly need, letting us in on the plans he took such delight in making. He set it all out before us in Christ, a long-range plan in which everything would be brought together and summed up in him, everything in deepest heaven, everything on planet earth.

11-12 It's in Christ that we find out who we are and what we are living for. Long before we first heard of Christ and got our hopes up, he had his eye on us, had designs on us for glorious living, part of the overall purpose he is working out in everything and everyone.

13-14 It's in Christ that you, once you heard the truth and believed it (this Message of your salvation), found yourselves home free—signed, sealed, and delivered by the Holy Spirit. This signet from God is the first installment on what's coming, a reminder that we'll get everything God has planned for us, a praising and glorious life.

"The Bible describes how God has brought many people back to life through a resurrection from the dead, but it doesn't ever describe him bringing anyone back from heaven. And speaking of bringing people back to life, you said heaven was so wonderful that people wouldn't want to come back to this life."

"That's true! Heaven is the reward of those who follow Jesus and we can't accurately describe its wonder or splendor," Kasy speaks glowingly about his faith.

"Well if that's true, then why don't those who are brought back from the dead complain about being brought back to this world. What the Bible doesn't say speaks loudly about our not going to heaven. We should pay attention to the noncomplaining of those resurrected back to this life," Isaac points out.

"You just refuse to see clear bible teaching."

"Please show me, where do you find that clear Bible teaching saying we have an immortal soul?" Isaac pleads.

"That's easy, we were created by God with one. I'm surprised you didn't know that," Kasy replies. Then reads the account of Adam's creation out of the Bible.

Genesis 2:7 King James Version (KJV)

7 And the Lord God formed man of the dust of the ground, and breathed into his nostrils the breath of life; and man became a living soul.

"See God created humans at the start as immortal souls," Kasy speaks triumphantly.

"That's a poor translation of the Hebrew word God inspired to be used. Nephesh is the same word God used for all the other animals. Man is described as mortal, the same as an animal," Isaac stressed. With fingers flying over the keys as he spoke, some scripture proof is displayed and read aloud.

Ecclesiastes 3:18-22 New International Version (NIV)
18 I also said to myself, "As for humans, God tests them so that they may see that they are like the animals. 19 Surely the fate of human beings is like that of the animals; the same fate awaits them both: As one dies, so dies the other. All have the same breath[a]; humans have no advantage over animals. Everything is meaningless. 20 All go to the same place; all come from dust, and to dust all return. 21 Who knows if the human spirit rises upward and if the spirit of the animal goes down into the earth?" 22 So I saw that there is nothing better for a person than to enjoy their work, because that is their lot. For who can bring them to see what will happen after them?

"When God drove Adam out of the garden of Eden, he kept man from the tree of life so they couldn't become immortal." Scripture is displayed before Isaac is finished talking. Isaac reads his proof.

Genesis 3:22-24 New King James Version (NKJV)

22 Then the Lord God said, "Behold, the man has become like one of Us, to know good and evil. And now, lest he put out his hand and take also of the tree of life, and eat, and live forever"— 23 therefore the Lord God sent him out of the garden of Eden to till the ground from which he was taken. 24 So He drove out the man; and He placed cherubim at the east of the garden of Eden, and a flaming sword which turned every way, to guard the way to the tree of life.

"And here God says, 'for you are dust'," a proof is displayed and read out loud by Isaac.

Genesis 3:19 New King James Version (NKJV)

**19 In the sweat of your face you shall eat bread
Till you return to the ground,
For out of it you were taken;
For dust you are,
And to dust you shall return."**

"God gives no possibility of immortality anywhere in the Old Testament. That's why the Jews are virtually the only society who don't believe humans possess an immortal soul."

"Now I know that's wrong!" Mr. Kasy protests. "I know for a fact that many Jews from after the second temple believed they possessed an immortal soul. I did a comparative religions study when I was in seminary about it."

"Yes, those Jews did start to believe in an immortal soul," Isaac agreed.

"So, you were just overstating your case to impress our audience I suppose?" Mr. Kasy looks directly at the King and warns, "he who is faithful in little, will be faithful in much."

"No. I wasn't overstating anything. The original Jews. The first temple Jews and those who received the word of God through Moses, they didn't believe in an immortal soul. The Jews you referred to were from the second temple, they did." Isaac clarified his statement.

"So those from the more enlightened period of the second temple understood better. Is that what you're afraid to say?"

"No. Not at all. The second temple Jews came out of Babylon. They had been exposed to many ungodly beliefs while in captivity and they brought many influences back with them into second temple Judaism beliefs. As the Greek language was pervasive in the larger culture, so was Greek philosophy. If you want to know if the Old Testament writings tell us we have an immortal soul, you only have to do an internet search on Jewish beliefs. The Old Testament is their Bible after all. Written in their mother tongue. They should know it best."

"What a good idea," The King interjects himself into the debate. "Let's take a bit of a detour and see what the original Jews believed about the immortal soul."

"Why should we concern ourselves with what other religions believe? We should follow what Christianity has to say, for it alone can provide salvation and eternal life," Mr. Kasy adds hastily.

"We should find out because you teach we were created with an immortal soul and Christians get the story of our creation from the Old Testament, which is the Jewish Bible," Isaac insists.

"I believe it would provide some clarity on the subject. I would like to know. So we'll do it!" The King directs.

"Absolutely your majesty," Kasy kowtows. "I just meant to underline the supremacy of the Christian faith and our savior Jesus."

The King does his own search on the internet and quickly finds an article on My Jewish Learning site that references Contemporary Jewish Religious Thought. The King summarizes as he reads aloud. "Bla, bla, bla. It says here the belief in an immortal soul is not Jewish, but Greek. It goes on to say, at the end times the dead will be brought back to life." The King mumbles as he skims the article for more relative facts. "The Idea of a disembodied soul is left curiously undeveloped; they speculate it's because of the belief in a resurrection. It seems as though the early first temple Jews didn't believe in an immortal soul after all." Mumbling incoherently the King reads on. "Bla, bla, bla, it's not until the middle ages that the idea of immortality creeps in and begins to dominate. Bla, bla, bla. Oh, this is interesting. Here they say the resurrection is only temporary. Then there is a second death of the body, but the souls of those who live well during their resurrected state get to live on as spirits, forever in the knowledge and essential nature of God. Bla, bla, bla. But the souls of the wicked are destroyed." The King stops talking after reading aloud and takes a drink from his glass. After an uncomfortable pause he continues with his thoughts. Directing his comments to Isaac the King says, "That sounds a lot like how you described the second resurrection. Only they do say we have souls."

"Yes! We do have immortal souls. Even they knew it!" Mr. Kasy exuberantly exclaimed.

"I'm amazed you believe in the immortal soul doctrine!" Isaac says. "We have just read how having an immortal soul is a pagan belief. It didn't creep into Jewish doctrine until the middle ages. I would think that basing your core religious belief on a pagan philosophy would be far worse than doing some physical exercises based in pagan worship. After all, you do claim to lead others by example, holding Godly truths paramount in your life."

"I teach the biblical Christian traditions regarding our immortal souls. Like our Jewish cousins said, we have souls," Kasy replies defensively.

"Yes, they refer to the soul. It's helpful to remember we are mortal soul's; we don't have an immortal one. S. O. S." Isaac says cryptically, referring to something only he saw as relevant. "Universal call of distress! Save Our Souls." His explanation starts to resonate with the audience. "We're all living souls. That's what a nephesh is," he emphasizes. "Job had faith he would see God with his own eyes. Job longed for his resurrection back to life where he knew he'd meet his redeemer in his own flesh."

Scripture was waiting on the screen before Isaac was finished talking. He reads it out loud.

Job 19:25-27 New King James Version (NKJV)
25 For I know that my Redeemer lives,
And He shall stand at last on the earth;
26 And after my skin is [a]destroyed, this I know,
That in my flesh I shall see God,
27 Whom I shall see for myself,
And my eyes shall behold, and not another.
How my [b]heart yearns within me!

Job 14:12-17 New King James Version (NKJV)
12 So man lies down and does not rise.
Till the heavens are no more,
They will not awake
Nor be roused from their sleep.
13 "Oh, that You would hide me in the grave,
That You would conceal me until Your wrath is past,
That You would appoint me a set time, and
remember me!
14 If a man dies, shall he live again?
All the days of my hard service I will wait,
Till my change comes.
15 You shall call, and I will answer You;
You shall desire the work of Your hands.
16 For now You number my steps,
But do not watch over my sin.
17 My transgression is sealed up in a bag,
And You [a]cover my iniquity.

Isaac continues, "unlike Job, as New Testament Christians we know how God covers our iniquity. The blood of his son covers us and washes our sins away. Jesus is our redeemer. The Jews knew God had a plan to save them but didn't know what it was. That's why the resurrection plan of God is so beautiful. Everyone who has ever lived will get an opportunity to accept Jesus and salvation if they want it. The love God has for us stretches past our mortal lives and will pursue us beyond our graves, through a resurrection back to life." Another verse is displayed, waiting to be read before Isaac is done talking.

Psalm 130:8 New International Version (NIV)
8 He himself will redeem Israel from all their sins.

"That's preposterous," Mr. Kasy loudly objected. "Your majesty, surely you aren't being swayed by this charlatan's tails of fancy. Regardless of what the Jews believed, the new testament tells us plainly that man only dies once. Not twice after a resurrection." Fumbling, Kasy finds and reads his proof.

Hebrews 9:27 King James Version (KJV)
27 And as it is appointed unto men once to die, but after this the judgment:

After reading Mr. Kasy continues, "the scripture is very clear here. Man only lives once, then we are judged, with the righteous going to heaven and the sinner condemned to hell." Gesturing towards Isaac, Kasy addresses the

King. "I fear for your immortal soul if you follow his path of perdition, your majesty. He's bound to lead you away from the love of Jesus. There's no telling what motives he's harboring in the blackness of his heart." Addressing the entire assembly Mr. Kasy states. "We know the New Testament is full of references telling us our immortal soul goes to heaven when we die. Just look at the thief on the cross. Jesus told him that very day they'd both be in heaven. When we accept Jesus as our savior we're guaranteed eternal life."

Isaac speaks up. "If man can only live once, what about all those who were brought back to life after dying that we've already talked about. For the Bible to remain uncontradictory you must be understanding those verses wrong. Yes, we're promised eternal life. The proof of that possibility is because Jesus was dead in the grave for three days and nights, then he was brought back to life. He didn't go to his father until after he was resurrected. Jesus told Mary not to touch him because he had not yet been to heaven the morning after his resurrection," scripture appears.

John 20:17 New King James Version (NKJV)
17 Jesus said to her, "Do not cling to Me, for I have not yet ascended to My Father; but go to My brethren and say to them, 'I am ascending to My Father and your Father, and to My God and your God.' "

"How could they have been in heaven the same day they died on the cross, if Jesus hadn't ascended to his father yet three days later? You must be misunderstanding something. As Christians we gain eternal life in the future, we don't possess it now. If we had eternal life from birth, why would we need to accept Jesus in order to get it?"

"Maybe our understanding of what it is to ascend is unclear," Kasy interrupts.

"We're heirs with the hope of eternal life. Heirs don't possess their inheritance now. They will inherit it in the future." Titus 3:7 New International Version (NIV) shows up on the big screen as Isaac talks, waiting to be read.

7 so that, having been justified by his grace, we might become heirs having the hope of eternal life.

Romans 8:17-19 New International Version (NIV)
17 Now if we are children, then we are heirs—heirs of God and co-heirs with Christ, if indeed we share in his sufferings in order that we may also share in his glory.
18 I consider that our present sufferings are not worth comparing with the glory that will be revealed in us.
19 For the creation waits in eager expectation for the children of God to be revealed.

"The glory will be revealed in us. Creation waits for us to be revealed. Future tense. We don't have it now, that would be present tense," Isaac stresses.

"I was heir to the throne," The King chimes in. "I waited as heir until my time came. My father died, then I became king. No longer an heir, I am now the ruler of my country."

"Exactly!" Isaac agrees. "We have to wait until our time arrives to inherit eternal life."

Chapter 19

Mr. Kasy breaks into the conversation. "What about all the people who have died, gone to heaven and then came back to tell us about their experience. Those stories alone make Christians sure there's a heaven and we go there when we die. There have been books and movies made about their encounters describing what they saw and how they felt."

"That's true. There have been many accounts written about those kinds of experiences. I'm not discounting those experiences, only how those experiences are being interpreted. If they truly are going to heaven, then why do people of all faiths share those experiences? In fact, one of the first recorded accounts is from a Greek soldier who lived centuries before the birth of Jesus. If these accounts of going to heaven and coming back are really proof that we go to heaven when we die, why do they happen to people who don't believe in Jesus. Some, happening even before his salvation granting sacrifice occurred. After all, only those who accept Jesus as their savior can get into the Kingdom of God."

"God works in mysterious ways, far beyond the comprehension of man. God isn't bound by the constraints of time. He controls time and space; it doesn't control him or his plans. You seem to forget God is sovereign over all, he can do whatever he wants. It must have been his will to grant those people a taste of heaven," Mr. Kasy speaks in a lofty tone as he goes on.

"Don't you know that even Paul had a similar experience, seeing the heavenly realm? Here I'll read it to you," Kasy finds the scripture passage.

2 Corinthians 12:1-4 New International Version (NIV)
Paul's Vision and His Thorn
1 I must go on boasting. Although there is nothing to be gained, I will go on to visions and revelations from the Lord. 2 I know a man in Christ who fourteen years ago was caught up to the third heaven. Whether it was in the body or out of the body I do not know—God knows. 3 And I know that this man—whether in the body or apart from the body I do not know, but God knows— 4 was caught up to paradise and heard inexpressible things, things that no one is permitted to tell.

"Paul's experience was like those who have been to heaven and back today. What more biblical proof do you need?" Kasy asks indignantly.

"That account describes exactly what I'm talking about. Paul himself wasn't even sure if he was there in body or spirit. His vision was so vivid, it felt like he was actually there. And yes, God is the supreme ruler over all. But he gave humanity his word in the Bible. He'll not stray from what he told us within its pages. Otherwise we could have no faith in it as his inspired word. Jesus told us that no man has ascended to heaven except for himself. He also told us he would come back and get all Christians, resurrecting them into eternal life when he returns and then they'll rule with him for a thousand years and on into eternity."

"That might be a possibility you believe in, but it's not what I believe. As I have maintained, we have an immortal soul that goes to heaven when we die if we're good, or to hell if we're bad. Just like Christianity has taught us for over two thousand years. The fact that you don't like my proof scriptures has no bearing on my beliefs. I'm not required to defend my beliefs to you. I follow Jesus as I see fit."

"That's true as well. You don't have to defend your teachings to me but a day of explaining will come. Salvation and Christianity has a very low threshold. All you need to do is accept Jesus as your savior and you can be saved. Until John wrote the book of Revelation and it was read by others, no one could put all the resurrections together in a coherent sequence of events. That means all the apostles probably didn't have a full grasp of what was coming. They saw the future through a dark glass, only knowing they had to have love, stay true to Jesus and keep his teachings."

"Exactly! I'm free to believe as I see fit and worship God in my own way. I can be a Christian and follow Jesus without ever having read, or even seen a Bible," Mr. Kasy agrees.

"Again, absolutely true," Isaac's fingers fly over the keyboard. He speaks with eyes fixed on Mr. Kasy. "You're free to do that as an individual, but God holds those who teach to a higher standard," verses appear on the screen. "Teachers who don't preach the truth Jesus taught, will be cursed by God."

James 3:1 New King James Version (NKJV)

1 My brethren, let not many of you become teachers, knowing that we shall receive a stricter judgment.

Galatians 1:6-9 New International Version (NIV)

No Other Gospel

6 I am astonished that you are so quickly deserting the one who called you to live in the grace of Christ and are turning to a different gospel—7 which is really no gospel at all. Evidently some people are throwing you into confusion and are trying to pervert the gospel of Christ. 8 But even if we or an angel from heaven should preach a gospel other than the one we preached to you, let them be under God's curse! 9 As we have already said, so now I say again: If anybody is preaching to you a gospel other than what you accepted, let them be under God's curse!

2 Peter 2:1 New International Version (NIV)

False Teachers and Their Destruction

But there were also false prophets among the people, just as there will be false teachers among you. They will secretly introduce destructive heresies, even denying the sovereign Lord who bought them— bringing swift destruction on themselves.

"Teaching immortal souls will dwell with God through any method other than going through the cleansing blood of Jesus, denies that Jesus alone is the way, the truth and the life. Believing all humans are born with an immortal soul teaches Jesus didn't actually die but was only extremely physically handicapped for our sins. His immortal soul along with his conscious personality, couldn't have died.

The proof Jesus gave for being our savior was his resurrection after being dead for three days and nights. Believing his spirit was alive somewhere rejects his proof. That's why we must cling to the truth God has given to us in the Bible. He tells us…" not even pausing for a breath before he reads the scripture that appears on the big screen.

"Ecclesiastes 9:5 King James Version (KJV)
For the living know that they shall die: but the dead know not any thing, neither have they any more a reward; for the memory of them is forgotten.

Psalm 115:17-18 King James Version (KJV)
17 The dead praise not the Lord, neither any that go down into silence.
18 But we will bless the Lord from this time forth and for evermore. Praise the Lord.

It's the living that praise God, the dead are asleep. God's word is the truth. We don't gain wisdom about God from any worldly source." More scripture appears, waiting to be read.

1 Timothy 6:3-5 New International Version (NIV)

3 If anyone teaches otherwise and does not agree to the sound instruction of our Lord Jesus Christ and to godly teaching, 4 they are conceited and understand nothing. They have an unhealthy interest in controversies and quarrels about words that result in envy, strife, malicious talk, evil suspicions 5 and constant friction between people of corrupt mind, who have been robbed of the truth and who think that godliness is a means to financial gain.

Ephesians 5:6 New International Version (NIV)
Let no one deceive you with empty words, for because of such things God's wrath comes on those who are disobedient.

Romans 16:18 New International Version (NIV)
18 For such people are not serving our Lord Christ, but their own appetites. By smooth talk and flattery they deceive the minds of naive people."

"You seem to be the one who wants to argue. Just because I can't produce the Bible proof for my beliefs right now, doesn't make them wrong. You've obviously been studying this subject for a long time. I've always emphasized the love of Jesus in my ministry."

Mr. Kasy's voice takes on a sweet, sentimental tone when talking about the love of Jesus. "Like the greats that went before me I preached the love of Jesus and his salvation, warning the lost souls of humanity about hell. Encouraging them to accept Jesus and heaven. I didn't get bogged down in all this mortal, immortal, bickering.

All you've talked about this morning is death and dying. My mission is to teach the love of Jesus to all I can reach."

"And that's what I'm doing as well. Showing those not called now how they can enter the Kingdom of God. This meeting has been called to discuss what happens to people after they die. Of course, I've been talking about death all morning. I also strive to bring the good news of the Kingdom and its resurrections to those called and not called alike. All people not called at this time should know God loves them, how his love will pursue them beyond the grave and how they'll receive the opportunity to learn about Jesus when God draws them to him. Through scripture I show those not called by God when their eyes will be opened to Jesus and his loving salvation. I try to show how maintaining an attitude of love will help save all people in their future life. A future life that comes through a resurrection of a mortal soul."

"There you go again, bashing the immortal soul truth. As long as the Salvation of Jesus is preached, what does it matter? Tomato tomoughto, potato potoughto."

"It matters because believing the immortal soul doctrine can lead to error. Billy Graham and Robert Schuller, to name a few, preached a similar message as you do their entire careers. Not understanding the true nature of our soul left them unable to see how people with love in their lives from all faiths will be saved. That misunderstanding led them to believe that people didn't have to accept Jesus, or even know about Jesus to be saved. Ultimately, leaving them to deny that Jesus is the sole path to salvation."

"I don't believe that! You should be ashamed of yourself for maligning those Godly men when they can't defend themselves. They were pillars of the gospel message. They knew how salvation worked," Kasy was indignant.

"I'm only stating publicly available information."

"Well I've never heard of such a thing. They knew people could only be saved by accepting Jesus into their hearts. They spent their lives preaching that very thing to the world, just as I have."

"I know. That's why I believe it's so imperative we get our beliefs in line with what the Bible teaches. Otherwise we'll go astray from God's path," Isaac spoke with passion about correct doctrine.

"And I suppose that makes you the expert. How convenient," Kasy says snidely.

"No, it makes the Bible the truth. That's why I keep asking you for the Bible proof to support your beliefs."

"Well it makes no sense. Why would those men say people don't need to accept Jesus into their hearts to be saved? That's fundamental to Christianity. I don't believe it; you better be able to prove this one."

"Well I can. Perhaps the King will be able to look up the incident on his computer?" Isaac looks to the King for assistance. "It's from an interview Robert Schuler had with Billy Graham on the Hour of Power in 1997, I think it was early spring. You should be able to find it."

The King starts to look up the interview. He starts to type then stops abruptly thinking he was getting a shock from his laptop. After inspecting the keyboard quickly, he starts typing again with the same results. After shaking his hands vigorously at his sides he begins to type, again with the same results. Resuming his search, this time expecting the tingling sensation, his hands seemed to have a mind of their own, flying over the keys at a rapid rate. As the King searched, Isaac continued to talk to Mr. Kasy.

"After travelling the world, meeting thousands of loving people who hadn't received God's call to know Jesus, I believe Mr. Graham, Mr. Schuler and many other Christians face the same dilemma as the King does. How do loving, caring, people who die not accepting God, escape the fires of hell? Believing in the immortal soul, that only has this life to follow Jesus, leaves no other option open to them for salvation. By not giving mankind an immortal soul, God gave those people the possibility of salvation through a future resurrection. There they get to choose Jesus and his offer of eternal life free of Satan's influence."

"I've only found a transcript of the interview," the King reports. "I could use some help reading it as there should be two voices." Looking out over the audience the King motions to Musa to come to the front, hoping he would read the account with him. Fearing public speaking, Musa turns around to see who the King was waving at behind him. Seeing nothing but the back wall Musa sadly came to the realization the King wanted him to come to the front and read to the crowd. With sweaty palms, Musa made his way onto the King's moderator stage.

"You read Mr. Schuler's lines," the King told Musa. "I'll be Mr. Graham." Seeing Mr. Schuler didn't have many lines, a relieved Musa nods his agreement and starts to read.

Mr. Schuler: Tell me what do you think is the future of Christianity.

Mr. Graham: Well Christianity and being a true believer. You know I think there's the, the, body of Christ, which comes from all, the Christian groups around the world. Or, outside the Christian groups. I think everybody that loves Christ, or knows Christ, whether they're conscious of it or not. They're members of the body of Christ.

And I don't think that we're going to see a great sweeping revival that will turn the whole world to Christ at any time. I think James answered that, the Apostle James, in the first council in Jerusalem. When he said that God's purpose for this age is to call out a people for his name, and that's what God is doing today. He's calling people for,,, out of the world for his name.

Whether they come from the Muslim world or the Buddhist world or the Christian world or the non-believing world. They are members of the body of Christ, because they've been called by God. They may not even know the name of Jesus, but they know in their heart that they need something that they don't have and they turn to the only light that they have. And I think that they are saved and that they're going to be with us in heaven.

Mr. Schuler. - What I hear you saying, that it's possible for Jesus Christ to come into a human heart and soul and life, even if they've been born in darkness and have never, had an exposure to the Bible. Is that a correct interpretation of what you're saying?

Mr. Graham. - Yes it is. Because I believe that. I've met people in various parts of the world in tribal situations, that they had never seen a Bible or heard about a bible. Never heard of Jesus. But they believe, in their heart that there was a God, and that, and they tried to live a life that was quite apart from the surrounding community in which they lived.

Mr. Schuler. - That's fantastic, I'm so thrilled to hear you say that there's a wideness in God's mercy.

Mr. Graham. - There is. There definitely is.

When the King and Musa are finished reading Isaac addresses the crowd.

"As I have been saying, not following the teachings God has given us in the Bible can lead us into error. Yes! God can call people from any community in the world. But to say we don't have to know Jesus, runs contrary to the Bible," Isaac then turns his attention to the King. "Your majesty," he begins humbly. "I was brought here because I had Bible based answers to questions you'd never found answers for. I've only used Bible scripture to explain what will happen to your ancestors. My answers must be different than anything you've ever heard before. If they weren't different, you would already have had your questions answered. To understand the afterlife God has planned for people you must first understand our human limitations. We've seen how the doctrine of the immortal soul is not a biblical one. Rather it comes from the philosophies of man, inspired by Satan when he first lied to Eve. You need to make up your own mind as God leads you." New verses are displayed on the screen, and Isaac reads them aloud.

Colossians 2:8 New International Version (NIV)
See to it that no one takes you captive through hollow and deceptive philosophy, which depends on human tradition and the elemental spiritual forces[a] of this world rather than on Christ.

Genesis 3:4 King James Version (KJV)
And the serpent said unto the woman, Ye shall not surely die:

"Yes your majesty," Mr. Kasy spoke up, addressing the King. "Your people and country need a strong leader such as yourself. Like we just read in Colossians, 'See to it that no one takes you captive through hollow deceptive philosophy.' Are you willing to throw away the faith of your childhood to follow some unpopular belief you've just heard about? A doctrine so obscure you've not heard about it until now in your later life. Be assured, just as there is a hell that the angels and sinners are put into, there is also a heaven for those who love the Lord," Mr. Kasy displays a scripture.

2 Peter 2:4 New International Version (NIV)
For if God did not spare angels when they sinned, but sent them to hell,[a] putting them in chains of darkness[b] to be held for judgment;

After reading the verse out loud Kasy goes on. "You alone set the standard for your people. Do you want them following some crazy belief no major Christian denomination endorses? Do you want your country's official beliefs to reflect those of some cultish, scrap metal dealer? Who'll lead your people in their walks of faith? Who'll guide them in their everyday life? My fellow clergy will never uphold, teach, or believe this new unfounded belief. No. You don't want to believe that.

Follow what you've been taught from childhood, those beliefs have kept your nation peaceful from its inception. The world is uncertain and storms can come out of the blue. Don't rebuff our spiritual help over disputes on these peripheral matters. Your nation needs as many friends as it can get."

Mr. Kasy's personal secretary discreetly waits at the side of the stage. When Mr. Kasy finishes speaking, he shyly hands a note to him with a slight bow. Kasy reads the note while Isaac is talking. A broad smile of expectant satisfaction spreads across his face.

"That verse seems incomplete," Isaac says dryly. "Let's read the entire chapter to fill in the story," scripture appears on the big screen.

2 Peter 2 New International Version (NIV)
False Teachers and Their Destruction
1 But there were also false prophets among the people, just as there will be false teachers among you. They will secretly introduce destructive heresies, even

denying the sovereign Lord who bought them—
bringing swift destruction on themselves. 2 Many will
follow their depraved conduct and will bring the way
of truth into disrepute. 3 In their greed these teachers
will exploit you with fabricated stories. Their
condemnation has long been hanging over them, and
their destruction has not been sleeping.

4 For if God did not spare angels when they sinned,
but sent them to hell,[a] putting them in chains of
darkness[b] to be held for judgment; 5 if he did not
spare the ancient world when he brought the flood on
its ungodly people, but protected Noah, a preacher of
righteousness, and seven others; 6 if he condemned
the cities of Sodom and Gomorrah by burning them to
ashes, and made them an example of what is going to
happen to the ungodly; 7 and if he rescued Lot, a
righteous man, who was distressed by the depraved
conduct of the lawless 8 (for that righteous man, living
among them day after day, was tormented in his
righteous soul by the lawless deeds he saw and
heard)— 9 if this is so, then the Lord knows how to
rescue the godly from trials and to hold the
unrighteous for punishment on the day of judgment.
10 This is especially true of those who follow the
corrupt desire of the flesh[c] and despise authority.
Bold and arrogant, they are not afraid to heap abuse
on celestial beings;11 yet even angels, although they
are stronger and more powerful, do not heap abuse on
such beings when bringing judgment on them from[d]
the Lord. 12 But these people blaspheme in matters
they do not understand. They are like unreasoning
animals, creatures of instinct, born only to be caught

and destroyed, and like animals they too will perish. 13 They will be paid back with harm for the harm they have done. Their idea of pleasure is to carouse in broad daylight. They are blots and blemishes, reveling in their pleasures while they feast with you.[e] 14 With eyes full of adultery, they never stop sinning; they seduce the unstable; they are experts in greed—an accursed brood! 15 They have left the straight way and wandered off to follow the way of Balaam son of Bezer,[f] who loved the wages of wickedness. 16 But he was rebuked for his wrongdoing by a donkey—an animal without speech—who spoke with a human voice and restrained the prophet's madness. 17 These people are springs without water and mists driven by a storm. Blackest darkness is reserved for them. 18 For they mouth empty, boastful words and, by appealing to the lustful desires of the flesh, they entice people who are just escaping from those who live in error. 19 They promise them freedom, while they themselves are slaves of depravity—for "people are slaves to whatever has mastered them." 20 If they have escaped the corruption of the world by knowing our Lord and Savior Jesus Christ and are again entangled in it and are overcome, they are worse off at the end than they were at the beginning. 21 It would have been better for them not to have known the way of righteousness, than to have known it and then to turn their backs on the sacred command that was passed on to them. 22 Of them the proverbs are true: "A dog returns to its vomit,"[g] and, "A sow that is washed returns to her wallowing in the mud."

"Yes, that is what the Bible has to say about your kind," Kasy speaks derogatorily to Isaac. "Your beliefs run contrary to official doctrine. Heresy like that won't go unpunished by us Christian authorities. We've been watching you."

"It's the official doctrine that's wrong. I thought you might be more concerned with what God has to say than man."

"Oh, I'm always ready to hear the voice of God. Just not your interpretation of God's voice."

"I don't think you'd believe man was mortal, even if God himself told you."

"Not so!" Mr. Kasey protested loudly. "I'll always believe God."

"Well then, what about this verse?" Isaac replies. Fingers flying over the keys, then scripture appears on the big screen.

Genesis 6:3 New International Version (NIV)
Then the Lord said, "My Spirit will not contend with humans forever, for they are mortal; their days will be a hundred and twenty years."

"Here, God himself is specifically telling us that man is mortal and has a limited life span," Isaac explains.

"He's referring to our physical mortal body. Not to our eternal souls," Kasey counters.

"We can't be both at the same time. We either have something that lives forever, which would make us immortal but potentially extremely physically handicapped, or we are mortal with nothing that can live separated from our living body. God describes us as mortal. The Bible repeatedly tells us so," Isaac stresses.

"Yes," Kasy says with a yawn. "That is what you've been going on about and that is the kind of talk that will soon be getting you into a lot of trouble."

"I'm more than happy to face what might be coming. Let God be true and every man a liar. The King can do as he pleases. As I've explained, Christianity is a calling from God, not the decision of man. We can only choose to faithfully follow that call or not. Do you have any comments on the interview transcript we just heard?"

"No. I don't feel the need to answer for others. Anyway, I'm growing tired of this facade, it's time I brought this meeting to a close," Mr. Kasy's voice is hard with cynicism and argence.

"Mr. Kasy!" The King speaks sternly to his old camp director. "I'm in charge here. I called for this meeting. I'll be the one to close it."

"Go ahead, pretend like you're in charge. I don't have to put up with it anymore. I'm done being at your beck and call. Groveling to these elite for a few crumbs that might fall off their tables," Kasy sweeps his arm, gesturing towards the crowd. "Even now in my retirement, after instructing your whelps for years, my livelihood is precarious. I'm forced to live on the coattails of your benevolence."

"Yes you do and you seem to be jumping off of those coattails," the King replied angrily.

"That I am. I'm finally being appreciated by someone in real power. I've been reporting to Prophet Father about the subversive activities going on in your kingdom. Accepting all those political refugees from around the world. Now bringing this convicted terrorist with his heretical theories here, giving him a platform to broadcast his poison. Well, my loyalty to the Empire has finally paid off. I have just received word..." Kasy waves the note delivered by his secretary. "that Monday morning I'll be starting my new role as the Empire's Chief Inquisitor for the African continent.

Tomorrow, Prophet Father will be establishing Jerusalem as his state capital for the Empire. Come Monday there'll be a new world order and I'll be playing an important part in it. God is finally blessing me, the way I deserve for my years of hard work in the world's backwater nations. I'll be the one you people come to begging for mercy. As Inquisitor, I'll be back for you," Kasy says pointing at Isaac, his voice deep and menacing. "I've given you plenty of rope and you've hung yourself with your words. I'll not rest until I hear you recant your beliefs. One way or another you'll beg me for mercy."

"That may all be true," the King says harshly. "but Monday is two days away. I'm still in charge here and now. Guards, take Mr. Kasy into custody." The royal guards at the King's side jump into action, seizing Mr. Kasy, they lead him away.

Mr. Kasy had barely left the conference room when the King started making plans to whisk the international volunteers into hiding. Knowing he would have only a short time before imperial SS troops showed up to free

Kasy, he sent dispatches to all the children's homes and farms, gathering all their foster parents and volunteers for immediate transport to safety.

"Musa my trusted friend, can I count on you for another mission of mercy?" the King asks after sending out his urgent dispatches.

"Absolutely!" came Musa's instant response. "It was my plan that brought them here in the first place. I want to see it through to the end. But where can we house them? The Empire won't rest until they find all of those loving people? Our country is so small, it'll be next to impossible to keep them all hidden."

"I was thinking of sending them north to the Grand Canyon. The special spot we found where the river washed out the entrance to that cave network. We could hide four times the number of people in there. There's plenty of year-round food and water, away from prying eyes"

"But your majesty," Musa interrupts. "that's not inside our country. You'll have no authority to protect them there."

"Musa, when we go hunting Antelope, how do we know where to go?" the King asks.

"We look for signs, scout the terrain for a water hole, then wait for the game to come to us."

"Exactly! We don't see the Antelope until the end of the hunt. Kasy will be looking all over my Kingdom for those refugees. Confident his quarry is here, he'll search everywhere until he has the satisfaction of prosecuting Isaac and his friends."

"The best place to hide is where no one will be looking for you," Musa notes, nodding his head.

"Now you're thinking. All we have to do is leave some signs for the SS to keep stumbling onto, enough to keep them looking here in our country."

"Meanwhile Isaac and the other refugees will be safely hidden away in a completely different country, where no one will be looking for them."

"Yes. That's my plan. Do you think it'll work?" the King earnestly asks his old friend.

"Well it's the best plan we've got and it's better than trying to hide them within our small country."

"For it to work we'll have to get all the refugees out of our country and into hiding up north. I was thinking of using Isaac as a decoy, convincing the Imperial forces the refugees are still here in our country."

"Unless I've seriously misjudged him, I'm sure Isaac won't hesitate to help," Musa confidently assures the King.

"Good. It may be dangerous. Would you help guide him through the mission and look out for him?"

"Absolutely! I think Isaac and I will be able to work well together."

"I'll send a security force right now to make discreet preparations. We'll send the refugees north disguised as tourists. We have contacts up there in the hospitality industry that will provide them cover stories." The King imagines how best to secure the safety of the refugees by surrounding himself with trusted government advisors who help him fulfill his escape plans.

Chapter 20

It had been five months since the scorpion stinging locusts came out of the great pit. Convincing world leaders he used his powers to get rid of them, Prophet Father was now declared by all, the redeemer of mankind. His deepest desire had finally been fulfilled. The Locust disappearing galvanized his place as the object of mankind's adulation. Knowing he could now do anything he desired unopposed, do to his unprecedented worldwide support, Prophet Father put the finishing touches on his plans to move into his new Jerusalem compound as soon as possible.

The next Sunday morning, Prophet Father enters Jerusalem with much fanfare in a surprise grand parade. Thousands of his faithful had spent months practicing to make his arrival a joyously spontaneous spectacle for the gullible worldwide viewing audience. Pre-empting scheduled programming, all forms of communication in the world are blanketed with the spectacle. Emergency broadcasts wake those asleep to the news which is hosted by the world's top personalities who run colour commentary in every language.

It appears to all that Prophet Father's white horse and robes emit light as he proceeds down the street, making him appear as an angelic being. Following his every move with handheld mirrors, hundreds of SS troopers discreetly reflect the bright morning sunshine down onto him from high vantage points. Reflective threads woven into his clothing, along with shorter fibers groomed into the coat of his Lipizzaner stallion, make them both glow supernaturally bright, even in the shadows.

Prophet Father's choice of clothing is inclusive of all the major faiths. His long flowing white Papal robes drift in the wind exposing the tailored salwar kameez. He randomly performs haute ecole on the energetic Lipizzaner, prancing down the road towards the tomb of the virgin. The white Buddhist Lama Gelug hat with a Tefillin squarely in the center of his brow stays firmly on his head even during the mezair, levade, courbette, capriole and croupade maneuvers. Wowing the crowds with his horsemanship, he holds an arrow in his right hand with the reins, while gripping Vishnu's Sharanga bow in his left and a quiver slung over his back.

Starting at the Mount of Olives he makes his way down Al-Mansuriya St. heading towards the Golden Gate. Christian and Muslim tradition both regard the Golden Gate as the entrance the messiah uses when returning to Jerusalem and Prophet Father was not about to let that expectation go unfulfilled. Desiring to be hailed as the world's savior, he embodies as many religious traditions as he can, dazzling the masses with signs and wonders.

After riding past cheering crowds for a kilometer, Prophet Father rounds the corner at the tomb of the virgin just in time to hear a series of explosions. The Golden Gate which has been filled in for over twelve centuries has just been blasted open in time for his arrival. Excavators and construction workers quickly transform the rubble into a trail over the adjoining graveyard that blocks the way from Al-Mansuriya street directly into Jerusalem through the Beautiful Gate. Showing no sign of skittishness, the Lipizzaner performs a perfect dressage walk over the loose rubble, carrying Prophet Father on the newly constructed pathway and up through the gates of repentance and mercy.

Having brought all the world's rulers willingly under his leadership by getting rid of the stinging locusts, Prophet Father brings stability to a fractured and squabbling world with an iron fist. Humanity is so weary of fear and terrorism, not to mention the stinging Locust, they gladly welcome Prophet Father as their savior. Trading personal freedoms, including thought, for safety, prosperity and stability, humanity eagerly performs his every edict and whim in complete obedience. They worship him as their savior god. Having gained the adoration and status he craved, Prophet Father now turned his sights on eliminating any and all worldly dissent to his omnipotence. He hadn't imagined the heavenly opposition headed his way.

"Hey you two! Hold it right there!" the huge security guard hollers loudly at a pair of individuals clad in traditional Israelite sackcloth. He quickly makes his way towards them crossing through the crowded main entrance of the Imperial Hall of Splendor. The two hooded figures stop. Turning towards the guard, they wait as he approaches them out of breath and red faced.

"You can't enter through the main lobby. You actors need to use the backstage door. This is going to be an evening with major announcements. You should know that you can't walk around amongst the audience dressed in full costume. Your instructions and entrance doors should have been sent to you along with your lines for this evening by your area assistant director."

"We don't have an area assistant director." the one cloaked figure replied politely.

"We're under the personal direction of the head director." the second shrouded individual said with wide, sweeping, hand gestures.

"Besides, we don't work off a script or orchestrated lines, so we never received any entrance protocol information. We were just told to show up here for this event," the first crudely garbed individual added.

"We just open our mouths and they're filled with what we need to say. There is no rehearsing," the second sums up.

"Oh. I see." Believing these two to be special celebrities, acting under the guidance of the overall head director of the day's events, the security guard is visibly intimidated.

"I, I beg your pardon, but I've been given strict orders to direct any stray actors to the rear stage doors. So, if you follow me this way," the guard motions towards a side exit with his arm. "I'll personally guide you to the backstage area where you can access the main stage and wait for your que."

As they walk towards the actors entrance the guard makes star-struck small talk with his two mysterious, presumed stars. "You know I've done some acting myself. Nothing big mind you, just some small, amateur, plays. Nothing as grand as performing on an Imperial stage with Prophet Father. I find acting therapeutic. It helps with my PTSD." The pair make no audible reply to the guard's overtures. He can only make out polite facial gestures as they proceed to the backstage entrance.

"I've always admired those of you who can do improv. I have a hard time remembering all my lines, let alone making them up on the spot. Wow! This is a real honor to be the one helping you two. Do you think you'd be able to give me any acting tips, later on maybe, after your performance?" Again, the pair just smile warmly back at the guard as they approach the checkpoint at the rear, outside, stage door.

A frail, angry young sentry barks gruffly at the crudely dressed couple. "Let's see your passes."

The large security guard escorting them steps to the front, confronting the small sentry forcefully. Getting right up in his face, the large man's personality instantly transforms into that of a psychotic killer.

"These two didn't receive their entrance instructions so they won't have any passes with them," he says through clenched teeth. "They'll be doing live improv with Prophet Father himself! I'll be personally escorting them backstage. As you can see, they don' t need to go to costuming, so they'll just wait with me in the wings for their que." Turning to smile pleasantly at the sackcloth pair, the security guard's face turns back to stone as he again addresses the small sentry. "You'd do well to address those you don't know with kindness and humility. It'll be much healthier for your future." Flexing his upper body muscles, making his bulky jacket stretch tightly around his chest and biceps, the guard demonstrates that his size wasn't due to an excess of donuts.

Swallowing hard, the small sentry nods fearfully as he buzzes the trio through the security door. Wiping the beads of sweat from his forehead with a hanky, he leans against the closing backstage door with a sigh of relief.

"How was that for acting?" the large security guard eagerly asked his pair of stars. "I think I made him wet his pants." He giggled, as a wide smile came to his face.

"You were very convincing," the oddly dressed couple replied. "Yes, even I was intimidated."

"Ya, but I got tongue tied. It'll be much healthier for your future. That was lame. I can't think on the spot like you guys. You improv actors make it seem so easy. How do you do it?"

"Well for us, like we said, we just open our mouths and they're filled with the words that need to come out."

"Man. What natural talent you must have." The large security guard stares at them in awe. "Let's wait over here, off to the side of the stage."

He directs them out of the stagehand's way, but with a good view of Prophet Father who had just started to address the live crowd as well as several cameras broadcasting to a worldwide audience.

Several minutes into Prophet Father's speech, a backstage grip eyed the odd-looking trio. He was going to hassle them for their passes until he recognized the large security guard from the front lobby. The large man's reputation for extreme aggression had followed him from his old SS days. Believing the security guard was in control of the situation, the grip left them alone and suggested the other backstage workers do the same.

"You know," the large security guard said to his drably dressed charges, "I just can't let it go. I've got to go back and properly threaten that weaselly little door man. You two stay here and wait for your que to go on stage. If I don't get back in time to see your performance, break a leg." With that, he turns and heads back the way he came.

"I'm the divine ruler of this world!" Floor monitors rang with the voice of Prophet Father. "I decide what is right or wrong. I alone built this prosperous and safe civilization. I grant forgiveness to those deserving. No one dares to challenge my ultimate authority," Prophet Father boasts pompously several minutes into his oratory. Up to this point the sackcloth clad pair stood motionless, but the self-aggrandizing by Prophet Father now made them step forward and onto the stage in full view of the live guests, Prophet Father and the worldwide audience.

"You aren't the divine ruler of this world. The Great God of Heaven is in full control. You rulers of this world govern at his pleasure," one of the shrouded pair spoke up loudly, momentarily silencing Prophet Father with surprise.

"Who are you to be speaking for the creator? I'm the only legitimate prophet to this world."

"You are nothing but a false prophet." The second mysterious figure declared, stepping forward aggressively. "There's nothing legitimate about you, for you belong to your father the devil, you carry out his evil desires. He was a murderer from the beginning, not holding to the truth, for there is no truth in him. When you lie, you speak his native language, for he is a liar and the father of liars."

"No! You two have no authority here. Like you said, I rule over this world at the pleasure of the God you say you speak for. You two are the frauds, not me. Shame on you for trying to beguile the world by undermining my God given authority. Who do you think you are?"

"We're the true witnesses of the Great Creator God, ruler of heaven and earth."

"Oh, how impressive!" Prophet Father replied sarcastically. "Funny, your all-powerful boss couldn't clad you in better clothing. That get up does make you stand out in a crowd, but it looks very itchy. Is that what you have to do to get attention? You mustn't be very good witnesses for your great creator God. If the world ever hears from you two again, you won't be known as the two witnesses, but the two false witnesses." Smiling at his own joke he motions for security to apprehend the mysterious pair. Prophet Father adds, "but I doubt you'll be making any encore performance. Take them away!"

Guards armed with the latest crowd control weaponry quickly surround the pair. Pointing their deadly thorium power disruptors at them, three guards step forward menacingly to subdue God's witnesses. The trio were only a step away when fire came from the mouths of the two witnesses, consuming the three in a flash, leaving only a slight smoke stain on the floor where they had stood.

Responding to the deadly provocation, the other guards fired their weapons at point black range. Skirting around the rough weave of the sackcloth worn by the witnesses, the energy discharge of the disrupters found other unintended targets. Leaving the witnesses unhurt, the wild, undirected charges were drawn back to the closest thorium disrupter, dispatching whoever was holding it. Seeing their comrades fall, more security guards scrambled into the fray, firing their own disruptors at will towards the two witnesses, having the same result. Soon the auditorium was littered with the smoking, charred remains of what was Prophet Fathers personal guard.

The auditorium audience sat motionless as the mayhem exploded around them. Not an eye blinked in the worldwide audience. All were glued to a screen as the action was projected live around the world. When the smoke cleared, the two witnesses picked their way through charred bodies to face Prophet Father.

"The Creator God has always been in charge of the earth. The things you do further his loving plans for mankind," gesturing to his fellow witness. "We'll be prophesying of his coming Kingdom, rebuking your falsehoods and punishing the rebelliously wicked of the earth."

"Well you certainly have my attention now," Prophet Father replied coolly. "Will you always be executing those who don't agree with you? That will teach mankind such a good lesson in God's love. It's sure to make everyone flock to him in adoring droves."

"We'll destroy with fire those who try to harm us. For the rest of sinful mankind, we'll withhold the rain, send plagues and turn the waters to blood. All these things will befall those who refuse to heed the words of the living God."

"Well, besides having fire come out of my mouth killing people, I can do those other tricks. Probably just as good as you."

"To prove our words are from God, we will withhold the rains for the next three days," one witness replied.

"Well, I'll see your three days of no rain and raise you a plague of flies." Prophet Father said tauntingly, eyes wide with delirium.

"You'll only be hurting yourself, along with those who follow you."

"I don't care! I'd cut off my own nose to spite my face if it diminished the grandeur of your power," Prophet Father declared derisively. "Every time you send a plague, withhold rain, or turn the waters to blood, I'll match it or trump it. The world will fear my power more than yours, but because you start it, they'll curse you and your God all the more." Now go! I've already given you two more publicity than you deserve."

"We'll be back. Correcting your errors through the word of God, along with warnings and prophecies. We'll declare the coming Kingdom of God throughout the entire world."

"We'll see about that as well." Prophet Father mumbles as the two witnesses make their way out of Jerusalem's Imperial Hall of Splendor.

Revelation 11 King James Version

1 And there was given me a reed like unto a rod: and the angel stood, saying, Rise, and measure the temple of God, and the altar, and them that worship therein.

2 But the court which is without the temple leave out, and measure it not; for it is given unto the Gentiles: and the holy city shall they tread under foot forty and two months.

3 And I will give power unto my two witnesses, and they shall prophesy a thousand two hundred and threescore days, clothed in sackcloth.

4 These are the two olive trees, and the two candlesticks standing before the God of the earth.

5 And if any man will hurt them, fire proceedeth out of their mouth, and devoureth their enemies: and if any man will hurt them, he must in this manner be killed.

6 These have power to shut heaven, that it rain not in the days of their prophecy: and have power over waters to turn them to blood, and to smite the earth with all plagues, as often as they will.

Back in his office Prophet Father vents his displeasure onto a group of trusted aids. "What was that?! And who were they?!" Prophet Father screamed, red faced. "It's bad enough they managed to get in, let alone end up on stage in front of a worldwide audience. But to have them dispose of my personal guard in such a miraculous way makes me look weak. We'll have to double down on getting rid of all dissension from those who follow God." Prophet Father starts to pace back and forth around the room as he tries to think of how he can salvage his reputation and leadership. "First off, ensure that the ID tattoo program is getting my mark on everyone. If we control the world's monetary system, I'll control its heart. Now addressing the matter at hand. How can I mold the world into my liking if I have to deal with those two fact checking everything I say? Someone better come up with a plan to neutralize their moral correctness quickly."

Looking around the room expectantly at his aids, he waits for someone to respond with a plan.

"How about we dig up or fabricate some dirt on those two. No one knows them yet, we could discredit them in the eyes of the world before they even get started," one counselor advised.

"That would take time to get all the backstories straight, otherwise everything will unravel and backfire on us," came a reply.

"And in case you missed it, they've already gotten started," Prophet Father complains. "Shooting fire from their mouths and burning those attacking them to a crisp has a way of getting everyone's attention."

"The way the disrupter blasts avoided hitting them... I've never heard of such a thing happening, let alone see it myself," an aid comments.

"And the discharges seemed to have a will of their own, randomly slamming into the other armed security guards."

Comments were coming from all the aids, marveling at what had just transpired.

"Yes, yes, yes! Those witnesses were just miraculous!" I know. I was there. Remember. I had the front row seat," Prophet Father angrily quietens the room. "But how do I get rid of them if we can't just kill them?"

"Maybe we're approaching this problem incorrectly," a senior aid speaks up thoughtfully. "What if we use those two to highlight your power?"

"A novel thought. How do you propose to do that?" a calming Prophet Father asks.

"Well, as the growing number of flies can attest, anything they can do, you can do as well."

"I can do better."

"Well, ok." Not wanting to rile his sovereign, the aid is conciliatory. "You can do better. So let them bring on their plagues, drought and rivers of blood. You'll out-do them every time. By more than doubling the calamity they bring, you'll prove your supremacy over them."

"Kind of like demonstrating how great the sacrifice of Jesus is to forgive sin, by sinning as much as possible. I like it." A smile returns to Prophet Father's lips at the thought of his favorite sins.

"More importantly, we must remove their moral authority," another aid speaks up.

"How can we do that? They claim to be speaking with the authority of God."

"But so do you my lord."

"Yes I know, but they have that fire thing going on to prove it."

"Perhaps we could write that off as some new, experimental, personal safety device."

"Well what about them fact checking what I say against the written word of God? How can I disprove the Bible?" Prophet Father questions his aids aggressively to test the viability of their ideas.

"No, you don't prove a thing. Make them prove their words are from the word of God."

"That wouldn't be hard to do," Prophet Father replies. "the internet is full of translations, commentaries, concordances and the like. No other book has been dissected and studied more than the Bible. All of it uploaded online for everyone to read and study."

"But what if the word of God wasn't so readily available? We bureaucrats have been in discussions on how to rid society of hate speech against ethnic and lifestyle groups. We've long viewed parts of the Bible, as fueling the hot beds of discrimination. We've developed viruses for eliminating the offensive parts we think should be sanitized from the Bible on all electronic devices. Once a device has been infected, the offensive texts will be wiped from the memory, we only need to implement the contagion."

"So, I wouldn't need to justify what I'm doing, because the witnesses would have no way of disproving any of it from the original Bible."

"Kind of. It could still be disproved if someone had an old paper copy of the text, but worldwide most of those have been discarded in favor of digital copies. The number of people who can or will bother to check the witness's assertions of wrongdoing, will never gain the popular worldwide support needed to threaten your rule. We should easily be able to spot dissenters, sending them off to reeducation camps as soon as they question your moral authority."

"Perfect! The witnesses can withhold the physical rain, but I'll cause the spiritual drought, resulting in a worldwide famine of the word of God. Many wolves have twisted the word of God in the past, but I'll erase his words from anyone who might use them against me."

"Exactly!" Exclaims another aid. "Not only that, but you could bring them with you every time you speak publicly."

"Why would I want to do that? They're dedicated to exposing me as a false prophet who leads the world away from God."

The aids start to brainstorm, and ideas are being tossed out by them in rapid succession.

"Ya, but they're boring! The world worships you as their god. No one will listen to them. The world will see them as a joke of your making. Every good comedian has a straight man. Treat them like the sideshow entertainment they are. Not to mention they can' t prove anything verifiable because of the famine of the word you'll create."

"Preaching the gospel of the great creator God of the Bible, those two witnesses will infuriate the other world religions. We'll encourage those other religions to assassinate the witnesses publicly on stage whenever they perform."

"The crowds will love that fire coming out of their mouth thing, burning people to a crisp will become the new spectator sport."

"Unless they are murdered, in which case it'll become our win, win scenario."

"We could make it a contest for people to see who can become the first one to succeed at killing them. We could run a highlight reel on TV every week of the burnings."

"We could call it the Burners Bloopers."

"Or maybe the Suicide Assassins."

"Historically those religions were good at getting suicide bombers to die for their causes. They should be able to work up some interest for this fight."

"Especially with the notoriety we can provide."

"We could start a go fund me campaign for the families the contestants leave behind."

"There'll be people volunteering for many reasons, all wanting to kill the Two Witnesses in front of a worldwide audience."

"It'll be great!" The aid table shouts in unison.

Prophet Father stops pacing and takes his place at the head of the boardroom table. Relaxing now that there's a firm course of action to be taken, he retrieves a large

Cuban from the humidor. Slouching in his chair, he blows smoke rings in the air and sighs delightedly. "I knew you'd all finally catch up to my ideas on how to deal with these Witnesses. I put on a show for you, allowing each of you to have a part in my new direction. Team building! That's the mark of a true leader. See how I got you all pulling together as a team towards where I already was. The trick was letting all of you believe you had an active part in the outcome. Damn, I'm good." Putting his feet up on the desk, Prophet Father leans back in his chair and savors his cigar as his aids breath a collective sigh of relief.

Amos 8:11-12 New King James Version
11 "Behold, the days are coming," says the Lord God,
   "That I will send a famine on the land,
Not a famine of bread,
Nor a thirst for water,
But of hearing the words of the Lord.
12 They shall wander from sea to sea,
And from north to east;
They shall run to and fro, seeking the word of the Lord,
But shall not find it.

Chapter 21

Prophet Father may have consolidated his power on Sunday morning, but Mr. Kasy's expectation that he would be hunting down heretics by Monday afternoon was a bit hasty. He languished in the royal dungeon for a week before Prophet Father's Imperial rule secured his release. Whisking him away to Jerusalem for a swearing in ceremony, where he and other continental chief inquisitors pledged their complete unquestioning loyalty to Prophet Father's version of Christianity and edicts. Kasey didn't return to Africa until the following week, giving the self-sacrificing refugees a big window of time to settle into their secret, rustic living accommodations in Africa's Grand Canyon.

Once he came back, Kasey was anxious to find Isaac and exercise his newly acquired authority. He had quickly grown accustomed to being treated with reverence by those serving him in the capital with Prophet Father. All the lower ranked plebs knew their place and followed protocol to the letter. Their discipline was enforced by the Beast's heavy hand and few dared stray into its path. Their attentiveness made Kasey feel like the special person he had always known he was.

Mr. Kasey was having a hard time getting the local Africans to acquiesce to his orders as obediently as the staff in Jerusalem had. He was sure that with the help of the embassy's SS officers, he would soon have the locals literally whipped into shape.

Reports of Isaac sightings had been coming into Kasey's office all week, but his SS troopers always seemed to miss catching him. Isaac was said to be teaching the gospel of the coming Kingdom of God to the local residents. Prophet Father's edicts expressly forbid all unauthorized public speaking and ordered the forcible roundup of all who had any unsanctioned viewpoints.

Wanting to snuff out all rebellious remnants of the loving church Jesus founded, Prophet Father sent an army of his best SS troops to be directed as Africa's Chief Inquisitor Kasey dictated. Making an example of others, and instilling fear was the explicit objective. No civilian body count could be too high. After running an algorithm from collected big data, Kasey believed Isaac would soon be appearing at the crowded national museum where he could spread his filthy lies. Positive Isaac would show up there soon, Kasey sets a trap and waits.

The analytics proved correct and no sooner had Kasey's plan been prepared that Isaac and his team unwittingly arrived. Satellite imagery showing an unusually high number of passenger buses converging within a six-block radius of the national museum alerted the SS to Isaac's arrival. From the number of arriving buses they surmised Isaac had brought all his refugee supporters with him for a mass rally, demonstrating their brazen defiance of the Empire's rule. The Chief Inquisitor was in the lead as his carefully planned trap was sprung.

Flanked by SS troopers with stun grenades at the ready, Kasey jumps out in front of Isaac, Musa and one other co-conspirator from behind one of the museum's large support pillars. Surprising them outside the winter sports wing of the museum, Kasey loudly demands Isaac and his companions surrender themselves to his legal authority.

"What legal authority do you have?" Musa demands. "This country is governed by an absolute monarchy, and I will only answer to my King!

Kasey quickly responds. "Well it's time you learned about two international laws. First is the golden rule. He who has the gold rules. The second, might makes right, is my favorite and the one I will soon be demonstrating on you. Your King and his pathetic little country will soon learn their place in our Empire's new world order."

"And I suppose you will be our loving teacher as you've always been."

"Loving to a fault." Kasey's voice reverted to the syrupy sweet tones of a kid's camp director. "As a loving father, having to bring harsh discipline to his errant child, I will gain no joy bringing tough love to you and your terrorist insurgents. World peace is too fragile right now to allow any dissension to the Empire's rule."

"Well you'll have to catch us first," Musa replies with a laugh as he directs Isaac and their driver to escape into the museum's sports wing. Turning to Isaac Musa says earnestly, "this may get deadly."

"We aren't born to get out of this life alive!" Isaac responds with a smile.

Splitting off to lead the SS away, Isaac and Musa head deeper into the museum as the bus driver cunningly slips away, blending into the sports museum displays. Hiding behind one of the pillars in the long corridor, Musa and Isaac pant hard as they lean against a column.

Knowing Kasey wanted these rebel leaders brought in alive for future interrogation, an observant SS soldier lobs a stun grenade beside the pillar, directly in front of Musa and Isaac. Isaac darts to the hockey display across from him. Grabbing the Northwood curved blade hockey stick from the number 21 Stan Mikita manikin's gloves, Isaac backhands the grenade down the hall into the middle of some startled SS troopers.

Another SS officer tosses, and a grenade lands three paces in front of Isaac who slap shots it. One timing it through a window, across from the displays, where another group of SS were clustered outside. The third grenade came in high. Isaac picks it out of the air with the stick, trapping it on the floor. Then he fires it back in the direction it came from with a wicked wrist shot.

Knowing he was running out of time before there would be a series of very loud explosions, Isaac jumps behind the column with Musa, where they duck and cover. When the dust cleared, the bewildered SS troops, along with Mr. Kasey, staggered out of the museum dazed and disoriented. Musa and Isaac had made their getaway.

"Who says road hockey skills won't help you later on in life." Isaac calls breathlessly to Musa as they run towards a waiting bus.

"I thought we were done for back there." Musa replied. "Do you think they're still chasing us?"

"They didn't bring an army not to catch us. Kasey won't stop now until he has us in chains."

"With the SS army closing in, I'm afraid there's just no way my King's plan will work out. But it's been a pleasure knowing you."

As they round the last corner before getting into the bus Isaac gasps to Musa. "It's been nice to know you too. And about there being no way the King's plan will work, I only have this to say. Yahweh."

Isaac follows Musa into the bus where the driver was waiting, ready to go. Spotted by SS scouts who report back to base command that Isaac is now on a passenger bus leaving the museum parking lot.

The bus Isaac and Musa are on heads towards the highway leading them southwest into the Lubombon district. Many similar busses funnel out of town at the same time. Coming from all directions, they fall into a convoy behind Musa's lead bus. They don't get far before helicopters are swirling overhead reporting their location to the army of SS which was mustering to give chase. Mr. Kasey is in the lead armored personnel carrier planning the rebel's demise. Still woozy from the grenade blasts, he shouts orders over the radio.

"Yes! I ordered all the troops to mobilize against them." Kasey screams into the mic. "We're going to chase them down and finish this. I have heard enough evidence to sign the death warrants for all of them. They can complain about their rights being infringed on or due process all they want, but I'm the law now. GO! GO! GO! But don't kill them all yet. I want to be the one to finish off the ring leaders, Isaac and Musa."

The long train of passenger buses head out of town with a growing pack of Imperial war machines coming up behind them. The Empire's only chance of catching the high-speed passenger buses was to get ahead of them and block the road they were on. Having brought mostly ground assault vehicles for the refugee roundup, Kasey deploys his two helicopters to set up roadblocks in front of the bus convoy. Reluctant to risk their lives by setting down on the road in front of speeding buses and hesitant to bomb one, not knowing which bus the leaders were in, the chopper pilots opt to blow up a short bridge the busses would soon have to cross.

Smoke from the bridge explosion blends in with the darkening clouds coming in from the west, cooling the hot afternoon sun. Seeing they couldn't go down the road much farther Isaac suggests they swerve off the road, through the ditch and onto the hot dusty Savannah, eastward away from the approaching storm.

"I don't remember all of this being in the Kings plans." Isaac hollers over the bus's roaring engine. "Let's go off road and see how all that armor fairs in the dirt."

Without hesitation the driver veers off the road and bounces onto the dry grassland, with the rest of the buses following suit. A large dust cloud swirls up from the busses that the Imperial forces doggedly follow, deep into the dry abyss. Winds buffet the bus convoy as they are hit by turbulence from the leading-edge of a large haboob quickly closing in on them. Soon they find themselves not only trying to outrun the Imperial army, but outrun a huge dust storm, blowing the dry Savannah topsoil eastward.

Barely three miles out onto the Savannah, the haboob starts to engulf the Empire's slower, light infantry vehicles. Still following Kasey's orders to take Isaac alive, the soldiers hold their fire to avoid hitting the leader's bus. Communication between the army vehicles breaks down as the statically charged dust and sand particles sweep over the war machines, making Kasey's new orders incomprehensible and updated data impossible to receive. The dark storm quickly engulfs the Empire's entire army, then swallows the refugee bus convoy.

Musa, Isaac and their team's bus is not only engulfed by the haboob, but it mysteriously starts bogging down as if it was driving through mud rather than on dry grass land. Soon the bus grinds to a halt as it sinks into the ground. It's not until they come to a stop that the vibrations of a large sustained earthquake could be felt. The ground's vibrations cause the ancient aquifer beneath the Savannah to mix with the parched soil. Liquefaction causes the soil particles to lose contact with each other, leaving the ground of the entire vast grassy plain unable to support the weight of any of the heavy vehicles on its surface.

Jumping clear of the lead bus, Musa, Isaac and the driver make it to an underground mountain top island of boulders jutting out of the Savannah. Without being swallowed up themselves, they manage to reach the rocks where they huddle amongst the boulders, trying to protect themselves from the swirling dirt of the haboob.

Hundreds of feet deep, the army vehicles as well as the refugee bus convoy, slowly sink through the gelatinous soil, coming to rest out of sight on the bedrock bottom. As gravity's pull is exerted on the last bus holding it firmly on the rocky bottom, the haboob blows itself out, leaving only a few stray dirt devils twisting over the now barren Savannah.

Revelation 12:6 New International Version (NIV)
The woman fled into the wilderness to a place prepared for her by God, where she might be taken care of for 1,260 days.

Revelation 12:13-16 Easy-to-Read Version
13 The dragon saw that he had been thrown down to the earth. So he chased the woman who had given birth to the child. 14 But the woman was given the two wings of a great eagle. Then she could fly to the place that was prepared for her in the desert. There she would be taken care of for three and a half years. There she would be away from the dragon.[a] 15 Then the dragon poured water out of its mouth like a river. It poured the water toward the woman so that the flood would carry her away. 16 But the earth helped the woman. The earth opened its mouth and swallowed the river that came from the mouth of the dragon.

Stealthily making their way further into the outback, Musa leads the trio through his familiar hunting territory before circling back towards a village. They discreetly hitch a ride back to town and make their way to a safe house where they're greeted by several compatriots.

"Brother, it's good to see you!" one of the rebels said as he hurried over to Musa, embracing him with an affectionate bear hug.

"We were following your lead bus on the Savannah. As we were engulfed by the haboob, our monitors kept sporadically blacking out. Luckily the bus's remote controls weren't affected and we could keep directing them. The army had overtaken the trailing bus when the earthquake started. We could feel the shaking here in the house. We didn't expect everything to sink into the dirt including the entire Imperial army. You three were the only rebels actually on a bus. We had no idea you had survived until now. We were afraid you had died."

Musa squeezes his friend tighter. "It was close, but here we are. It's a good thing you and the others were driving by remote control. We barely escaped from the lead bus. If anyone would have been on those busses further back on the Savannah, away from the rocks, they would have perished for sure."

Securely hidden in their safe house from the few SS still alive in the country, those resisting Prophet Father's rule celebrate their victory and narrow escape, recounting the day's adventures well into the night.

Chapter 22

The next morning a stunning, well-dressed woman arrived at the safe house in a tourist rental Jeep to collect Isaac and Musa. She was clothed fashionably in modern attire that enhanced her ebony skin tones and athletic physique. Isaac didn't recognize her from the hotel at first, all dolled up and out of her drab maid's uniform, but he was still a guy, and he definitely noticed her now.

"The King needed a volunteer to discreetly take you two north to the camp caves." She explained. Her voice was pleasant without the hint of an African accent. "I volunteered, thinking we'd look like tourists if I was with you. A foreign biracial couple, and their local guide. What could be more touristy? I even brought a Jeep with camping supplies for our big five safari, cameras and all."

She noticed Isaac's face flush as he smiled shyly at the mention of him being in the biracial duo.

"But you'll need to dress the part if we're going to be successful." She hands them each a bag with shoes and clothes. Musa and Isaac take the bags and disappear into the back of the safe house to change. When they reappeared they looked their parts.

"Good thinking." Musa spoke up. "I like your spunk. I've seen you around the hotel, but I don't believe we've ever met." He extended his hand in greeting. "I'm Musa, the King's aid. This is Isaac. I rescued him from a beheading so he could help answer an old question for my King."

Isaac stood in awkward silence behind Musa. His eyes riveted on the woman.

"I'm Dorit," she replied, confidently shaking Musa's hand. I've heard the hotel staff talk about Isaac and I attended the debate with Mr. Kasey. That's mostly why I volunteered to come. I would like to hear more of what Isaac has to say as I too have unanswered questions."

"I'll be as helpful as possible answering them." Isaac stammered eagerly, finally finding his tongue.

"The King must trust you. How did you get to know him?" Musa asked warily. Unsure of her loyalties, he kept himself in front of Isaac.

"I met the King at the Reed ceremony two years ago. I'm friends with one of the girls he was interested in as another wife. He didn't pay me much attention as I was fully clothed, unlike the rest of the girls. He did admire the way I organized the dinner though. The kitchen staff got the meals mixed up and I stepped in to straighten things out. He told me I should come work at the Royal hotel and that he would look forward to seeing me at the next Reed ceremony in more traditional attire."

"Did you go the next year in traditional attire?" Musa asks with a smile, eyeing her up and down.

"No. My traditions have more modest roots. My parents immigrated here when I was twelve and I was brought up with a different system of personal values than my friends who were born here."

"Yes, I recall the King complaining about that dinner."
Musa chuckled, relaxing with hearing her story. "So, do
you run the dining room at the hotel?"

"No." Came her reply. "The management are paranoid
about losing their positions. They think I'm a spy for the
King and don't trust me. I'll never get off the ladder's
bottom rung if I stick around there."

"So you volunteered to get out and get ahead." Musa
surmises.

"Yes. A girl's gotta do, what a girl's gotta do." She
says with a wink and a smile. "But I've heard Isaac
speak." She earnestly speaks directly to Isaac. "What
you've been saying makes sense to me. I'd like to come
along and learn more."

"Well, as you planned, now we look like a foreign
biracial couple on safari with our trusty guide." Isaac
notes eagerly. "We'd be short one if you didn't come
along."

"Why do you talk without a local accent? Musa asks
not fully convinced he should trust her.

"I've always enjoyed playing around with accents."
She replies as a local. "Like Trevor Noah. I study the way
people talk and mimic them." Sounding now like a Boer
from South Africa. "I'm a bit of a Chameleon that way."
Switching to impersonate a mandarin investor. "It's cheap
entertainment that I'm good at. People enjoy it." She now
sounded like an imperial spokesperson.

"Well, you seem to have a gift for the gab, I hope you
like camping." Musa replied, satisfied with her stories. "I
suppose the guide better drive. You two can sit in the

back and take in the scenery. You'll see further from the back seat." He says jokingly like a dad as they head for the Jeep.

They drive for hours making their way to the safety of the north. The whole time Dorit peppers Isaac with questions about his beliefs, trying to find holes in his logic, or scriptural contradictions. Although she was well versed in biblical theology it had never occurred to Dorit to connect the scriptures together the way Isaac did. But now that she took a fresh look at the scriptures, she could see errors in her old beliefs.

"Of course!" Dorit said with amazed enlightenment. "If everyone has an immortal soul at birth, then John 3:16 can't be right. We wouldn't need Jesus to give us eternal life as we would already have it and eternal life couldn't be reserved only for those who love Jesus."

"Exactly!" Isaac said triumphantly.

"But why would God make his plans like that when he only created everything to display his glory?"

"Oh I don't agree. Displaying his glory is worthless if it's not displayed to someone else who can appreciate it. Why would God display his glory to himself? God had no beginning, he would have been alive forever before he started creating things."

"I don't fully see your point."

"Well I think God was lonely. I think he wants to share life and love with others. He created man because he wants a relationship with us. He wants family."

"But that means God would want, or desire something. If he desires something, that would diminish his sovereignty. God is in need of nothing, he can create anything he might want." Dorit expresses her belief.

"I agree, God is the sovereign creator. However the fact he created anything should prove he wants something and there is one thing he can't create by fiat. He can't create love or make a sentient being love him. That's something we must do willingly. Humans who willingly follow him, through Jesus, have the potential to become more valued by God than anything else. Love is the one thing God can not create. Love has to be grown, developed through active participation."

"You make it sound like we have a choice if we should choose sin or follow God. Adam made the choice to sin for us, condemning all mankind to a life of sin ever since. What free choice could we have if humans are hardwired to sin, it's our default setting." Dorit passionately states.

"The Bible tells us that God won't punish the children for the sins of their fathers. If we have no free will to decide not to sin, then our sins wouldn't be our own fault. The sins we commit would be forced upon us by external forces and we wouldn't be responsible for them. Following that line of thinking will lead us to believe we don't need Jesus to cleanse our sins as those sins were a result of Adam's bad choice not ours. In the judgement to come, mankind would cry out to God, it isn't not our fault."

"Everyone needs to accept Jesus if they want their sins forgiven."

"Exactly!" Isaac agrees. "We need to accept his sacrifice to cleanse us of our sins. But if those sins were made because I had no choice but to make them how can they be mine? Without freedom to choose we wouldn't be self thinking beings. We'd just be sinning because we have to, robots doing as we're programmed. But we have the choice not to sin, we just don't make that choice often enough. Choosing sin just once still sentences us to death. That's why the sinless life of Jesus was so amazing. He came as a human and did what no other human could do. He never chose to let his human desire to sin, control his decisions. He lived the only perfect life, choosing to never sin." Isaac insists.

"Well of course he did! He was fully human and fully God."

"No, not the way I think you mean it, both at the same time. Yes, he was fully God when he was with God from the beginning, but he freely gave that up to become a humble servant in human form. He proved it was possible for a human to live a sinless life against the pulls of the flesh and our desire to sin. If his perfect life had been lived through the power of God, it would only show it's impossible for a human to live sinlessly and that God was asking for more than was possible, even for himself. God would be unreasonable in condemning us for sinning if it was impossible for us not to sin."

"That's not what I've been taught!" Dorit replies sceptically. "I've always been told that Jesus was both God and man, both at the same time."

"Then what made the life Jesus lived so special. As God, he would have had no problem not sinning. Just because you weren't taught this before doesn't make it wrong. I'd bet you were taught you have an immortal soul as well."

"Yes, that is the dominant Christian belief."

"Well if Jesus was fully God and Fully man at the same time he could have raised himself from the dead. We're told several times that God the father raised Jesus from the dead, and speaking of death, if Jesus was fully God, would he ever have been completely dead, or was he conscious the whole time and just extremely physically handycapped, but not fully dead?"

"Oh, I believe he was completely dead for the three days. That was his proof of messiahship."

"Exactly! Would he have been dead if he was still fully God?"

"I'll need to fully research this topic and study Bible scripture to find the truth about those points." Dorit said sincerely.

"I'm glad to hear you build your beliefs on the word of God and not on the teachings of man." Isaac said with a smile.

"Yes. I want to follow what the Bible tells me, not what some man like yourself has to say." Dorit looked critically at Isaac.

"Hopefully we'll have lots of time to explore those scriptures together when we get to our place of safety up north. My desire is to follow the word of God as well. My opinions can change. They don't have to be right, but I won't be indifferent to the word of God. I want to follow him in truth and love." Isaac says with a warm smile, with Dorit shyly smiling in reply.

"But this doesn't explain why God would create everything like he has. What's his plan?"

"I believe he wants a family full of love. Isn't that what most of us want? The loving companionship of family."

"The Bible does tell us we will become the children of God." Dorit points out agreeably.

"Just what I was going to say." Isaac was enthusiastic. "Children have to be born into a family after growing inside the mother. It's at their birth that they become viable children. When we're called by God to follow Jesus we start that gestation period. When Jesus returns we'll be born into the family of God as spirit beings, just like our big brother Jesus. Accepting Jesus as king over our lives is the first start. When we're resurrected, born as spirit beings, we'll become kings and priests in the Kingdom of God"

"Well I only have one king in my life and he's the King I have faithfully served my whole life." Musa speaks up loudly to be heard over the noisy Jeep. Unnoticed by Isaac and Dorit, Musa had been listening to their conversation and was eager to get a word in. "I've known about Jesus since I was a child but I've not felt any calling from God. I'm a good and fair man, respected within my country by its citizens and my King. I treat others with respect because that's how I was raised not because I heard a calling from God. I know people from many different religions who are good people just like me."

"Yes. I know many who are like that." Isaac responds, sitting forward in his seat so he could see Musa better.

"That's why God has laid out his plan the way he has. So all mankind will get an opportunity to accept Jesus as saviour. He will call to everyone at some time within his planned resurrections."

"This is a bigger topic than I had imagined." Dorit comments with surprise. "One topic seems to be entwined with another, like a plate of spaghetti. I hope we will have time to unwind them all when we get to the wilderness camp. I need to write these idea threads out on paper to keep them all straight."

"I'll enjoy doing that with you." Isaac responds positively. "It's not everyday I find someone interested in studying and believing what they discover the Bible to be saying. Most seem to only want to make the scriptures fit into what they already believe."

"Well you two can count me out!" Musa declares matter-of-factly. I'll be far too busy taking care of things around the camp to spend time reading and talking about God." Musa regrets getting involved in a conversation he didn't fully comprehend. "We're going to have to stop for gas. I'll get us some food at the same time." Musa talks loudly, looking at his passengers in the rearview mirror.

"Good. I need to use the restroom." Dorit replies as a colonizing Belgium debutante.

Musa pulls the Jeep up to the gas pump of a disheveled lean-to store front, in a small frontier village. A group of unsavory looking locals were lounging on the stoop, playing cards at a rickety table. They take no notice of the Jeep until Dorit elegantly strolls towards the latrine. They all turn their heads in unison and watch her until she's out of sight. They don't notice Isaac getting out of the Jeep to stretch his legs. He walks around the opposite side of the shack, watching some kids playing on a tire swing. Isaac isn't there long before the youngest girl falls off the tire, hitting the ground hard.

Isaac reacts instinctively and is by her side brushing the little girl off. Helping her up, he gives her a consoling hug as she wails out her pain. Her cries bring her mother running with the local men from the porch, hot on her heels.

"Hey cracker!" The lead one hollers at Isaac. "What are you doing to that little black girl."

"She fell off the swing," Isaac explained. "I was trying to help her. I didn't notice she was black, only that she needed help."

Isaac's soft answer of sincerity took the men by surprise.

"Well we can never be sure about you pale strangers." Another man says, "we always seem to get exploited by some invader."

"Maybe we need to teach you some respect for the locals." The biggest man says tapping a long, thick stick on the ground, like a batter would his bat.

"That won't be necessary boys." Came a strong confident Sotho voice from behind them. "This one's mine and I don't want him broken."

Dorit brushes past the small bunch of locals. Taking Isaac by the arm she cuddles up to him and runs her fingers through his hair lovingly. "It takes a lot of hard work to get a man trained the way a girl wants. He meant no harm and was only trying to help. We're on safari, looking to get pictures of the big five. Not hurt the locals."

Rattled by hearing their mother tongue, the men stared at Dorit in amazement. "Where you from girl and how'd you end up with this one?" came a startled question.

"Oh, that's a longer story than we have time for I'm afraid." Dorit went on in the Sotho language. "We're expected at our hotel soon. They won't hold dinner and my favorite is on the menu tonight. We really need to get going. We only stopped in to get gas." Dorit smiled sweetly as she flipped her hair with her free hand.

"You can take the time," came the reply. "We really want to know. You'll have to have leftovers."

Just then the Jeep pulled up two feet behind Isaac and Dorit. "Come on you two." Musa called to them. "We don't have time for visiting with the locals. We still have a ways to go."

"Well maybe we're not done with them," the bigger man with the stick said menacingly.

Musa rests his hand on the extra-large can of pepper spray strapped to the dash. "No, we need to go now," Musa replies forcefully. The second the men hesitate, Isaac and Dorit scramble into the back seat. They're feet were barely off the ground before Musa had the Jeeps wheels spinning on the dry dirt, leaving the locals in a cloud of dust, with the sobbing little girl.

Once back on the road heading north and sure they weren't being followed, the trio start to relax as they speed towards safety.

"Wow that was tense." Isaac said, in between controlled breaths. "You really saved my bacon Dorit. I'm sure glad you liked to play with languages as a kid."

"No problem. Nothing I wouldn't do for any friend eh." She said in perfect Canadian.

"You were great too Musa. You saved both of us from an uncertain future."

"Well a good safari guide needs to keep his charges safe from all predators."

"You sure did that." Dorit replied. "I got the feeling, those guys weren't interested in talking, no matter what I sounded like."

"Just what did you say to them as you ran your fingers through my hair."

"I told them you were mine and not to hurt you as men are hard to train."

"That was ballsy," Musa said. "I'm sure they've never heard a local girl talk like that before." Speeding towards safety he starts to laugh infectiously and soon they are all roaring with laughter at their close call with danger.

Chapter 23

In his Jerusalem headquarters office, Prophet Father's personal aid cautiously approaches with urgent news.

"Good Father." The aid says, stooping low as he enters the room.

"Yes. You may approach." Prophet Father replies, holding out his right hand in recognition of his attendant.

The aid comes forward, kneeling in front of Prophet Father he kisses the ring on his master's hand. "Great merciful Father," the aid humbly starts. "May you forever reign," the aid rises to his feet at Prophet Father's encouragement.

"What is the trouble my trusted adherent?" Prophet Father asks benevolently with a sincere smile.

"News from Africa my liege."

"Ah, good. I trust my chief inquisitor has finished dealing with those who would dare rebel against my edicts."

"Well, yes my lord. I'm afraid he is finished."

"Ah! Good. No need to be afraid. No rebel body count could be too high. I want this episode to be a warning to all mankind. It's time everyone learns who's in control of this world."

"But Sire, I don't think you fully understand."

"You aren't supposed to think. It's above your pay grade. I'm the one who does all the thinking. And who are you to tell me I don't understand?" Father's voice is stern.

"I, I didn't mean to be presumptuous, your majesty," the aid stammered. "But. But, I haven't told you all the news from Africa."

"Well then, you'd better enlighten me while you still have breath to talk."

"The news isn't good my Lord. Your African Chief Inquisitor and the SS army are lost."

"Lost? What are you talking about you imbecile? They're in that worthless Podunk south African country I sent them to, I know exactly where they are."

"But that's just it, Primate. They all seemed to have vanished off the Savannah while in pursuit of those rebels."

"What about Kasey? He was in charge of the campaign, he should know what's going on. Get a hold of him for me and I'll ask him myself."

"I can't, Supreme Pontiff. He's with the missing SS. They've all disappeared together."

"What about all the armament? Surely it couldn't have disappeared without a trace. There's no place big enough there to hide all that equipment."

"Last we heard, the army was catching up to the rebel busses when they were engulfed by a giant dust storm. All electronic surveillance was lost, we were blind. When the dust settled, they had all vanished. The army, the rebel busses, Kasey, everything had vanished. All that was left out on the Savannah was wet soil. They're searching for any trace of them now. There's nothing more to report."

"Then go. Go! Keep me posted. Go! And next time give me a full report the first time."

"Yes, yes my Liege." The aid grovels as he retreats backwards, bowing his way out of the room.

Prophet Father paces around the office for a moment, then sits contemplatively in his large leather office chair as he plans his next move.

Later that afternoon the aid finds Prophet Father before he meets with his regional governors.

"News just came in from Africa your majesty. They've located the army."

"Good. What does Kasey have to say for himself?" He snaps.

"Mr. Kasey has nothing to say. He…"

"What do you mean he has nothing to say. Tell him I want a full report on my desk before sunset!" Prophet Father cuts in.

"No one has been able to talk to Mr. Kasey," the aid explains.

"Why not? You said they've been found. You tell him I want a progress report on those rebels. He was given orders to destroy those refugees, meeting together as if they were some loving church. I want them snuffed out before more adherents are converted to their so-called ways of love. I gave him an army to do it, now I want results."

"The military vehicles and the rebel busses have been found. It's assumed the SS personnel, rebels, along with Kasey are with those vehicles."

"Great. Arrest the rebels and have Kasey report to me before the end of the day."

"But my Potentate. The vehicles are buried hundreds of feet below the Savannah. They were found using ground penetrating radar, electromagnetic conductivity and multi-frequency surveys. It's believed everyone in those vehicles sunk down to bedrock below the Savannah in a quicksand event, caused by an earthquake, while our surveillance was blinded by a dust storm."

"So, you're telling me that everyone is dead and buried under the sand?"

"Yes, your Excellency." The aid replies timidly, bracing himself for the rage of his master.

"Well that's great." Prophet Father replies with glee. "The rebels have been liquidated. Their loving church has been buried: that turned out good. It's a shame we didn't get much live media coverage of the events and it's too bad about the SS army, but I did say no body count would be too high to snuff out that church. I'll have my media specialists put a favorable spin on this news." Prophet Father talks to himself more than the aid as he works through the handling of the matter. "Maybe play up the patriotic SS sacrifices made while fighting those cowardly rebels."

Starting to pace in circles, Prophet Father formulates his response to the new updates. "Keep me informed of any fresh developments. I'll stamp out any seed that may try to sprout from that church of love. I'm sure many have been infected by their personal examples and stories. They'll be hard to find, scattered throughout the population, but I'll root them out. If they want to follow sacrificial love, I'll let them be sacrificed, baptized in their own blood."

He laughs maniacally, envisioning more state sanctioned torture chambers incorporated into existing re-education camps and new ones springing up throughout the world, martyring the churches seed along with those who would question his moral supremacy.

Revelation 12:17 New International Version

Then the dragon was enraged at the woman and went off to wage war against the rest of her offspring—those who keep God's commands and hold fast their testimony about Jesus.

"I'm sure the Franciscan and Dominican orders will eagerly pick up the cause as they did with the ancient inquisitions."

Prophet Father's personal aid stands nodding his head empathically, patiently waiting for him to finish ranting before he discreetly slips away.

Urging the world's population to turn from their sins and repent, the witnesses, sometimes teaching, sometimes explaining, rebuke an ungodly world and through Bible scripture they're always correcting the biblical errors of Prophet Father. Hearing them explain God's plan for mankind's salvation, most listen only to reject them as fools. Those who try to find the Bible verses used by the Two Witnesses are frustrated by not having accurate Bibles to study from due to a famine of accurate scripture. Scattered few heed the message to repent and are soon swept off for Imperial re-education.

Following their mission and declaring the soon coming Kingdom of God through the power of His name, the Two Witnesses crash a second Imperial rally hosted by Prophet Father. This time Prophet Father had a plan, expecting they'd be stopping by. Noticing them standing just offstage, he pauses his speech, then introduces them to the worldwide audience, welcoming them onto the stage.

"And look who we have with us today!" He talks directly to the camera, making eye contact with everyone in the video audience.

"It's the Two Witnesses!" The large red applause signs flash above the stage, cueing the live audience how to respond.

"Yes. Let's bring them on stage with a big round of applause." Casually walking over to them Prophet Father claps his hands enthusiastically, then warmly directs them over towards the podium.

"For those folks who may not know our guests, let me introduce the self-proclaimed Two Witnesses of God." Again, the applause signs flash.

"I see you've both dressed in your finest for this occasion." Prophet Father jokes, pretending to brush dust and lint off of them as he straightens up their hooded sackcloth tunics.

"Do you two share the same tailor by any chance? Or were these outfits prepared especially for you by God?" The signs switch to 'laugh' and the live audience join in with the pre-recorded laughter coming through the house speakers. Prophet Father sounds upbeat like a late-night talk show host. "So what have you two been up too since we last met?" Prophet Father queries.

"We've been prophesying." Came the reply.

"Oh!! Well that sounds very ostentatious. Is that your mission? Prophet Father continues condescendingly.

"Yes. God spoke to us. He told us to prophesy to the world!" The other witness spoke up, taking turns answering.

"Well! You heard it here first," Prophet Father played up the answer. "They're on a mission from God." Oo's and aw's come from the monitors as the crowd starts to jeer.

"Did others happen to hear God give you your instructions."

"No. I don't think so. We were alone, hiking in the mountains when God spoke to us."

"Well, did you pack enough water? Dehydration can play havoc with your mind you know." The audience laughs spontaneously at the witnesses' expense. "Did you both actually hear the audible voice of God?"

"Yes, we had plenty of water." One answered. "We both heard God at the same time." The other added.

"Well. You two must be very special to be the only ones called by God for this special task. I'd bet you were top students. Did you have to take any special prophet training?"

"No, not at all. We've never had any special training of any kind." "We just open our mouths and God fills it with what he wants us to say."

"Well it takes a lot of courage and bravery to stand before a worldwide audience, exposing their sins and telling them to repent."

"I don't know about that," they replied. "It doesn't take bravery or courage. It takes faith."

"Well it's a shame no one else was there to corroborate your story about God calling you. We'll just have to take your word for it I suppose."

"God thought of that for us. As you've seen, we have divine powers to stop the rain, turn water to blood and send plagues."

"Yes, yes, I've experienced those firsthand. But this is a new worldwide audience, some will be tuned in for the first time. How are they supposed to be sure? Do you think you two could give us a demonstration now, broadcast live throughout the entire world?"

"God's power is to be used to further his plans, not to entertain the masses." A Witness responds contemptuously.

"Well what about that fire thingy you do? Will you always be doing that when someone tries to harm you? It was very impressive last time you graced my stage, dispatching my personal SS by speaking fire out of your mouths, not to mention the way you dodged all those lithium powered blasters."

"Yes, that's true. Anyone who tries to harm us will be destroyed in the same manner."

"Well that would be a good proof of your God given mission. The way you handle trouble looks very miraculous. Very miraculous indeed."

"We try not to resort to that. We'd prefer to avoid trouble when we can."

"Ah, yes. Take the loving, non-combative course of action. Speaking of courses, how do you two chart yours? It must be hard to personally go everywhere, after all your message is for the entire world. What do your travel plans look like, or do you just plan to keep showing up on stage with me?"

"We go where the Spirit leads." One Witness explains. "And you do have a worldwide audience." The other points out.

"Well if you two are going to be showing up all the time anyway, why don't we just plan for you to have a regular spot with me. It'll give you a stage from which you can electronically proclaim your message around the world. I'll even take you with me when I travel to do live rallies."

"Why would you do that?"

"If you truly are sent from God, it'll do me no good to fight you, and if you aren't sent by God, someone will kill you. Anyway, don't you know the saying, 'keep your friends close, but your enemies closer'? Either way you have nothing to lose and a worldwide audience to gain."

"What would we have to do for you?"

"Nothing at all. Just be yourselves. Contrasted against you, I look good. Mankind was born for sin. It's their default setting. They love me and hate the way you two tell them how bad they are. With you acting as The Two Witnesses for your God, my approval ratings will never go down."

"Alright, we agree to prophecy the words of God from your stage." "And as you'll see, we are sent by God." They respond.

"Good! For your sakes I hope you are sent by God. But to prove it, we'll just have to put you to the test, now won't we?" Turning to address the crowd, Prophet Father asks. "What do you all say, should we put them to the test?" Prophet Father hollers, waving his arms to get the crowd riled up.

The audience chants back to him spontaneously, "Test! Test! Test! Test! Test!"

Prophet Father Holds his hands up, quieting the audience. Turning back to the Two Witnesses he exclaims. "You heard them! They want a test. How can I say no?" Gesturing backstage he motions for someone to come forward. "This brings us to a segment of the program I like to call; Can You Kill Them?!"

The Two Witnesses' eyes grow wide. "Oh, I know." Prophet Father explains. "You feel cheated because you didn't get to prophecy yet. But I promise," he says earnestly, "if you're still with us, next time we'll make it up to you by giving you double the prophesying time. A new show must build its fan base. We need to give the population a reason to tune in next time. But don't worry, if what you say is true, you'll have nothing to worry about."

A man walks on stage brandishing an old-fashioned AK47 machine gun. He approaches the Two Witnesses warily, like a wolf stalking its prey.

"Last time the SS were using modern thorium powered disrupters. I thought giving some older technology a try might produce better results," Prophet father explains to the Two Witnesses.

Turning to the gunman he adds, "make sure you point that thing away from the audience and me. You are shooting bullets. We don't want to get hit by accident."

The gunman nods as he puts Prophet Father and the audience at his back. Walking menacingly towards the ill dressed Witnesses, who slowly retreated, trying to reason with him.

"This isn't a good idea. We don't want to hurt you, but we need to defend ourselves. Just stop and think through your actions before it's too late."

The gunman stops, heading their words to think through his actions, he holds up his gun and scrutinizes it carefully. Releasing the safety, he smiles and nods his appreciation to the Two Witnesses. Giving them a thumbs up gesture, he once again firmly grips the gun and points it at them. His finger squeezes the trigger, but just before the bullets fly, fire erupts from the Two Witnesses' mouths, incinerating him instantly.

The audience holds its collective breath, taking in what has just transpired. Prophet Father didn't miss a beat. Smiling and clapping loudly he walks to center stage.

"Well how about that folks! That was amazing!" Pointing to the smoldering corpse. "He didn't even get off a round." The audience reads the flashing applause sign and joins him in revelry. "Talk about a decisive victory. You two are the quick draw champs for sure."

Looking straight into the camera for a closeup he continues. "Now if there are any of you at home who want to have a crack at defeating these two and become quick draw champs yourselves, or maybe you want to prove that the Two Witnesses' God is a fake. Just sign up for your chance to be immortalized. The number will be displayed at the end of our show. And of course," Pointing at the Two Witnesses.,"there'll be a hefty reward for the person who defeats these two notorious killers. Keep tuning in to stay up with all the latest action, we'll be running live colour commentary by your favorite on air personalities, as well as the best of highlights and a bloopers reel."

The Two Witnesses stand disappointedly as the live audience claps and shouts wildly at the dawning of the world's new bloodsport. As the cameras pan the enthusiastic audience, bringing the show to a close, an announcer's voice exuberantly broadcasts the contact information displayed on the screen.

"That's right. To have your very own chance at killing the Two Witnesses live before a worldwide audience, just dial 666 on any communication device and leave your personal information with us. That's right, just dial 666 for your chance at worldwide fame. That's 666 on any communication device. Operators are standing by." Then much faster he continues. "Contestants must be within the legal age of consent and accept all liabilities associated with this contest, holding the Empire completely blameless for any and all personal injuries or losses, including death.

Soon there is a flood of applicants vying for the bounty, stardom, or notoriety, as well as those from other religions wanting to disprove the supremacy of the God, the Two Witnesses boldly proclaim.

The next day, a private luncheon at an Imperial banquet hall, honoring the members of the small research group that discovered when the stinging Locust would die off. Prophet Father hosts a banquet for them and several hundred of their extended families and friends. Sparing no expense, the Empire puts its best foot forward.

"I wanted to personally congratulate all of you for your outstanding work on this file." Prophet Father said after the meal had concluded. "The Empire owes you a debt of gratitude for all your work and sacrifice." Some of the members are fussing with their rambunctious children and infants as Prophet Father heaps praise on their small group of researchers.

"Although those directly working on the project are sworn to secrecy, it's only natural that someone may have let an errant word slip to a friend or relative. I'd like to extend my personal appreciation to your family members and friends for their understanding and support. We want to assure you all that the Empire and I are stronger now because of the support provided to those researchers working on this case. My heartfelt thanks goes out to you all." The room is filled with chatter as parents, siblings, friends, aunts and uncles, looked appreciatively at each other and at the researchers around the room. They were all honored and proud to be included in the celebrations.

"No other research has propelled the Empire ahead like the research you all were a part of. Some actively, others passively in a supportive role. I know that most of you were unaware of the nature of research that was being done, however it is vital that the knowledge of this research end here today. I humbly thank you all for the sacrifices you have made personally for the Empire. I also know you all want to succeed in life like everyone else, enjoying the fruits of your hard-earned labors, sharing them with your families well into your old age. Sadly, this is not the outcome that any of you will be experiencing. The need for secrecy is just too great to allow any of you to make a slip of the tongue. The Empire can't tolerate even the hint of a scandal on this file. I hope you have enjoyed this fine meal we prepared for you, as it will be your last. Again, I do appreciate all the sacrifices you've made for the Empire, especially this final, ultimate sacrifice. The poison should start taking effect, right, about, now." Prophet Father informs the shocked audience, checking his watch as the timer starts to buzz.

The infants are the first to fall silent in the room, followed by those with a lower body mass. Soon even the rotund are slumped over in their chairs, face first into their plates, around the banquet hall.

"Well. That takes care of that." Prophet Father remarks to his aid as he leaves through a side exit. "We just couldn't risk the truth coming out." Giving his aid a sideways glance, he adds. "Just you remember that."

"My lips are sealed, your Eminence. You know I suffer from terminal memory loss."

"Well keep it that way. Have them put a torch to this place so there's nothing to discover. It'll be a shame how everyone died in such a deadly fire, after such fine festivities."

"Of course, Sire. It will be handled with the utmost discretion." The aid helps Prophet Father into his vehicle, then dutifully returns to the banquet room to prepare the pyre.

Months turn into years for Isaac, surviving in safety and relative comfort with the rest of the loving volunteers. The wilderness encampment became their home, tucked away from the tribulation going on in the rest of the world. Isaac was reunited with his mom, who had been one of the original volunteers to come help the King's orphans. She happily watched as Isaac and Dorit made their pledge of faithfulness to each other before God. She was also there to greet her twin grandchildren.

Raising all the children took a group effort, as the little ones ran and played carefree in the safety of their forest, hemmed in by steep cliffs, raging water and foreboding caves. Dense tree canopy coverage gave them ample protection from visual or electronic air surveillance. The misty waterfalls, along with lush foliage, purified the air of its deadly toxins. An abundance of fish thrived in the pure headwater of the tributary. Bubbling up from distant mountain fed springs, it naturally irrigated edible berries, vegetables, nut and fruit trees, then flowed into the main river system.

With food and shelter easily accessible within the camp perimeters, the band of volunteers would dry fish in the sun, curing them before adding berries, roots and vegetables, making a type of ultimate survival food. Oblivious to the outside world, they thrived for three and a half years within this lush compound, waiting for the second coming of their savior.

After Prophet Father rid the world of the Scorpion stinging Locust, the nations from Asia were pleased to proclaim him their savior along with the rest of the world. They looked to him as their spiritual leader, weaving him into their religious tapestries. However, after years of the Two Witnesses preaching their God as the one and only true God, the maker of heaven and earth, the nations of Asia had reached the end of their patience with Prophet Father. They blamed him for enabling the Witnesses to spread religious exclusivity at his live rallies and continuously around the world electronically. They also believed he was secretly keeping the Two Witnesses alive as hundreds of their faithful followers tried to kill them, only to be consumed by fire. Those martyrs believed killing the Two Witnesses would prove them wrong and their God impotent.

Finding the economic terms agreed upon with the Empire were not being honoured, they had reached their breaking point. Still having regional control of their own armies, the leaders of these nations held clandestine meetings to air grievances and plan. Now, after nearly Three and a half years of Imperial rule under Prophet Father, the time to act had come. Knowing that only an overwhelming show of force would get results at the negotiating table, these Asian nations funnel their combined armies of 200,000,000 over the Silk Road, close to Jerusalem, threatening Prophet Father. Killing a third of mankind as they came, they overwhelm the outnumbered Imperial troops and elite SS. Poised to overthrow Prophet Father and his Holy Roman Empire, they demand new terms be implemented for a new world order.

Seeing this newly formed army was made up of many factions, Prophet Father shrewdly finds a way to divide them politically, by negotiating terms that best suit his desires. He forms a deal that eliminates the Asians's largest source of complaint, the Two Witnesses. Eliminating the Two Witnesses would bring the Asian factions back under Imperial control. Prophet Father wastes no time before consulting the Beast on how to best achieve his plans.

"My organization has a long proud history," the Beast explains. "For security reasons, we haven't kept any written records on how or why each Chairman handled a particular situation. We have oral traditions, passing down stories. One story I remember was how a Chairman got special divination from spirits, saving him from certain failure."

"This is no time for fireside ghost stories," Prophet Father snaps. "I have to kill those Two Witnesses to stop the Empire from unravelling. We've tried everything over the last three and a half years and nothing has worked. I thought for sure someone would have killed them by now, but it's always the same fire from them that wins. I just don't know what to do!"

"Well. Like I was saying. There is this story about a Chairman who got himself in a pickle, kind of like what you're in. He tried everything he knew to get himself out of it, but each time he tried he'd fail. He finally realized he was trapped in the Dunning Kruger effect. He just didn't know what he didn't know, and he was making decisions beyond his ability."

"So you're saying I'm ignorant and need more knowledge?" Prophet Father replied angrily.

"Now that's a cognitive breakthrough. You're really making progress. You've acknowledged what you had just told me, 'I just don't know what to do'. Your exact words. Now that you understand your ignorance and need for more knowledge, you can move forward. Realizing your need for help is the first step in recovery."

"Well you should know, you've taken those twelve steps many times." Father's voice is thick with sarcasm.

"You don't need to be mean, I'm only trying to help."

"Is that the end of your story? How did this Chairman acquire his newfound wisdom?"

"Like I said." The Beast went on. "He consulted the spirit realm to get him out of trouble."

Prophet Father is defensive, "it's been obvious for years the Two Witnesses are doing the will of their God, the maker of everything. How do you expect me to fight against that?"

"I don't know, but I've made a few inquiries to those spirits myself with good results. At times I can feel them working inside my mind as I give myself over to them. I just sit back and watch as they take control of me," the Beast replies.

"Hum. I like being in control of things, but it seems like the only way to get out of this jam is to try it. I don't have very long to kill the Witnesses, otherwise the deal with the Asians is off. I can't let that happen."

Directing Prophet Father to his private meditation room, the Beast replies. "Come, let me lead you. We'll go to my spirits together and they'll guide us to the truth. We'll be able to sit back and watch as they take control, working through us as we surrender completely to their will. It's worked for me in the past and I know they won't let us down now."

Prophet Father nods his head, desperate to do anything that would result in success, he follows the lead of the Beast and sits awkwardly on the office floor. Opening his mind as a blank page, he invites the spirits to come and take over his consciousness.

"Try this. I find it helps to clear my mind into a blank slate. OOOHHMM." The Beast chants.

Prophet Father again nods his head like a dutiful apprentice. Closing his eyes, he relaxes and disengages with himself. "OOOOHHHMMM." His voice blends with Beast, as they drone on.

Revelation 9:13-21 New International Version (NIV)
13 The sixth angel sounded his trumpet, and I heard a voice coming from the four horns of the golden altar that is before God. 14 It said to the sixth angel who had the trumpet, "Release the four angels who are bound at the great river Euphrates." 15 And the four

angels who had been kept ready for this very hour and day and month and year were released to kill a third of mankind. 16 The number of the mounted troops was twice ten thousand times ten thousand. I heard their number. 17 The horses and riders I saw in my vision looked like this: Their breastplates were fiery red, dark blue, and yellow as sulfur. The heads of the horses resembled the heads of lions, and out of their mouths came fire, smoke and sulfur. 18 A third of mankind was killed by the three plagues of fire, smoke and sulfur that came out of their mouths. 19 The power of the horses was in their mouths and in their tails; for their tails were like snakes, having heads with which they inflict injury. 20 The rest of mankind who were not killed by these plagues still did not repent of the work of their hands; they did not stop worshiping demons, and idols of gold, silver, bronze, stone and wood—idols that cannot see or hear or walk. 21 Nor did they repent of their murders, their magic arts, their sexual immorality or their thefts.

Prophet Father returned to his office reinvigorated and as some of his aids thought, his personality was different, more intense and foreboding. He announces his plan to his team.

"I've discovered how to kill the Two Witnesses." He informs them eagerly. "All this time we've been trying to kill them using weapons made by man. When we should have been using weapons made by God for killing those who deserved death."

His team stared blankly back at him, unsure of what he was talking about.

"The answer is repeated in the Bible numerous times." Father explained. "Using the first weapons made by God is the only way we have yet to try." Prophet Father went on, hoping someone would guess the answer. Silence filled the room, finally Prophet Father exasperatedly exclaimed. "Stoning. We've never tried to stone them to death. Rocks are God's original and most primitive weapon. David mastered them, putting smooth stones to deadly use on several occasions."

"But who will put this theory of yours to the test? It may be hard to find a volunteer willing to risk their life on your hunch." Came a nervous reply.

"I will do it personally." Prophet Father replies proudly. "I want the world to know that I alone have the power to kill those Two Witnesses. Making me more powerful than even their God. The world will see and worship me for the divinity that, 'I Am'."

Most of humanity are oblivious as the two witnesses proclaim God; they only watch for the comedic entertainment value, the spectacle of human incineration, or to find out when more punishment is coming their way. For 1260 days the world has endured their prophesying, rebuking and punishing. Weary of them, the world now longed for relief from the pair of doomsayers.

During today's broadcast at the, Can You Kill Them segment, the Witnesses brace themselves for yet another attempt on their lives, by some religious zealot, or extreme sports junkie, chasing the ultimate adrenaline rush. They are shocked when Prophet Father announces that he will finally be the one to put the Witnesses to death.

"I alone am the true god of this world," he brags, looking directly into a camera and making eye contact with everyone watching a screen. "I alone am the one who will vanquish these two and their God. I will display my power for all the world to see. Then I alone will receive all the glory and honor I am due."

Father proceeds towards the witnesses with a bag of stones and a sling. Using David as his example, he hurls two stones in quick succession. Both find their mark, the Two Witnesses crumble to the floor dead. The audience, caught off guard for an instant from the lack of fire, or smell of charred flesh, erupts in exuberant exaltation. Desperate to finally be free of the Witnesses, the crowd pleads to bury them in hastily dug graves, but they are refused.

"No! I want them left in the street to rot," came Prophet Fathers decree. "I want all to see, smell and remember what happens to those who challenge me. Have cameras broadcast their decaying bodies around the world, until there's nothing left but their sun-bleached bones. I'm establishing a new worldwide holiday to commemorate this day. Death Day will be celebrated around the world as a joyous time of merriment. I want people to exchange gifts and celebrate, remembering this joyous day as the day I delivered them from those two evil Witnesses."

The world's inhabitants party for days singing, 'peace, peace, peace has finally come to the earth'.

Revelation 11:7-14 King James Version (KJV)

7 And when they shall have finished their testimony, the beast that ascendeth out of the bottomless pit shall make war against them, and shall overcome them, and kill them.

8 And their dead bodies shall lie in the street of the great city, which spiritually is called Sodom and Egypt, where also our Lord was crucified.

9 And they of the people and kindreds and tongues and nations shall see their dead bodies three days and an half, and shall not suffer their dead bodies to be put in graves.

10 And they that dwell upon the earth shall rejoice over them, and make merry, and shall send gifts one to another; because these two prophets tormented them that dwelt on the earth.

Always on the lookout for approaching meteorites, Imperial telescopes monitor around the earth's location in space. Scientists are alarmed when an unpredicted blip appears on their computer screens. Unsure what it might be, they send the alert up the chain of command. With the early warning given by long range scanners and computer modelling that predict the trajectory, every camera available is focused on the Jerusalem sky.

Undeterred by the approaching object, the party carries on for three and a half days. One day for every year the Two Witnesses delivered their message of God to the world, and yet in all that time the world would not repent or turn from their sins. After three and a half days of watching the Two Witnesses decay into a stinky oose, the party abruptly ends. The Two Witnesses are mysteriously resurrected victoriously back to life with the call of God. Within the same hour, the rumble of a great earthquake could be heard devastating the city.

11 And after three and a half days, the spirit of life from God entered into them, and they stood upon their feet; and great fear fell upon them which saw them.

12 And they heard a great voice from heaven saying unto them, Come up hither. And they ascended up to heaven in a cloud; and their enemies beheld them.

13 And the same hour was there a great earthquake, and the tenth part of the city fell, and in the earthquake were slain of men seven thousand: and the remnant were affrighted, and gave glory to the God of heaven.

14 The second woe is past; and, behold, the third woe cometh quickly.

Astonished, every eye in the world was glued to a screen to see the freshly resurrected Witnesses as well as scan the Jerusalem sky. Watching intently, not wanting to miss a thing, the world held its collective breath as history unfolded before them that day in Jerusalem. The clouds begin to part and every camera reveals what looks like a man riding on a white horse approaching from space. As this apparition approaches, the resurrected Two Witnesses rise into the air from where they stand, towards the arriving horseman.

Before they get more than 80 feet into the sky, a great shout is heard around the world, followed by the deafening blast of a trumpet. Soon the Two Witnesses are overtaken in the sky by mysterious phantoms rising simultaneously out of the earth and sea around the world. Starting out as wispy sinews, they flesh out into complete bodies as they rise into the air, rendezvousing with the Witnesses.

These were the followers of Jesus who had died and were asleep in their graves, their bones and bodies had long since rotted, ashes to ashes and dust to dust, into soil. Having a perfect memory and knowing each one intimately, God had no trouble in reanimating their personalities, memories and psyche essence back to life just as they were, but into new spiritual bodies. Their first conscious thought since they died, is when they rise up, greeting Jesus as immortal children of God. With shouts of praise and excitement they gather around him.

1 Thessalonians 4:15-16 New King James Version (NKJV)

15 For this we say to you by the word of the Lord, that we who are alive and remain until the coming of the Lord will by no means precede those who are [a]asleep. 16 For the Lord Himself will descend from heaven with a shout, with the voice of an archangel, and with the trumpet of God. And the dead in Christ will rise first.

Prophet Father was in a panic, not knowing what to do. His illusions of world supremacy seemed to be slipping out of his grasp with the Two Witnesses coming back to life and this new extraterrestrial arriving. The Beast calms him with reassuring words that strengthen his resolve.

"Come my friend. Let's seek the guidance of our spirits. They were right about how to do away with the Witnesses, if we give ourselves completely and unreservedly to their will, they will lead us into our final reward. One deserving of all the gains we've brought to mankind." The Beast leads Prophet Father to a quiet room and into a calm mindful state. OOOHHHMMM they start to chant.

From mankind's vantage point, the sound of the trumpet blast startles them, but not as much as the mysterious figures that emerge from under the dirt and water. Wherever they lay, they rise with shouts of praise. These phantoms are followed by a smaller group of figures that also rise, merging to join the arriving apparition appearing in the clouds. Isaac, Dorit and others, redeemed by Jesus are in this second wave of newly resurrected saints. This is the resurrection Isaac and the followers of Jesus that were still alive had been waiting for. Those who were asleep in their graves, including the Two Witnesses, rose first, followed by those who were still waiting at the coming of Jesus.

"Dorit this is it!! Jesus has finally come for us!"

"Yes! I can see! We're going to be reborn into spirit. We'll see Jesus as he is because we'll be like him."

Dorit comes to a sudden realization. "The children. The children! It never occurred to me before, but the children will be left here alone, still physical." As the thought is spoken aloud, all the parents are comforted by a familiar loving voice they had trusted for the past three and a half years.

"Don't worry about the children!" Musa reassures. "I always knew there would be a good reason why God hadn't called me to Jesus yet." Musa said matter of factly. "Me and a few others have the privilege of staying and taking care of them. I've faithfully served King Mark my whole life so far. Now it looks like I'll have a new King to serve faithfully for the rest of it. Maybe you will introduce me to your King and big brother."

"It will be our pleasure!" Came the joyously spontaneous, response from Dorit and Isaac just before gravity loses its hold on them.

The children of those caught up alive to the returning Jesus, are left to be cared for and protected by trusted family or friends who hadn't been called to Jesus by God.

As Isaac Dorit and the others from the place of safety rise to meet their saviour in the air, they are changed into the type of spiritual body that the coming Jesus has. They pass through the tree cover that kept them hidden for the last three and a half years. But rather than going around the thick leafy branches they simply pass right through them as if they or the trees weren't made of solid material.

1 John 3:1-2 New International Version (NIV)

1 See what great love the Father has lavished on us, that we should be called children of God! And that is what we are! The reason the world does not know us is that it did not know him. 2 Dear friends, now we are children of God, and what we will be has not yet been made known. But we know that when Christ appears, we shall be like him, for we shall see him as he is.

"Did you see that Dorit?" Isaac exclaimed. "When we went through the tree canopy I could see inside the branches and leaves. It was fascinating to see their internal workings."

"Yes! I saw it too," came Dorit's reply. "Do you feel a tingling running through your body?"

"Yes. It's like the tingling I felt in my fingers when I was debating Mr. Kasey and I feel like I'm using all my senses to the fullest."

"I know exactly what you mean. Not only my senses but I even have all my memories and they are as vivid as if they just happened, I even remember being dried off at birth."

"Yeah." Was all Isaac could reply as he was silenced by the grandeur of being changed in the twinkling of an eye.

1 Thessalonians 4:17 King James Version

Then we which are alive and remain shall be caught up together with them in the clouds, to meet the Lord in the air: and so shall we ever be with the Lord.

Revelation 1:7 New International Version
**"Look, he is coming with the clouds," and "every eye will see him,
even those who pierced him"; and all peoples on earth "will mourn because of him." So shall it be! Amen**.

1 Corinthians 15:52 King James Version (KJV)
In a moment, in the twinkling of an eye, at the last trump: for the trumpet shall sound, and the dead shall be raised incorruptible, and we shall be changed.

As the mysterious figures slip through gravity's grasp, they join the horseman as He approaches through the clouds. With a trumpet sounding in their ears, the world's inhabitants try to understand the unprecedented events unfolding before them. The rider is now surrounded by a host of white robed figures in the sky. Some people are so fearful of the events they hide in caves and rocks, crying out to the mountains to cover and shield them from whatever else was to come.

Their fear is justified, judging by the rider's appearance. His intent to rule is obvious, from the crowns he was wearing on his head, to his blood drenched robes, looking like he had already been in a brawl. His flaming eyes and the rod of iron by his side, both invoked fear in the earth's population. But the most terrifying thing about this coming invader was the flaming sword that came out of his mouth. It seemed like it would divide soul and spirit, joints and marrow, and marrow from bone.

Revelation 11:15 New International Version (NIV)
The seventh angel sounded his trumpet, and there were loud voices in heaven, which said:

"The kingdom of the world has become the kingdom of our Lord and of his Messiah, and he will reign for ever and ever."

Revelation 19:19 New King James Version (NKJV)
And I saw the beast, the kings of the earth, and their armies, gathered together to make war against Him who sat on the horse and against His army.

Revelation 19:11-16 New King James Version (NKJV)
Christ on a White Horse
11 Now I saw heaven opened, and behold, a white horse. And He who sat on him was called Faithful and True, and in righteousness He judges and makes war. 12 His eyes were like a flame of fire, and on His head were many crowns. He [a]had a name written that no one knew except Himself. 13 He was clothed with a robe dipped in blood, and His name is called The Word of God. 14 And the armies in heaven, clothed in [b]fine linen, white and clean, followed Him on white horses. 15 Now out of His mouth goes a [c]sharp sword, that with it He should strike the nations. And He Himself will rule them with a rod of iron. He Himself treads the winepress of the fierceness and wrath of Almighty God. 16 And He has on His robe and on His thigh a name written:
KING OF KINGS AND

LORD OF LORDS.

Controlled by their invited spirits, Prophet Father and the Beast rally the armies of the world to attack this new extraterrestrial invader coming to rule over their planet. They address the awaiting armies through a live broadcast that goes out to the world's inhabitants:

Prophet Father speaks forcefully into his mic. "It's good that our brothers from the Asian armies are here to join with our Imperial troops. Shoulder to shoulder we'll win this battle to save the world. Obviously, the scientific pundits were wrong about the strange atmospheric plagues this world has gone through over the past 7 years. The conspiracy theorists were right after all. The Earth is being invaded by Extraterrestrials! Planning to reign over us, they've subverted human turncoats to join them. They lived here among us, learning our weaknesses until now! Now as they launch this full-scale invasion.

This is a fight for humanity's freedom! If we fail, it'll be the end of the world as we know it! Fight these galactic invaders! Fight for your families! Fight for your country's survival! Fight for your personal freedoms. Fight to keep all we've built as a human race! ARE YOU READY! This will be a fight for your lives and all you hold dear! Give Us FREEDOM or Give Us DEATH!"

Joining Prophet Father at the podium is the Beast. Shaking their fists above their heads as they rally mankind against the invaders, they both shout defiantly.

"ATTACK!!!"

About the Author

Clayton and his wife live in the Okanagan Valley of southern British Colombia, Canada. They have two adult children and enjoy getting out to explore the outdoors, camping and quading. Clayton started his working career as an owner-operator in the trucking industry. After an industrial accident he retrained as a heavy duty mechanic and driving instructor. He enjoys working with his hands. Being a tradesman provides a good living for his family, but his passion is to study the Bible as the Bereans did, proving what is true from the scriptures.

Clayton is a published freelance author within the Christian genre. He writes articles and Bible studies for the www.biblists.com web site, and has audio books and articles appearing on various podcast websites.

Study the Bible with Clayton Carlson

Contact Clayton through his website at:
www.biblists.com

Ask a question about the content in this book, study the Bible with Clayton in Kelowna BC, Canada or online by visiting Biblists.com for scheduling information.

Books by Clayton Carlson

Biblist Apologetics
Heading Home
"In The Beginning" Chronologically Speaking. Bible Supports Richard Dawkins
My Baby Died. Where is My Baby?
Searching For Immortality
The Eden Conspiracy
Thy Kingdom Come, The Next Big Thing.